A Thousand
Tomorrows

Just Beyond
the Clouds

KAREN KINGSBURY

A Thousand Tomorrows

Just Beyond the Clouds

CENTER
STREET

New York Boston Nashville

Compilation Copyright © 2011 by Karen Kingsbury
A Thousand Tomorrows Copyright © 2005 by Karen Kingsbury
Just Beyond the Clouds Copyright © 2007 by Karen Kingsbury

Karen Kingsbury is represented by the literary agency of Alive Communications.
7680 Goddard Street, Suite 200
Colorado Springs, CO 80920
www.alivecom.com

Center Street
Hachette Book Group
237 Park Avenue
New York, NY 10017
www.centerstreet.com

Center Street is a division of Hachette Book Group, Inc.
The Center Street name and logo are trademarks of Hachette Book Group, Inc.

A Thousand Tomorrows originally published in hardcover by Center Street.
Just Beyond the Clouds originally published in paperback by Center Street.

Printed in the United States of America

First Compilation Edition: January 2011
10 9 8 7 6 5 4 3 2 1

Library of Congress Control Number: 2010928664
ISBN 978-1-59995-402-8

A Thousand Tomorrows

Donald, my Prince Charming: The dance is a beautiful one; I only wish the music would play forever.

Kelsey, my forever laughter: Thanks for letting me into the most tender places of your heart.

Tyler, my sweetest song: When the spotlight hits you, honey, your dad and I will be there in the front row.

Sean, my silly heart: It feels like you've been in my heart forever.

Josh, my gentle giant: Our plan was two adopted Haitian boys; God's plan was three. I'm so glad He brought you to us.

EJ, my chosen one: Watching you come into your own, growing and stretching with the years, has been one of my greatest blessings.

Austin, my miracle boy: Your days are speeding by, precious youngest child. I can't slow the march of time, but you remind me I can savor every beat.

And to God Almighty, the Author of Life, who has—for now—blessed me with these.

Acknowledgments

Novels do not come together without a great deal of help. For that reason, I'd like to thank several people who helped make *A Thousand Tomorrows* possible.

First, a special thanks to Maureen Egen and Rolf Zettersten for taking me under your wing at Center Street and believing that maybe the whole world needed to know about this story. Your encouragement and faith in me have made all the difference. I appreciate you more than you know. Also, a thanks to my other friends at Center Street, especially my editor, Leslie Peterson, and my publicist, Andrea Davis. You are amazing in the way you think outside the box. I'm grateful beyond measure to be working with you.

Also, thanks to the people who helped lend credibility to this novel. A year ago, I shared a cross-country airplane ride with professional bull rider Ross Coleman. That four-hour conversation became the inspiration for Cody Gunner, the main character in *A Thousand Tomorrows*. Since that conversation, Ross Coleman and his family, along with dozens of rodeo competitors, cowboys, and professional bull riders including the all-time great Tuff Hedeman, helped make the world of rodeo real to me, and for that I am grateful. You lent accuracy to this story; any errors in detail are mine.

In addition, a thanks to those who shared their cystic fibrosis stories and information. I join you in praying for a cure for this disease, and for believing that in time research and funding will continue to add tomorrows every day.

Thank you to my family, especially Donald and the kids, who don't mind tuna sandwiches and quesadillas two weeks straight when I'm on deadline. You're the best support system I could ever have! Thanks also to my mother, Anne Kingsbury, who is my assistant and best friend. And a thanks to my dad, Ted Kingsbury, who continues to be my greatest encourager.

In addition I'd like to thank my friends and family who surround me with love and prayer and encouragement, especially Susan Kane, Trish Kingsbury, Lynne Groten, Ann Hudson, Sylvia Wallgren, Sonya Fitzpatrick, Teresa Thacker, Kathy Santschi, Melinda Chapman, Christine Wessel, Vicki and Randy Graves, Marcia Bender, and so many others.

A special thanks to my agent, Rick Christian, at Alive Communications. You are brilliant at all you do, acting in so many roles as you lead me in this writing adventure. You care deeply about my career, but more than that, you care about me in my role as a wife and mother. Thanks for working out the details with that in mind. You're amazing, and I'm the most thankful author in the world to be working with you.

Chapter One

Mary Williams never saw it coming.

She became Mike Gunner's wife the summer of 1972, back when love was all the world needed, big enough to solve any problem. So big no one imagined it might end or die or drop off suddenly the way the muddy Mississippi River did ten yards out.

The wedding was small, held on a hillside in Oxford not far from Ole Miss, a stone's throw from the grassy football field where Mike had been king. Marriage, they told themselves, wouldn't mean losing their independence. They were just adding another layer to their relationship, something more diverse, more complex. As a reminder, during the ceremony they each held something that symbolized themselves—Mary, a book of poetry; Mike, a football.

A football.

Looking back that should've been a sign, because football was Mike's first love, and what sort of man could be married to two lovers? But at the time—with half the guests in flowing tie-dyed gowns and flower wreaths—holding a football and a book of poetry seemed hip and new, a spit in the face of tradition and marital bondage. No three-piece suits and starched aprons for Mike and Mary.

Mike had an NFL contract with the Atlanta Falcons, and a pretty new house a few miles from the stadium. Mary was a runaway, so leaving Biloxi meant cutting ties that were already frayed. They would live as one, him in a Falcons uniform, her with a pen and paper, ready to capture the deep phrases and rhymes that grew in the soil of her heart.

Babies? They would wait five years at least. Maybe ten. She was only nineteen, a child herself. Marriage would mean finding new and heightened ways to love each other. Sundays cheering from the stands while her husband blazed a trail down the football field, and lazy Tuesdays, barefoot and sipping coffee while she recited to him her latest creation.

That was the plan, anyway.

But God didn't get the memo, because Mary was pregnant three months later and gave birth to a baby boy shortly before their first anniversary. Cody William Gunner, they called him. Little Codester. Mary put away the pen and paper and bought a rocking chair. She spent her days and most nights walking a crying baby, heating up bottles, and changing diapers.

"Sorry I'm not around more," Mike told her. He wasn't used to babies. Besides, if he wanted to keep up, he needed more time at the field house, more reps with the weights, more hours on the track.

Mary told him she didn't mind, and the funny thing was, she really didn't. Life was good at home. Mike was happy about being a father, because Cody was all boy from the moment he was born. His first word was *ball*, and Mike bought him a pair of running shoes months before he could walk.

The years that followed were a blur of vibrant reds and happy yellows. Mike was coming into his own, each season showing him faster, more proficient at catching the long bomb. There had been no warning, no sign that life was about to fall apart.

In the spring of 1978, when Cody was nearly five, Mary learned she was expecting again. Still, it wasn't the coming baby, but a bad catch one October Sunday that changed everything. Mike was all alone, ten yards away from the nearest defender, when he reached for the sky, grabbed the ball and came down at an angle that buckled his knees.

A torn anterior ligament, the hospital report showed. Surgery was scheduled; crutches were ordered. "You'll miss a season," the doctor told him. "To be honest, I'm not sure you'll ever run the same again."

Six weeks later Mary gave birth to Carl Joseph.

From the beginning, Carl was different. He didn't cry the way Cody had, and he slept more than usual. His fussiest moments were during feeding time, when milk from the bottle would leak out his nose while he was eating, causing him to choke and sputter and cough.

Mike would look at him and get nervous. "Why's he doing that?"

"I'm not sure." Mary kept a burp rag close by, dabbing at the baby's nose and convincing herself nothing was wrong. "At least he isn't crying."

Either way, Mike wanted to be gone. As soon as he could, he got back in the training room, working harder than ever to make the knee well again. By the next fall, he was cleared to play, but he was more than a second slower in the forty.

"We'll try you at special teams, Gunner," the coach told him. "You've got to get your times down if you want your spot back."

His future suddenly as shaky as his left knee, Mike began staying out with the guys after games, drinking and coming home with a strange, distant look in his eyes. By the time Carl Joseph was two, Mike was cut from the Falcons. Cut without so much as a thank you or a good-luck card.

By then they knew the truth about Carl Joseph.

Their second son had Down syndrome. His condition came with a host of problems, feeding issues, developmental and speech delays. One morning Mary sat Mike down at the breakfast table.

"You never talk about Carl Joseph." She put her hands on her hips. "You act like he has the flu or something."

Mike shrugged. "We'll get him therapy; he'll be fine."

"He won't be fine, Mike." She heard a crack in her voice. "He'll be this way forever. He'll *live* with us forever."

It was that last part that caught Mike's attention. He said nothing significant at the time, nothing Mary could remember. But that summer, he was gone more than he was home. Always his story was the same. He was traveling the country looking for a tryout, getting a few weeks' look in one city and then another, working out with a handful of teams, trying to convince coaches he hadn't lost a step, hadn't done anything but get stronger since his injury.

But one weekend morning, when Mike was still asleep in their bedroom, Mary found a Polaroid picture in his duffle bag. It was of him in a bar surrounded by three girls, one on each knee, one draped over his shoulder.

When Mike woke up, Mary was in the kitchen ready to confront him. He would have to stop traveling, stop believing his next contract was a tryout away. Bars would be a thing of the past, because she needed him at home, helping out with the boys. Money was running out. If football had nothing more to offer, he needed to find a job, some other way to support them. She had her speech memorized, but it was all for nothing.

He took control of the conversation from the moment he found her at the kitchen table.

"This…" He tossed his hands and let them fall limp at his sides. His eyes were bloodshot. "This isn't what I want anymore."

"What?" She held up the Polaroid. "You mean this?"

Anger flashed in his eyes. He snatched the picture from her, crumpled it, and slammed it into the trash can. The look he gave her was cold, indifferent. He gritted his teeth. "What I do outside this house is my business."

She opened her mouth, but before she could tell him he was wrong, he slid his wedding ring from his left hand and dropped it on the table between them.

"It's over, Mary. I don't love you anymore."

Carl's cry sounded from upstairs. Slow and monotone, the cry of a child who would always be different. Mary looked up, following the sound. Then she found Mike's eyes again. "This isn't about me." She kept her tone calm, gentle. "It's about you."

A loud breath escaped his lips. "It's not about me."

"It is." She sat back, her eyes never leaving his. "You were on top of the world before you got hurt; now you're out of work and afraid." Compassion found a place in her voice. "Let's pull together, Mike." She stood, picked up his ring, and held it out to him. "Let me help you."

Carl's crying grew louder.

Mike closed his eyes. "I can't…" His words were a tortured whisper. "I can't stay here. I can't be a father to him, Mary. Every time I look at him, I…I can't do it."

Mary felt the blood drain from her face and the cheap linoleum turn liquid beneath her feet. What had he said? This was about Carl Joseph? Precious Carl, who never did anything but smile at Mike and long to be held by him?

Mary's scalp tingled, and the hairs on her arms stood straight up. "You're saying you can't stay married to me because of…because of Carl Joseph?"

"Don't say it like that." He pinched the bridge of his nose and hung his head.

Carl's crying grew still louder.

"But that's it, right?" The truth was exploding within her, spraying shrapnel at her heart and soul and leaving scars that would stay forever. "You want out because you can't be a father to Carl Joseph. Or because you're embarrassed by him. Because he's not perfect."

"I'm already packed, Mary. I called a cab; I'm flying to California and starting over. You can have the house; I'll send money when I get a job."

In a small, less important part of her mind, Mary wondered where Cody was, why he was so quiet. But she couldn't act on her curiosity. She was too busy reminding herself to breathe. "You're leaving because your son has Down syndrome? Do you hear yourself, Mike?"

But he was already headed back up the stairs.

When he left the house ten minutes later, he mumbled a single good-bye to no one in particular. Cody came tearing into the entryway from the living room, his eyes wide, forehead creased with worry.

"Dad, wait!" Cody ran out the door, his untied tennis shoes flopping with every step.

Carl Joseph in tow, Mary followed, horrified at the scene playing out. The cab waited out front, and without turning back, Mike helped the driver load both his suitcases into the trunk.

Cody stopped a few feet away, chest heaving. "Dad, where are you going?"

Mike hesitated, his eyes on Cody. "Never mind."

"But Dad—" Cody took a step closer. "When're you coming home?"

"I'm not." He looked at Mary and back at Cody. "This is it, son." Mike moved toward the passenger door. "Be good for your mama, you hear?"

"But Dad...I got a baseball game Friday; you promised you'd be there!" The boy was frantic, his words breathless and clipped. "Dad, don't go!"

Mike opened the door of the cab.

"Wait!" Mary stormed barefoot across the damp grass toward the cab. Carl Joseph stayed behind, rooted in one spot, watching, his thumb in his mouth. Mary jabbed her finger in the air. "You can't leave now, Mike. Your son's talking to you."

"Don't do this, Mary." Mike shot her a warning look. He lowered himself a few inches toward the passenger seat. "I have nothing to say."

"Dad!" Cody looked from Mike to Mary and back again. "What's happening; where're you going?"

Mike bit his lip and gave a curt nod to Cody. "Good-bye, son."

"Fine!" Mary screamed the word, her voice shrill and panicked. "Leave, then." She bent over, her knees shaking. Tears ran in rivers down her face. "Go ahead and leave. But if you go now, don't come back. Not ever!"

"What?" Cody looked desperate and sick, his world spinning out of control. He glared at his mother. "Don't say that, Mom. Don't tell him not to come back!"

Mary's eyes never left Mike's face. "Stay out of this, Cody. If he doesn't want us, he can go." She raised her voice again. "Do you hear me, Mike? Don't come back!"

What happened next would be a part of all their lives as long as morning followed night. Cody's father looked once more at the three of them standing on the lawn, then he climbed into the backseat, shut the door, and the cab pulled away.

"Dad!" Cody screamed his name and took off running.

The sound frightened Carl Joseph. He buried his face in his hands and fell onto his knees, rocking forward and calling out, "Mama…Mama…Mama."

Mary went to him. "Shhh. It's okay." She rubbed his back. Why was this happening? And why hadn't there been any warning? She was dizzy with shock, sick to her stomach and barely able to stand as she watched Cody chase after his father's cab.

Never did the cab slow even a little, but all the while Cody kept running. "Dad! Dad, wait!" Five houses down, seven, ten. "Don't go, Dad! Please!"

Each word hit Mary like a Mack truck. When she couldn't take another minute, she screamed after him, "Cody, get back here!"

But he wouldn't come, wouldn't stop running. All the way to the end of the block, with a speed he'd gotten from his father, he ran until the cab was long gone from sight. Then, for ten minutes, he stood there. A dark-haired eight-year-old boy, standing on the corner staring after a cab that wasn't ever coming back.

In some small way, Mary was almost glad Mike was gone.

Sure, a few hours earlier she'd been willing to fight for their marriage. But that was when she thought things were simpler. She could understand his confusion, what with his football career in limbo.

But to be embarrassed by Carl Joseph?

Carl was her son, a part of her. Because of his disability, he'd never be capable of the kind of low, mean-spirited act his father had just committed. No, Carl would always have a kind, simple heart, but Mike would miss that—the same way he'd missed everything about Carl Joseph since the day he was diagnosed.

Even as she stood there, willing Cody to turn around and come home, not quite believing her marriage was over, she felt her resolve building. There was no loving a man who didn't love his own son. If Mike didn't want to be a father to Carl Joseph, she'd love the boy enough for both of them. She would survive, even if she never heard from Mike Gunner again.

She focused on Cody once more, his little-boy shoulders slumped forward as he waited, facing the empty spot where the cab had disappeared. He was crying, no doubt. She could almost see his smudged, tearstained cheeks and the slack-jawed look on his face. Was he feeling the way she felt? Abandoned? Overcome with despair?

A strange thought hit her, and suddenly fear had the upper hand.

Because the thought was something she hadn't considered until that moment. Yes, she would survive, and certainly Carl Joseph would be okay without Mike. But Cody adored his father; he always had. And if the boy's slumped shoulders were any indication, Cody might not bounce back the way she and Carl would.

Rather, he might never be the same again.

Chapter Two

Cody's sides hurt from running.

He dug his fingers into his waist and stared down the empty street. "Dad!" The picture filled his mind again. The cab slowing down, stopping for a minute, then making a gradual left turn. "Dad, come back."

A breeze hit him in the face and he realized he was crying.

"Dad!" Cody gasped, grabbing at any air he could suck in. Why did he leave? Where did he go? Dad took trips all the time, but he always came home. Always. What had he said? He wasn't coming back; was that it? His dad's words rumbled around inside him, making his chest tight, filling his heart and soul and lungs with hurt. Every breath was a struggle.

His dad was gone.

He was gone and there was nothing Cody could do about it. *Come back, Dad!* The words stayed stuck in his throat this time, and he stared down. *Stay, feet. Don't move. He'll come back; he will.*

Cody lifted his eyes to the place where the cab had turned. Any second, right? He'd turn around, come back home, tell them all he was sorry for getting so mad, right? Cody waited and waited and waited. And then he remembered the thing his dad had said about Carl Joseph.

I can't be a father to him...

Eight years was plenty old enough for Cody to understand the problem. Carl Joseph was different. He didn't look right or talk right or walk right. He was happy and really good at loving everyone and he almost never got mad, but their dad maybe didn't notice that. That's why, this time, having his dad leave was more serious.

Because he didn't want to be a daddy to Carl Joseph.

Cody stared down the street. *Come back, Dad...turn around.* He waited and watched for a long, long time.

Nothing.

No movement, no sounds of cars turning around and coming back. No yellow cabs. Just the quiet dance of twisty green leaves above him and the hot summer song of unseen crickets. Or something like crickets.

Later his mother would tell him that she cried for him, standing there all that time, waiting for his father to come back. But after a while, Cody wasn't just standing there waiting; he was swept up in a feeling he'd never known until that day.

It started in his feet, almost as if it were oozing up through the cracked bumpy sidewalk. A burning that flooded his veins and pushed higher, past his knees and thighs, into his gut, where it swirled and mixed and grew until it filled his heart and mind, and finally his soul.

Not until it fully consumed him, not until it took up every spare bit of his young body, did he realize what had come over him, into him.

Cody knew what hate was because of Billy Bloom in his second-grade class. Billy was bigger than everyone else. Bigger and meaner. He tripped kindergartners, and stole the ball from the kickball game at recess, and laughed at Cody when he got a wrong answer in math. Cody hated Billy Bloom.

But what he was feeling now, this was something new, something so powerful it burned in his arms and legs and made him feel heavy and slow and trapped. All the other times Cody had used the word hate, he'd been wrong. Because *this*—what he felt for his father—was hatred.

CODY NEVER TOLD anyone, but that morning he felt his heart shrivel up and die, all except the piece that belonged to Carl Joseph. His little brother thought Cody was Superman and Christopher Robin all rolled into one. As the weeks passed, every morning was the same routine. Carl Joseph would scamper down the hall to Cody's room, slip inside, and stand next to the bed.

"Brother…" He would pat Cody's shoulder. "It's a new morning."

Cody would stir and blink his eyes and find Carl Joseph there. "Yep, buddy. A brand-new morning."

"Is Daddy coming home today?"

Cody would grit his teeth and sit up some. "Not today, buddy. I don't think so."

For a minute worry would cast shadows on Carl Joseph's face. But then a grin would fill his round cheeks and he'd make a funny chuckling sound. "That's okay, 'cause know why, brother?"

"Why?"

" 'Cause I have you, brother. I always have you."

Cody would hug him around the neck. "That's right, buddy. You always have me."

The two of them were inseparable. Carl Joseph followed him around the house, waiting for him at the front window on school days. He didn't talk as clear as other kids, and he had those puffy bunches of skin under his eyes. But he was the happiest little guy Cody ever saw. He loved with abandon, and after a few months he walked into Cody's room one morning and didn't ask about when Daddy would come home.

That day Carl Joseph worked his way into the deepest part of Cody's heart. He still wasn't sure exactly what was wrong with Carl Joseph, but whatever it was, Cody had a feeling there wouldn't be many people in his little brother's life. If their dad didn't want Carl Joseph, maybe no one would.

No one but Cody. Whatever else happened, Cody would love Carl Joseph, and maybe that was all he'd ever love. He had no use for his mother; she was a grown-up, the only one with the power to keep Cody's father home. Instead, she'd stood right there on the grass and told him to go. Told him to go and never come back.

The rest of that year, Cody would wait until Carl Joseph was asleep, then he'd creep up to his room without saying good night to his mother. He'd lie on the bed and stare at the wall. Sometimes tears would come, sometimes not. Always he would start at the beginning.

Hearing his dad talk to his mom about leaving, about not wanting to be with Carl Joseph. Then seeing his dad with a suitcase and following him out into the front yard and watching him head for the yellow cab.

"Good-bye, son. Good-bye."

The story would run again and again in his head, playing out on the blank wall beside his bed. Almost always his mother would find him there. Most of the time she didn't ask about why Cody went to bed early or why he was lying on his side staring at the wall or why he never told her good night or what he was feeling about his dad being gone.

But once in a while she would try.

Cody remembered one night the next spring when his mom came up to talk to him. She opened the door and took a loud breath. Then she moved a few steps toward him. "I hate that you hide up here, Cody. You're not the only one hurting."

"Yes, I am!" Cody turned over and sat up. His heart skittered around in his chest. "Carl Joseph doesn't remember Daddy."

"I miss him, too." She sat on the edge of his bed. Her eyes were red and swollen, and her voice was tired. "I love him, Cody. It's not my fault he left."

"It is too your fault!" Cody closed his eyes and remembered

his father leaving. When he opened them the anger inside him was bursting to get out. "You told him to go!"

"Cody." His mom touched his foot. Her fingers were shaking. "I didn't mean it."

"Yes you did!" His voice got louder. "You told him to go and never come back."

"Because I was mad. I didn't really want him to go."

But nothing she said that night or any other time was enough to convince Cody. She told his dad to leave, and not only that, she did nothing to make him stay. Maybe if she'd been nicer to him, helped him find another football job. Made him better dinners. Anything to make sure he didn't walk out the door.

Even when it no longer made sense, long after his childhood days blended into middle school, Cody blamed her. Because it was easier to dole out blame than it was to unravel the knot of hatred and sort through the loose ends of a lifetime of bitterness.

By the time Cody was in seventh grade, the football coach approached him.

"You're Mike Gunner's boy, right? Atlanta Falcons back a few years ago?"

Cody bristled, his spine stiff. "Yes, sir."

"Well." The coach gave a few slow nods. "I've watched you out with the other boys." The man hesitated. "You're good, Cody. You play just like your dad. The varsity coach over at the high school wants you to join 'em for practice a few times a week. How does that sound?"

Cody made a hurried attempt at trying to sort through

his emotions. *Just like my dad?* He swallowed, not sure what to say.

The coach raised his brow, as if maybe he expected a different reaction. "What can I tell 'em, Gunner? You interested?"

"Yes, sir." He coughed and his words got stuck in his throat. Was that why he loved the game, loved the way the ball felt in the crook of his arm, tucked against his ribs, the way his feet flew down the field? Because he was Mike Gunner's boy? The anger that lived and breathed in that dark closet of his heart roared so loud it took his breath away.

If football was his father's legacy, he wanted nothing to do with it.

The coach started walking away. "Okay, then. I'll tell him you'll be there."

"Sir?" Cody's face grew hot. He waited until the coach turned around. "What I mean is, no, sir. I won't go; I'm not interested."

The coach gave him a strange look. Then he laughed. "Of course you're interested, Gunner." He twisted his face. "Football's in your blood."

"No, sir." Cody's mind raced, desperate for an answer. "I'm…I'm going out for band."

"Band?" The word clearly left a bad taste in the coach's mouth. "You're kidding, right?"

"No, sir." Cody tried to look serious. "I…I love band." He hesitated. He would no sooner go out for band than dye his hair pink. Cody felt himself relax; he stood a little taller. "Band's what I live for."

The coach studied him, a frown deepening the lines in

his forehead. Then he shrugged and took a step back. "Suit yourself, Gunner. I'll tell 'em you have other plans."

As Cody watched the man leave, a certainty filled his soul. He would never pick up a football again as long as he lived. No matter his feelings for the game, if seeing him with a pigskin reminded people of his father, he wanted none of it.

Later that year he fell in with a group of 4-H kids, guys who needed help with their farming or livestock. Cody was a quick study, and after a few months he could handle a horse as well as the kids who'd been on them for years.

One night just before summer, he and the guys met at the fairgrounds to watch the high school rodeo team practice. They moved close to the fence and Cody breathed it in, the heavy smell of bull hides. Cody knew about bull riding, but that night was the first time he ever saw a cowboy ride. The guy was a junior, a scrawny kid Cody had seen around town. Slow and careful, the cowboy lowered himself onto a jet-black bull, and in a blur the gate flew open and the animal burst into the arena.

Wild and out of control, the bull bucked and jerked and reared his head back. It was all the cowboy could do to hold on, and after six seconds, he slid to one side of the animal's back and fell hard in a heap to the ground.

"No good!" an older cowboy shouted. The man was in his late twenties, maybe. The rodeo coach, no doubt. "You need eight, Ronny. Eight seconds."

The kid picked himself up, dusted off his loose-fitting jeans and pressed his cowboy hat onto his head. His voice held a type of respect Cody admired. "Yes, sir. Eight seconds."

Five bulls stood together in a stock pen. The black one, two brown, one gray- and white-spotted, and one that was broad and yellow with a hump between its shoulders. One after another Ronny and a handful of high school cowboys took on the bulls while their instructor shouted out advice.

"Find the seat, Taylor, find it and keep it!...Move your legs, Ronny....Kevin, bring your hand up higher over your head! Okay, good."

Cody barely heard any of it.

He was too busy watching the bulls, studying them, hypnotized by their fury. Those eight seconds, while the cowboy was on the bull's back, were the picture of a battle he knew intimately. The war he waged every day against the anger and rage within him. The way the rider struggled to stay on through the violent bucking, looking for the center of a ride that was never even close to controlled. It was the same way he fought to stay on top of the emotions that boiled inside him.

Before he could voice what he was feeling, without saying a word to his buddies, he followed the fence around the arena and walked up to the man still barking orders at the cowboys.

"That's better, Ronny; can you feel it? Keep it centered!"

"Sir?" Cody squared his legs and crossed his arms.

The man gripped the crown of his hat and looked over his shoulder. "Whadya want, kid?"

Cody didn't hesitate. "I want to ride."

"Yeah?" The coach smiled and a sarcastic chuckle sounded deep in his throat. "What are you, eleven?"

"Thirteen." The anger grew a few degrees hotter. He straightened himself. "I'll stay on any bull you've got."

The man leaned into the fence and sized him up. "What grade you in? Seventh?"

"Yes, sir."

"Another year before you can ride for me." He turned toward the action in the arena.

Cody stared at the man's back and clenched his teeth. He didn't need anyone's permission to ride a bull. It was his own thing; between the bull and him. He continued around the arena to the chutes.

One of the cowboys shot him a look. "Hey, kid, get lost. This is for cowboys only."

"I'm a cowboy." He nodded the brim of his hat toward the coach. "He wants to see what I can do."

The kid frowned, but then his expression eased. He raised one shoulder. "Okay. Take the next one."

He should've been scared, at least. The bulls had no horns, but the animals were massive. One slip beneath those muscled legs, and there wouldn't be any ride to remember. Cody worked the muscles in his jaw. As long as the coach didn't see him in the chutes, he'd be all right.

When it was his turn, he glanced at the coach and felt himself relax. The guy was talking to three riders, his back to the chute. Cody held his breath. He wasn't leaving the arena without getting on a bull.

"Take your ride, little man," one of the bigger cowboys shouted at him. "We're waiting."

Cody bit down hard and steadied himself. Then he did

what he'd seen the other cowboys do. He climbed into the
chute, one foot on either side of the bull, and fumbled with
the rope. His hand had to be wrapped to the bull somehow,
right? He flipped the rope around, trying to make a loop.

"Oh, brother. Ain't you ever done this?" The cowboy on
the gate leaned over. "Which hand you ridin' with?"

Which hand? Cody gulped and thrust his right hand out.

"That'll do." The cowboy set to work wrapping Cody's
hand, palm up, until it was tight against the bull's back. "Slide
forward."

Cody did as he was told. That's when he noticed the look
in the bull's eyes.

Lifeless, hard eyes, trying to catch a glimpse of whichever
mortal had dared climb on his back. Cody stared at the beast.
The anger in the animal's expression was rivaled only by
his own.

"Ya hear me, cowboy? You ready?"

Cody blinked. What was he doing, sitting on a bull? Was
he crazy? Fear tried to say something, but anger kicked it in
the shins. *Come on, bull, give it all you got. Your fury's nothing
compared to mine.* He nodded. "Ready."

The chute was open.

Stay centered, wasn't that what the coach had told the
other riders? *Keep your seat; stay centered.* He focused on the
animal's back, and suddenly he wasn't fighting to stay on a
bucking bull. He was taking on his father, battling the loneliness and rejection and abandonment, focusing all his rage
on the beast.

How many times had thoughts of his dad made him want

to punch his hand through a wall or rip a door from its hinges? Running helped some, but nothing eased the rage in his heart.

Nothing until now.

The buzzer sounded. Cody pulled his hand free and swung his legs over the side of the bull. Something was making its way through his veins, but it took a few seconds to realize what it was.

Relief.

For the first time since his father walked out, his heart didn't feel paralyzed with rage. The reason was obvious: he'd left every bit of emotion on the back of the bull.

Only then did he hear the coach bellowing in his direction. One of the cowboys herded the bull back into the chute, and a hush fell over the arena. Cody turned and stood frozen, facing the man. His buddies had moved closer. They were clustered outside the fence, eyes wide.

"Stay there, kid. Don't move!" Even in the shadowy arena lights, the coach's cheeks were bright red. He stormed up to Cody until their faces were inches apart. His voice fell to a dangerous hiss. "I told you to go home."

"Sorry, sir." Cody swallowed hard, but he didn't break eye contact. "I...I had to ride tonight. I *had* to."

The man twisted his face into a sneer aimed at Cody. Then, bit by bit, his face unwound and he took a step back. "Where'd you learn to ride like that?"

He couldn't lie to the man now; not if he wanted to ride again. "That was my first ride, sir."

"Your first..." The coach narrowed his eyes. "That was your first time on a bull?"

"Yes, sir." Cody pulled himself a bit straighter. "I'm sorry, sir."

The man hung his thumbs on his belt buckle. "What's your name, boy?"

"Cody. Cody Gunner."

"You going to Jefferson High, Gunner?"

"Yes, sir." He looked at the ground for a moment. "When I'm old enough."

"You wanna be a bull rider, is that it?"

A bull rider? Cody hadn't considered the idea before. But he wanted to climb back on a bull more than he'd ever wanted anything. Cody exhaled, still catching his breath, his eyes on the coach again. The rush from the ride was wearing off. "Yes, sir. I want that."

The coach hesitated. This was the part where he'd kick Cody out of the arena and tell him he'd never ride for Jefferson's rodeo team. Not ever. Cody waited, unable to blink under the man's stare.

But instead of ordering him home or threatening him for his actions, the coach gave a single nod. The hint of a rusty old smile tugged on his lips. "You know something, Cody Gunner? I think you'll be a pretty good one."

After that, there was no turning back.

Cody's birthday was three weeks later, in June. He wanted just one thing—tuition and transportation to a bull-riding school in Colorado.

"Bull riding?" His mother frowned. "Cody, that's the craziest sport on earth." She crossed her arms and tapped her foot. "You can do anything but that." She turned back to the dishes she'd been doing. "Play football like your daddy. At least then you'll go head-to-head with a boy your size. Not a bull."

Football like his daddy? Cody felt his gaze harden. He had nothing but contempt for his mother. After all this time she still didn't get it, didn't understand him. Sure, she was easy on him. She didn't give him rules the way other boys had rules from their parents. Instead she gave him whatever he wanted, and peppered him with questions. "Cody, how are you?" "Cody, what're you thinking?" "Cody, what are you feeling?" "Cody, what's wrong?"

He was sick of her questions, sick of her trying to make up for the fact that he didn't have a dad. She never hassled him about his attitude or lack of kindness, even when he secretly wished she would.

But if she could suggest football, she didn't even know him.

Carl Joseph must've heard the conversation because he pushed his way between them. He was eight by then, as sweet and simple as he'd been at two. "Cody, brother, c'mere!"

The heat in Cody's anger cooled. Carl Joseph was his best friend, the only one he could trust. Cody couldn't count the times he'd wished it were he and not Carl Joseph who'd been born with Down syndrome. Because at least Carl Joseph was happy, too simple to understand even that their father had gone away, let alone the reasons why. Carl Joseph's eyes were honest and full of light, and his enthusiasm knew no limits. He called Cody "brother," and Cody called him "buddy."

Carl Joseph grabbed his hand and pulled. "C'mon, brother, talk to me."

"Just a minute, buddy." Cody glared at his mother. "It's Mom's turn."

"No, Cody!" Carl Joseph grinned big and tugged a little harder. His voice was loud, excited.

This time Cody couldn't resist. He gave his mother a look and let himself be pulled into the next room. When Carl Joseph thought they were alone, his eyes sparkled. "You gonna ride a bull, Cody?"

Cody's heart swelled at the transparent look in his brother's eyes. A look of thrill and pride and expectancy. "Yes, buddy. I'm gonna be a bull rider."

"Remember, brother? We watched bull riding on TV?" He rocked back and forth, nervous, anticipating.

"We sure did, buddy." Cody put his arm around Carl Joseph's shoulders and gave him a sideways hug.

Carl Joseph let out a whooping victory cry. He slid from Cody's grasp, marched his feet up and down and moved in a tight winner's circle around Cody. His arms punched at invisible targets. "Bull riding! Brother's gonna be a bull rider!"

As Cody watched Carl Joseph that familiar fierce protection reared up in his heart. Once, a few years after their father left, a kid in his class pointed at Cody and laughed. "*His* brother's a retard! He lives in my neighborhood."

Never mind that the kids were taking a spelling test. Cody had the guy pinned before he had time to cry for help. It took the teacher and a passing custodian to pull Cody off the boy. It was the last time anyone at Davis Elementary said anything mean about Carl Joseph.

Watching him now, the determination in Cody's heart grew. No one better ever harm Carl Joseph, not ever. His brother stopped, drawing loud, exaggerated breaths. "I'm tuckered out, brother."

Cody smiled. "Yeah, you look like it."

So what if his mother didn't approve? He'd already made up his mind. The fact that Carl Joseph was excited only made him that much more sure.

Cody brushed his knuckles along the top of Carl Joseph's head. "We'll talk later, okay?" He made a face. "Mom's waiting."

"Right." Carl Joseph nodded, and did his best imitation of Cody's grimace. "Mom's waiting."

Cody grinned. What wasn't there to love about Carl Joseph? He turned and found his mother waiting in the kitchen. Her arms were crossed.

"What was that all about?"

"Carl's happy for me." Cody stuck out his chin. "I'm fourteen in a few weeks, Mom. I wanna go to bull-riding school. That's all I want."

Her look said everything her words didn't.

She wanted to be mad, wanted to tell him all the things any mother would tell her son if he came home wanting to be a bull rider. People were killed riding bulls; trampled and maimed and paralyzed. A body could age four decades in as many seconds in a sport that violent and unpredictable. But she must've seen the determination in Cody's eyes, because she blinked.

And that single blink told Cody he'd won.

The arrangements came together quickly, and by the time he arrived home from bull-riding school, he couldn't think of anything but getting a seat on the next bull.

Quickly Cody learned something about bull riders. The very good ones rode because they loved the sport, because they'd loved it since they were old enough to jump on the back of a sheep. For those riders, every go-round was an unequaled adrenaline rush, an addictive high that knew no match.

Cody was nothing like those cowboys.

Through middle school and high school, past his eighteenth birthday when he qualified for his Professional Rodeo Cowboys Association card; through event after event when sheer fury drove him to stay on bulls that couldn't be ridden; through the first two seasons when he first noticed Ali, the first two seasons when people started whispering that maybe there was no better bull rider than the independent Cody Gunner and no better barrel racer than the untouchable Ali Daniels, through all the travel and women and rank rodeo stock, he couldn't get one thought out of his head:

His father walked out of Carl Joseph's life because the kid had Down syndrome, because something was clearly wrong with that son. Cody had heard him say so. But what about the other son, the older son? What about him? The man had left Cody, too, and the thing Cody could never quite figure out was this: What, exactly, was wrong with him?

It was this question that stoked the coals of his anger, even when his past seemed forever behind him. No, Cody didn't ride bulls because he loved the rush. The rush was there, and it was real enough. Cody rode because battling a two-thousand-pound bull for eight seconds was the only way to live with the rage.

And as Cody Gunner moved into the public limelight, as he became the talk of the Pro Rodeo Tour, the invincible, undefeatable cowboy, it was that part he kept a secret. The fact that he didn't ride for the love of the sport; he rode because he had to.

Chapter Three

Ali Daniels sat in her trailer, not far from her mother, and stared out the window.

"This is my year." She gripped the arms of the swivel chair, her eyes unblinking.

"Yes." Her mom stood. "I can feel it." She opened a cupboard next to the miniature sink and pulled out a bulky vest. "Here." She handed it over. "Let's go, Ali. It's time."

A slow breath eased across Ali's lips. "Okay." She took the vest, slipped one arm through, then the other, and zipped it. A few more snaps and she was ready. She looked out again and saw a group of bundled-up cowboys making their way across the snow-covered parking lot toward Stadium Arena. They laughed, listening to the shortest one in the group, hanging on to whatever story he was telling. Not far back, three couples followed, headed the same way.

This was Denver in late January, the season opener; festivities at the National Western Stock Show and Rodeo would start early and end late. Ali didn't mind missing the hoopla, as long as she was ready for her ride. The ride was all that counted.

She sat at the edge of her chair and kept her eyes on the people; so many people. Good for them for coming out, for cheering on the deserving professional rodeo riders and wranglers. But Ali didn't need them. She would've competed in an empty arena.

Anything to fly across the dirt, power and grace, an extension of the horse she'd spent years training. Sometimes she wasn't sure which of them loved the ride more, she or the muscled palomino horse she'd raised from birth.

"Ali?" Her mother touched her shoulder. "You okay?"

"Yeah." Her answer was quick. The walls of her chest ached, tighter than usual. Every breath was difficult, intentional, but what else could she say? How she felt wasn't a part of the equation; it never had been. "I'm fine."

"All right." She hesitated. "I'll get ready."

Familiar thoughts swirled about in Ali's heart.

Her popularity was building, not only because she was winning rodeos. She was a mystery, someone they'd dubbed beautiful and unreachable. She leaned forward and winced; the vest was tighter than usual. Yes, the public, the media, all of them held her up and examined her in the limelight. But there was very little she let them see.

She kept to herself, in her trailer with her mother or in a quiet corner of the locker room just long enough to change into her riding clothes. Friendships would be nice, but the less time she spent in the arena the better. She arrived in the tunnel minutes before each ride, and after the event she gathered her things and gave her horse a quick cooldown. Then she changed and headed back outside. The other barrel racers thought her distant, haughty, too good for them.

That wasn't it, but she couldn't explain herself. Not without giving away her secret, not without solving the mystery.

Her routine, her last-minute entry and quick exit from the arena, meant no time for cowboys, either. Just about all the single rodeo men and a few of the married ones had tried to hit on her in the past two years. Once in a while she would catch a smile or a glance from a cowboy who seemed nice enough. But there was no point, nothing she could offer in return.

Not when she was singly focused on two goals: staying healthy and being the best barrel racer in the world.

But the thing that really set her apart was something no one on the tour would ever know about. At least not while she was still competing. People wouldn't understand; they'd ask questions and make pronouncements about the risks and dangers. Before long the story would be out, and everyone would stop seeing her as the most promising barrel racer in rodeo.

Instead, they'd see her for her battles.

That would never happen; Ali was determined. Pro Rodeo would never know about her battles, her secret. They would never find out that she did something no other barrel racer did:

She held her breath when she rode.

From the tunnel around each of the three barrels, and

back, she didn't draw a bit of air. The hooves of her horse would keep time with her heartbeat as the seconds played out, one after another. By the time she hit the tunnel again, she was desperate for air, her lungs screaming for relief.

Small wonder that she regularly clocked in at less than eighteen seconds. Whether she was riding at the arena back home or racing for the national championship, every bit of her strength—even the energy it took to breathe—was focused on the ride. The fact that Ali held her breath when she raced was something only her parents knew about. Given the circumstances, they agreed that not breathing during the ride was her best chance of remaining a competitor.

It would be their secret.

So after two full years on the tour, Ali Daniels remained a curiosity, a blue-eyed rider with a thick ponytail of pale blonde hair, black hat and jeans, blazing across the arena on a horse as fair as she was. Reporters would ask her questions after a win, but her answers were never more than a few words. The details of her life went unknown.

The way they would stay.

ALI DREW A slow breath and adjusted the vest. It was never comfortable; especially just before a ride, when all she wanted was to break free, run outside, saddle up Ace, and ride like the wind around the outside of the arena.

She bit her lower lip. Patience. There was no riding without patience.

The truth was, she shouldn't have been here at all—not

her, and not Ace. Ace was a quarter horse so small at birth his owner was willing to give him away. Only Ali had seen the horse's potential, rearing him and coaxing him and hand-feeding him until he was as big and strong as any horse on the tour.

That alone was shocking, because Ali's parents never wanted anything to do with horses.

Ali and her younger sister, Anna, grew up on a cattle ranch in Colorado, where her father made the rounds on an ATV quad-runner. Horses were off-limits, too much dander and dust, too many allergens, too great the chance that Ali and Anna might get sick. Because of their allergies, the sisters took their lessons at home in rooms cleaned by air purifiers. They were taught to read and sew and play the piano. Outdoor time was kept to a minimum.

But in the evening, when their parents were busy, Ali and Anna sat by the bedroom window and dreamed of another life. Ali remembered one time more clearly than the others.

"You know what I wanna do?" Anna's eyes sparkled that evening. "I wanna race through the forever hay fields and play hide-and-seek out by the tallest pine trees, and jump on that palomino horse next door." Anna was eight that year; Ali nine. The idea seemed wild and outrageous and terribly exciting. "Wouldn't that be something?"

"Yes." Ali squinted at the world beyond their sterile confines. "One day we will, okay, Anna? One day."

But the chance never came.

One afternoon when Anna was ten, she caught a cold. Something must've blown into the house from the garden, their mother always guessed. The cold became bronchitis, quick and fast. An asthma attack sent her to the hospital, and by the next day she had a respiratory infection. Within forty-eight hours her fever raged out of control. Pneumonia set in and because of her situation, no doctor or antibiotic could do a thing to help her. All their attempts at safety, all the years spent watching life through a window, had done nothing to save Anna. Three days later she was gone.

Anna's death changed everything for Ali, and she made up her mind. She would not watch life from a window; she would live it to the fullest, doing everything Anna had dreamed of doing.

The memory dissolved and Ali adjusted her vest again. She tried to draw a deep breath, but it wouldn't come; not fully.

She still had a few hours before her ride, so remembering helped pass the time. The season opener always stirred up the past, bringing reminders of how fortunate she was, how hard she'd fought against the odds and how easily this season-or any season—could be her last.

The pretty horse next door had a foal, and the foal became Ali's closest friend. He was the color of caramel custard with a mane the same pale blonde as Ali's long hair. She named him Ace, and against the odds, against the doctor's warnings, she spent every spare moment with him and grew stronger for it. With the neighbor's help, she broke him and trained him and learned to fly across the fields behind her parents' home.

Eventually she discovered barrel racing, and her father

built an arena and a barn, with a custom air-filtration system to reduce the allergens from damp hay and horse dander. Ali remembered once when her aunt and uncle asked how her parents could be a willing party to something that might shorten their daughter's life.

Ali never forgot her father's answer. "Riding horses *is* Ali's life," he told them. "It's that simple."

So it was.

On Ace she not only had a purpose—to round the barrels faster than anyone had before—but she felt vibrant, all of life bursting within her. And that feeling defied any sense of reason, because doctors and medicine and statistics said she should be dying.

The mystery was this: Ali Daniels had cystic fibrosis.

Cystic fibrosis—with all its terrible limitations and its lifetime sentence of having her back pounded two hours each day so she could cough up the thick secretions that would otherwise choke her. CF, the doctors called it, the same condition Anna had been born with. The disease in which every cold could go into pneumonia; and every bout of pneumonia could mean death.

Ali's parents never told her the prognosis for people with cystic fibrosis. She found it for herself—on the Internet. Patients with CF usually died as young adults, and though the life expectancy had risen, the outcome was certain.

One day, not too far off, the disease would kill her.

Ali adjusted her position again. The vest was tight against her ribs, tight and uncomfortable. It wasn't for protection, the way the bull riders' vests were, though hers was customized to look like theirs. Rather, it was a compression vest. Powered by electricity, the vest had a series of air chambers, which rhythmically compressed Ali's lungs. The vest did mechanically what used to be done only by Ali's parents pounding on her chest and back.

One way or another, her lungs had to be cleared.

She leaned forward and let the vest work its magic. Ten more minutes and she'd be done. A series of coughs came over her, productive coughs. The type that kept her healthy. When she was finished, she closed her eyes and remembered again.

Her first rodeo came before her fourteenth birthday, the first time she and Ace tore around the barrels for a winning time. Three years later she hit the Pro Rodeo Tour, and she'd been hard to beat ever since.

Same as Cody Gunner.

The two of them were alike, both quiet, distant. Mysterious.

Ali was no longer amazed at how the crowd responded to Cody, how whole sections of women in the stands would wave their arms and chant his name when Cody received another saddle or a buckle. The sight of a six-foot-two bull rider with short dark hair, unrelenting blue eyes, and a confidence bigger than the arena left them collectively breathless.

Ali wasn't blind; the attraction was there for her, too. But that was as far as it went. As far as it would ever go. She'd shared the winner's circle with Cody too many times to count, and still they'd never said more than a polite hello to each other. Other cowboys would tip their hats or smile in her direction. Several made attempts at conversation.

Only Cody Gunner never tried, and that suited Ali fine. Cody was an island, a loner—just like her. He didn't flirt with the barrel racers or grin at the cowgirls who hung out near the stock pens; he didn't tend to the throng of female fans who waited for him after every rodeo.

The longer she rode the tour with him, the more Ali thought she understood him. The fact that he kept his distance didn't mean he was unkind, any more than she was unkind for keeping hers. On occasion, when their eyes met, Ali thought she saw a glimpse of something familiar in Cody's soul. A respect, maybe. A sameness. Whatever drove Cody Gunner to ride bulls for a living, Ali guessed it wasn't far off from what drove her. A passion born of something intensely private.

So while she didn't get weak at the knees in his presence, she quietly admired his independence, the way he didn't need people or trappings or success, but just the bull. Just the ride. He had placed second last year, just as she had.

This year—for one more season at least—they'd share the tour and the limelight with a single goal: a national championship. There was talk that Cody then might leave the tour, join Tuff Hedeman's upstart Professional Bull Riders circuit where the stock was more rank, the purses potentially bigger. If Cody was going to leave, this could be the last year they'd tour together.

Not that it mattered. That cold January day, the beginning

of her third season in the PRCA, Ali Daniels had more important details to mull over than whether this was Cody's last season with the Pro Rodeo Tour. This was her year, the year she would stay healthy and strong and break record after record on her quest for the championship.

Ali and Ace, making history.

Her heart had room for nothing else.

Chapter Four

The season was three weeks old, and Cody Gunner was riding better than ever. The tour was in San Antonio, and his draw that night was a good one—a bull named Monster Mash, ridden just once in twenty-two attempts. A rider who could stay the course was guaranteed a score in the high eighties. Make it pretty and anything was possible.

Cody didn't worry about the judges. Scores didn't matter nearly as much as the eight seconds. If he got bucked off, Cody's anger would swell and grow, desperate for release. But if he stayed on for eight, he could beat the demons that battled him—if just for the night. There was the practical side, too. Winning meant enough money to keep playing the game.

Cody hung his rope in his locker, shoved his gear bag inside, and headed down the tunnel. Like most of the winter events, this one was at an indoor arena—the Joe and Harry Freeman Coliseum. It was his fifth season in the PRCA, so Cody knew his way around most of the venues. He tucked his shirt in as he walked, making sure the buttons lined up with his belt buckle.

Before he could stretch, before he could focus on the ride, he needed to know where he was in the lineup. He came into the clearing and turned right toward the information table, the place where the judges sat in a row, their paperwork spread out in front of them.

That's when something caught his attention.

A few feet away, leaning against the wall, was a fellow bull rider, a Brazilian who had taken first place from him three times the year before. Next to the cowboy was an older man with the same eyes, same cheekbones. The rider's father, Cody figured. He'd seen the two of them together before, in a handful of cities.

Cody watched them, watched the way the older man put his hand on the bull rider's shoulder, whispering something that made the cowboy smile. Probably some bit of encouragement or advice, something only a father could bring his son in the hour before a bull ride.

That was the way his own father had been with him before he walked out, wasn't it? Kind and compassionate, there with words of encouragement when Cody was up at bat in Little League or working on a school project?

Cody clenched his fists and turned from the scene. A young woman at the information table smiled at him.

"Cody Gunner, what can I do for you?"

Images of the Brazilian cowboy and his father burned in his mind. Cody focused on the woman. "Where am I in the order?"

The woman checked a list, grabbed a scrap of paper, and scribbled something. "Here." She handed it to him. "Good luck tonight."

Cody took the slip, nodded at her, and headed back down the tunnel. Halfway to the locker room he opened the paper. The woman had written that he rode second to last that night. At the bottom she'd scribbled her phone number.

He ripped the paper in half and went to his locker. It was time to stretch, even if his ride wasn't until the end. But he couldn't focus yet, couldn't let go of the picture in his head, the one of the rider and his dad.

What would it be like to ride bulls with his dad around, to get a dose of wisdom and confidence from his father before every ride? Cody opened his locker, pulled out his worn deerskin riding glove, and slammed the door shut. He dropped to the bench, hung his head, and closed his eyes.

Of course the thought would haunt him today. There was no way around it, not after his mother's call that morning. She knew better than to call him the day of a ride, but she did it anyway. The news had made Cody sick to his stomach, unable to force down more than a piece of toast and an apple all day. Her call played in his mind again.

"He found us." Her voice was nervous, mixed with fresh hope.

"Who?" Cody had still been in bed, the hotel sheets a mess from the night before. He blinked back a hard night's sleep and tried to focus. He was alone, though he hadn't been a few hours earlier. What was his mother talking about, someone finding them? Had Carl Joseph wandered off? "Tell me later; I'm tired."

"Cody, you need to hear this." His mother's voice grew stronger, happier. "Your father found us, Cody. He called a few minutes ago; he wants to see you and Carl Joseph."

Cody had sat straight up in bed. His heart pounded hard, sending shock waves through his chest and throat and temples. It wasn't possible. "My *father* called? After thirteen years he looks us up and you sound happy about it?"

Silence stood between them for a moment.

"He's sorry, Cody. Life hasn't been easy for him, either." She hesitated. "We had a long talk; he wants to see you."

Her words hit him like a load of buckshot, ripping at the places in his heart that still cared, still ached for his father no matter how much he told himself otherwise. A sound came from him, part laugh, part moan. Was she serious? How could she consider letting him back into their lives after what he'd done?

Cody leaned over his knees, the sheets loose around his waist. "I don't have a father."

"Cody, that's not how you feel, and—"

"I won't see him." His tone was sharp. "I need to go." He slammed down the phone, flopped back onto the pillow, and stared at the ceiling. The nausea hit him then. How dare he walk back into their lives now? How could he complain about his own life being hard when the whole mess was his fault?

Cody pressed his fists into his stomach and forced himself out of bed. What was the problem, anyway? He'd told her the truth; he didn't have a father.

But the conversation marred the entire day.

Normally the afternoon of a ride was marked by quiet preparation and nervous anticipation. In this case, he had both a hangover and his mother's phone call to shake off. The buildup felt flat, and all day he fought a headache.

Voices sounded outside the locker room door, and Cody hunkered down on the bench, his eyes still closed. The other cowboys would guess he was lost in concentration, readying himself for the ride. They'd leave him alone.

He pictured his father—however he must look with thirteen more years on him. Mike Gunner had played the field for more than a decade, shirked every ounce of family responsibility, and now—maybe because his son was a famous bull rider—he wanted back into their lives.

Worse, his mother was entertaining the possibility.

Adrenaline mixed with fury and ran hot through Cody's veins. He wanted to put his fist through the locker door, but he held back. *Save it for the bull, Gunner. Save it for the bull.* His eyes flew open. He stood, grabbed his rope, and headed down the tunnel.

The barrel racers were competing. He climbed a fence so he could stretch and watch at the same time. Over the loudspeaker the announcer was introducing the next ride.

"Ali Daniels is up, riding her longtime horse, Ace. Ali's on a streak of top-three finishes this season, and looking for the win here tonight. Anything less than fourteen-point-five seconds should do it, ladies and gentlemen."

He droned on about Ali's statistics, her intrigue and mystery.

Cody spread his legs wide until he felt the stretch along

the inside of his thighs. Ali Daniels didn't need an introduction. Next to him, she was the most well-known competitor on the tour. Beautiful, strange, and mysterious. She rode with a reckless abandon that Cody understood innately, an abandon he admired.

From the first time he saw her compete, Cody wanted to go to her, wanted to be with her and ride with her and know everything about her. She was quiet and reclusive, confident and masterful in her talent. For all the girls who gave him no resistance, Ali was the ultimate challenge.

But he didn't allow those feelings to be anything more than fleeting. His success on the tour depended on his anger. He was twenty-one, too young to fall for a girl. Not even a girl like Ali Daniels. And so he ignored her at every rodeo— except when she competed.

Cody leaned to the right, focusing the stretch on that leg. Just then, Ali tore out of the tunnel, her head close to her horse's mane. She wasn't hard-looking like some of the barrel racers. Black hat and black jeans, a starched white shirt, her light blonde ponytail flying behind her, eyes intent on making the turn. Tight around the first barrel, then she blazed across the arena and around the second.

The crowd was already on its feet.

Every time Ali rode, there was the possibility of her setting a new record. That night was no exception. She rounded the third barrel and leaned forward. She and her horse blazed across the barrier at 14.35 seconds.

"Ladies and gentlemen, we have a new arena record! Ali Daniels shaved two-tenths of a second off the previous fastest time for barrels in this arena. She's sitting pretty safe for first place. Let's show her our appreciation."

Again the crowd cheered.

Cody wanted to peer into the tunnel, watch her pull up and dismount the way other cowboys watched Ali Daniels. But he wouldn't. Times like this he was glad he'd kept his distance. He didn't need any distractions.

He shifted his weight to the left leg, feeling the stretch stronger than before. Forty minutes passed, while the anger he harbored rose and grew within him. Forty minutes of picturing Carl Joseph's face as their mother explained the obvious—their father was gone. Forty minutes of hating him for walking out, for not making it clear to Cody what he'd ever done wrong, how he might've been responsible for making his daddy leave.

Forty minutes when Ali Daniels was just another rider on the tour, when his mother and even his brother might as well have been a million miles away, when nothing mattered in life except the battle, the damage he was about to do to a bull named Monster Mash.

"You got yourself the best draw of the night, Gunner." One of the cowboys slapped his back and took a step toward the chute next to Cody's. "You ready?"

"Ready."

"Let's get 'em." The cowboy nodded at the spectators. "It's a good crowd tonight; they deserve a show."

"Nothin' but eight."

The bull riders were lined up by then, gathered near the chute of whichever cowboy was next out. One at a time the riders flew into the arena, half of them making the eight seconds, the other half bucked off. Cody cheered them on, because that's what cowboys did. They pulled for one another. Bull riding never pitted a cowboy against his fellow rider. The contest was against the bull, only the bull.

But even as he cheered, his heart was back on a street corner the summer of his eighth year, watching for that yellow cab.

Cody zipped up his protective vest and spread his legs. Stretching was crucial; he'd been loosening up for an hour already. He bent at the waist, nose to his right knee, two, three, four, five. A little farther, and he switched sides, nose to his left knee, two, three, four, five. A shift to the center, straight back, palms to the ground, two, three, four...The whole time he kept his eyes on the bull.

An announcer was introducing the matchup.

"Monster Mash is a Texas Brahma bull, genetically engineered by the best in the business. Wicked horns, and a twist—about to keep a cowboy guessing."

The other announcer broke in. "Now remember, this is a bull that hasn't been rode ever. Not once. A killer beast with an average score of forty-eight-nine. Twenty-three cowboys on; twenty-three off."

"And Cody Gunner wants to change all that."

Cody tuned it out.

He felt himself slipping into the zone, the place where his little-boy disappointment, his unchecked rage and pent-up hatred, could be released. If only for eight seconds.

Finally it was his turn.

He pressed his cowboy hat onto his head, low over his brow, ran a few steps in place, and climbed the gate. One leg over the top of the chute, then the other. A push and he braced himself with his hands until he was straddled above the bull. Monster Mash was an ugly beast, mottled gray with uneven coloring and evil black eyes. His horns weren't much threat, but the hump on his back had knocked out a cowboy or two. Cody knew this, but he didn't think about it, didn't think about the bull's tendencies or any of the things most riders thought about.

All that mattered was this: The bull wanted to kill him.

Cody saw it in the way those dead eyes watched him, anxious, waiting. The bull had an innate sense, an ability to spot the cowboy, sniff out the next sacrificial victim. The animal shouldered the gates and pawed at the ground. Those awful eyes never let up, never blinked.

If there'd been a way through the bars, the bull would've found it.

Van Halen's "Jump" pounded out a rhythm that grew and built and filled each of the fifteen thousand fans with a frenzied anticipation. Bull riding was the last event, the biggest draw. Rodeo fans loved it. Loved the energy and intensity and possibility of horrific wrecks, the idea of mere mortals going head-to-head with an untamable beast.

"That's right," Cody glared at the animal, "go ahead and try it."

The bull jerked his head, shark-like eyes rolling back into his skull. Cody could picture it, knew what would happen the instant they opened the gate. The bull would become two thousand pounds of snorting, sweating muscle, writhing and twisting and flying through the hot summer night driven by one desire: Kill the cowboy.

The bull rider didn't need the announcers to tell him; he knew the score. Monster Mash couldn't be ridden, wouldn't let a cowboy sit on his back four seconds, let alone eight. Five guys stood on the outside of the gate, two of them holding tight to Cody's jacket, ready to pull him out if the bull went psycho. But Cody was ready. He lowered himself a foot, not quite touching the animal, his feet still on the steel rungs.

"Yeah, you want me." Cody gritted his teeth. The hatred was growing, filling him with a burning intensity, a seething red-hot rage. Everything but the bull faded from view, the bull and the profile of a face.

His father's face.

How could he walk out on us?

The hatred bubbled within him, mingled with liquid intensity and spilled into his icy veins, pumped through his ready limbs.

"Let's go, Gunner." A cowboy on the gate grabbed his arm and slapped his back.

It was time.

He lowered himself onto the bull, just down from the animal's shoulder blades. The beast's muscles trembled, furious, his hide hot and sweaty and loose over his bony spine. Monster Mash was famous for his damage in the chute, and today was no exception. The animal shifted all his weight sideways and Cody bit into his mouth guard.

He smacked the bull's shoulder. Fiery pain shot through

his knee, the same knee he'd had pinned in the chutes six times this season. He couldn't leave the chute until he had his hand wrapped; couldn't wrap the hand until the bull let up, moved to the center, and freed his leg. Another whack and another. Fire shot up through his thigh. The deeper the pain, the more intense his hatred.

He was just a little boy, eight years old, full of laughter and love and kindness and goodness, and his little brother...

His little brother.

The rage tripled.

He shoved the bull's head. "Get outta there!" The animal moved three inches to the side and Cody jerked free. He shoved his right hand through the rope, palm up. Someone handed him the lead and he wrapped it hard, yanked it tight.

Cody wasn't sure if Monster Mash would spin to the outside or buck first. Films were available on every bull, and most riders memorized that sort of detail. Not Cody. He wanted his bulls unpredictable, because fury and hatred and rage were unpredictable.

The bull rattled the chute again, jerking his head back and snorting, spraying the legs of the two closest guys, sounding like the beast he was, hating the cowboy. Cody slid forward to his tied-down hand, checked to make sure his knees weren't trapped. He locked his eyes on the animal's neck and gave the signal—a quick nod. A click of the latch, and the gate flew open.

"Go, Gunner!" another cowboy yelled.

He was one second into the ride when Monster Mash

threw himself into a convulsion, all four hooves off the ground, twisting and snorting, kicking up dirt and dung in all directions. One-point-five seconds…two…two-point-five. The bull crashed down on his front feet, and already the animal's body was contorting in another direction, frantic to get the cowboy off his back. Cody kept his seat centered within a fraction of an inch, his legs tight around the bull.

Every late night wondering where his father was, why he hadn't called. Every birthday and Christmas and summer vacation without a gift or a card or even a call. All of that hatred poured from him, releasing the rage that would otherwise strangle him.

Monster Mash was off the ground again, flying in a circle, kicking his backside up into the air, but Cody wasn't going anywhere. He leaned back, staying with the ride, holding center. A buzzer sounded and suddenly it was over.

With a flick of his wrist to release his riding hand, he kicked his feet over the side of the bull. But something was wrong. His hand was hung up, and with the animal's next arch of his back, Cody flopped like a rag doll alongside the bull's belly.

This had happened before; Cody didn't panic. No matter what the bull did to him now, he was the winner. He'd already won the battle. From both sides he felt the bullfighters rush in, one of them grabbing at the end of the rope, trying to free his hand. The other waving something to distract the bull. The men might be dressed like clowns but they were willing to sacrifice their own bodies to keep a cowboy from danger. Cody was still caught up, still trying to free his hand, his body still being jerked along the side of the bull.

That's when he heard it.

A snap in his riding hand. At the same time, Monster Mash whipped his head back at him. The hump on his back caught Cody square in the jaw and that was all he remembered. When he woke up, he was lying on a bench with the rodeo doctor staring at him.

"Cody…" The man was in his mid-thirties, the first one on the scene of any wreck on the Pro Rodeo Tour. "Can you hear me? Cody?"

"What?" His head hurt, but his heart and soul reveled in the release. He'd stayed the course, ridden Monster Mash for eight, and nothing could change the way that felt. He massaged his fingers into the sides of his head. "What was my score?"

The doctor chuckled. "On the knockout or the ride?"

Cody gave his head a slight shake. "Forget the knockout. I'm fine."

"You got an eighty-nine." The doctor shone a small flashlight into his eyes. "How're you feeling?"

"Better." Cody ran his tongue over his lower lip. "Eighty-nine?"

"Yes." The doctor frowned. "Lift your hand."

Cody tried to move it, and that's when he understood the doctor's frown. He winced, and supported it with his left hand. "It's just sprained."

"X-rays will tell."

Half an hour later, Cody had his bags packed for a two-week visit to his mother's house. A small bone in his hand was fractured, and he had a mild concussion. The doctor ordered two weeks off the bulls—minimum. Cody was given a splint for his hand and instructions to lay low.

He was on his way out of the training room when he spotted Ali Daniels.

Every other time they'd passed each other—for two years straight—they barely looked up. Today, though, Ali paused.

"Want some advice?" She took another step toward him, a bridle flung over one shoulder.

Too stunned to answer, Cody stopped and sized her up. She was five-foot-six, maybe five-seven, and up close her eyes shone like summer lake water. He leaned against the nearest wall and grinned at her. "Okay."

"If you can stay on eight, stay on nine." She smiled and started walking again. "At least until your hand's free."

She was gone before he could recover, before even a single comeback formed on his tongue. Was she kidding? Did she think she had information that might help Cody Gunner ride bulls better? And why did she talk to him now, after so many events where they had never connected?

Cody had no answers. Maybe it was a delusion; concussions could do that to a person. He watched her leave and let the comment pass. He didn't have time for Ali Daniels or any of the other girls who would be waiting for him outside the arena. He had something far bigger ahead of him—two weeks to talk sense into his mother. That way, the next time his father called she could do what she should've done the day before.

Hang up on him.

Chapter Five

Mary Gunner loved having her older son home.

Out on the road, riding a slate of bulls every weekend, meant that bad news was always just around the corner. Mary knew the sport well enough to know the possibilities, and they terrified her. So when Cody showed up with his hand in a splint needing two weeks of rest, she was grateful.

Quietly grateful.

Cody wouldn't have it any other way. His anger at her hadn't dimmed from the days after Mike left. Never mind that his blaming her made no sense. The moment he entered the house he looked around, his expression tense.

"Where is he?"

Mary held his eyes for a moment, then she turned toward the stairs and cupped her mouth. "Carl Joseph! Your brother's home."

The sound of pounding footsteps came in response. "Brother!" the voice bellowed from an upper room.

"I'm down here, buddy!" Cody went to the foot of the stairs and looked up.

"Coming, brother!" Carl Joseph was fifteen now, still attending a special-education program where they were teaching him menial tasks. Most days Mary was grateful for Carl Joseph's Down syndrome. It meant that at least one son would always love her. One son would keep her company the way Cody never did.

Carl Joseph barreled down the stairs and gave Cody a long bear hug. When he pulled back, his eyes danced. "How's the bulls, brother?"

"Well..." Cody held up the hand that bore the cast. "Not so good this weekend."

"Ooooh!" He touched Cody's cast and shook his head. "You be careful, brother. You be careful."

Cody chuckled. "I will." He put his arm around Carl Joseph's neck and led his brother into the next room.

For two weeks straight the two were inseparable. They played checkers and backgammon and watched videotapes of bull riding on TV. The morning after Cody left, Carl Joseph found Mary reading a book in the living room.

"Mom, I have a question." He came a few steps closer.

Mary held her hand out to him. "What, honey?"

"How come Cody doesn't like you?" Carl Joseph cocked his head, his mouth open. "How come, Mom?"

The question tore at Mary's heart, but it was an honest one, proof that Cody's bad attitude wasn't only her imagination. She cleared her throat, searching for a way to explain the situation. She couldn't mention Mike. Carl Joseph didn't remember his father, and if Mike wanted back into their lives—the way he said he did—she didn't want to taint Carl Joseph's image of him.

"Cody loves me." Mary bit her lip, fighting tears. "But sometimes his heart doesn't work the same as yours."

"Brother's heart doesn't work right?" Carl Joseph thought about that for a minute. "You know what I hope?"

Mary slid to the edge of her seat, her eyes damp. The compassion in Carl Joseph was every bit as intense as the hatred in Cody. "What, honey?"

"I hope that Cody's heart will get better, just like his hand."

Mary hugged her younger son. "So do I, honey." He couldn't know that's what she'd hoped and prayed for years, what she prayed for even now—that one day Cody would meet someone who would teach him more than horses and rodeos and bull riding. Someone who might teach Cody the most important lesson of all.

How to love.

CODY WAS BACK on the tour, riding as if he'd never hurt his hand at all. Yes, he was using a lot of tape, wrapping his hand and forearm tighter than before. But a little pain was nothing. It made the battle that much more intense. Fighting not just the bull, but pain and injuries, too.

He was in second place in the standings, ten points below first despite two missed weekends. Regaining the lead was as sure as morning. His nighttime hours were different, too, fewer beers and women, cleaner, the way they always were after a few weeks with Carl Joseph.

His mother called twice in the next few weeks.

"Your father's been by," she told him during the first phone call. "Carl Joseph likes him. They played football in the backyard."

Football? The idea made Cody's gut ache. Mike Gunner, big former NFL player, loses thirteen years of his kids' lives and then shows up and tosses a ball around? Like nothing ever happened?

"He's asking about you, Cody," she told him the next time. "He wants to watch you ride."

"Tell him no." Cody was in the locker room. He dropped to the bench and gripped the edge of it, his voice low so the other cowboys passing in and out wouldn't hear him. In the background Lynyrd Skynyrd was singing "Sweet Home Alabama" over the arena speakers.

"I won't do that, Cody." His mother sounded impatient.

Cody pinched his eyes shut. What was the feeling tearing at him? Hatred, right? More anger and fury? But it didn't feel like only that. It felt like little-boy sadness, too. A sadness that didn't make sense because he'd banned it from his heart the day the yellow cab drove away.

"Cody, when can he see you?" His mother sounded tired, as if she knew his answer before he said it.

"Never." He pursed his lips. "I have nothing to say to him."

Whatever his mother wanted to accomplish by calling him, the end result was a good one. That weekend and the next, he took first and second, and now he had the lead heading into the final go-round in Houston at the Reliant Center. The barrel racing was under way, and Cody took his spot on the fence, stretching the insides of his legs and the muscles that lined his groin.

As always, he watched Ali's race. She was every bit as fast as usual, but this time something was wrong; her face was red and puffy. He looked around but no one along the fence looked worried, as if maybe he was the only one who saw that she was in trouble.

He was off the fence, jogging toward the tunnel before she crossed the barrier. He stepped into view just in time to see her hop down from her horse and lower her head between her knees.

She was coughing so hard she couldn't catch her breath. Cody stared for a minute. Was she sick? Was it asthma? Maybe she was choking. He grabbed a cup of water from a nearby cooler. With no one around, Cody wasn't sure what to do. He took tentative steps closer until she looked up.

"Ali?" He closed the distance between them and held out the cup.

She hacked again. "Thanks." She took it and downed it in a single swig. A few more coughs and the redness in her face started to fade. She leaned against her horse, clearly exhausted from the struggle. "I'm okay. I…I guess I have a cold."

"I guess." He took a step back. "I've never heard anyone cough like that."

She folded her arms in front of her and stared at him, eyes

wide. Then she nodded her chin toward the arena. "Your ride's coming up."

"Yeah." He tipped his hat to her. "Get better." He trotted off for the chutes, surprised by one thing.

Ali Daniels wasn't superhuman after all; he'd seen a vulnerable side of her. It was all he could do to shut her image out of his mind while he rode. The first bull that night tripped and fell to his knees, giving Cody a re-ride. He lasted eight on the second. His score wasn't great, but it was enough to win, and less than half an hour after her coughing episode, Ali Daniels stood next to him in the arena while they both accepted their championship buckles.

They were headed back down the tunnel when Cody fell in beside her. "Hey…wanna go out? Get something to eat?"

Ali hesitated. She met his eyes but only for a few seconds before staring straight ahead. "I can't; I have plans."

"Plans?" Cody allowed a smile into his voice. It wasn't that he doubted her, but she traveled with her mother, and the two of them were in her trailer before ten o'clock every night. What plans could she possibly have?

"Yes, Cody Gunner." She angled her face, teasing him. Her eyes didn't look quite right, maybe the cold she was fighting. "I have a hot date, okay?"

Cody wanted to laugh out loud, but he couldn't. He didn't know her well enough to assume she was kidding. Instead he shrugged and winked at her. "Suit yourself."

He held the door open for her and they headed into the night—her to her mother's trailer and whatever hot date she had that night, and Cody to the nearest bar to meet up with the other cowboys.

But it was another early night for him.

Dinner was good, the beer was flowing, and half a dozen girls made themselves available. But he wasn't interested. No matter what they looked like or how they presented themselves, or what they had to offer, Cody couldn't help but compare them to Ali Daniels.

And since they all fell short, he did the right thing. When he turned the key of his hotel room that night he was by himself, except for the place in his memory filled with the blonde, blue-eyed barrel racer.

A girl whose level of mystery had doubled in a single conversation.

Chapter Six

The hot date was a private plane ride to Denver General Hospital.

Ali had been expecting the visit since the second week of the season, and it frustrated her. This was the year she didn't want to miss a single event, the year she planned to keep herself healthy so she wouldn't need any downtime in a hospital bed.

But her body had other ideas.

It was Monday night now, and her mother was in the chair beside her bed. Dr. Bryce Cleary was due any minute, the same doctor who had treated Ali since she began riding horses. The visit wasn't any surprise, really. Since early in the season, her coughing had been more intense, the spells closer together.

The lives of cystic fibrosis patients are directed by test results. Bacteria analysis, lung function, nutritional deficiencies, enzyme levels. All have to be closely monitored. When one or more of Ali's readings fell into their respective danger zones, it was time to see Dr. Cleary.

In the hospital she would be on constant oxygen and intravenous antibiotics. Her body would get the rest it needed, the infection she was fighting would clear up, and after a week she could get on with living. At least that's how it had always played out before.

Ali rolled onto her side and studied her mother. "You look worried."

"I'm not much for hospitals; you know that." She reached out and took Ali's hand.

"Me either."

They were quiet for a minute. Ali knew what her mother was thinking—the same thing she was thinking. Anna died in a room like this one, her body trying to find the way back to daylight. They both know cystic fibrosis patients weren't admitted to the hospital unless their situation was serious.

There were no guarantees, no certainties that this would be merely another tune-up, another pit stop between rodeo appearances.

Her mother leaned back in her chair. "After your win the other night"—their eyes met—"why was Cody Gunner talking to you?"

A smile lifted the corners of Ali's mouth before she could stop it. "He asked me out."

"Cody Gunner?" Her eyebrows lifted, creasing her forehead. She still held Ali's hand, but now she loosened her grip. "Why didn't you tell me?"

"I couldn't breathe; I guess I was distracted." Her smile softened. For a minute she could see Cody's face as he walked next to her. "It's okay, Mama. I'm not interested."

Her mother hesitated. A slow breath came from her. "You know I have hopes and dreams for you. That you'll live long enough to be loved, that when the time's right you'll meet someone. Someone who'll sweep you off your feet and take you away from horse dander and dusty arenas and damp hay." She looked at the ceiling. "But heaven forbid it be someone like Cody Gunner."

Ali laughed, and the effort brought on a wave of coughs. "Mama…I told you I wasn't interested." She gulped, catching her breath. "Wish for my health, but don't wish that I'll meet someone." She stroked her thumb along her mother's hand. "I am loved—by you and Daddy. I have the life I want—me and Ace, winning on the rodeo tour, flying across arenas in every city on the schedule." She felt her expression soften. "That's all I need."

Her mother looked at her, a look that went straight to her soul. "Ali, before you die, I want you to be loved the way your father loves me. Loved by a man who would give anything for you." She paused. "Horses can't compare to a love like that."

Ali didn't respond. Her mother was wrong, of course. Horses were enough; they had always been enough. But there was no changing her mother's mind. They had this discussion at least once a month. Ali believed her mother was less interested in her meeting a man than she was in her leaving the rodeo tour.

She bit her lip. She'd already told her mother the way she felt about falling in love. She wouldn't do it. She'd dated once, the year before she joined the PRCA. After a series of colds and a hospital stay, the boy told her he couldn't handle her being sick. And he didn't even know about her cystic fibrosis.

The experience convinced her that dating was a waste of time. She didn't want to disappoint someone every time she got sick; and in the end, any relationship would end too soon. That was the way of life for a cystic fibrosis patient.

Riding Ace was enough; it was all she wanted. Her mother could dream twenty-four hours a day, but nothing would change Ali's determination. She would stay on the Pro Rodeo Tour until her body gave her no choice but to quit. Then she would live with her parents until the end. No sad good-byes other than the ones she would have with them and Ace.

There was a knock at the door and Dr. Cleary entered the room. "Hi." He had a manila file in his hand. "How're you feeling, Ali?"

"Better." She rolled onto her back and released her mother's hand. "My lungs are still full, though. I can feel them."

"Yes." The doctor came to the foot of her bed and looked at her. "Your numbers could be better. You've lost some weight, so I'm increasing your enzymes."

"That's what the nurse said." Ali managed a smile. The routine was the same every time. Eat more, take the enzymes, adjust the medication. She wanted him to get to the good part, the part where he told her how long until she could be released, until she could be back at her next rodeo.

"Is it worse than before?" Her mother's lips were pale, narrow and pinched. Her fear was palpable. She forced a tight smile. "You know Ali. She thinks these visits are tune-ups." She paused. "Is this one different?"

"Well…yes." The doctor opened the file and sorted through several sheets. He looked up and met Ali's eyes. "It's different because after two full days of treatment, her lungs aren't responding the way I'd like."

Ali's heart missed a beat. She had grown up around doctors and hospitals; nothing in the medical world frightened her. But what was Dr. Cleary saying? She propped herself up. "So increase the medicine, right? Is that what's next?"

The doctor closed the file and let his hands fall to his sides. "Ali, your lung tissue is losing elasticity. You've always known this was where you were headed."

Her mother lifted her chin, her back stiff. "So, what does that mean? She stays in the hospital longer?"

"We'll increase her medication and keep her for a week, like always." He pursed his lips. "The problem is, at this point, her lungs can't rebound as well. Every time her numbers get bad, she'll lose some of her lung capacity permanently. Some of the bacteria won't ever go away. That's where we're at."

Ali swallowed against the lump in her throat. The doctor was wrong; he had to be. Her lungs weren't worse than usual; the feeling was the same as always. "Isn't there anything… can't you give me something to bring them back all the way, like before?"

"Yes." The doctor's tone was gentle but stern. "I can give you an order, Ali. When you leave the hospital this time, go home and stay home. Sell your horse and take up piano again. You have to stay away from all irritants if you want to slow this thing."

Ali shook her head, her mind spinning. The doctor's

order was out of the question. Impossible. She glanced at her mother. Was that relief in her eyes? Did she pay the doctor to come up with such a crazy suggestion? She leaned on her elbows and met the doctor's eyes straight on. "I'm in the middle of a season, Doctor. I'm not quitting."

The doctor clutched the file to his middle and looked at her, silent. Something in his expression told Ali he was being straight with her. Remorse fell into the mix of feelings burying her. She couldn't blame Dr. Cleary. The news wasn't easy for him either.

Finally he drew a slow breath and looked at them.

"Let me make it clearer." He opened the folder again. "The dust and molds and allergens at horse arenas have done permanent damage to your lungs. If you don't stop riding, you'll need a lung transplant in a year or less."

A lung transplant? Things were that bad?

Ali's heart raced and the mattress beneath her felt wobbly and off-balance. Cystic fibrosis patients didn't get lung transplants until their situations were dire. Unless…She held her breath, hopeful. Maybe things were different now, maybe a lung transplant would cure her. "Would that make me better?"

Her mother hung her head and shaded her eyes. This was the worst possible news; the news all of them had dreaded since Ali started riding horses.

The doctor took a step closer. "Nothing's changed." He patted Ali's hand. "A transplant buys you three years, maybe four. Less if you don't take care of yourself."

"Doctor…" Her mother lifted her head. Tears pooled in

her eyes. "Are you saying if Ali doesn't stop riding she *could* need a transplant, or she *will* need one?"

The doctor brought his lips together and exhaled in a way that filled his cheeks. He gave a sharp sideways shake of his head. "Anything could happen, Mrs. Daniels. There's a chance she could return to riding and not see things get worse for more than a year. Two or three years even. But eventually it'll catch her. I'm completely certain of that."

Ali was trembling. What were all the tubes attached to her, anyway? She wanted to rip them from her arms and run from the room, from the awful news. But something the doctor said caught her attention. "So you could be wrong? About needing it within the year?"

"You can hear what you want to hear." The doctor's expression was soft, sympathetic, but he sounded defeated. "I'm advising you to stop riding—the sooner, the better."

Ali stared at him. Then she let her head fall back against the pillow. "I won't stop." She closed her eyes. "Please, do everything you can to make me better. I'll finish this season, and then I'll decide."

The doctor knew not to argue. He'd recommended against horses since she was eleven. "Very well." He took a few steps back. "I'd like to run tests on your parents; see if they'd be a match. We're doing transplants with live donors these days, but it takes two people to pull it off."

"Live donors?" Her mother looked hopeful, and Ali's heart hurt for her.

"It's a serious ordeal, Mrs. Daniels. One donor gives the lower right lobe, the other gives the lower left. Anyone who donates a lobe will experience a permanent loss in lung function."

"That wouldn't be a problem." She nodded. "We'd like to be tested right away."

With that, the doctor was gone. Ali wanted to scream and cry and bury her head in the pillow. She didn't want her parents going through something that drastic, a difficult surgery and the loss of lung function. Not when it had always been her decision to keep riding, to put her health at risk.

She opened her eyes and looked at her mother. "I'm sorry, Mom." She reached out and took her hand again. The doctor could check all he wanted; she wouldn't take a lung from either of her parents. It wasn't their fault she was sick. It was her own. Her determination to keep riding.

"Ali"—her mother's eyes pleaded with her—"You're the best in rodeo. Isn't that enough?"

"I haven't won a national championship, Mama. Ace and I can do it. It might still happen this season." Her lungs hurt from the emotion building within her. "I can't stop riding; you know that."

Instead of yelling at her or demanding she stop, her mother dabbed at her eyes and stared at her folded hands. "I don't know how we'll tell your father."

Ali felt the victory all the way to her soul. "He'll understand."

She looked up and their eyes held. "I understand, too. I just want to keep you around a little longer."

"I know. Thanks, Mama."

She was released from the hospital a week later with a

stronger arsenal of medicines and inhalers and strict orders to use her vest two to three times a day. Especially at rodeos.

The next week while she recuperated at home, watching old movies with her father and helping her mother in the kitchen, Cody Gunner's name never came up.

Except in Ali's mind.

She'd told her mother the truth; she wasn't interested. Not in Cody or anyone else. Despite her mother's prayers to the contrary, she would not get involved with a man; not when she had so little time, when her sport demanded every spare moment.

Still, her first night out of the hospital, when her parents had turned in and sleep wouldn't come, when the prospect of getting off Ace for good or being relegated to a lung transplant left her too frightened to close her eyes, she found comfort in one thing alone. The memory of Cody Gunner leaving his place on the fence to bring her a cup of water. The sound of his voice, the feel of his body a foot from hers in the tunnel, the guarded kindness in his voice as he asked her out.

By morning, she shook off the crazy thoughts and promised to never entertain them again. Cody Gunner? Any thought of him was ridiculous, unwanted. She didn't care a bit for the guy. He was a player, a renegade who needed no one. It was one thing to ride horses against her doctor's orders. But to have feelings for Cody Gunner?

Even she wasn't that crazy.

Chapter Seven

Cody hated himself for worrying, but he couldn't help it.

For two straight events, Ali Daniels hadn't shown up and that could only mean one thing. Her cold was worse than he'd thought. Maybe it wasn't a cold, but pneumonia. Maybe she was in the hospital.

Thoughts of her distracted him, and he rode below what he was capable of at both events, taking a fourth place and a no-score. The third weekend, he spotted her trailer and felt himself relax. Whatever the problem, she must have recovered.

He saw her that Saturday morning, several hours before the spectators were scheduled to arrive. She was riding her horse in the field behind the arena, tearing up one way, circling imaginary barrels, and then racing like the wind back toward the edge of the parking lot.

Cody loved horses, but he didn't own one. Most of the

time he flew to events and stayed in hotels. Ali and the other competitors who relied on their horses traveled in motor homes, pulling horse trailers. He wandered toward the stock area and borrowed a horse from one of the steer wrestlers. In an easy motion, he swung himself into the saddle and galloped out to the field toward Ali.

She looked healthy and tanned; her cheeks clear of the puffy redness.

He pulled up near her. She turned two tight circles, then stopped and faced him. He held her gaze. "You've been gone."

"Yes." Without tugging on the reins, the animal leaned his head back, and she rested against his neck. She was breathless from the workout. "Did you get hung up while I was away?"

A strange feeling worked its way through Cody's gut, a feeling he couldn't quite identify. He allowed the hint of a smile. "I would've." He leaned forward, his hands covering the saddle horn. "But I got the best advice."

"Really?" Her expression was light, easy.

"Really." He danced his horse sideways a few steps. "Someone told me if I could stay on for eight, I could stay for nine. You know, use the extra second to untie my hand so I wouldn't get hung up."

"Well?" She shifted back in her saddle. "Did it work?"

"Like a charm." He lifted his hands so she could see them. "No more casts."

"Hmmm." She raised one eyebrow. "Imagine that." Her

heels pressed against her horse's belly. And without further warning, she was off, flying down the field, clearly intent on finishing her workout.

Cody watched her, and the challenge was too great to pass up. He switched the reins from one side of the horse's neck to the other. "Yah!" And suddenly he was tearing up the field after her, mesmerized by her speed and ability. He didn't catch up with her until she reached the far side.

She brushed her hair off her face, her cheeks ruddy from the exertion. "Are you chasing me?"

He held the reins tight against his waist. With the sun on her face, exhilarated from the ride, she wasn't only beautiful. She was irresistible. He waited until he had his breath again. "Do you want me to?"

"No." A laugh came from her, one that sounded like the most delicate wind chimes. "There's no point."

"Why not?" His words were slow, the conversation unhurried. They were far enough from the arena that no one could see them, no one would wonder why Cody Gunner was talking to Ali Daniels.

"Because"—she smiled—"I don't want to be caught." She set her horse in motion again. "See ya."

There was laughter in her voice. She was kidding, of course. All girls wanted to be caught. But maybe Ali was different in this, too. He didn't ride after her. Instead he set out at a diagonal, back toward the stock pen. He returned the horse and headed to the hotel for breakfast.

It took him an hour to stop replaying their conversation

in his head. He chided himself, hating the way she'd distracted him that morning. If she didn't want to be caught, fine. He wouldn't chase her.

He needed his focus, needed to stay angry, in touch with the rage. Nothing in his riding regimen had room for the strange feelings she stirred inside him. But after their encounter that morning, he couldn't get into a rhythm, couldn't find the way back to the pain that kept him centered on the back of a bull for eight violent seconds. He was bucked off an easy ride, a bull that had been ridden 70 percent of the time.

He was walking down the tunnel, disgusted, when he saw Ali sitting by herself outside the locker room. She was coughing, but she stopped when she saw him.

"Ready for more advice?" She stood and leaned against the wall.

Normally after a buck-off, he wouldn't talk to anyone. But his frustration had no staying power in her presence. He stopped and crossed his arms. "Let me guess, don't fall off, right?"

"No." She pushed the toe of her boot around in the dirt. A smile lifted her lips. "That would help, but you should anticipate more. The way you ride, it's all about reacting. You should balance that. Focus on the feel of the bull's shoulders and anticipate his next move. Anticipation first; then reaction." She lifted one shoulder and fell in alongside him. "Couldn't hurt."

He stopped just before the men's locker room door. "Thank you, Ali." His tone was dry, mildly sarcastic. He was still dusty from being bucked off the easiest bull at the rodeo. She couldn't expect him to be cheerful. "How did I get along without you?"

"That one"—she pushed the door of the women's locker room and grinned—"I can't help you with."

Cody waited outside the arena for her, but she never showed.

He was on his way back to the hotel when two bull riders and a half dozen scantily dressed girls met him in the parking lot. He hung with them for a few hours, but just before midnight—when one of the girls moved onto his lap—Cody called it a night.

As he fell asleep, he promised himself he wouldn't lose another go-round because of Ali Daniels. She wasn't interested, and neither was he. That was reason enough to put her out of his mind.

The next day he was getting ready for his ride when his heart dropped.

Not ten yards ahead of him stood his mother and his brother and a man who looked very much like his father. Cody glared at the man. Was it really him? Had he come without being invited? Cody wanted to walk up and punch him in the face, release on the man a fraction of the rage he felt when he climbed on a bull. But not in front of Carl Joseph. He was about to turn around when his mother spotted him.

"Wait, Cody." She wore jeans, and a red sweater he'd never seen before. She took light running steps toward him. "Don't leave."

He shook his head and took a step back, but it was too late. Carl Joseph saw him. "Brother! Hi, brother!"

Cody stopped. He gritted his teeth and ordered his heart to kick into a normal beat. When his mother was inches from him, he leaned in, his voice strained. "Why'd you bring him?"

"He wanted to come." She wore sunglasses, but he could see the fear in her face. "You're his son, Cody. You need to talk to him."

Carl Joseph was loping up. "Brother! Guess what?"

"Hey, buddy." Cody couldn't let his brother know he was mad. "You gonna watch me ride tonight?"

"Yeah, and guess what?" He jumped a few times in place. "I met my dad. He's your dad, too!" Carl Joseph pointed at the man, still waiting ten yards back. "See, brother. That's him. That's our dad!"

The excitement in Carl Joseph's voice made Cody furious. The nerve of the man, coming back into their lives and getting Carl Joseph's hopes up. When he walked out the next time it would change the kid forever, just as it had changed Cody.

Carl Joseph tugged on his arm. "Come meet him, brother. He wants to talk to you."

A seething hatred consumed him. He shot another angry look at his mother. It took all his effort to keep his tone even. "Listen, buddy, I need to get ready for my ride. I'll talk to him later, okay?"

"Okay." Carl Joseph gave him a dramatic high five. "Have a good ride, brother!"

Without saying another word to his mom, without another glance at his father, he turned and headed fast in the opposite direction. That night—intently aware that somewhere in the stands his father was sitting next to Carl Joseph—the ride was easier than it had been in weeks. Cody rode out his rage, taking every bit of it out on the bull. In the process he kept a seat on a beast known for its violent wrecks.

Cody's score for the night was ninety-three—his highest of the season, and enough to put him in the championship round.

He stayed in the locker room until he was sure his family was gone. When he was ready to leave, he exited to the outdoors. There would be no partying for him that night; not when he had a decade of emotions to sort through. Before turning in, there was something he had to do. He made his way through the parking lot to Ali's trailer and gave a light knock on the door.

She wore jeans and a sweatshirt, and in the moonlight she looked impossibly beautiful. "Cody...what're you—"

"Ali." He tipped his hat, a grin tugging at his mouth. "Just wanted to thank you for the advice. My win tonight...it was all you."

With that he turned and headed for the hotel across the street. He was gone before she could respond.

Chapter Eight

Cody avoided Ali as much as possible.

They were midway through the season, and points were crucial if he wanted to take a lead into the summer. After seeing his father, he had no trouble focusing, no difficulty identifying the demons only bull riding could battle. He won three straight and by the first part of June there was no one close.

His mother still called, but he didn't mind. Every conversation about his father was fuel for the fire, another reason to attack the bull, to go the distance no matter how violent the ride. The guy was serious about coming back. He took a job coaching at a small college a mile from their house. The story was the same with every phone call. His father was desperately sorry, anxious for a second chance.

"The call of every Christian is to forgive," his mother told him one morning. "Please, Cody, give him a chance."

"That's funny." Cody wanted to laugh. "I thought the call

of every Christian was to love." He tightened his grasp on the cell phone. "Remind him of that, why don't you."

His mother didn't miss a beat. "What would you know of love, Cody? You don't love anyone but Carl Joseph. No one else gets in."

"I don't need anyone else."

"You do, Cody. You'll waste your whole life fighting make-believe battles if you don't turn around and see the truth. We all love you, Cody. Carl Joseph and I, and even your father."

Cody was shaking by then. "Don't mention his name again or I'll hang up."

The battle raged.

Cody could only guess how the situation with his parents would turn out, but he was sure of this: He wouldn't go home again. Not until his father was out of the picture. The man had changed the course of his life, sent him chasing after death every weekend of the year. He should've been playing football for some college team by then, but instead he was crippled with rage.

A rage that was worse than ever, one even bull riding barely eased.

※

ALI COULD TELL Cody was staying away.

He was winning, but he looked angry as he stormed around the arena, angry and distant. The two of them hadn't spoken to each other in weeks.

That was okay; Ali was fighting her own battles.

Despite an arsenal of stronger medications and inhalers, she was struggling during events. She could still hold her breath during the ride, but afterwards, when she grabbed that first bit of air, she would slip into a coughing spasm that sometimes lasted five minutes.

Other riders had begun to notice. Whereas they typically kept their distance, reacting to her aloofness, now a few of them expressed concern.

"You should see a doctor about that cough," an older rider told her the day before. "You sound like you have pneumonia."

If they only knew.

That day, Ali added a third session with the compression vest. The treatment helped, but a few hours later she finished her ride with one of her slowest times of the season, and afterwards she lapsed into a series of coughs that wouldn't let up.

She was doubled over near her horse when she felt his hand on her shoulder.

"Ali...here." This time Cody handed her a full water bottle. "Maybe you're allergic to dust."

"Maybe." Ali took a long drink. She had her own water, but it was twenty yards away, near the back of the tunnel. Another swig and she could feel her lungs relax, feel the air making its way into even the stubborn areas that were no longer soft and pliable. "I'm fine." She wiped her brow and met his eyes. "Thanks."

He studied her for a minute. "I have to go."

"Yep." She smiled. "My advice is still paying off."

Cody grinned and let his gaze fall to his boots. When he looked up, his eyes were more vulnerable than before. "Can I ask you something?"

"You just did." She lowered her chin, her eyes big. It felt fun to tease him.

"I'm serious, Ali." He looked over his shoulder at the arena. The last barrel racer was about to go. His ride was coming up.

"Okay." She took another drink from the bottle. She could breathe now; but she needed to get out of the tunnel. The dust there was almost as bad as it was on the barrel course. She squinted at him. "Ask."

"Why do you ride sick?"

The words skipped across the surface of her heart like a series of smooth stones. She met his gaze, unblinking. "Why do you ride angry?"

He mulled over her question and finally gave her a slow nod. "The answers are somewhere, aren't they?"

"Probably."

"Let's talk tonight." The teasing faded from his eyes. "Can we do that, Ali?"

The truck was circling the barrel course now; a handful of cowboys tossing the bins in the back, clearing things for the bull riders. Ali knew what her mother would think. Anyone but Cody Gunner...She looked at the arena. "You need to go."

"Tell me, Ali. We'll find someplace and talk for an hour. Nothing more."

Ali bit her lip. She needed to wear the vest for an hour

before she could do anything. "Come by my trailer around eleven. Knock once on the door; I'll be waiting."

For the first time in weeks, the anger lifted entirely from Cody's face. "Me, too."

Ali rarely stayed in the arena long enough to watch the bull riders. If she wanted her lungs to bounce back from a race, she needed to get Ace out to the stock pens so she could breathe fresh air. Then, as soon as possible, she would return to the trailer and slip on the compression vest.

Her mother would already be there, waiting.

But that night, she wanted to watch Cody ride. So she took care of Ace and headed back down the tunnel toward the arena. Bull riders were crazy. Ali had always thought so. It was one thing to ride a horse around a pattern of barrels. But to sit on a bucking bull, to think for a minute it was possible to master two thousand pounds of muscled beast, that was crazy.

Crazy and dangerous.

One of the riders that night got hung up on a bull's horns. He was almost free when the bull jerked his head back and hit the rider's face square on. It wasn't as bloody as it could've been, but the rider was knocked out, cold.

The bullfighters rushed in and distracted the animal, saving the rider's life. When it was safe, a stretcher was brought out. Even the announcer—usually optimistic in the face of injuries, sounded concerned. Two riders later a cowboy was bucked off and landed on his head. He lay motionless for nearly a minute before giving a weak movement with first his hands, then his feet.

Two more riders and then it was Cody's turn.

The announcer was commenting on Cody's luck, how he always seemed to draw the rankest bulls. That was a good thing because half the rider's score came from the bull's ability to buck. The best stock could twist in more than one direction and keep their front and back feet off the ground at the same time, flying through the air.

Ali read the reports. Cody had a knack for drawing that type of bull at least once every rodeo. She watched him climb onto the bull, and that's when she saw it. She was right; he rode angry. From the moment he straddled the bull, his jaw was set, his eyes narrow. They showed his face on the big screen, and his expression was so colored with rage it made her take a step back.

The chute opened and Cody held on, focused and intent. The seconds ticked off, and Cody didn't give the bull a single centimeter's edge. He stayed perfectly centered, his left hand in the air no matter what the bull did to buck him off.

His ride brought him an eighty-six, good enough for second place heading into the final go-round the next day. Ali hurried out of the arena, her stomach in knots. What was the feeling inside her? The strange fluttering of her heart when he survived the ride and pumped his fist in the air? Was it the oneness, the sameness Ali had recognized in him before?

Ali had no answers as she darted through the rows of trailers and RVs. When she reached theirs, her mother was outside waiting. "Where've you been?"

"Talking." Ali walked past her, up the few stairs and into

the trailer. She found her vest, eased her arms into it, and zipped it up.

"Ali..." Her mother followed her back into the trailer. She sounded more tired than angry. "Your lungs can't take it; you know that."

"Mama..." She flipped the compression switch. The machine made a gentle whirring sound and the vest began to inflate. "I've gone two years riding this tour without so much as a friend." Her tone was soft; she had no desire to fight. "I think it's okay if I hang around one time to talk, don't you?"

Her mother hesitated. Then she kissed the top of Ali's head. "I want you well, Ali. As long as possible."

"I know." Their eyes met. "I'm sorry."

Ali spent the next hour angry with herself. She shouldn't have asked Cody to come. She was wrong to invite him; wrong to make him think she was even a little interested. A friendship with him wouldn't lead anywhere, not when her health was so unstable. There was no reason to involve him.

The knock came at eleven on the dot.

Her mother was long since asleep. Ali pulled a jacket on over her sweater, opened the door and slipped outside, down the steps so that she was standing in front of him. "Hi."

"Hi." Cody took a step back, giving her space. He wore his heavy PRCA jacket, jeans, and a cowboy hat. It was easy to see why the girls never left him alone.

"My mom's asleep." Ali shut the trailer door.

"Oh." He stuck his hands in his pockets.

The night was the warmest it had been all season, and

a slight breeze played in the distant trees. The parking lot floodlights were off. The only glow came from a canopy of stars and a sliver of the moon hanging on the horizon.

"Follow me." She led him around the front of the trailer where two canvas chairs were set up. It was the place where she and her mother would sometimes sit and talk while they waited for Ali's events.

She took one of the chairs and he took the other, sliding it so it would be closer to her. "I got eight." His voice was a whisper.

"I know." She angled herself so she could see him better.

"You left."

"I came back." Ali studied him. Was he interested or only curious? Either way she had no business leading him on. "You were good."

A smile danced in his eyes, one she could see even in the dark. "Just following advice, ma'am." He shrugged one shoulder. "Sure glad you said something."

She grinned. "I do what I can to help." Her lungs wanted a full breath, but she could only take in so much air. She should've felt better after an hour with the vest. Her grin faded. It was a reminder she should keep the conversation brief. "Okay, you wanted to talk."

He hesitated. "You were gonna tell me why you ride sick." He leaned closer, his voice quiet. "Maybe you should get an inhaler or something."

She smiled. Four inhalers lay in a drawer inside the trailer. "I ride because I love it, Cody. Same as all of us." Her hair blew in the breeze and she caught it, smoothing it back. A tinny Hank Williams song played from a nearby trailer, and the smell of horses hung in the air. "I just get sick more." She hesitated. How much should she tell him?

Cody stretched his legs, his boots almost touching hers. "Doesn't it make you worse, riding when you're sick?"

"If you were sick, you'd ride anyway." She stared at the moon for a minute, then back at him. "Right?"

He leaned back, locked his fingers together and placed them behind his head. "I guess." He narrowed his eyes, more concerned than curious. "Why are you sick so much?"

She blinked, waiting. "That's the question I never answer."

"I know." He angled his head, his eyes searching. "That's why I'm here."

"Hmmm." She pressed into the canvas chair. For the wildest moment, she actually considered it. What if she told him? Her secret had belonged to her and her parents all these years, but somehow—in the dark night with Cody Gunner—she wanted him to know. Maybe then he would lose interest; it would be easier than telling him later.

One thing was sure. Her secret would be safe with him. Cody talked to no one, same as her. If anyone could keep her situation under wraps, he could.

"Tell me, Ali." He leaned closer.

The smell of him was intoxicating. Leather and cologne, and something Ali couldn't make out. Confidence and charisma. The intangible that made every bull rider larger than life. The scenario played out in her mind. What would it hurt? She could have a friend on the tour, couldn't she? Someone who would know what she was up against?

Her hands trembled and her heart raced. She sat up straighter in the chair and met his eyes. "I have cystic fibrosis." There. She'd said it. She pulled her knees up and hugged them to her chest, her eyes still on his. "It's a lung disease."

Cody stared at her, his eyes wide. "Cystic fibrosis?" His expression changed from shock to anger and back to shock again. "Is it bad?"

Ali wasn't surprised at his question. Most people her age didn't know about CF unless they had a reason to know. "Yes." She rested her chin on her knees, but it did nothing to ward off the chill in her heart. "Cystic fibrosis is always bad."

His expression was frozen, as if he were waiting for her to laugh out loud and tell him it was all a bad joke. "You're serious?"

"Serious." She felt herself relax. Relief and a new sort of camaraderie flooded her soul. It felt wonderful to finally tell someone the truth. "That's why I cough so much; it's why I ride sick." She smiled. "I have no choice."

He was still motionless. His mouth was open, but it took a long while for the words to come. "Will you die?"

"Everyone dies." She kept her tone light. He didn't need to know everything.

"I mean it, Ali. How sick are you?" This time something vulnerable flashed in his eyes, a depth of emotion that couldn't have been easy for someone as private as Cody Gunner.

"I'm sorry." She sat straighter and gripped her knees, not sure what to say. Was she really having this conversation with him? Sitting beside him in the dark parking lot outside the arena, sharing secrets she'd kept all her life? She bit the inside of her cheek. "CF doesn't have a pattern. It'll shorten my life, yes. But no one knows exactly how much."

He stared at her for a few more heartbeats. Then he stood and walked a few feet away, his back to her. His outline was impressive in the shadows, the cowboy hat and jacket only adding to his image. He wasn't going to stay, she could tell. Her honesty had frightened him. They probably wouldn't talk again after this.

"Cody?"

He turned, hung his head for a moment, then straightened and returned to his chair. A long sigh left his lips as he looked at her again. "I'm sorry."

"Don't be." She lowered her voice. If they weren't careful her mother would wake up. "I'm doing what I love. How many people can say that?"

"Riding horses." He lifted his hat and pushed his fingers up his forehead and into his short hair. His voice was tinged with pain and frustration. "That can't be good for you."

The breeze was picking up, the temperature dropping. "Anything that makes me feel that alive is good for me." Ali eased her feet back to the ground. "I get sick once in a while, but the doctors know what to do for me."

"That's why you were gone a few weeks ago?" The reality of her situation was settling in. The shock was gone, and now his eyes held a helplessness, a futility.

"Yes. I spent a week in the hospital. Sort of a tune-up." Ali turned toward him in her chair so she could see him better. "I wear a compression vest three times a day. Otherwise my lungs will get worse."

"So that's…" He swallowed, his eyes wide. "That's why you go straight to your trailer."

"Mm-hmm." She felt utterly at peace. How wonderful to finally tell another competitor the truth, more wonderful than she could've imagined. Hiding her sickness had allowed her to compete like anyone else; but the journey hadn't been easy. Everyone wondered about her; they guessed about what made her different from the others.

Now Cody knew.

She explained how she held her breath when she rode, how she took only a few inhalations in the tunnel to keep from breathing in too much dust, and how she'd kept the entire ordeal a secret. "I never wanted anyone to leak it to the press. I wanted people to know me for the way I run barrels, not my sickness."

"Why me, Ali?" His eyes softened. "Why'd you trust me?"

"You asked." She looked at the silhouette of the nearby mountains against the sky. Then she found his eyes again. "You're a lot like me, Cody. All you need is the ride."

"Yes." Cody thought about that. "Can I do anything to help? Anything that would make it easier for you?"

She grinned. "Sure. Don't talk to me in the tunnel." She pointed toward a clearing a few yards away. "And could you ride your bulls out here so I could watch?"

His smile broke the tension of the moment. "If they'd let me, I'd do that every night. I hate the crowds. They're not why I ride."

Silence sat between them for a time.

"That brings us to you, Cody Gunner." She lived with CF every day of her life. She was finished talking about it for now. "What makes you so mad? I watched you tonight, all that anger. It has to come from somewhere." She waited. "What are you fighting out there?"

Cody studied her for a minute. "You should get in; you have goose bumps."

"I'm okay." She paused, wanting his answer.

"No. It's late." He reached out his hand to help her up. "I don't want you getting a cold."

The minute his fingers touched hers, she felt it. A current of something new and wild and exciting. Something that touched her heart and soul and body all at the same time. As soon as she was on her feet, she let go and the moment was over. Her cheeks were hot, and she was glad for the darkness.

"Okay." She swallowed. Was he really worried about the cold air, or had her honesty scared him? Either way, he was right. She needed to get inside. "Maybe some other time."

"What about tomorrow?"

"Tomorrow?" Her heart soared.

"If it's okay. I'll meet you here, same time?"

"Okay."

They stood, facing each other. For a long moment she searched beyond his eyes. She'd been wrong earlier. He wasn't afraid of her disease. They had found a friendship, and she was completely comfortable with that. He wouldn't tell anyone her secret. Besides, it didn't matter as much now. Dr. Cleary was right; her time on the tour was short.

Eventually everyone would know the truth about Ali Daniels.

"Thanks for talking." He slid his hands into his pockets again. "Go in and get warm."

He hesitated, and she wondered if he was going to hug her. But then he took two steps back and tipped his hat. "Good night, Ali."

"Good night."

She was inside before she acknowledged the subtle ache in her chest. She was breathless, flushed, the way she felt when she needed her inhaler. Only this time the feeling was different, and Ali knew why. She wasn't breathless because of the night air or the long day or the battles she fought with cystic fibrosis.

She was breathless because of Cody Gunner.

ALI DROVE HIM in ways he didn't dare tell her.

That first night was the beginning of many. Through summer and into fall, for the rest of the season, Cody was driven by a different set of feelings. He enjoyed the bulls more, embracing the adrenaline rush and smiling more often when he lasted eight seconds. After a good ride, he would raise his fists to the crowd and grin at their applause, or toss his hat at a bull that had given him a winning ride. For the first time, Cody identified with the other cowboys on the tour. It was a rush, riding bulls, a rush Cody had missed too often in the years when every ride was consumed with thoughts of his father.

Now, when the familiar anger kicked in while he was lowering himself onto a bull, when it churned in his gut and made him grit his teeth during his final seconds in the chute, it was less about his father than something else, something new.

A lung disease called cystic fibrosis.

He and Ali talked about everything, and their talks became a lifeline, the difference Ali made in his life too big to measure. Because of her, he didn't go through the day angry, he didn't waste the nights putting out the embers of hatred with a six-pack. Rather he spent his days waiting for the one night each weekend when he and Ali could be together.

Always he'd known that if he fell for a girl, his riding days would be numbered. Because love was a light that wouldn't allow darkness to reign in his soul. And without the darkness, what reason did he have to battle it? To get in the arena with a snorting beast and fight for his life? Without the rage? There would be no point.

But with Ali it was different.

What he felt for her was more pure and honest, more intense. And it made everything about riding bulls more intense, too. It wasn't love, not in the conventional sense. His feelings for Ali were deeper, stronger, the same sort of emotions he felt for Carl Joseph. He would've protected Ali

Daniels if it meant jumping in front of a train or taking a bullet in the chest.

Feelings that strong.

As the season played out, the two of them stayed near the top of the leaderboards. Since talk on the tour flowed like cheap wine, Cody kept his distance during the day. Neither of them wanted their names linked for any reason other than the obvious—they were both among the best in the business.

But at night, after the championship buckles had been handed out and the crowds had gone home, Ali and Cody would sneak out and take their places in the familiar chairs in front of her trailer. There they opened themselves to a world neither of them had ever known before.

The world of friendship.

He told her the story of his childhood, how his father had left, and how there would always be the struggle to forgive the man. Some of the more private details he kept to himself, sparing her the part about Carl Joseph's handicap and running after his father's cab and how he felt no connection with his mother.

Still, what he did share was more than he'd ever told anyone.

No matter how late they stayed up, whispering in the moonlight, they never ran out of things to talk about. Once in a while a comfortable silence would fall between them and Ali would smile at him, her eyes dancing.

"You aren't chasing me, right?"

He would raise his eyebrows in mock surprise. "Chase *you?*" His chin would lift a few inches. "Come on, Ali. I don't chase girls. You know that."

"Good." She'd pull her feet up, her voice full of teasing. "I don't want to be caught, remember?"

"Yes, Ali, I remember." He'd hold his hands up in surrender. "You're safe with me; I don't want to be caught either."

Ali Daniels was the most serious girl he'd ever known. But after a few weeks, he found ways to make her laugh. Before turning in for the night they'd sometimes be in tears from trying to stifle their bouts of laughter, keeping quiet so they wouldn't wake her mother.

By the end of the season they both qualified for the National Finals Rodeo in Las Vegas. Usually after a long year, Cody was anxious to get to the NFR, ready to take a shot at the title and head home. But this year he had no home to go back to. His father had moved in, and from what his mother said he was sleeping in Cody's bedroom. There was even talk that the two of them might get remarried. Apparently, Carl Joseph was thrilled.

Cody wanted nothing to do with any of them.

So instead of looking forward to the season finale, he was dreading it. Ali was coughing harder, looking tired more often. She wanted a national championship in the worst way, but her times had been a whole second or two slower in the past weeks. They would compete like crazy and when the final buzzer sounded he had no idea what he was going to do.

But that wasn't why he was dreading the final. He dreaded it because after the finals he wouldn't see Ali again until late January in Denver. The truth was something he recognized. He could barely last a week without her.

How was he going to survive two months?

Chapter Nine

For Ali Daniels, there was no worse place to compete than Las Vegas.

A constant wind blew across the desert floor, stirring up dirt and pushing the smog from one side of the valley to the other. The National Finals Rodeo was held at the Thomas and Mack Center, a huge indoor arena that sat more than fifteen thousand fans. Not only would the dirt be softer, more likely to fill the air, but NFR organizers used indoor fireworks before each day's events.

And the NFR didn't happen in a weekend like other rodeos throughout the year. It ran ten days straight. Ten days of racing barrels through dust and fireworks smoke and the stuffy confines of one of the biggest indoor arenas of the year. Even the locker rooms were worse, because officials at the University of Nevada at Las Vegas covered the tunnel and locker room floors with plastic. That meant the dirt wasn't packed down the way it was in most arenas.

No wonder she hadn't done well at her first two NFR showings.

This year, though, she had a plan. She would wear the compression vest ninety minutes, three times a day. The longer she spent in the vest, the more relief she felt, and the longer that relief lasted.

It was the first day.

She and her mother had found a nice spot at Sam's Town for their trailer, an oversized space with trees along one side. Ali liked that; it would give her and Cody privacy for their late-night talks. Cody had a room at the hotel next door, so after the rodeo each night, they wouldn't have trouble meeting up.

Ali slipped on her vest and zipped it up. She and her mother had spent the past two weeks at home, the first three days in the hospital. The doctor's warnings were just as strong as before, but he stopped short of badgering her. When the season was over, when she had her national championship in hand, then she could think about quitting.

Not until then.

She flipped on the compression switch and felt the vest fill up. At the same time, the door opened and her mother walked in, a bag of groceries in her arms.

"Again?" She set the bag down and began unloading it. "Didn't you get an hour earlier?"

"Ninety minutes. I'm going longer for the next ten days."

Her mother was quiet, unusually so. She finished putting away the food and took the chair opposite Ali. "Honey, we need to talk."

Ali felt her heart skip a beat. Her mother was easy. Whatever hardships being on the Pro Rodeo Tour caused, however difficult it was being away from home, her mother never let on. She wanted Ali to be happy. It was the reason she'd agreed to travel with her in the first place. But the concern written into her expression now was something Ali almost never saw.

"What's wrong, Mama?"

A tired breath made its way from her. "I was in line at the store, and two bull riders were in front of me."

Two bull riders? Ali wasn't sure what to say. She waited for her mother to continue.

"They were talking about Cody Gunner. One of them laughed about how tame he was these days, none of the partying and loose women he used to associate with."

Ali had a feeling about what was coming. But how could anyone have known? They hadn't so much as shared a conversation in front of the other riders. She swallowed. "Okay...I guess that's good, right?"

"There's more." Her shoulders dropped a notch. "The other cowboy said, 'You know what happened to Cody, right?' And the first guy nodded and said, 'Ali Daniels, that's what happened to him.'"

She blinked, searching her mind's list of possible replies.

"I'm with you all the time in the arena, Ali. Ever since that first night when you and Cody talked, I've watched you and seen nothing. Absolutely nothing between you." She turned her hands palms up. "Have I missed something? Are you dating that boy behind my back?"

Her secret meetings with Cody were never supposed to be anything but temporary, small chances for a friendship that had made the entire last half of the season her best days of all. From the first she'd looked for a way to tell her mother about her time with Cody.

Now she was getting her chance. She cleared her throat. "We're not dating, obviously. You'd know if I was."

"Then what? Why would they say that?"

"Because ..." The vest made it harder to talk in whole sentences. She didn't want Cody to come between them. She closed her eyes tight and then opened them, her tone flat. "Because sometimes Cody comes by our trailer at night."

It took a minute for Ali's words to sink in. "What?" Her mother's voice was tight, disbelieving. "After I'm asleep?"

"Yes." Ali winced. Sometimes she had to remind herself. The vest wasn't squeezing the life out of her; it was pressing life back into her. "Yes, after you're asleep he comes by and we ...we sit outside in the folding chairs."

Her mother's expression was a study in control. Shock and surprise added to the fine lines around her eyes. She wasn't angry. Hurt, maybe, but not angry. For a while the only sound between them was the steady rhythmic whirring of the vest as it worked on her lungs. What was she thinking? Was she disappointed, frustrated? Was she ready to take the two of them home for good?

Finally Ali couldn't handle another minute. "Mama? Say something."

Her mother leaned her elbows on the arms of the chair and looked at Ali. "Do you love him?"

The question made Ali hesitate, and that hesitation terrified her more than anything her mother could've said or
done. Did she love him? Of course not, right? The idea was
absurd, falling in love with a reckless bull rider like Cody
Gunner.

But then why did she hesitate?

Ali ran her tongue over her lower lip. "No, Mama, it's not
like that. He's my friend; nothing more."

Her mother's words were calm, deliberate. "Then why
hide your visits? Did you think I wouldn't approve?"

"Do you?" Ali's answer was sharper than she intended.
Her heart melted and she felt her expression soften. "I kept
thinking about what you said. Heaven forbid it be someone
like Cody Gunner. I didn't think you'd want me talking to
him."

Her mother drew a slow breath, her eyes searching Ali's.
"How much have you told him?"

If she was going to be honest, she couldn't stop now.
"Everything. He knows about my CF."

"Well..." her mother slid back in her chair. She turned it
so she was facing the opposite window. "It'll be all over the
tour by January, if it's not already out there. If that's what you
want, then I guess it's okay if—"

"Mama!" Ali was supposed to relax when the vest was
on, work with the compressions so they were more effec-
tive. But she was too upset to relax. She flipped the switch
and the machine fell silent. "Turn around and look at me.
Please!"

Her mother spun around. "Don't use that tone with me,

young lady. Cody Gunner's reputation precedes him. In the arena and out. He's not your type, not our type."

"Be quiet, Mama." Ali's voice rang with passion. "You don't know him. He won't tell a soul about my CF." She pressed her hand against her chest. "He'd do anything for me. Anything at all."

Her mother's mouth hung open. "Dear me." The words were the slightest whisper. "You're in love with him and you don't even know it."

"I'm not in love with him. He's my friend. The first friend I've had since I started riding professionally." Ali's throat was tight, her lungs heavier than usual. "Can't I have that, Mama? One single friend?"

For years, her mother had been forced to hold back her opinions, forced to let Ali make her own decisions about the way she spent her time. Even when those decisions might take years off her life. Now, Ali could see the same struggle playing out. Her mother didn't want Cody Gunner around any more than she wanted Ali on a horse.

She crossed the small space between them and knelt at Ali's feet. With gentle movements, while her eyes filled with tears, she put her hand on top of Ali's knee. "I'm sorry, honey. I never meant to upset you."

Ali put her arms around her mother's neck. "I don't love him, Mama. I promise." Tears filled her own eyes, because it wasn't fair. She was twenty years old and she wouldn't see thirty. Tears because her mother had given so much, and now she was afraid Ali would somehow share what was left of her time with Cody Gunner.

"It's your life, Ali." She whispered the words against Ali's cheek. "I promised you a long time ago—I won't tell you how to live it."

There it was. The bottom line, the thing her mother always said whenever they had these discussions. After Anna's death, when the idea of horseback riding seemed suicidal, time and again when Dr. Cleary insisted that barrel racing would cut years off her life, and now—when Ali wanted the green light for a friendship with Cody Gunner.

Ali closed her eyes and a stream of hot tears spilled onto her cheeks. Her mother's words ran through her mind again. *It's your life, Ali...I won't tell you how to live it.* Exactly what she needed to hear.

"It's okay, honey." Her mother took her hand and squeezed it three times. Their silent way of saying the three most important words of all, *I love you.* "It's okay."

She sniffed and blinked her eyes open. "Can I have him come earlier tonight? Before you go to bed."

"Yes." Her mother reached out and dried her cheeks. "I'd like that."

Ali took second that night, putting her in position to make a run for the championship. She had only a minute to pull Cody aside and tell him about the conversation with his mother.

"She must hate me for keeping you out late."

"No." Ali shook her head. "Give her a chance. She's on our side, Cody. Really. Come by early tonight; you'll see."

At 10:30 he knocked on their trailer door, and Ali let her mother answer it.

"Cody." Her mother hesitated, but her voice was warm. "Come in."

From the back of the table where she sat, Ali felt herself relax. Everything was going to be fine, once her mother got to know him.

"Yes, ma'am." Cody's voice rang with cowboy respect. "Thank you."

Ali's mother stepped back and gestured toward the small table where Ali was sitting. "How'd you ride tonight, Cody?"

"I took third, ma'am. The bull could've been better."

"We'll be pulling for a better draw tomorrow." She gave him a smile that eased the tension. "Iced tea?"

"Yes, ma'am, that'd be nice." Cody shot a nervous glance at Ali. "I appreciate you having me."

Ali's mother was at the small refrigerator, pouring three glasses of tea. "Well..." She looked at him over her shoulder. "It's about time you saw the inside of our trailer."

The silence was interrupted by Ali's giggles, and not long after, her mother and Cody joined in. After that, the ice was broken. Their evening visits continued to be early every night that week, and always, sometime around eleven, Ali's mother would turn in. Ali would get into her sweatshirt, and she and Cody would find their familiar places in the chairs outside.

Over the next few days, most of their talk was about the competition. Cody held a strong second place, but Ali was frustrated with her times. She wasn't riding as fast as before, and she didn't know why. Her times had her sitting at fourth overall, but she would need a few first-place finishes in the remainder of the races if she were to have a chance at the championship.

"You're still holding your breath?" Cody was sitting beside her, closer than when they first started meeting together.

"Definitely." She frowned and stared straight ahead. "I do the ride in my mind a hundred times a day; I can't figure out how to catch that extra step."

"Hmmm." Cody stretched his legs out and folded his hands behind his head, the way she was familiar with now. A grin started in his eyes and made its way down to his mouth. "Someone once told me the secret was anticipation." He bumped her arm with his elbow. "Sound familiar?"

She chuckled, careful to be quiet. "Must've been someone smart."

"Yes." He tapped her head, letting his fingers run along her hair for a few seconds. "And did I mention focus. She thinks focus helps, too."

"Ah, yes. Focus." Ali did an exaggerated frown. Focus had been easier before, back when her mind didn't share time between racing and thinking about her conversations with Cody Gunner.

At most rodeos they talked for a few hours a weekend. At this one, they were together that long every night. By the sixth day, she met him outside the arena.

"You're right." She anchored her hands on her hips and squinted at him. The sky was bright blue, the December day as sunny as any in July.

"Right about what?" He smiled at her, studying her.

"About my focus; it isn't there." She shifted her weight, hoping he wouldn't take this wrong. He needed to understand. "Let's take a few nights off, turn in early. We can talk when it's over. Maybe that'll help me concentrate."

"I'm a distraction, huh?" He gave a light laugh, but disappointment colored his eyes. He kept his tone upbeat. "Sure, Ali. Whatever helps."

"You understand, right?" She felt funny trying to explain herself. Neither of them owed the other anything. "This championship means...well, it means everything to me. I've waited all my life for it."

The next four rides were the best either of them had all season. Still, the competition was tough. Ali was in third heading into the final round, Cody a few points shy of first. He was the defending champion, but for him it would come down to the draw.

Minutes before her race, Ali climbed onto Ace and ran her fingers over his coarse blond mane. She spoke to him, low and gentle near his ears, the way she always did before a ride. "Atta boy, Ace. It's all yours tonight. All yours."

A million thoughts fought for her attention. Anna sitting by the window looking out at the neighbor's farm. *I wanna race through the forever hay fields and play hide-and-seek out by the tallest pine trees, and jump on that palomino horse next door.* And her mother agreeing finally to let her have the baby foal. *It's your life, Ali. I won't stop you...won't stop you.* And Cody Gunner with those crazy blue eyes wanting to talk to her. *Just once, Ali. Tell me why you do it; why you ride so sick?*

She cleared her mind.

People in her position talked often about sacrifice, all they'd given up to get where they were. For Ali, of course, the sacrifice was something more than a missed childhood or the cost of spending hours a day on the back of a horse. The sacrifice would come later—in the years of life she would lose for her decision to ride.

From the first time she watched a rider race around barrels she'd believed she was better, faster. That one day the championship would belong to her. And now here she was, minutes away from taking it, owning it. This would be the fastest ride of her life; she could feel it in her bones, in the center of her being.

It was her turn to take her mark.

Like always, Ace was spirited, desperate for the go-ahead, the chance to tear out of the tunnel around the course he loved. He nodded and pranced sideways. "This is it, Ace," she whispered. "Faster. Faster and stronger."

She sucked in a full breath and held it just as they tore down the tunnel and into the arena. The two of them flew around the first barrel, cleaner, faster than ever, and Ali knew it was happening. The thing she'd dreamed of since she was eleven years old was happening here and now, and no one could stop them.

Ace pushed himself, his hooves barely making contact with the soft dirt as he rounded the second barrel. *One more, just one more.* Ali pressed into him, willing him to move. They were almost around the third barrel when it happened. Ace's foot caught the barrel's edge.

"No!" Ali screamed, and as she did she sucked in a

mouthful of dusty air. She lunged toward the barrel, desperate to keep it upright. But it was too late.

In the corner of her eye she watched the barrel crash onto its side, taking with it her only chance at the title. A spilled barrel was something Ali rarely dealt with; certainly never in a National Finals Rodeo. The mistake meant a five-second penalty, and a score that wouldn't be in the top six for the round.

She couldn't feel Ace beneath her as she raced into the tunnel. It was all a nightmare, right? She was dreaming, and any minute she'd wake up and it would be time to go to the arena. Her eyes closed before she came to a stop. *No...no, that didn't happen. It can't end this way.*

That's when she realized something else was wrong. She couldn't breathe, couldn't draw a breath. Never mind the race or the lost championship, suddenly she couldn't think about anything but drawing in oxygen, meeting her body's desperate need for air. She must have taken in too much dust when she took a breath out on the course, and now she couldn't stop coughing.

She dismounted and grabbed her water bottle. Her knees were weak, and it took all her energy to stay on her feet. Dark spots danced in her eyes and she held on to Ace, coughing with no relief, certain she was about to faint and not sure if it was because her heart was breaking or because she couldn't quench the burning in her lungs.

She sucked in a long swig of water and forced herself not to draw a breath. *Calm, Ali. Be calm.* The coughing wouldn't let up, and she sprayed the mouthful of water across the floor.

This had happened one other time, and the doctor had told her above all not to panic.

But even Ace was nervous, whinnying and giving her anxious glances.

She was too far down the tunnel to get anyone's attention, but clearly she needed help. The coughing had kicked into an asthma attack. She needed her inhaler, the one she kept in her equipment bag for emergencies. Only this was the first time she'd ever needed it after a race, and she wasn't even sure where her bag was.

Nausea welled up in her and she grabbed at a shallow breath. More coughing, and now she was doubled over. She was about to drop to her knees when she heard his voice.

"Ali!"

Her face was burning up, red hot from the exertion. She met his eyes, and saw the inhaler in his hand. She couldn't speak, couldn't do anything but grab it and shove it up against her lips.

The first two puffs, she could hold the medication for no more than a second. But then, slowly, she felt her airways relax. The third puff lasted longer and by the time she took her fourth, the coughing subsided. Everything ached, even her bones. She was dizzy from the lack of oxygen, and just as she swayed Cody caught her arm and led her to a bench a few feet away.

He took the spot next to her, stroking her back, brushing his cool knuckles against her hot cheeks. "Ali, you scared me."

She was too tired to keep her head up, so she let it fall

on his shoulder. For all their late-night talks, this was the closest their bodies had ever been. Ali couldn't get a rope around her thoughts. She'd lost the biggest race of her life, but somehow her heart soared with possibility.

"I...I lost."

"I know; it's all right. You can get it next year, Ali." He gulped and she caught a strange look in his eyes, something she hadn't seen there before. "Are you okay?"

Ali took in a slow breath. "I couldn't...couldn't stop coughing."

"I saw the whole thing." He smoothed a section of hair off her forehead. "The barrel went over and you breathed, didn't you?"

A sense of awe joined the emotions already having their way with her. She sat up straight and looked at him. "You saw that?"

"Yes." He exhaled, and she caught a look at his legs. He was trembling. "I knew you were in trouble; I ran for your bag, and your mom was already on it. She handed me your inhaler because I could get it to you faster." He ran his hand along her back again. "You sure you're okay?"

"I'm fine." Her heart rate was fast, but her breathing was as good as it would get inside the stadium. "Thanks."

He shot a look toward the arena. The floor was cleared already, the bull riders getting ready. When he spoke, his teeth were clenched. "I hate that you suffer like this, Ali. It isn't right."

Tears stung at her eyes, but she refused them. Rodeo riders didn't hold on to the hurt very long. It was part of their way, their lifestyle. She gave him a gentle push. "Go ride. At least one of us can be champion."

Cody hesitated, looking into her eyes. "Later?"

"Yes." She didn't have to ask what he meant. They'd avoided each other the past four days, and in the end it hadn't done her any good. She didn't have a national championship, but she had a friend.

He gave her one last look, a grimace that shouted fierce determination. Then he stood, pressed his hat onto his head, and took off down the tunnel.

Her mother came through the locker room door at the same time, her face tight with worry. "I knew you were coughing. I gave Cody your inhaler; he could reach you first."

"Yes." She stood and faced her mother. The way her throat closed up, it was much worse than coughing, but there was no reason to say anything now. "Thanks."

They were talking around the obvious, but the pretense could only last so long. Her mother knew more than anyone how much the championship meant. Her health wasn't holding up the way she wanted it to, and unless she found a way to get stronger, she might not be well enough to compete next year.

Her mother's eyes grew watery and she held out her hands. "Come here, Ali."

Ali was tough so much of the time, determined to push ahead, bent on being the best barrel racer in the world. But right now, she didn't feel tough or determined or even close to the best in the world. She took a few steps and leaned into her mother's embrace, but even then she kept the sobs at bay.

She wanted to head back down the tunnel, find a spot with a good view and watch Cody ride. He'd drawn a tough bull, one that would give him the win if he lasted eight seconds. But at that moment, still buried beneath the weight of her defeat, in all the world she really needed just one thing.

To be held by her mama until everything felt right again.

Chapter Ten

S ling Shot was the best draw Cody had gotten all week. The animal was the biggest, meanest bull at the NFR, a bull with thick, curved horns and shoulders that could toss a cowboy across the arena in a single violent motion.

It was the exact draw Cody had been hoping for.

The rage he felt when he thought about Ali was almost frightening. She was an angel, a delicate flower with a grace and strength on horseback that would take the breath from anyone with eyes.

No one knew she was sick, because she didn't look sick. Her skin was tanned from the summer season, her pale blonde hair long and healthy. How would any of the others have known that the cough she battled wasn't a cold or an allergy, but a dreaded disease?

Ali Daniels shouldn't have had cystic fibrosis. She should've been dreaming of another five years on the tour, and then a life that was nothing but blue skies and flaming red sunsets. It wasn't fair, the disease. The ride beneath him was no longer tied in any way to his hatred for his father, but to cystic fibrosis, with all the merciless damage it was doing to Ali. Because it was that—combined with a reckless abandon for the rush of the ride—that had Cody riding better than ever in his life.

Cody positioned himself over the bull and stared at the animal's center. If only he could battle her disease the way he was about to battle the bull.

"Ready, Gunner?"

"Ready." Cody worked the muscles in his jaw and slid his mouthpiece in place. His blood boiled hot through his face and neck, down his arms. He lowered himself onto the animal's back, wrapped his hand tough and fast, and slid forward. Sling Shot reared his head back and lifted off his front feet.

Cody smacked the bull's neck, and the animal dropped, startled. "That's right." Cody seethed the words. No disease would ever hurt Ali Daniels, not if he had anything to say about it. This time he didn't wait. He shoved his crotch against his riding hand, leaned forward, and nodded hard.

The latch opened and the bull took to the air, spinning halfway around before ever touching ground. He was already twisting in the other direction as he pushed off his back feet. Cody kept his seat, his body so balanced he didn't feel like he was riding the bull, but floating above him.

A jerk of his neck and the bull was airborne again. Adrenaline surged through Cody's body and in that moment he believed he was actually stronger than the bull. Stronger and smarter.

Fight me, bull; try it. Ali would get on a horse again next season. Nothing would stop her, not even cystic fibrosis. Twice more the bull spun and bucked, arching through the air, and suddenly Cody knew. He had this one, the ride was his. He heard the buzzer. He'd made it; he'd ridden a bull that was responsible for some of the worst wrecks in the PRCA, and it had felt easy.

He leaned forward, readying himself. Next time the bull bucked he'd make the jump. The animal rocked back and then slammed down on his front hooves, his back legs snapping behind him. Cody pushed off, but as he did, the bull snapped his head back and caught Cody in the forehead with his horn.

A splash of dark spots filled his vision, but only for a few seconds. He felt one of the bullfighters at his side, helping him out of the arena. The other one must've been distracting the bull. Cody blinked and the stars faded. Blood was dripping down his face before he could get back to the gate. The doctor was at his side in three seconds with a cloth and a stitch kit.

He handed Cody the rag and helped him press it against his head. "Nice gash." He led Cody down the tunnel to the training room. "You okay?"

"Yeah." Cody wasn't sure what he felt. His head hurt, but it was nothing compared to the way his heart felt. Yes, he was the national champion bull rider, an award he'd won before, one he'd earned. But what about Ali? She'd wanted the title more than any other rider. How was that fair?

She was the best barrel racer on the tour, no matter what

the final standings showed. He took a seat at the trainer's table. Like so much about her life, she deserved more than a seventh-place finish.

The doctor took the bloody cloth from Cody and studied his head. "It's deep, but not too long. Most of it's in your hairline." He chuckled. "We won't need to make a mess of that pretty face of yours. Not this time."

"I guess."

The doctor went to work, and Cody didn't flinch as the stitching got under way.

"You cowboy up better than anyone out there, Gunner." He wiped a clean cloth along Cody's brow, and dropped it on the floor. It was bloodred. "Blow like that should've knocked you out."

"I'm fine." He played the doctor's words in his mind again. *Cowboy up.* It was the slogan of the Pro Rodeo Tour, the slogan of bull riders and rodeo competitors at every level of the game. No matter how hard the hit, whatever the level of injury, a cowboy didn't stay down. He got up and shook off the pain.

Cody had ridden with broken ribs and a separated shoulder. He'd seen cowboys get knocked out, stitched up, and taped together and an hour later be rubbing resin into their rope, ready for the next go-round. Guys would laugh off the injuries, slap one another on the back, and say it again: "Cowboy up." The words had come to define the cowboy mentality, the rodeo way of life. Riders had two choices: cowboy up or go home. If cowboys didn't look past their injuries, the rodeo would no longer exist. Everyone rode hurt; it was the nature of the sport.

But the doctor was wrong. Cody wasn't the toughest cowboy on the tour, not by far. Not him or any of the bull riders or saddle bronc guys. He knew a competitor who could cowboy up better than any of them.

The rider was Ali Daniels.

Who else would consider competing week after week, knowing that every day on her horse took days off her life? Where was there another rider who raced without drawing a breath, who spent hours in a compression vest just so lungs would carry her through fifteen seconds of competition?

The doctor finished up and Cody headed back down the tunnel toward the arena. In a ceremony fitting of the NFR, Cody was named champion bull rider, and the crowd rose to their feet as he accepted his buckle. He grinned and held it up, waving first in one direction, then the other, giving them the reaction they expected. The reaction they deserved.

But all he could think about was Ali. How was she feeling? Was her breathing back to normal, really back to normal? And what was she doing right then? He scanned the crowd, looking for her along the fence, but he didn't see her.

For the next hour he smiled for two dozen cameras, gave eight interviews, and signed autographs. The questions were the same every time. No, he wasn't hurt; yes, Sling Shot had been a good draw. Yes, of course he'd be back next year. No, he wasn't making the shift to the PBR, not yet. No, he didn't have any special secrets to staying on a bull—none he would talk about, anyway.

They were boring answers, and not altogether true. But

they were the answers Cody always gave. The whole time Ali was on his mind and in his heart. He'd gladly trade in his buckle and prize money, his championship, if she could have another chance to ride, to prove no one was better. And since he couldn't do that, he'd do what was second best. He'd help her stay healthy; push her so she'd win it next year.

It was after 11:30 when Cody finally stepped out of the pickup truck of one of the steer wrestlers and headed for the Sam's Town RV lot. The air was warm that night, warmer than it had been all week. He wanted to take Ali out to dinner or go for a walk with her. But the casinos were terrible, thick with smoke and people. And it was too late to take a walk.

He heard high-pitched voices behind him. "Cody... Cody, wait!"

Girls. He glanced over his shoulder. Four of them were running toward him, three blondes and a brunette, and all looked to be in their late teens. One of them was waving something that looked like a hotel key. Disgust smacked him in the face. How many times had he taken advantage of a situation like this?

"Ladies." He waved once, tipped his hat, and kept walking. His pace was faster than theirs, and eventually they gave up. The last thing he needed was a group of fans following him to Ali's trailer. He pressed his hat low onto his head, careful not to tear the bandage off his forehead.

Be awake, Ali. Please. He squinted in the darkness and even from fifty yards away, he spotted her trailer and the single light she left on. The light that meant she was waiting for him. He jogged the rest of the way, and knocked just once on her trailer door.

She poked her head out and tiptoed down the steps. For a long time she looked at him. "Okay." Her eyes shone in the moonlight, the disappointment from earlier gone completely. "So I was wrong."

This was what he loved about her, that even when things could've been dark and somber, she found ways to play with him. The serious girl she'd been when they first started talking was gone forever.

He leaned against her trailer, breathless and grinning. "The nine-second thing?"

"Yeah." She winced and lifted his hat enough to see the bandage. "Maybe eight's enough after all."

"That'll teach me to listen to you." He adjusted the brim again. "Does that mean you were there?"

"Mama and I watched it from the press seats." She angled her head, her eyes full of admiration. "You deserved the win, Cody. You were brilliant tonight."

"Thanks." He gave a quick look over his shoulder, making sure the fans hadn't followed him. He'd been waiting all day for this time with Ali. He led her toward the chairs. "Let's move to the other side; it's quiet there."

They each grabbed a chair and set them up between her trailer and the trees. Her mother's room was on the opposite end, so there was no danger they'd wake her. Before they sat down, he turned to her and felt his smile fade. "I'm sorry about earlier. You..." He looked down for a minute, the frustration back in full force. "You deserved it, Ali. What happened was wrong."

"I've thought about it." Her voice was clear and sweet, quiet against the night breeze. "It was my own fault. I tried to cut the last corner."

He looked up and met her eyes, and there in the moonlight he could see to the very center of her soul. "You have to come back, try again, okay?"

She swallowed, hesitant. "I will."

Something in the air between them changed. He was more aware of her than ever before. They were inches from each other, hidden in a place where no one could see them. "I wanted you to win, Ali." He looked down at her, his words a whisper. "You have no idea how much I wanted it for you."

She nodded. "Me, too." Her eyes held his, and this time he could see the sorrow, the depth of the loss and all it had meant to her.

Since he got there, he'd wanted to take her in his arms. And now he couldn't wait another moment. "Ali...don't give up." He put his hands on her shoulders and then pulled her in, folding his arms around her, holding her close.

In the past they'd been careful with the line between friendship and something more. In Cody's mind, the line was a wall, solid stone and ten feet high. A hug like this one would be over as soon as it started.

But neither of them was letting go.

Seconds passed, and the feel of her body against his shot a fire through him, a fire that was way beyond his control. This was territory they hadn't explored, and the dangers were there for both of them. Still, he couldn't let go of her, couldn't find the strength to pull away.

"All my life I've wanted that title." Her body trembled, her arms still tight around his waist. She pulled back enough to see his eyes. Her chest rose with every breath, and a mix of fear and desire filled her eyes. "But you know what?"

"What?" He could feel himself drawing her closer.

"I want this more."

"Ali..." What were they doing? They'd agreed things wouldn't go this way, not ever. But then why was he helpless to stop it? He ran his fingertips along her brow, her cheekbone. He inhaled, shallow and ragged. "This is when you're supposed to ask me."

Her eyes melted into his, and she brought her hands up alongside his face. "Ask you what?"

"Whether I'm chasing you." His knees were weak. He wanted to kiss her; he couldn't hold out much longer. His mind bounced between walking away, telling her good night and forgetting they'd ever come even this close—or giving in to his desire.

"Except"—her voice was breathy—"guess what?"

"What?" Cody swallowed, trying to believe she was really in his arms. He couldn't take his eyes from her. She was so beautiful, inside and out, more beautiful than anyone he'd ever known.

"It's okay." She lifted her face to his. Lilacs grew among the trees that lined their trailer space, and the late-night air was sweet with the smell of them. Then without waiting, she drew him closer and kissed him. It was a soft kiss colored with question marks, framed in uncertainty. The kiss of sweet inexperience and uncontrollable desire. "It's okay." She drew back, her eyes dark. "Because you already caught me."

Her kiss was still fresh on his lips, but this time he took the lead. Slow and deliberate, he shaded her with the brim of his hat and brought his lips to hers. He let the kiss build, guiding her, showing her the way until she was as involved in the moment as he was.

A minute passed before she started to squirm and then in a rush, she pulled back, her breathing fast and uneven. "Cody..." She stared at him, eyes wide, frightened. "I'm sorry. I can't..."

"It's all right, Ali." He moved closer.

"No." She spun around and took three steps toward the trees. "I didn't mean it." Her ponytail was loose; strands of blonde hair spilling onto her red sweater. She turned and faced him. "I didn't mean it, Cody. I don't want to be caught."

"Ali..."

"I don't." Her voice was louder than it should've been. She paced a few steps in each direction and then found his eyes again. "That..." She waved her hand in the air. "The way that felt...it scares me to death."

Cody hesitated. "Why?" This was the reason he hadn't crossed the line before tonight. He could handle being just her friend. But he couldn't stand her being afraid, upset.

Tears filled her eyes and she shook her head. "You don't understand."

"Yes, I do." He closed the distance between them. "You

never wanted to need me, right?" His words were quiet, calm. "That's it, right, Ali?"

"No." She hung her head, the fight gone from her voice. "We'll both lose, Cody." She looked up. "If we let this happen, we both lose."

"You're wrong." He was closer now. "We both win." He wove his fingers into her hair and eased the band from her ponytail. Her hair fell loose around her shoulders, and with the slightest pressure from his fingers, he pulled her to him once more.

"Be my friend." She pressed her head to his chest, keeping a fraction of an inch between them, and at the same time clutching at his back, her heart and mind at odds.

"I will, Ali." He crooked his finger, placed it beneath her chin and lifted her face to his. "After tonight, okay?"

That was all he needed to say. Going against everything she was asking of him, she kissed him again. Long and with an intensity that hadn't been there before. When she came up for air, she searched his eyes and the understanding was clear.

They would have this night, this single time to pretend they could be more than friends, to believe that she wasn't sick and he wasn't determined to remain a loner. Cody leaned against the fence, the tree branches creating an alcove that belonged to them alone. Cicadas played softly in the distance, and a ribbon of cool air mixed in the breeze. He drew her close and for the sweetest hour they kissed and whispered and held each other, allowing the intensity between them to build until Cody couldn't take another minute.

"Ali..." He stepped around her and flopped into one of the canvas chairs a few feet away. He stared at the sky, his body burning with an intensity he'd never known before. A long exhale came from him and he chuckled, trying to cool off. Did she have any idea how she made him feel? "I have to go."

She looked at the ground, her expression shy and a little embarrassed. "I know...it's late."

His body screamed to return to her, but he had to get back. If he didn't stop now, if he didn't return to his hotel room, he would cross other lines. Lines he would never dream of crossing with Ali Daniels, at least not in sane moments. He rubbed the back of his neck and grinned at her. "That wasn't so bad, was it?"

"No." The shyness left and a grin tugged at the corners of her lips. "Not too bad." She brushed the back of her hand against her lips. Her eyes were still dark, her voice throaty. "We haven't talked about the Christmas break."

"No." Cody forced himself to stay in the chair. "I'm not going home this time."

"Where then?"

He shrugged. "One of the steer wrestlers has a cabin on his ranch. Maybe there."

"Hmmm." She came to him and took the other chair. "I have an idea."

Cody took her hand in his, running his thumb along the soft inside of her palm. He waited, watching her.

"My dad's looking for someone to help out on the ranch." Her voice was hesitant, but she continued. "He wants to be with me over the break." She met his eyes. "We have a guest-house. What do you think?" She raised her brow. "Wanna spend Christmas with us, Cody?"

Two months on Ali's ranch? Days and hours of conversations and long walks and quiet laughter with her? Cody let the idea take root, and as it did the strange feeling came over him again, the one he couldn't quite pinpoint. He slid his boot alongside hers and tapped her toe. "Are you sure?"

"Mmm-hmm. I talked to Mama earlier today. She's fine with it; Daddy, too."

He leaned back in the chair, his eyes still on her. "What happened tonight, that won't happen again, right? That's the way you want it?"

Sorrow cast a shadow over her. "It's the way it has to be, Cody. I wish I could explain it better."

"I understand." He gave her a half smile. "At least I'll try to understand." Two months on Ali's ranch as nothing more than her friend? The situation would test his will. But the alternatives weren't even a consideration. He had no choice; he would take whatever she gave him. "When do we leave?"

A smile filled her face, the biggest smile he'd ever gotten from her. "First thing in the morning."

"I'll be here." He brought her hand to his lips and kissed it, the most tender kiss he could manage. His heart soared, breaking through the clouds of gloom and doubt and loss, all the feelings he would've had if this were good bye. "See you tomorrow, Ali."

It was on the way back, halfway to the hotel, that Cody had a sudden realization. Since he'd known Ali, he hadn't been able to make out the strange feeling in his chest, the way she sometimes took his breath away and left him weak at the knees. Admiration, companionship, definitely. But this feeling wasn't that. It wasn't even lust.

Now, after an hour in Ali Daniels' arms, he knew exactly what the strange feeling was, and the realization made his head spin. He would have to keep the truth from her; otherwise she'd run scared away from him, as fast as she could in the opposite direction. The feeling was bound to scare her, because it scared him, too. She was sick, after all. Cystic fibrosis meant she wouldn't live as long as other people. But the fear wasn't enough to keep him away, not with this new understanding of his heart's feelings.

It was a feeling he'd promised himself he would never have, not for anyone other than Carl Joseph. But it was too late now. The way he felt for Ali ran deeper than what he felt for his brother, deeper than anything he'd ever experienced. His feelings for her were raw and alive and all-consuming.

Never mind his tough-guy image, or all the ways he'd been invincible on the back of a bull. There was nothing he could do to stop the way he felt. No matter what he told her in the coming months about being content with her friendship, he would be lying. The truth was, he didn't care about Ali Daniels only as a friend.

He was in love with her.

Chapter Eleven

From the beginning, Ali believed it was possible.

She could bring Cody Gunner home and enjoy his company, watch him work the cattle in the fields, talk with him at night and still keep her distance. She had to, really. Because first place in her life didn't belong to her or Ace or the Pro Rodeo Tour. It didn't belong to Cody.

First place belonged to cystic fibrosis.

The disease would determine the number of her days and the quality in the number. But it wouldn't determine the way she spent her life. Cody knew she wouldn't live as long as other people, but he had no idea how little time she had.

So it was up to her to keep things between them platonic.

It was their third day back, and they were in Dr. Cleary's office, Ali seated between her parents. Over the phone, he had recommended a hospital stay—four days at least. But Ali convinced him she was just as well off at home. She could stay inside where the air was clean, use a portable oxygen tank, and increase her medications. Besides, she'd be around Cody and her family. That had to be better than the hospital.

Now, they were talking about the possibility of a lung transplant.

"We have the test results back from earlier. Your father was a match." He checked his chart. "Your mother has the wrong blood type. The problem is, we need two donors if we do a live-donor transplant."

"Couldn't we do just one?" Fear lined her mother's face. She could barely speak. "Wouldn't that help a little?"

"No. The healthy lobe would quickly be infected by the diseased lung." He shook his head. "I'd want to remove her lungs completely. She'd need two donors." Another pause. "And I've checked your insurance. The transplant will cost tens of thousands of dollars out of pocket."

"We'll find the money." Her father gave a curt nod. The cost of cystic fibrosis was something he never talked about, something he seemed determined to protect her from. "Somehow we'll find it."

"Very well." The doctor went on about the other details. Already he'd put her on a list, a registry through the University of Colorado Hospital in Denver where a computer would match donors with recipients. Most of the donors would come from cadavers, so there would be little warning if she was chosen.

The news was hard for all of them, but especially for her father. He was a quiet man, tall and strong. He'd missed out on much of Ali's barrel-racing career because they needed him back at the ranch, working the cattle. But during the times Ali was home, nothing would keep him from spending entire days with her—playing pinochle and backgammon and Scrabble while Ali told him stories from her year on the road.

But as Dr. Cleary delivered one blow after another, her father began to massage his throat. His cheeks got red; then his chin began to quiver. She'd never seen him cry, but when the doctor reached the part about the cost, and the last part—the part about still needing another donor to pull off a live transplant, two tears rolled down his leathered cheeks.

He cleared his throat and crossed his arms hard in front of him. "When…when will she need the operation?"

Dr. Cleary's lips formed a straight line. His eyes didn't waver as he looked at her father. "She needs it now, Mr. Daniels. Her lungs aren't getting any better."

"Maybe they will." Her mother put her hand on her father's knee. She tried to sound hopeful. "After she rests some."

Ali agreed with her mother. She was a week off one of the biggest rodeos of her life. If she could race barrels ten days straight, she couldn't be too sick.

"To be honest, I'm not hopeful." The doctor frowned. "Let's talk about the chances of getting a call from the donor registry." He crossed his arms, his jaw set. "Recipients are ranked according to their need. Ali needs a lung, but she'll live awhile without one. That means she won't be at the top of the list right away. The trouble is, once she's there, she won't have much time."

"What can we do, Doctor?" Ali's father took hold of her hand.

Dr. Cleary lowered his brow. "Live donors need the right blood type and they must be in good health. Healthy lungs have five lobes, two large lower lobes, and three smaller lobes. Ideally, donors should be bigger than the recipient, since their two lobes will replace five."

Her father had his hand near his throat again. "But if her mother isn't a match..."

"Then we need to find another donor." He looked from her father to her mother and back again. "Is there anyone in the family, an uncle or a cousin, someone who might consider being a live donor?"

Ali felt sick to her stomach, her head spinning. It was her fault they were having this discussion. She shook her head. "No. We can't ask that of anyone." She squeezed her father's hand and met his eyes. "We'll just hope for a call from the registry."

The doctor went through a few other pieces of advice and warnings, how important it was for her to stay inside and stay off her horse during the break, that sort of thing.

When the meeting was finished, Ali thanked the doctor. But she didn't say another word on the journey home. Her parents sat up front, with her in back. It was a seventy-mile trip to the hospital from the ranch, a trip she and her parents had made far too often. Ali kept her eyes on the road.

She needed to be moved up the registry list; then everything would work out.

Her mother turned around. "What are you thinking?"

"Nothing."

For a little while, her mother was quiet, watching her. Then she reached back and put her hand alongside Ali's face. "God has a plan. He always has a plan."

Ali nodded and turned back to the window. She wasn't sure what to say. If there was a plan in her having CF, she didn't see it. After a while she looked at her mother. "I wonder if Anna's riding horses in heaven. You know, since her plan didn't include riding them here on earth." The sarcasm felt strange and bitter on her tongue, but her parents seemed to miss it.

"Well..." Her father adjusted his grip on the steering wheel and sighed, the type of tired old sigh that seemed to come from way down in his dusty boots. "I reckon she's riding the prettiest horse of all."

She glanced at her father in the rearview mirror. "How's the cattle work going, Daddy?"

He looked at her, his eyes dull, lifeless. "Cody, you mean?"

"Yes, sir. Is he working out?"

"He's a polite boy, hard worker." He stroked his chin, thoughtful in his appraisal. "I like him." His eyes caught hers and he managed a smile. "So long as you don't."

"He's my friend." She looked in the rearview mirror and grinned at her mother. "Right, Mama?"

Her mother looked slightly exasperated. She raised an

eyebrow. "I have my doubts." She paused and her tone grew more serious. "You haven't told him, have you, Ali?"

"Told him what?" She wished her father would go faster; she wanted to get home and let Cody know the good news. No hospital stay for now.

Her father glanced back at her. "You haven't told him the truth about your health." He hesitated. "You're very sick, Ali. He doesn't know that."

"He knows." She kept her tone light. "I told him I have cystic fibrosis."

"But he doesn't know you could…you could be gone in a year, right?" Pain filled her mother's words. She didn't say them easily.

"Anyone could die in a year."

Ali's answer was quick, but her parents were right. Cody had no idea how sick she was, and she owed him the truth. They were quiet for a while, her parents letting the weight of their concern set in. As her father turned right onto their winding driveway, she let out a sharp breath. "Fine. I'll tell him."

"I just don't want him surprised." Her mother turned and met her eyes again. "You think the two of you are friends, but I've seen the way he looks at you. The boy's crazy about you, honey. Plumb crazy." She paused. "You need to tell him."

Ali agreed, but as she climbed out of the truck, as she spotted Cody on Ace a couple hundred yards away, she wanted only to run to him, climb up behind him and race like the wind across the fields, as far from the doctor's warnings as possible. She would tell him one of these days, before the next season started. Just not yet. Not with Christmas com-ing, not while they had eight weeks of good times ahead.

"Ali..." Her father stood near the passenger door. He seemed to notice the way she was watching Cody and Ace. "Go in now, ya hear? You need a treatment and a few hours of oxygen."

"I will, Daddy." She motioned toward the field. "I just wanna tell Cody we're back."

"That's not what Dr. Cleary—"

"Ali." Her mother cut in. "Do it fast. Please."

"I will." Their eyes met and what Ali saw made her heart swell. Her mother understood. It didn't matter if every out-door breath cost her an entire day, nothing could keep her from Cody. The connection between them was that strong.

Her mother linked arms with her father and led him toward the house, her eyes on him. "A few minutes won't hurt; she'll be okay." Over her shoulder she looked back at Ali. "I'll get your vest ready."

"Thanks, Mama." Ali headed toward the field, but Cody wasn't where he'd been before. Maybe he'd seen them pull in and he was putting Ace in the barn. Ali kept her pace to a fast walk, dormant frostbitten grass crunching beneath her feet. Nothing that would make her breathe too hard. This was a period of recuperation, so any time outdoors was counterproductive.

She made her way to the barn and peered inside. He was there, leading Ace into one of the stalls. He turned when he heard her come in, and his face lit up. "You're back!"

"Yes." She wanted to go closer, but barns were the worst place for her. Even this one, with the air purifier.

Cody knew that. He left Ace and jogged across the hay-covered floor. "Let's get you out of here."

She nodded and followed him out the door and around the far side of the building, along the wall that faced the open land instead of the house. They stopped after a few yards and faced each other, leaning their shoulders against the wall. She stared at him, soaking him in.

"They didn't admit you." His voice was low, each word a caress against her soul. Barely a foot separated them.

"No." She grinned and raised her eyebrows. "I'm home for good!" She could barely remember the conversation at the doctor's office, not while she was looking at him, drawn to him. He smelled of cologne and hay and Ace's sweaty back.

He grinned. "That means you're doing good. Kicking CF in the shins, right?"

"I guess." She did a small shrug and suddenly, as it had the last time they were alone this way, the air between them changed. A stillness hung there, cold and crisp. Snow was in the forecast. Christmas was ten days away and everything about the moment was surreal, magical in a way Ali had never known before.

Cody felt it, too, she could tell by the way he looked at her. A force came between them, bigger than either of them, bigger than both of them combined. It drew them closer, paying no heed to common sense. Cody took his gloves off.

He stuffed them in the pocket of his coat and touched her face, her shoulder.

Before she could think about what she was doing, she was in his arms.

"Ali—" He looked into her eyes, searching her heart, her soul. His voice was husky, thick with emotion. "How can you ask me to be your friend? All I can think about is that night in Vegas."

She had no answers. She wasn't sure how she'd lasted this long. Every spare moment since that night near her trailer, even while she was telling herself she could keep her distance, she had longed for him, to be with him like this again.

Her eyes found his and her words were more of a cry than a whisper. "Kiss me. Please, Cody."

He leaned into her, his fingers warm against her face, and they came together in a kiss that was drawn out and fueled by desperate need. She nuzzled her face against his, refusing to pull away. He deserved to know what the doctor said, but she couldn't bring herself to tell him how little time she had. Not when all that mattered were the minutes they had right then, when she could still draw a good breath and he was so alive and strong and warm in her arms.

He kissed her again, brushing his lips along her neck, stirring up feelings wild and unfamiliar. "Ali…" He drew back and his eyes touched parts of her heart she didn't know existed. "I can't be your friend."

She let her forehead fall against his chin. "Yes, Cody. You can; you have to be."

"I can pretend, but don't you see?"

Her eyes lifted to his and her heart skittered into a strange pattern. The air was colder now, but it didn't touch the heat between them. "See what?"

His breath was sweet against her face, making her forget everything else. "I love you, Ali. We can take this as slow as you want." He kissed her forehead and both cheeks, looking like he was trying to memorize her with his fingers. "But nothing will change the fact that I love you."

Ali held on to him tighter. What had he just said? He loved her? Her feelings soared and dropped wildly in opposite directions, a part of her giddy, taken with his words. But an equal part terrified, because now, no matter what she said or did, there was no turning back, no way to pretend about a friendship when their hearts had moved miles beyond.

"I'm scared." She pressed in closer, sheltered by his presence, his feelings for her.

"Don't be." He found her lips again. His eyes met hers and she felt a strength, a power she could draw from, one she was no longer capable of. "Everything's going to be all right."

"Okay." She kissed him again. She wanted to tell him she felt the same way, that she loved him as he loved her. But the thought scared her to death. So instead, with every ounce of her resolve, she pulled away. "I have to go; my parents are waiting for me."

"Don't be afraid." He kissed two of his fingers and pressed them to her lips. "We can do this; we'll take it slow."

She nodded and moved another few steps back. Then she turned and walked quickly, steadily toward the house. Her cheeks had to be fiery red; certainly her parents would know what she'd been doing. But as she found the gravel path and headed for the back door, she wasn't worried about her parents.

She was worried about herself.

Because no matter what Cody said, he couldn't promise her everything would be okay. And what kind of person was she, letting him think they could be more than friends, letting him believe that love had a fighting chance between them? She was horrible, rotten, and selfish, but she could do nothing to stop herself. Her feelings for Cody were like a potent drug, and she the crazy overnight addict.

But that didn't make it right. Only Dr. Cleary could make promises at this stage in her life. And his words earlier that day meant just one promise remained for her and Cody. The promise that after today, only one thing could ever come of their time together.

Complete and utter heartache.

Chapter Twelve

For Cody, the days were torture.

Riding the fields of her family's ranch, tending her father's cattle, and all the while wanting to be inside with Ali. Once or twice a day Cody would go inside for a drink or a chicken sandwich, and always the sight of her took him by surprise.

She was set up in the living room, small plastic oxygen tubes running from a canister near her feet up along the side of her chair and into her nose. Most of the time she wore the vest, but once he walked in while her mother was beating on her back.

He stopped, horrified.

Mrs. Daniels had her hand cupped and in a methodical fashion, she pounded on a section of Ali's ribs. The blows came in small tight circles and when she had fully pounded on one area, Ali's mother would drop down a few inches and start making circles again.

After a minute, Ali saw him there and gave him a weak smile. Her mother stopped and met his eyes. "Cody." She nodded, out of breath from the effort. "The vest can't get everything up. Sometimes we still have to do this."

Cody managed a brief nod and a quick glance at Ali, then he went to the kitchen for water. He gripped the kitchen counter and hung his head over the sink. Was this what she had to go through? Were the secretions Ali talked about that hard to remove? He couldn't imagine hitting Ali that hard, and yet…obviously the treatment worked. If someone didn't help her, her lungs would pay the price.

The scene made working with the cattle that much harder. He wanted to be inside, sitting next to her, reading with her or watching movies. She looked well enough, and the doctor's report had been good. But seeing her with the tubes in her nose, watching her mother pound on her back, Cody felt a thread of terror weave itself around the edge of his heart. She was okay, right? Better than before, wasn't that what the doctor had told her?

Nights were the best.

After her last treatment, she'd come off the oxygen for an hour or more. They would sit on the sofa, side by side, until her parents went to bed. Then they'd share quiet kisses and whispered thoughts.

Christmas came and they exchanged gifts. Cody gave her a white gold bracelet with a tiny row of diamonds, and she gave him a red scarf. Something she'd been knitting while he was at work outside. Two more weeks went by and Cody couldn't think of anything but her, his love for her.

She seemed to be getting stronger every day, her lungs more able to handle another round of rodeos. They talked about the upcoming season and how this would be her best chance to finally win the championship. But he couldn't imagine another year of hiding his feelings, sneaking out to see her for an hour or two.

It hit him one day, a realization as clear as the Colorado sky. He didn't want to be her secret friend; he wanted to be her husband.

The next morning he borrowed the Ford and headed into town. There, he picked out a brilliant white gold solitaire and had the inside engraved with one word: *Forever*. That night he wanted to talk to both her parents, but her father turned in early and Cody couldn't wait. Ali was upstairs taking a bath, so now was the time. With the ring in his jeans pocket, he found her mother in the kitchen stirring something in a green glass bowl.

"Mrs. Daniels..." He stood in the doorway, his heart racing.

She turned and looked at him. "Hello, Cody." A dishtowel hung over her left shoulder; her hair was pinned up.

"Ma'am, can I talk to you?" Cody walked the rest of the distance into the kitchen and anchored himself a few feet from her.

"Sure." She set the big plastic spoon on the countertop, blew at a wisp of hair, and turned to face him. "What's on your mind?"

"Well." His hands were sweaty. He wiped them on his Wranglers and reached into his pocket. The ring was there and he pulled it out, keeping his fingers tight around it. "Has Ali told you anything about the two of us?"

"Yes." Sarah Daniels' expression closed off some. "She tells me the two of you are friends." She raised one eyebrow a bit. "Nothing more."

He gave a nervous chuckle and ran his thumb along the ring, keeping it hidden in the palm of his hand. "To be honest with you, ma'am, things have changed. They've been changing for a while now."

"Changing?" She leaned against the counter.

"Yes, ma'am. See..." This was the hardest thing he'd ever said. Ali had been sheltered all her life because of her health. What would her mother think of her sick daughter falling in love with a bull rider? Cody clenched his teeth and continued. "I love her. I'm in love with her. We have...we have very strong feelings for each other."

Mrs. Daniels crossed her arms, her knuckles white. "Does Ali know you're talking to me?"

"No." Cody's answer was quick. "I went into town today and I bought this." He held out his hand and opened it. The ring caught the light and sprayed it across the kitchen. It was even more beautiful outside the velvet box. "I want to marry her, Mrs. Daniels. I wanted to talk to you and her father first, but since he was asleep I thought I'd show you the ring and—"

"No, Cody." She held her hand up and made short desperate shakes with her head. She brought her fingers to her face and covered her eyes.

Her obvious distress stopped him from saying anything else. He held the ring between his thumb and forefinger, and let his hand fall to his side. Was she that surprised, that upset about the idea? Was he such a poor choice for a husband that she couldn't hear him out?

Through the cracks between her fingers he could see the color leaving her cheeks. Her forehead was creased in a strong mix of grief and sorrow Cody hadn't expected. He felt his heart sink. Whatever the future held for Ali and him, it wouldn't be easy.

Finally, she folded her arms and drew in a shaky breath. When her eyes met his, he saw there were tears on her cheeks. "We asked Ali to tell you."

Cody felt light-headed. What was she talking about? Ali didn't need to tell anyone anything; that was his job. He was the one who wanted to ask the question. He blinked twice. "Tell me what?"

Ali's mother came closer and put her hands on Cody's shoulders. "Ali's dying."

He took a step back, letting her hands fall from him. Why would she say that, especially now? Ali was fine. She was better than she'd been at the end of the season. He shook his head, his eyes holding tight to hers. "That's a terrible thing to say, ma'am. Her doctor told her she was doing better."

"Cody." The woman's voice was tired, but steadier than before. Fresh tears filled her eyes. "For years I've prayed Ali would fall in love, that someone might come along to make her forget about horses and barrel racing. Someone who would keep her indoors, where she could be safe." She made a sound that was more cry than laugh. "Instead, she met you. Someone who loves rodeo as much as she does."

"Ma'am"—he was shaking from head to toe, his world spinning out of control—"Ali told me about her disease. She said it would take years off her life, but she could live a long time still. Decades, even, right?"

"No." The sadness in her eyes was deeper, stronger than before. "Ali doesn't need a wedding, Cody. She needs a lung transplant. Otherwise…" Her voice caught and she brought the back of her hand to her mouth. Two sobs filled the space between them. She hung her head. "Cody, I'm sorry; Ali… Ali should've told you."

He couldn't draw a breath, couldn't feel himself standing there. It wasn't happening; he wasn't hearing this. He bent over, his forearms on his knees. *Breathe, Gunner. Get a grip.* Nothing was going to happen to Ali, nothing. He straightened and stared at Ali's mother. "What are you saying? She's sicker than she's let on?" His tone was angrier than he intended. "Is that it?"

Mrs. Daniels still had her hand near her mouth. She moved it now, her lips quivering. "Ali will be dead in a year without a lung transplant. *That's* what the doctor said the last time he saw us." She hugged herself and three more quiet sobs shook her shoulders. "We've all known it was coming."

Cody felt the wood floor beneath his feet buckle. Her words didn't make sense, didn't connect with the conversations he'd had with Ali even the day before. She was feeling better, anxious to get back on Ace, making plans for the coming season. Ali Daniels wasn't dying, not even close.

But that reality clashed hard with the one before his eyes. Her mother was crying, weeping for Ali and the pain she clearly believed lay ahead for all of them. He began to shake and sway a little. He couldn't get his words to come. Was it true? Could Ali have known this and kept it from him? Upstairs, the water was still running. Ali wouldn't be down for a while.

"Mrs. Daniels..." He waited until she opened her eyes, until he could see for himself whether Ali was as bad off as she'd said. "Ali won't live another year without a lung transplant? Is that right?"

"Yes, Cody." She looked at him, and in that moment he knew. "We've talked about a live transplant, but that won't work." A catch sounded in her voice. "She's on a donor list; that's all we can do."

Cody's head was spinning. It was true, all of it.

Ali's lungs really were that bad, no matter what she said or how she felt or how determined she was to be at the season opener in January. She was dying. And suddenly all the fuzzy lines of their relationship came into crisp, clear focus. Of course she hadn't wanted to be more than friends.

What had she told him that day, half a year ago, when he saw her riding Ace in the fields behind one of the arenas? She didn't want to be caught, right? But he'd gone after her anyway, even after she told him straight-up not to chase her. Only he couldn't stop himself.

And once he caught her, she couldn't stop herself, either.

A suffocating pressure settled on his chest, and he leaned his hip into the counter closest to him. There would be no wedding, no future together, not if she only had a year. Ali would never agree to it. She would cling to her thought that if she told him no, if she pulled away, she could somehow spare them both the pain that would eventually come.

The reality was still sinking in, still exploding through his heart and soul. Ali Daniels was dying. She was dying, and there was nothing he could do about it. Nothing he could—

What had her mother said?

Think, Gunner. There was a solution here; there had to be. She was on a donor list, but there was something else, right? Something about a live transplant, wasn't that it? *Live* had to mean someone living could give her a lung, at least it sounded that way. That would be serious, of course, but it could be done. And if it could be done then there was still hope; there had to be. He sucked in a full breath.

"Okay." He grabbed the thin string of hope and clung to it with his whole being. He studied her mother's face. "Let's get her a lung transplant. Then she'll be fine, right?"

Ali's mother closed her eyes and shook her head. New tears splashed onto the floor. "She's on a waiting list, but she's not a top priority, not yet."

His mind raced. He pinched the bridge of his nose, demanding his mind to focus. "Tell me about this live transplant thing. Why won't that work?"

She sniffed and brought her fist to her lips for a moment. "They can do a transplant with two living donors. Her father's a match, but I'm not." She shook her head and opened her eyes. "We've never been close to Ali's two aunts, and besides, she doesn't want to ask. She says it isn't anyone's fault but her own that she needs a transplant this soon."

Defeat deepened the lines on her forehead. "Without a second donor the idea of a—"

"Wait!" The answer was easy. "I'll give her one of mine." Cody's heart pounded with hope. That was the answer. Of course it was. He could get by on one lung, couldn't he? People did it all the time. Hadn't he read about a rider who took a horn to the ribs, lost a lung, and kept riding? Or what about his grandfather? The man had lung cancer and lived another decade with just one lung. Possibility rushed through him. "I'll do it, Mrs. Daniels. I'll give her one. Then she can get better."

"Cody." Ali's mother came closer, her eyes begging him to understand. "Ali won't ever get better." She sucked in four quick breaths and gave another shake of her head. "A new lung will buy her three years at best. Three years, Cody."

Three years? Cody held his breath. It wasn't long enough, but it was better than one. And maybe sometime during those three years they'd find a cure, a way to help cystic fibrosis patients live longer.

Three years was an eternity if it meant keeping Ali alive.

"Mrs. Daniels"—his tone was calmer now, marked with a steely determination—"I've measured my whole life in seconds." He took her hands and squeezed them. His mind was made up. "On the back of a bull, eight seconds feels like a lifetime." A catch sounded in his voice. "Three years…?" He studied her. "That's a thousand tomorrows, ma'am. Forever to a cowboy like me."

Ali's mother tried, but nothing she said after that came close to changing his mind. He turned in early, not sure he could face Ali without letting her know the truth—that her secret was out.

His conversation with her mother stayed with him as he headed for the guesthouse and long after the lights were out. He would give Ali a lung, and maybe she would get back five years or ten. Maybe someone really would find a cure. They could get married and force a lifetime of love and memories into whatever time she had. The more he thought about it, the more he was sure it would happen. And if it only bought them three years then so be it.

Because three years with Ali was better than all of eternity without her.

Chapter Thirteen

Before he could do anything else, before he could think about the future, he had to know if he was a match. The first test was simple. If his blood type matched hers, if he was healthy and bigger than her, he could be a donor. After that more specific testing would mix a sample of his blood with a sample of hers, to check for compatibility.

The next day he drove into Denver and headed for the office of Dr. Cleary, the man who knew how bad off Ali really was. A receptionist made him wait half an hour, but finally the doctor saw him. When Cody explained the situation, he was happy to draw the blood.

Cody had no anxiety while he waited. He knew the answer long before the nurse presented him with the results. He was a match; of course he was. He and Ali were so close their hearts beat in time with each other. How could his blood type have been anything but the same as hers? The other test results wouldn't be available for several days, but Cody felt confident.

That afternoon as he walked up to the house, he heard loud voices inside. He opened the door quieter than usual and listened.

"I don't care! You had no right to tell him."

"Ali, he loves you; he had to know." It was her mother. Cody sank against the doorframe and listened.

"I would've told him, can't you see that? How am I supposed to face him now?" She was crying, her breaths short. He wanted to go to her, but he steadied himself, waiting, listening.

"Ali, calm down. You do yourself no good by getting upset."

"I don't care!" She uttered a cry. "So where is he now, huh? Where'd he go?"

"I told you; he's getting a blood test." She sounded tired, deliberately calm, the sorrow from the previous night hidden, no doubt for Ali's sake. "Ali, he *wants* to give you a lung."

"No!" She shouted this time, her voice ringing with anger and fear. "I won't take it!" He heard footsteps and then the sound of the back door opening and slamming shut.

"Ali!" He heard her mother open the door again and shout after her. "It's too cold out there! Come back and talk to me!"

That was all Cody needed to hear. He ran into the house, grabbed Ali's black wool jacket from the chair, and exchanged a glance with her mother. "I'll bring her back."

"Please, Cody." Relief rang in her voice. "Get her inside."

Cody tore through the door in time to see Ali sprint across the backyard toward the barn. She was going for Ace, no doubt. Ali hadn't been on him since they'd been home, and he knew how badly she wanted to ride.

He had never seen Ali run on anything but a horse. Watching her now, he wasn't surprised. She ran fast, a picture of grace and beauty, the same way she was on Ace's back. He picked up his speed as she turned and dashed through the barn doors. By the time he made his way inside, she was already saddling Ace. She turned, startled by his presence.

"Cody!" She pulled the cinch strap tight, put her boot in the stirrup and swung herself into the saddle. Shame darkened her features. She led the horse a few steps toward him. A wheeze sounded between her words. "Go away...I want to be alone."

"I'm not leaving." He held tight to her coat. Then he closed the distance between them, grabbed the saddle horn and swung himself up behind her.

"Fine." She didn't skip a beat, but dug her heels into Ace's sides and leaned forward.

The horse took off like lightning, tearing out of the barn and out into the open fields. He could feel her shaking, shivering from the combination of cold and fury. His body sheltered hers, but it wasn't keeping her warm, not with the wind in her face. He leaned in and yelled loud enough for her to hear him. "Stop! You need your coat."

"No!" She shot the word at him over her shoulder, and leaned closer to Ace's neck. "Yah!"

The horse kicked into another gear. *Come on, Ali.* He gritted his teeth and hung on to the saddle with one hand. With the other, he draped the coat over Ali's shoulders, holding it in place so it wouldn't fly off. She kept Ace running, flying across the rolling hills and rocky bluffs toward the far end of their ranch. Only when she'd ridden past the cattle, out to the barbed wire, did she pull to a stop.

Without looking at him, she dismounted and walked to the nearest fence post. The coat was still hanging on her shoulders, and she bent over, coughing long and hard. Cody felt the fear rise in his throat. He didn't have her inhaler, didn't have any way to help her. They were too far out to get help if she couldn't catch her breath.

His heart pounded against his chest. "Ali!" He jumped down and headed for her. "Breathe out; it's okay. You can do this."

She was bent in half, coughing, gasping for breath. "Cody...I'm sorry...I didn't mean to...to hurt you."

"Don't, Ali. It's okay. I'm here; I'm not mad."

Her coughing was getting worse. The cold air and exertion must've kicked her into a spasm, because she couldn't catch her breath. She was heading into a full-blown asthma attack, the kind Cody had seen her suffer before. That meant she needed her inhaler, the one back at the house.

Her gasps were more strained now, frantic for air.

"Ali, breathe out. Come on, you can do this."

But she couldn't, and he had a decision to make. He could get her back on Ace and go for help, but that would take ten minutes. Ten minutes they didn't have. If only she could relax, maybe the air would come.

His hand ran over her back, up and down in small circles. "Breathe, Ali. Please, breathe."

"I...I can't." Her coughing was horrendous now.

Terror filled him, paralyzing his ability to move or think or do anything but watch her fade away. He clenched his fists and shouted into the afternoon wind. "Help me!" His voice was lost among the rustling of pines overhead. "Make her breathe! Please!"

Ali coughed three times, but not as hard as before. She drew in a slow breath; it was raspy, but it was air. A tingling worked its way down Cody's spine from his neck to his lower back. He put his hand on her shoulder. His voice was quieter this time. "Ali, keep going! Keep breathing!"

"Cody..." She straightened some, her gasps farther apart. Now that he could see her face, the sight of her made him weak. Her skin was pasty gray, her lips a frightening shade of blue. "I'm okay."

He rubbed her back, leaning into her. "Slow breaths, Ali. Slow and easy. Blow out; you're getting through it."

She rested against the fence post, shaky and weak. Her breathing wasn't normal but it was better. "Thank you."

He was stunned, speechless. If things had been different, she could be passed out on the frozen ground by now, minutes from death. He shuddered. "Here." He helped get her arms into the wool coat. "Let's get you home."

Their conversation came later that night, when she

was rested and medicated, when all that was left from the terrifying afternoon was the memory of her anger.

They sat on the sofa, and Cody took the lead. "I heard you and your mother."

She crossed her arms and looked at her lap. "I wanted to tell you." Her eyes met his. "It was my job."

"It doesn't matter, Ali. I know the truth, and guess what?" He slid closer and took her hand in his. "I'm a match! As soon as you're ready, I'll give you one of my lungs. And maybe in the years after that they'll find a cure for CF and—"

"You can't." The anger was gone, but she shook her head anyway. "I won't let you." She bit her lip, her eyes damp. "You live for those eight seconds on a bull, Cody. I won't let you give that up."

"I don't have to." He smiled, his tone confident. She couldn't change his mind any more than her mother could have. He was more convinced with every passing hour. "I called one of the rodeo docs and asked. He said a bull rider could compete with one lung." Cody didn't tell her the rest of what the doctor said. Riding with one lung was very risky; it meant less room for error. A punctured lung could be deadly in such a situation.

"But when, Cody?" She lowered her brow. "You can't take time off during the season."

"I won't have to." He ran his knuckles along her cheek-bone. "You feel good, right?"

She studied him, puzzled. "So…"

"So we'll do the season together next year. When it's over, when we both have our buckles, we'll check into the hospital and I'll give you a lung." He kept a calm exterior, but inside he was holding his breath, pushing for her to tell him yes.

"Cody…" She angled herself toward him. "I don't want you to do it. You need your lungs."

"Come on, Ali." A grin tugged at his lips. He brushed a strand of hair back from her face. "We're talking about Gunner lungs here. One would be better than two on most riders."

She couldn't keep from smiling, even if fear still had the upper hand. "You're crazy."

"Yes. About you." He hesitated, watching her, waiting until the fear faded. "I'm doing this, Ali. I'm giving you a lung. I've already made up my mind."

"Cody…" The conviction was gone from her voice.

When she didn't go on, when she didn't argue or tell him she didn't want his offer, he knew he'd won. And with that, his heart shifted gears. He pulled the ring from his pocket. "Ali…" He leaned in and kissed her. "I don't care if you're sick, or how many years you'll get from a lung transplant." He kept his fingers on the sides of her face. "I love you."

The fear in her eyes turned to surprise, and the surprise to a sort of joy he hadn't seen in her since they came home from Las Vegas. "You really do?"

He slid her to the edge of the sofa and dropped to one knee. "I found out something today." He ran his tongue over his lower lip. "I found out I can't live without you." He kept the ring in his hand, tight against his knee. With the other hand, he covered her fingers. "But something else. Ever since my dad left, my mom has believed that someday I'd learn to let go ...that I'd learn to love." He studied Ali, the picture she made. He would never forget the way she looked, sitting in front of him, healthy and whole. "And now look at me."

For the second time that night, a smile played on her lips. Her eyes held the now familiar adoration she hadn't allowed herself to feel since her angry ride the day before. She messed her fingers through his hair. "What am I going to do with you?"

He reached into his closed palm and lifted the ring for her to see. "Marry me, Ali."

Her mouth hung open for a moment, but her surprise gave way to a certainty that told him all was right with their world. She wasn't going to run or push him away. It was too late to keep from falling for each other. They'd fallen, and from this day on there would be nothing else.

Here, now, they wouldn't borrow sadness from some far-off day. Not when they'd found something so rare together. She slid closer to him and put her arms around his neck. "Cody Gunner, I have a question."

He brought his lips to hers, the gentlest kiss. Then he found her eyes, his voice barely a whisper. "Ask it."

"Okay." She watched him, her eyes full of light and love. Her smile started there and made its way to her mouth. "Are you chasing me?"

"Always." He grinned.

Her smile faded. "Don't ever stop." She kissed him with a slow certainty, a kiss that told him she had as much hope as he had about their future. When she pulled back, her eyes held a strange mix of starry-eyed dreams and smoldering desire. "Now I need to answer your question."

"Yes." He pressed his face against hers, holding on to the feel of her soft skin against his. "I'm waiting."

She giggled and leaned back, looking beyond his eyes and straight to the places of his heart that were no longer closed off. "Yes, Cody." Her eyes shone like never before. "I'll marry you."

He drew her closer, holding her tight not only in his arms, but in his soul. "I love you, Ali."

Her face grew serious. "I love you, too." It was the first time she'd said it. But once the words were out, the truth about them filled her expression. "I love you with all I am, Cody Gunner."

It was a moment that might've been marked by tears. But as they kissed, as she held up her hand and let him slide the ring past her knuckle, they laughed and held each other and whispered about what her parents would say, and whether he would even tell his. They cuddled on the couch, talking about wedding dresses and handwritten vows and honeymoons and the future, their eyes clear and dry.

Cody thought he understood why.

The story they were starting was bound to have sad scenes. The ending would be saddest of all. So why not smile and laugh and love as long as they had today? Why not admire her ring and kiss her and hold her, breathing in the feel of her against his chest? Today was no time for crying. Cody wasn't willing to lose a single happy moment with Ali Daniels. Soon enough down the road, the tears would come. For now, today belonged to them.

Today, and another year of rodeo, and after that a thousand precious tomorrows.

Chapter Fourteen

The Pro Rodeo season started out like the one Ali Daniels had always dreamed about. But even then she had a sense the good times wouldn't last.

She set a record at the opener in Denver, and took first place at all but two of the first seven stops. But along the way she could feel herself shutting down. Every breath required deliberate thought. Not just the breathing she did in the arena, but all the time, even after a long session in her compression vest.

They carried oxygen in her trailer, and Cody rarely left her side. He was first in the standings, riding with as much fury as ever—all of it somehow directed toward cystic fibrosis. At least that's what he told her.

At night he no longer stopped by for an hour. He slept on the sofa with Ali ten feet away in her room. She was surprised at the boundaries he kept for them. When their kissing stirred new and unspeakable passions in her, he would quietly pull away and bid her good night, even if it left them both trembling.

"I've done this my way before," he told her once. "You're different, Ali. I'd wait forever for you."

They set a date for their wedding—the third Saturday in May. There were no rodeos that weekend, and so they'd have most of the season to focus on gaining the lead in their respective rankings. The wedding would be small. A simple ceremony outdoors, atop a grassy bluff on her parents' ranch. Her mom and dad would attend, of course, but she wanted his parents to be there, too.

"Cody, you need to tell them." She'd bring it up every few days, but he shut down whenever she asked about it.

It wasn't until a California rodeo in mid-April that Ali saw for herself how angry he was with his parents. The arena was outdoors that week, and Ali was in the stands talking to her mother, the sunshine beating down on them, when a woman walked up and introduced herself.

"Ali Daniels?" The woman fidgeted, casting an anxious look over her shoulder. Behind her stood a young man with Down syndrome.

Ali smiled. "Yes?" She was approached by fans at every rodeo; especially now that she and Cody were an item. Half the time people wanted her to give him a message or have him sign something. But the woman didn't have the look of a fan, and something in her blue eyes was familiar.

"Ali, I'm Mary Gunner, Cody's mother." She held out her hand and gave Ali a nervous look. "I'm not sure my son would want me talking to you."

The boy behind her, the one with Down syndrome, was that Cody's brother, Carl Joseph? The one he had talked about? Her head spun and she struggled to find her voice. Why hadn't Cody ever said anything about his brother's disability? Ali felt an immediate warmth for Mary Gunner.

"Please"—Ali slid over—"sit down." She took her own mother's hand. "Mama, this is Mary Gunner, Cody's mother."

"Nice to meet you." Mary gave them a partial smile. She turned and motioned for the young man with her to take a seat. "This is Carl Joseph, Cody's brother."

"I've heard about him." Ali looked around Mary to the young man and waved. He had Cody's dark hair, but that was all. Carl Joseph's eyes were brown and deep set. He was thicker, stouter than Cody. "Hi, I'm Ali."

Carl Joseph raised his hand quickly and dropped it again. He struggled with eye contact, shy and grinning. "Hi, Ali. You're pretty."

"Thanks."

Mary patted her younger son's knee. Then she looked at Ali. "I got a call from someone in rodeo." She hesitated. "You and my son are engaged, is that right?"

"Yes, ma'am." Ali's heart went out to the woman. She wanted to hug her and apologize for the way Cody had shut her out. "We're getting married in May. I keep pushing Cody to call and invite you."

Mary folded her hands and let out a tired breath. "It isn't me he's mad at; it's his father." She hesitated. "We're back together now; we remarried over the Christmas break. But

Cody can't think of his daddy without thinking about how he walked away. He won't return my calls, won't talk to either of us." Her eyes grew damp. "Mike Gunner's a different man now."

"Is he?" Ali had wondered about Cody's father. Whatever the man had done, Cody rarely got specific with the details.

"Oh, yes." Mary's smile reached all the way to her eyes. "He's wonderful, Ali. If Cody only knew ..."

"Mary ..." Ali's mother leaned forward so the two could see each other. "Ali has cystic fibrosis. I wasn't sure if you knew that or not."

Cody's mother froze, her mouth open. The news took a few seconds to sink in, but as it did, her shoulders slumped some. Clearly she understood the ramifications of cystic fibrosis better than Cody had. Mary shifted her eyes to Ali, and placed her hand on Ali's knee. "I'm sorry; I had no idea."

"We've kept it a secret, but not for much longer." Ali's mother was stronger now, more accepting of the situation. "Ali has to have a lung transplant. We're planning the operation for December."

The pain in Mary's eyes was genuine, and Ali felt for her. After all the hurt the Gunners had experienced as a family, now this. Her son was marrying someone with a terminal illness. Next to her, Carl Joseph was blissfully unaware of the conversation. He cheered on the team ropers, caught up in the excitement of the arena.

Ali's mother wasn't finished. "There's more, Mary."

"More?" Heartache rang in her quiet voice.

"She needs a lung from two people, and I'm not a match. So...one will come from her father. The other...Cody wants to give her one of his."

Mary drew back a few inches, shocked. "Cody?"

"We tried to talk him out of it, but his mind's made up. He's been cleared by the doctor; he's giving one of his lungs to Ali."

A soft gasp came from the woman, and she looked from Ali to her mother. "Then...then that's the answer."

"The answer?" Ali's mother had tenderness in her voice. The situation was hard for all of them.

"For years I've wanted to believe that...that one day Cody would learn to love and now..." Her words caught in her throat. "I'm sorry. This is amazing."

Something caught Ali's attention and she looked up. Cody was coming toward them, staring at his mother, his eyes blazing. Ali stood. Maybe if she headed him off before he reached her, maybe then they could avoid a scene. "Cody..."

He stopped and waited, breathing hard, his eyes on the place where their mothers were talking. Carl Joseph remained focused on the arena. At that instant, the women both noticed him, and Mary started to stand. But before she could, Ali put a hand on her shoulder.

"I'll talk to him." The announcer was saying something about hot dogs being half price and Ali could barely hear herself. She raised her voice as she met Mary's eyes. "Thank you for introducing yourself. I...I hope one day we can work all this out."

She gave her mother a glance that said she'd be back.

Then she went to Cody. He had his hands on his hips, his faded white cowboy hat dipped low. When she reached him, she took his hand. "Can we talk?"

"What's she doing here?" he hissed, his voice low.

"Follow me." She headed up the stairs and then down onto the dusty track that surrounded the arena. People were watching them, so she moved fast, leading him past the busy concession stands through the competitors' gate, to a quiet sun-splashed corner where they could be alone.

The whole time she could feel Cody fuming beside her.

She faced him now, her heart pounding. "What is it, Cody? Why do you hate her?"

His eyes narrowed. "You don't know everything, okay?" He seethed with each word, his anger reaching a level she'd never seen in him before.

But it wasn't enough to stop her.

She'd never pushed when it came to his parents, never dug deep enough to find out why his feelings ran so cold against them. She felt her own frustration building. "I might not know everything, Cody, but your mother loves you." She pushed her finger at his chest. "She loves you, Cody!" Her voice was louder than she intended, but she was too worked up to stop. "I saw that the minute she came up and said hello."

"Is that right?" He stood and glared at her. "Well, let me tell you something you didn't see." He was still furious, but he wasn't shouting. Other riders were looking their way. "You didn't see your father throw his suitcase into a taxicab and drive off without looking back. You didn't scream for him to stop, and run down the street after him. And you didn't stand on the corner watching that yellow cab disappear and never come back."

His chest was heaving, and anger wasn't the only thing in his tone. He had the eyes of a young boy, hurt to the core by the things he was sharing. Ali reached out and tried to take his hand. "Cody ..."

"No!" He jerked away. "I'm not finished!" He turned away from her, took two steps, and faced her again. His cheeks blazed from the intensity of his emotions. "You know about Carl Joseph now, right?"

"You should've told me he was—"

"No." He dropped the brim of his hat another inch. "I didn't tell you because to me he doesn't have Down syndrome. He never had it. He's just a big kid with a big heart, but you know what my father said about him?" His words were fast, a string of bullets. "He said he couldn't be a father to a kid like Carl Joseph." Cody's eyes were damp, but he clenched his jaw, too angry to cry. "You wanna know why I'm mad? Why I can't run back home and pretend everything's okay? My dad left us because he couldn't love the most loving kid in the world, Ali. That's why."

Tears poked pins in her eyes, too. Her chest was tight, her airways too narrow, the way they got when she was upset. But she didn't want to move, didn't want to interrupt the moment by grabbing the inhaler from her boot. She didn't want to do anything but let him finish.

"Ali, you have no idea." He moaned and looked straight up at the sky, then just as fast his eyes found hers again. "You know what I never understood? The thing that drove me onto the back of all those bulls week after week after lousy week? I could see why someone shallow might not love Carl Joseph. Carl wasn't the perfect boy child, he wasn't the sort of kid a former NFL star could be proud of." He pounded his chest with his open palm. "But what about me, Ali? What was wrong that he couldn't love me?"

Cody dropped down slow onto his heels, and stared at the ground.

"There was nothing wrong with you." Ali coughed three times and then willed herself to wait. He deserved her full attention. She took hold of his shoulder; this time he didn't pull away. Three more coughs shook her chest. "It was your father, Cody. Something was wrong with *him*." She hesitated. "But maybe he's better now; maybe he's changed."

Cody jerked his shoulder from her reach. He lifted his head and glared at her. "Never mind." Disgust rattled his tone. His eyes were ice cold, the hurt from a moment earlier replaced by walls thick and immovable. He stood, gave her one last look, and turned around. Without saying another word he headed hard toward the stock area, his boot heels kicking up a small dust cloud with every step.

"Cody, wait..." A series of coughs seized her, but she was on her feet anyway. She ran a few steps. "Cody..."

He stopped sharp and turned around. "Don't follow me." He spat the words, unconcerned with the way people stared and took paths around them. "You don't understand." He tossed his hands in the air. "No one'll ever understand."

"Hey..." She took another step closer, close enough to see the way his hands trembled. Panic took the tightness in her throat to a new level. She didn't have long. An asthma attack was coming. But right now the pain in her lungs was nothing to the ache in her heart. "That's not fair."

"But it's true." He spat the last few words at her. Then he turned and continued making his way toward the pens.

She coughed twice and watched him leave. There was no point following him, not if he wouldn't listen to her. She reached into her boot for her inhaler. What was he thinking? She was the only one who knew what drove him to ride. She'd spotted his anger before they had a single conversation. Of course she understood him.

One breath at a time she sucked in the medication, and eventually she felt her airways respond. She needed another session with her compression vest, but she was running out of time. The first round in the barrel racing was less than an hour off, and Ace wasn't warm yet. She turned and walked in the opposite direction, out to where Ace was tied up in a pen.

She tightened his saddle and checked his bridle. Then for the next half hour she loped with him across a field at the back of the parking lot. Ace was such a good horse, dependable and strong. Always there for her.

But what about Cody? Why couldn't he see that she was on his side? If he didn't make peace with his parents, the rift would always come between them. Family was family. It was wrong to go through life hating the people you were supposed to love most.

The air was humid that day, humid and thick. The pollen must've been high, as well, because Ali could almost feel herself breathing more than air. Usually the medication brought at least some relief. But this time her lungs were tight, stiff and unresponsive. The trouble was, she couldn't use the inhaler again, not for four hours.

"Okay, Ace, that's all," she cooed near his ears, resting her head on his. "Let's slow it down."

She walked with him a few minutes longer and then headed for the arena. Her race was sixth that afternoon; it was time to report to the judges. This rodeo was a big one for her and Cody. They both needed wins to head into the summer season in the lead.

Her chest hurt, and she drew a breath that didn't come close to filling her lungs. Warnings sounded in her mind. What if the race pushed her past the point of bouncing back? How would she get her mama's attention if she needed help? Ali checked her watch. Maybe she had enough time. She could go back to the trailer, use one of the vapor mist medications, maybe that would help.

Across the field she heard the announcer.

"Now's your time to get some popcorn, ladies and gentlemen, because we've got a treat up for you next. Some of the finest barrel racers in the business, including—"

Ali had heard enough, and in that moment she made up her mind. There wasn't time to go back. Her airways weren't in great shape, but she could get through the ride. Hold her breath and tear around the cloverleaf pattern. Then go back to her trailer and use the compression vest. Everything would be fine. In fact, as she rode Ace to the check-in point, as she readied herself for the race, she wasn't worried about herself at all.

She was worried about Cody.

Chapter Fifteen

He was an idiot.

No matter how angry he was at his parents, he had no right to take it out on her. What he'd said was right; Ali didn't understand. But that wasn't her fault. She hadn't lived a lifetime wondering why her father didn't love her. If she and her parents had ever disagreed or been mad at one another, they would've worked it out by the next day. Of course she would want him to patch everything up.

So why'd he have to get mad at her? How could he have yelled at her, Ali Daniels, a girl who'd never fought with anyone? He was an idiot. Cowboy pride, that's what it was. Stubborn cowboy pride.

He should've turned around and run after her, taken her in his arms and told her he was sorry. Instead he'd let her go off, coughing and sputtering. Now he'd have to wait until after her race to talk to her.

The stands were almost full, but he found a spot on the

top row and kept his hat low so he wouldn't be recognized. From there he could see his mother and Carl Joseph, still sitting next to Ali's mother. He forced himself to watch the barrel racers instead.

Times for the first five riders were all decent. She would need a great ride to put herself at the top. *Come on, Ali...I'm up here, pulling for you. Give it your best.*

The announcer introduced her just as she tore into the arena. Her blonde ponytail flew behind her like pale silk, her trademark black hat and black jeans standing out in stark contrast to her palomino horse.

"Look at her go!" The announcer was excited, keeping the crowd on the edge of their seats. "If she gets this last barrel she could have herself a record-breaker, folks."

Ali flew around the final barrel and blazed back through the gate, but something was wrong. She didn't look right; something in her eyes and the gray color of her skin. Cody stood up, adrenaline flooding his veins. She looked faint, beyond sick. The whole arena had to see that.

"She did it!" The announcer hooted out loud. "Ali Daniels has the new record, ladies and gentlemen!"

The crowd was on its feet, clapping and cheering for Ali, but Cody climbed on top of the bench and peered over them. He had to see her, needed to know that she was okay. Cody squinted hard, scanning the area where the barrel racers were gathered until he saw her. She was still on Ace, still making her way from the arena. She came to an abrupt stop and then, in a sickening sort of flop, she fell onto the ground.

"Ali!" He tore down the steps, his eyes glued to the place where she lay, motionless. It was his fault; he'd upset her before the race, and now she couldn't breathe. He cursed himself as he took the stairs two at a time. Every step was a frantic plea. *No, not now...not yet...help her, please. Help her breathe.*

Even from across the stadium he could see people snapping to action around her. Two riders moved in at her side, and a couple of cowboys ran into the arena waving their arms. "Get an ambulance! Hurry!"

A hush fell over the crowd, all eyes trained on the place where Ali had fallen. Cody picked up his pace. Behind him he heard steps and turned to see Ali's mother, her face pale, eyes wide. "Run, Cody...don't wait for me!"

He took off, tearing around the fence toward the competitors' area. Rodeos kept an ambulance on hand. By the time Cody reached the small crowd that had gathered around Ali, the ambulance was just a few yards away.

"Ali!" His voice was lost in the chaos. Emergency personnel were at the center, but there were too many barrel racers and other competitors in the way for him to see what they were doing, whether she was conscious or not.

"Move!" he shouted, and a few people cleared a path. If she needed her inhaler, why hadn't she taken it? What could've made her collapse like that? And why wasn't she getting up?

He had to part his way through the crowd to get to her. By the time he reached the inner circle, they were loading her limp, beautiful body onto a stretcher. Someone was holding an oxygen mask over her face, and through it he saw her blink. She was awake!

"Ali!" He pushed his way to her side and grabbed her hand. "Ali, I'm here." He moved in time with the paramedics, walking beside her toward the ambulance.

She mumbled something and pushed the oxygen away from her face. "Cody..." She was pasty gray, her breathing tight and shallow, the way it had been at her ranch that day. "I'm fine..." Her words were breathy and weak, barely understandable. "Don't...don't worry about me."

"I'm sorry." His heart screamed within him, pounding out a fast and terrible rhythm. *Don't let her die. Please...*Why had he gotten her so upset? They were at the ambulance door now; he had only seconds. "I didn't mean it, okay?"

"It's not your fault." She blinked and the movement was slow and fading. "Go ride."

It wasn't his fault? Even now she was thinking of him, reading his mind. Of course it was his fault. He'd gotten her upset; he'd let her walk away coughing when he could've helped her. Whatever happened, he was completely responsible.

Ali's mother ran up. She spoke to the paramedic, and Cody distantly heard him grant her permission to go along for the ride. He shot a look at the other medic, the one closest to him. "Take me, too. She needs me."

"Her mother's going." He lifted the stretcher and slid it into the back of the ambulance. "Only next of kin is allowed; I'm sorry."

"Is she okay?"

The man looked at his partner and then at Ali. "She needs to be seen, but she's stable."

Cody felt himself catch a full breath. "Okay." He met Ali's eyes. "I'll be right behind you. I'm leaving now."

The technician wanted to put the oxygen over her face again, but Ali turned away. "No, Cody. Stay…" Sweat drops dotted her face, and the skin around her mouth was still blue. "Ride…you can come later. I'll…be fine." Her eyes locked on his, and despite the commotion and crowd and frenzied attempts to help her, everything faded away. Everything but her. "I love you, Cody."

Her words were too soft to hear, but he heard them all the same. Heard them to the core of his being. He took a step back, his eyes still on hers. "I love you, too."

Someone closed the ambulance doors and the driver gave three short bursts with the siren, clearing a path through the crowd. And then she was gone. She and her mother, leaving him alone on a patch of dusty rodeo ground, his head spinning. What city were they in, anyway? And what was the name of the hospital? How could he find her if he didn't know where she was?

A bull rider came up beside him and put an arm around him. "They'll take care of her, Cody. Probably just the heat."

The heat? He stared at the guy and opened his mouth to explain that it wasn't the heat; it was her CF. But then he remembered. No one knew, not one of them. Ali looked as healthy as ever. Why would anyone think she was dying of a fatal lung disease? He'd promised Ali he would keep her secret, and even now he wouldn't betray her.

The rider was waiting, but Cody only gave him a quick slap on his shoulder. "Thanks, man. You're right."

Cody didn't know what to do. He started in one direction, stopped and turned around, and stopped again. Why was he at the arena when Ali needed him? He had to find his way to her. The other barrel racers were finishing up now, and the announcer explained that Ali had been taken in for a check.

"Bull riders should report at the judge's table," he said. "That's right, folks, hold on to your hats. We've got the best bull riders on the tour about to take a seat on the rankest bulls around."

Cody had a great draw for the final go-round of the day, and he was third to ride. What was it Ali had told him? Ride first, then come see her, wasn't that it? He paced to the far chain-link fence, grabbed it and stared at the highway beyond. Someone would know where they'd taken her, maybe someone at the announcer's booth.

Riders talked about the adrenaline rush of getting on a bull.

It was nothing to the way he felt now, stomach aching, limbs on fire, head spinning. *Please...*

He clenched his fist and drove it into the fence. Fine. If she wanted him to ride, he'd ride. What would eight seconds matter? The paramedic said she was steady, right? He could ride and he'd still be fifteen minutes behind the ambulance. The moment he was finished he'd find out where she was and take her truck. It was unhooked from their trailer; the keys on the floorboard where she always kept them.

In a burst, he turned and jogged toward the chutes. He wasn't stretched out, but that didn't matter. He'd never been more focused in his life. He would ride for Ali, because she wanted him to. After all he'd done wrong that day, the least he could do was turn in a winning performance. He was halfway there when his mother stepped out from the crowd and blocked his path.

"Cody..." Fear colored her eyes. "Is she all right?"

A part of him wanted to cry at the sight of her, run to her arms and let her rock away the hurt the way she'd done when he was a little boy. But in the war that was their family existence, she'd chosen sides. He stopped only long enough to nod his head. "She's fine."

He started to move again, but she took hold of his arm. "Let me help, Cody. I'll take you to her."

"No!" He hissed the word. "I can get there myself."

Then he turned and stormed to the area behind the chutes. He grabbed his rope and slipped on his vest. By the time he reached the pen and climbed up the fence, it was his turn. He climbed in, steadied himself over the bull, and dropped onto the beast's back, shoving his mouth guard in place. The animal snorted, pawing the ground. "Not today, mister."

Three cowboys sat on the fence around him, holding on to his vest. Cody wrapped his hand in record time, grabbed the chute with his free hand, and nodded. The ride was wild, twisting him in tight circles and sending him airborne on top of the bull, his arm straight up, legs in perfect position. The bull snorted and Cody felt the spray against his face, smelled the animal's fury.

Not today, bull. Not this cowboy. Cody kept his eyes on the bull's shoulders. Nothing was going to happen to Ali, nothing.

The ride was crazy, more intense than any Cody could remember. Adrenaline filled him, flooding his senses until there was only Cody and the bull, Cody and the ride. Eight seconds passed in a blur, and when the buzzer sounded, Cody jumped off and headed straight for the gates.

He was halfway to Ali's truck when he heard the announcer shout, "Cody Gunner gets a ninety-three, folks; you can live a long time and never see a bull ride like that one! Let's hear it for..."

Cody tuned it out.

He climbed into Ali's truck and used her cell phone to call information. There was one hospital in town. Cody phoned for directions as he drove through the parking lot toward the exit. Ten minutes later he walked into the emergency room and spotted her mother.

"How is she?" He was still dirty from the ride. "What's wrong with her?"

"She's okay, Cody. They're giving her oxygen." Her mother squeezed his hand. "Dr. Cleary told her it would get like this."

"But they can make her better, right, get her well again?" He couldn't think, couldn't breathe until he knew she was going to be all right.

"Yes. She'll have to stay in the hospital awhile. Four days, maybe." Ali's mother looked tired. "How'd you ride?"

The matter was so small compared to Ali's health.

"Ninety-three." He looked past her, toward the double doors that led to the hospital rooms. "Can I see her?"

Her mother hesitated. "The doctor said only—"

"Ma'am, please." He looked at her again.

She gave a nervous glance at the receptionist's desk. "Okay." She motioned to him. "Stay with me."

They went back and found her in the third room on the right. She was by herself, hooked up to an intravenous bag and oxygen. As soon as he saw her, he felt himself relax. Her color was back. Her mother was right; she was going to get through this. One more time, one more chance.

"Hey, you." He moved to her side.

She looked tired, but she found a smile for him. "Did you stay on?"

"Yeah." He stroked her hair, searched her eyes. "What happened back there?"

"I couldn't get a breath." The weariness lifted. "Did you hear? I set a record!"

"I heard." He bent down and kissed her cheek. He didn't want to talk about their events. "You couldn't breathe? You mean after the race, after holding your breath?"

"Right." She closed her eyes and opened them, more slowly than before. "I'm okay, Cody. They gave me something; I can breathe now."

"It's because you were upset." He ran his fingertips along her brow. "I'm an idiot. I shouldn't have gotten mad."

"No." She swallowed and cleared her throat. "It was the humidity, Cody. Really."

She was wrong, but he wasn't going to push. No sense upsetting her further. "You can breathe okay now?"

"Yes." She put her hand over his. "I'm fine, Cody. Just another tune-up." Concern flashed in her eyes. "You have another ride tonight."

"I can turn out; I don't need this event."

"Cody Gunner!" She placed her hand over his. "You've never turned out in your life." She looked at her mother, standing a few feet away. "Tell him, Mama. He can't help me sitting here in a hospital room."

Mrs. Daniels came a step closer. "She's right; go ride, Cody."

"I don't need to." He wouldn't take his eyes off her.

"Yes, you do." She closed her eyes, too tired to keep them open. "Go win it."

They talked a few more minutes, until she convinced him she was feeling good, that all she really wanted was a nap. It wasn't until he reached the arena and reported in, that he got the news.

News that made his heart turn somersaults in his chest.

Chapter Sixteen

Night rides always involved the rankest stock, the toughest bulls. It was that way on purpose, designed to bring in the higher-paying crowds and give them a better show. When Cody returned to the arena he got the news he'd been waiting for since he earned his pro card. The bull he'd drawn was none other than the legend, the meanest bull on the tour, a bull so violent and crazed, his owners competed him as often as possible, making a killing off him.

The bull was Chaos.

Of the twenty-three times he'd been ridden in the past two years, Chaos had bucked off twenty-three riders. But that wasn't all. The bull wielded his horns like weapons. In his wake were a trail of broken ribs, concussions, and a spinal injury. On the Pro Rodeo Tour no greater challenge existed than the challenge of riding Chaos. Before Ali, Cody would've paid a year's winnings for a chance on this bull. Just one chance.

But now...

Now he carried something inside him that would give Ali another three years. He didn't care if Chaos hurt him; that was part of bull riding. But what if the bull jabbed him in the ribs, what if he punctured his lung, Ali's lung?

His mind reeled.

Should he take the draw, maybe pull off the ride of his life? If he did, it would be the pinnacle of his career, no matter how long he rode. Riding Chaos would guarantee him a win and put him in position to coast into the finals. He paced up and down the alley behind the chutes. Every few minutes he stopped to stretch, thinking about the possibilities.

The smell of burned popcorn and greasy corn dogs filled the air and mixed with the scent of livestock. What should he do? How much of a risk was he willing to take? He refused to scan the stands, afraid his mother was still there. If she was, Carl Joseph would see him this time, and then he'd have no choice but to deal with her, as well. Not that he expected her to come looking. He wasn't even sure she was still there. He didn't care. The only thing on his mind was the wild bull ride ahead, his chance at making history.

And the damage it could do to him if he didn't.

Cody was slated to ride last, and the situation was clear to everyone. Stay eight on Chaos and he'd be first not only at this event, but in the standings. First with no one close behind him.

Still...he couldn't get Ali out of his mind. He wore a path behind the chutes, stretching and trying to convince himself it would be okay. Ali would want him to ride, to take his shot at the bull no one could beat. But as he climbed the fence and stared in at the bull, he shuddered.

He already knew what would happen. The bull would fly through the air, bucking him onto the ground and coming back to finish him off. Chaos wasn't content with sending cowboys to the ground; he wanted to kill them. Before Ali, that would've been fine. Let the beast try. He'd ridden unridable bulls before.

But what if he *did* get hurt? What if he had a wreck that damaged his lungs?

He could risk his own life, but not Ali's.

And with that he made his decision. Cody hopped down behind the chutes and headed for the judges' table.

"Gunner, what're you doing?" one of the cowboys shouted after him. "Your ride's up in a few minutes."

Cody didn't stop. He reached the table and stood in front of the oldest judge in the business, a veteran, pure class and character.

"Cody Gunner?" He gave Cody a curious frown. "You need to be in the chute, young man. How can I help you?"

"I'm turning out, sir." He grabbed his number off the back of his vest and thrust it onto the table. "I can't ride tonight."

"But that's the best draw of the—"

"Thank you, sir."

He didn't say another word until he was at Ali's side.

"I can't believe you turned out." She held his hand and smiled at him. "Everyone's going to think you've lost your edge."

"I don't care." He leaned down and kissed her lips, slow and tender. "As long as I don't lose you." He brushed his nose against hers and drew back a little.

"You won't, Cody. I'm fine."

"Right." He bit his lip. He didn't tell her why he turned out; left her thinking it was his deal, that he couldn't get focused with her in the hospital. He couldn't tell her he wanted to keep his lungs safe. It was better if she didn't know, less upsetting to her.

They talked about the standings, and after a while, her mother came in from the cafeteria. "Your father says hello. He'll call you in the morning."

"Thanks, Mama." Ali gave her a lopsided smile.

They made small talk for half an hour before the doctor came in, a clipboard in his hands, his face dark.

Cody sat on one side of the bed, Ali's mother on the other. He wanted to tell the doctor to leave; they were doing fine without anything else to think about.

"Hello." Mrs. Daniels spoke first. "Have you talked to Dr. Cleary?"

"Yes." The man came to the foot of her mattress and touched her toes. "Hi, Ali. You doing okay?"

"Mmm-hmm." She was breathing easier, but she looked exhausted.

The doctor shifted his look to Ali's mother again. "I ran the test results by Ali's doctor, and, well…the news isn't good."

Cody steeled himself. Hadn't he known this was coming? No matter what Ali said about this being another tune-up, they all knew she was getting worse. The coughing, the extra medication, the frantic times when she couldn't breathe. The signs were there for all of them.

"Her functions are bad, right?" Ali's mother took hold of Ali's forearm. "I can tell."

"It's more than her function tests, Mrs. Daniels." The doctor released a heavy breath. "Her lungs are shutting down. She's finished barrel racing."

Ali reached for Cody's hand. She closed her eyes, squeezing his fingers. He wanted to cover her ears, shelter her with his body. Anything to erase what the man had said. This was the day she'd dreaded all her life. She wasn't being given a warning; it was more of a pronouncement.

No more barrel racing. Not ever.

Cody could only imagine the heartache exploding through her, because his heart was breaking, too. She was finished racing? Done with the dream she'd chased since she was eleven? Never again would she race around the barrels, faster than every other rider. She and Ace were finished, finished with the Pro Rodeo Tour, finished traveling around the country, finished climbing the leaderboard.

Ali Daniels would be remembered for blazing onto the barrel-racing scene and staying in the top handful of riders the whole time she competed. But her promise would never be fulfilled; there would be no national championship.

He let his head fall against her hand, willing some of his strength into her. The doctor was going on, saying something about recuperating and using the next few months to get stronger. Then he said something that made Cody sit straight up.

"Dr. Cleary tells me you're planning a lung transplant in December." The man's face was stern, tense.

"Yes." Ali's mother continued to be the spokesperson for the three of them. She hesitated and looked his way. "Cody's one of the donors. Her father's the other."

"That's what I need to talk to you about." The doctor opened the file he was holding. "We rescheduled the transplant for June. Dr. Cleary believes that's as long as we can wait. After consulting with our specialists, I have to agree." He read the file. "Ali would stay a few more days here, and then return home. We'd like her to gain some strength over the next eight weeks, so that she's in the best possible shape for the transplant."

June? Cody froze for a moment, but there was no hesitation. June was perfect. The sooner the better. That made his decision about the season an easy one.

Ali opened her eyes and the three of them stayed silent, the news suffocating them like a desert dust cloud.

"Doctor"—Ali's mother sounded drained, resigned—"could you give us some time to talk?"

"Yes, certainly." He looked from Ali's mother to Ali and finally to Cody. "I wish I could give you some options, but there are none. This is the only plan left."

As soon as the doctor was gone, Ali turned to him. "You don't have to do it, Cody. Someone else could give me a lung; I'm still on the donor list and my case will be more urgent now. June is the worst time for—"

"Ali." He pressed his fingers to her lips. "I'm done with the season."

"No, Cody." Her mother looked at him. "Ali's right. You're at the top of your sport." She clutched the arms of her chair. "You're healthy and whole; if we put her back on the donor list she might get a lung right when she needs it."

"Listen." Cody's tone was calm, convinced. He slid back in his chair. "I'm doing this. Nothing can change my mind. I *want* her to have my lung."

No one said anything. Then Ali reached out and took his fingers. "We could try to wait, Cody. The doctor might be wrong. What's a few months if it'll let you win the championship again?"

"Hear me, Ali. Please." He leaned close and kissed the inside of her wrist. "My season's over whether you have the transplant in June or December. I won't get on another bull until it's over."

"Why? I…I don't understand." Her voice was quiet, weak. "I don't need you at home with me, watching me breathe from a machine. I'd rather have you winning rodeos, Cody. Doing what you love."

"I can't." He ran his fingers over her engagement ring and pressed her hand to his face. He didn't want to tell her, but he had to. "I've never worried about getting hurt on a bull, because I only had myself to think about." He shrugged. "I don't know, maybe I wanted the challenge. The pain of a pulled shoulder beat the other pain, the one inside." He found her eyes and held them. "But everything's different now." He sat up and put her hand to his chest. "One of my lungs is already yours, Ali. It's not mine. I'm not worried about myself, I'm worried about the part of me that belongs to you."

Ali's mother covered her face with her fingers. She was crying, doing her best to hide the noise.

Tears filled Ali's eyes, too, spilling down the bridge of her nose onto her pillow. And that's when he knew he'd won. It was time to go home and get Ali well again, time to dream about the days the transplant would buy them. It was possible, wasn't it? A cure could be found while she was living on borrowed time, right?

He leaned over the bed and hugged her. No matter that Ali and her mother were crying, he couldn't bring himself to feel sad. So what if he missed a season of Pro Rodeo? He'd earned plenty of money that year already, and he could always go back when the surgery was behind them.

Ali was going to get better, stronger, and after her transplant anything could happen. She was a survivor, a fighter. If anyone could beat cystic fibrosis, it was Ali Daniels. And now they would be together every day back at her ranch. Ali and her mother were upset now, but Cody could feel nothing but joy over the fact. And then in just a few weeks when she was well enough, they would celebrate the happiest moment of all.

Their wedding day.

Chapter Seventeen

She found the dress at an old boutique in Denver, a small store she and her mother visited on the way back from a meeting with Dr. Cleary. Ali knew the moment she slipped it on. It was perfect, the only dress she could wear to marry Cody Gunner.

It was May, and warm temperatures had come to Colorado. The dress was full-length, layered satin covered with delicate lace, cap sleeves that fell an inch off her shoulders. She tried it on in front of a three-way mirror, and her mother covered her mouth, her eyes dancing.

"Ali, you're a vision." She came up and gave her a sideways hug as they both looked in the mirror. "Remember when I told you how much I hoped and prayed for this?" She turned and faced her. "For you to live long enough to fall in love?"

"Yes, Mama." She angled her head closer to her mother's. "I remember."

"I told you heaven forbid it be Cody." There was a catch in her voice. "Ali, I was wrong, honey. Cody loves you the way I only dreamed you might be loved."

"I know." She smiled at the reflection of the two of them. "I'm the luckiest girl in the world."

The days passed quickly and a few nights before the wedding, Ali and Cody were outside on the front porch, sitting in the old swing.

"Hey." He looked at her. "I just thought of something; I haven't got your wedding present yet."

"That's okay." She looked out at the winding drive, the one they'd driven down so many times on their way to a rodeo. It was still impossible to believe those days were behind her; it was the hardest part of her new reality. She shifted and caught Cody's eyes. "I don't need a wedding present; you're enough."

"That's not right, Ali. You deserve a wedding present."

She wove her fingers between his and rested her head on his shoulder. A wedding present. She hadn't given the idea much thought, but now that he mentioned it…"Okay, tell you what."

"What?"

"After we get married, ride with me out to the far end of the ranch. Out there I'll tell you what I want."

"In your wedding dress?"

"Yes." She set the swing in motion again. "The minute the ceremony is finished."

He wanted to argue with her, she could see it in his eyes. But he wouldn't. There was too little time to argue over anything now.

The morning of the wedding arrived, bursting with sunshine and new life. Ali went to her bedroom window and looked out. What would it be like to wake up next to Cody, to feel the strength of his body alongside hers? She could hardly wait. If she were smart she would've married him last Christmas when he proposed to her.

A bluebird landed on the tree outside her window. He cocked his head and looked straight at her. Then he hopped three times along the branch and flew off. Something about the bird made Ali think about her sister.

Anna had been her best friend, the sister who was her other half. Together they sat in their safe, clean room with the pastel wallpaper and dreamed of everything they'd do when they got better. Because back then they believed little girls with cystic fibrosis would get better, that one day they could skip across grassy hills and play hide-and-seek around the bushes and craggy rocks and outcroppings of pine trees. That come some autumn afternoon they might ride horses from sunup till sundown without worrying even a bit.

But it hadn't happened. Anna never got the chance to grow up or find her way out of their bedroom or skip across the grassy hillsides or ride horses. Anna should've been there that day. She would've worn pale blue, her favorite color. Her dress would've been long and slender, and she would've placed baby's breath and miniature daisies in her hair. The daisies that grew outside their bedroom window.

She would've loved Cody, loved the way he cared for her and her family. Cody and Anna would've been fast friends, and together with Ali and their mother, the four of them would've played hearts and spades and dreamed of the future.

Ali gripped the windowsill. Tears welled in her heart.

Anna should've been there beside Ali that day, her maid of honor, her best friend. And the fact that she wasn't, that instead she was buried in the cemetery down the road, made Ali mad with a fierceness she'd hidden for a decade. It had been easy to place it all in a box and let it lie there, her sorrow, Anna's death, all of it. Easy to never lift the lid and examine exactly who was to blame, to never even try to make sense of it.

But now…now everywhere she looked she saw Anna, and not just Anna, but life and hope and a future full of promise. She'd had a decade of horseback riding and barrel racing, parents who let her follow her dreams, and now the most amazing thing of all.

Cody's love.

Coincidence could explain a lot of situations, but Cody? The fact that his lung was a perfect match for her ailing body? A love that made it hard to know where she ended and he began?

None of it was by chance.

She'd been granted all her dreams but one, and what was a national championship compared to the sweet season she was about to share with Cody? It was a miracle she was even standing there that morning. She could've died her first year on horseback. Dr. Cleary had told them that, hadn't he?

She never should've survived the years she spent on Ace, the friendship she shared with her horse. Ace had taken

Anna's place, easing the loss and giving Ali another chance at life. Ace didn't treat her differently for being sick. He didn't take it easy on her or hold back. No, he flew when she was on him, sometimes for whole afternoons before either of them would get tired.

None of that should've been possible.

And then there was her mother's dream. That she live long enough to fall in love, to know the love of a man who cherished her beyond even himself. Who would've thought that Cody Gunner would be that man? But there was Cody, loving her, adoring her, giving himself completely for her.

If he could've taken her disease onto himself, he would've done it. That was the kind of love Cody had for her.

And what about the time out by the back fence, when she couldn't catch her breath? She could've died then, and she never would've known this day, never would've been preparing to stand on a hillside and promise her love to a man whose soul was intertwined with her own.

She'd been spared so much. She drew a breath and smiled. Her lungs would hold up today, she could feel it in her bones. She lifted her eyes to the sky and peered beyond the blue, to the place where her sister must live. As long as she drew breath she wouldn't understand why Anna had to go so young, why she couldn't be here now to celebrate this day with her.

But she couldn't be mad about it, not anymore.

Tears stung at her eyes and she moved closer to the window, the blue sky filling her senses. She sniffed, overcome by a wave of sorrow bigger than the ranch out back. "Can I ask

You something?" Her voice cracked, but she kept her eyes toward heaven. "Would You let Anna watch today, please? Give her a front-row seat." Ali closed her eyes. She ached for Anna more today than ever before. "One more thing. Tell her I miss her."

WITH HER PARENTS watching from a few feet away, Ali glided down the stairs. She held a bouquet of red roses, cut that morning from her mother's garden. Cody waited on the landing below in dark jeans, a white button-down shirt, and a wool suit coat. He looked like the prince he would always be.

She didn't have to ask him what he thought of her dress or of how she looked that day. It was written across his face, spilling over from his heart. However long she had left, she would never again look at Cody without seeing his eyes the way they shone as she came to him.

They embraced, Cody's arms strong and protective, one around her waist, one along her upper back. She breathed in the smell of him, his cologne and shampoo and minty breath mixing in a way that was sweetly intoxicating, hinting at all that was to come that day, that night.

Before he released her, he whispered near her ear, "This is the best day of my life."

The pastor and his wife were there also, not far from her parents. The pastor was thick and bearded with a guitar slung over his shoulder. His wife held a camera and a Bible. She took pictures, several of Cody and Ali, others of the two of them with her parents.

Ali pulled the woman aside before the group headed out. There was a song she'd remembered that morning. It was an old hymn, one of her mother's favorites.

"Can you play it for us, at the end, when we're married?" Ali kept her voice low. The song would be a surprise.

"Definitely." The pastor's wife knew Ali's mother. The significance of the song was clear in her expression. "I'd be honored."

"Thank you." Ali found her father then and linked arms with him.

They led the way, with Cody and Ali's mother next, and the pastor and his wife last. The procession took them over freshly mowed grass, past the tomato garden and rosebushes to the bluff, fifty yards from the house. It was a spot made of rock, covered with patchy grass, a place where she and Anna had dreamed of playing when they were little.

Everyone took their places. Cody and Ali in the center, her parents—the attendants—on either side. The pastor adjusted his guitar and tuned it for a few seconds. His wife stood near him and the first song began.

It was one that captured everything about the two of them. It spoke of a dream being like a river, the dreamer like a vessel, and how even when it was impossible to know what was ahead in the journey, the dreamer had no choice but to follow the dream.

A light wind danced across the ranch that afternoon, and wisps of Ali's hair fanned her face. Without turning her head, she studied her father, tall and proud, stoic. He had stood by while she chased her dreams, paying the price of loneliness and uncertainty, but always believing in her. How amazing that his frame was so like Cody's, that they might test so similar in their blood types and compatibility.

The doctors were wrong. She would live far longer than three years with a set of lungs from Cody and her father. They were the strongest men she knew; their lungs would keep her going for a decade at least.

She felt a stirring at her right elbow, and her mother leaned in. Her voice was the softest whisper. "I'm so happy for you, sweetheart."

"Me, too." Ali kept her response low. "It's what you asked for."

"Yes." Their eyes held a moment longer. "Exactly what I asked for."

When the song was over, the pastor opened the Bible and read about love.

"Love is patient and kind..."

Ali looked at Cody. The words seemed to be coming straight from his heart to hers, as if what they'd found together was the picture of what love was supposed to be. She handed her bouquet to her mother and took hold of his hands. They had much ahead in the coming weeks, the transplant and a month of recovery. Dangers would always exist for her, but here and now, lost in Cody's eyes, love—the type of love being spoken of now—was all that mattered.

The pastor was finishing the reading.

"Love always protects, always trusts, always hopes, always perseveres." He paused and looked at them. "Love never fails."

It was time for the vows. They'd each written something special and unique, and then together they'd written the last part.

Ali and Cody faced each other, and Cody went first.

"I take you, Ali Daniels, as my wife." He drew a breath and steadied himself. "If I have ten years with you, or a hundred, our time together would never be enough. With you, I'm something I've never been before." He paused. "I'm whole because you complete me. My love for you means I'm no longer sure where I end and you begin." He ran his thumbs along the tops of her hands, his tone steady even as his eyes filled. This last part they'd written together. "Ali, I promise you everything I am, everything I have, as many days as we share together. No matter what tomorrow brings, I will be here. I will stand by you and stay by you. I will be strong when you cannot be strong, and I will hold you up when you cannot stand. My love, my life, is yours, Ali, from this day on."

He slid a delicate white gold band onto her finger and covered her hands with his.

She hesitated, his words still washing over her. Finally she swallowed and found her voice. "I take you, Cody Gunner, as my husband." Everything faded but the man before her and the connection she felt with him. She waited until the lump in her throat relaxed. "I was not looking for love, but you came into my life and brought it. You opened my heart to feelings I'd never known, my eyes to colors I'd never seen. You taught me that love is measured not in years or decades, but in smiles and dreams and shared bits of laughter, in quiet walks and tender embraces and late-night talks." Her voice cracked, but she continued. "Cody, I promise you all of me every day, as many days as we have together. No matter what tomorrow brings"—she touched the place over his heart— "I will be here." Behind her, she could hear her mother sniffling. Tears blurred her own eyes, and she blinked so she could make out his face, his eyes. "I will stand by you in your dreams and stay by you in spirit. I will be strong in heart when you cannot be strong, and I will hold your hand when neither of us can stand. My love, my life, is yours, Cody, from this day on."

She slipped a thicker matching band onto his finger and in the distance she saw a blue jay, just like the one she'd seen that morning. And suddenly she knew her prayer had been answered. Somewhere up in heaven, Anna was cheering for her, cheering and waving her hands and dancing because of what Ali had found with Cody Gunner.

The pastor said a few words about marriage and the commitment it involved. He closed with another reading.

"And now, these three remain: faith, hope, and love. But the greatest of these is love." He paused, his smile lifting the mood. "It is my pleasure to pronounce you husband and wife. Cody, you may kiss your bride."

Again a gentle breeze played in her hair, sending fine wisps of blonde across her cheeks. Cody brushed them back, taking her face in his hands. Then, in a way that mixed delicate tenderness and smoldering passion, he kissed her.

The pastor took a step back and smiled. "Mr. and Mrs. Gunner, I'd like to be the first to congratulate you."

Her parents circled them, hugging them and making the moment last. In the background, the pastor picked up his guitar and started playing. His wife's voice rang full and clear across the place where they stood. The song grew and built and filled Ali's heart with hope and possibility.

Ali caught her mother's eyes. She leaned close and whispered near her ear, "I love you, Mama. I do."

Her mother hugged her, rocking her, the two of them swaying in the breeze. "Everything's going to be okay, honey. Keep believing."

"I will." She drew back and returned to Cody's side. It was time for the part Ali had asked for, the part that made both her parents and Cody nervous. She was supposed to be using these weeks as a time away from horseback riding.

But Ali wanted this, and none of them could refuse her. Not on her wedding day.

She nodded at Cody and smiled. He hesitated, then broke away from the group and headed for the barn. A few minutes later, he galloped out on Ace, cowboy hat in place, headed for Ali. When he reached her, he extended his hand, and with the help of her dad and the preacher, Ali climbed onto Ace and pressed herself snug against Cody's back. She sat sidesaddle, her long dress flowing just past the white lace-up boots she'd chosen for the day.

"You ready?" Cody adjusted his hat, his eyes bright with emotion.

"Ready." She turned and the pastor took their picture. She waved to her parents, and they were off, Cody at the reins.

He took them slow and steady, and she melted into him,

enjoying the feel of his body against hers. After several minutes, they were out of sight of the others, and Cody slowed Ace to a stop.

She faced him. "Congratulations, Mr. Gunner."

He tipped his hat to her. "And you, Mrs. Gunner."

"See"—she gave a light giggle—"I was right."

"About what?" He ran his fingers along her spine.

"You *were* chasing me."

"Yes." His eyes caressed her, held her. "And now I'm not letting you go."

The sun was warm against her face, splashing bright rays over a moment that was already brilliant. She worked her hands around his waist and leaned her head on his chest. "I can't believe we're married."

"Me neither." He kissed the top of her head. "Okay, so this is when you tell me what you want for your wedding present, right?"

"Right." She eased herself up, studying him. "Now's the time."

She watched his face, checking for his reaction. Maybe this wasn't a good idea. She didn't want anything to mar the moment, to cast a shadow on their wedding day. Not even something as important as this. She leaned up and kissed him, a kiss that promised more for later when they would drive to the secluded resort in the Rockies, the place where they would spend three nights before coming home and facing the transplant.

He brushed his nose against hers, shading her from the sun with the brim of his hat. "I'm waiting, Mrs. Gunner."

Her smile faded as she found his eyes. "This is serious, okay?"

"Okay." He brushed his knuckles against her cheek, the way he'd done from the first time they kissed. A grin tugged at the corners of his mouth. "I'm very serious."

He wasn't, but he would be. "Okay, this is what I want." She took a slow breath. "I want you to forgive your parents. That's what I want for my wedding present."

She watched her words work their way from his heart to his head and back again. He chuckled, his tone thick with disbelief. "Ali…"

"I know you don't want to, but it means so much to me." She took hold of his jacket lapels, hoping her words would breach the walls he'd built in his heart. "I want them on our side, Cody. They're my family now, too."

The muscles in his jaw flexed and for a moment he looked to the side, across the sloped fields and foothills that ran toward the Rockies. Finally he unclenched his jaw and caught her eyes again. "That one…might take a while."

"Fine." She kissed the tip of his nose. As long as he was open to the idea, reconciliation was bound to come. A sweet sense of victory flooded her veins, victory and a peace she'd been searching for since that conversation with Cody in the competitors' area the day she had her last barrel race. "Just try. That's all I want."

He searched her eyes. "You know what I want to give you?"

"What?" She put her hands on his knees, steadying herself.

"Time." His lips were tight, his chin strong despite the sudden storm in his eyes. "I want to wake up with you in my arms tomorrow morning and find out that CF was only a bad dream." He ran his fingers lightly down her side. "That you're as healthy on the inside as you look on the outside." He cupped her face in his hands. "I want time to have babies and raise them and grow old with you."

She leaned her shoulder into him and rested her head against his heart. "I want that, too."

They talked for a while longer, about the transplant and her fear that he wouldn't ride again. "You have to, Cody. You have to win another championship." She tugged on his hat. "Win it for me this time, okay?"

He nodded, but his look didn't fool her. It would be a long time before Cody climbed back in the chute with a bull. Not because of a missing lung, but because he didn't want to lose a minute of their time together.

Ali couldn't blame him. As much as she wanted him to ride, she wanted him with her more. They were about to head back home when Ali stopped and turned to him. "I almost forgot your wedding present."

"Mine?" Cody cocked his head. "That's crazy, silly." He lifted her chin, meeting her eyes straight-on. "I have you, that's all I need."

"And something else." Ali gathered the reins and handed them to him. "Here."

"Ali, I don't…" Confusion clouded his eyes. "I don't understand."

"I'll still ride him. As long as I can walk I'll ride him." She smiled through her tears. "But after today he's yours, Cody. I'm giving you Ace."

He didn't say anything. Rather, he folded his arms around her and held her for a long time, moving only to pat Ace on the neck now and then. She was giving him Ace? Her most precious possession? Her friend? It was more than Cody could take in.

When they started back toward the house, it was in the silent understanding of all they'd shared that day, all they would share in the days and months to come. There would be pain, yes. But first there would be love. A love that would always protect, always trust, always hope, always persevere.

A love that would never fail.

Chapter Eighteen

T he weeks flew by in a blur of unspeakable passion and tender moments, until finally the lung transplant that would stave off Ali's death was only minutes away.

Cody lay on a hospital gurney, prepped and waiting. Ali and her father were ready, too, in separate nearby rooms. The doctor had promised he could see Ali once more before the surgery. Not because he had fears; he didn't. He was convinced the operation would be a complete success. But because he wanted to make sure she wasn't afraid.

The cost became an issue as they neared the transplant date. Ali's parents cashed out the stocks they'd been saving, but they were still short. As soon as he was aware of the situation, Cody paid the difference. Most of his winnings were bankrolled. Other than the cost of riding every week during the season, he didn't need much.

He shifted on the gurney. He had expected to feel the

adrenaline, the same sense of heightened alert he experienced whenever he climbed onto the back of a bull—ready to fight for his life. Instead, he was antsy with anticipation, anxious to get the transplant over with.

Ali was much worse now. She couldn't sing or take a walk without getting winded. Even a shower was impossible because the humidity made it too difficult to breathe. The bacterial infection in her lungs wasn't going anywhere; the lung transplant was her only hope.

Cody would've done it back when she first grew worse, but the procedure took time and preparation. Fewer than a hundred live-donor lung transplants were performed each year, most with huge success. Still, the surgery was rare. The right team of doctors at the University of Colorado Hospital in Denver had to be assembled and ready in order for it to be the success they were looking for.

The sun beat on the window of Cody's room, but in the spray of light all he could see was Ali's face, the way she looked the night before when he held her, stroking her hair and memorizing her. It would go well; it had to. They hadn't come this far to run into trouble now. It would be okay for all of them and when transplant and recovery were over, Ali would be stronger, more alive than ever.

He adjusted the sheets and shifted to his side, his back to the door. As he did, he heard someone walk in. Probably another nurse, looking for a sample, ready to poke him with another needle. He turned and what he saw made his stomach drop.

"Hello, Cody..." His father shut the door behind him

and took a few steps closer. His sleeve was rolled up, and a bandage ran around his elbow. "The doctor told me I could have a few minutes with you."

Cody stared at him, unblinking. How dare his father come now, when he was lying on a gurney, when he couldn't run away, couldn't do anything but face the man? This was a private time between him and Ali and her parents. What would his father know about the sort of love he and Ali shared? Why had he come—and how could his mother have allowed it?

With everything in him, Cody wanted to be mad.

But after a month of being married to Ali, after waking with her in his arms and knowing the intimacy of her touch, it didn't matter how much he wanted to be angry.

He couldn't remember how.

His father took another step. "I'm sorry, Cody." His eyes shifted to the smooth tiled floor. When he looked up again, defeat was written across his face. "You don't have to forgive me; I don't blame you."

Cody blinked and the moment changed. He wasn't in a hospital room a few feet from the father he hadn't talked to in almost fifteen years. He was a boy again, and his father was throwing his things into a yellow cab, walking around to the passenger door and waving good-bye. *This is it, son...be good for your mama. This is it...* And he was watching his father climb into the cab and shut the door, watching the cab drive off down the street, and he was running after it, as fast and hard as his eight-year-old legs would take him.

And suddenly he thought of something he hadn't thought of in all those years without his father. Why had he run so fast and hard? Why had it mattered so much that he catch the cab, that he stop his father from walking out of his life? The answer came swift and certain, choking his soul and making his eyes blur. The reason was obvious. He ran after him because he loved him, loved his father with an intensity he hadn't known again until Ali Daniels.

Mike Gunner was a pro football player. What little boy wouldn't have thought him bigger than life, a hero who came home and shared a dinner table with them. But Cody's father had been so much more than an image. Back when they were together, Cody was the happiest little boy in Atlanta. He and his father played make-believe football games, and Cody would savor the long afternoons when his dad threw him a ball or tackled him on the living room floor. The sun rose and set on the man because that's how much Cody loved him.

That's why he ran after the cab that day.

For some crazy mixed-up reason, he had blamed his mother for the loss, as if she were at fault for letting him go. But even all of that had been fueled only by the crazy love of a little boy for his daddy. A bond that even hatred couldn't sever. In fact, his hatred for his father was equaled only by the love he'd once felt for him, the love he'd lost. A love that was still alive, because Cody could feel it rushing to the surface, taking away his ability to speak or cry or even breathe.

His father cleared his throat. "I came to say a few things; I might as well get them said." He rubbed the back of his neck, a gesture Cody recognized as his own. Their eyes met and his father's were marked by a vulnerability, an openness that seemed to bare his heart. "I was selfish and wrong when I left you; I couldn't see anything but me." He turned his hands palms up. "It was all my fault, Cody. I couldn't let you…" He gestured toward the hospital room. "I couldn't let you go through this without telling you how sorry I am. You and Carl Joseph, you deserved better."

"We…" Cody pressed his lips together to keep from crying. "We needed you, Dad."

"I know." Only a few feet separated them, and his father closed the distance. He reached toward Cody with his bandaged arm and held his hand out. "I'm sorry."

Somehow this attempt was different from the time his father showed up at the rodeo. There it felt like a stunt, his way of cashing in on Cody's success and popularity. But here…Cody coughed, working out the thickness in his throat. He pointed to the bandage on his father's arm. "What happened?"

He grabbed the spot with his other hand and shrugged. "I gave blood. In case you or Ali or her father need it during the surgery."

Cody blinked, too stunned to move. His father had done what? He'd given blood for them? Not knowing whether Cody would even talk to him, he'd flown to Denver and given blood?

Voices talked in hushed tones in the hallway, and buzzers from a nearby room filled the air. Cody barely noticed. In painful slow motions, the walls in his heart came crumbling down. He still loved his dad, he actually did. No matter how many years the rage had consumed him or how hard he'd tried to battle it into submission. The love was there as long as the little boy in his heart still lived. Tears spilled onto his cheeks. He couldn't speak, couldn't tell his father the things he wanted to say, things that were still awkward. But he did the one thing he could do.

He reached out and took his father's hand.

ALI COULD BREATHE again.

This was her first sign that the surgery was over, and that it had gone well. She was still sedated, still not quite awake. But she could breathe. For a long while she lay there, savoring every breath, every sweet, life-giving breath.

The rest of her days she would have a part of Cody inside her, a part of him, and a part of her father. Their gift would give her the chance to think about riding again or having a family or beating CF once and for all. The chance to think about tomorrow and all it might offer. Her father had always been a part of her. But now and forevermore, Cody's life would course through her, giving her strength and hope and time. Giving her a future.

She heard someone walk into the room and come close. "Hello?" Her throat sounded dry, her voice thick and hoarse.

"Ali, sweetheart." It was her mother. The clear, kind voice of her mother. "How are you feeling?"

"Mama..." Sleep hung over her, making her eyelids heavy. But she fought to open them. When she did, she squinted, trying to make out her mother's face. "How's Daddy and Cody?"

"They're wonderful, honey." Her mother kissed her cheek. "The surgery was a success for everyone."

Ali closed her eyes, relief adding to the other wonderful feelings awakening throughout her body. But none of them meant anything if she couldn't see him, couldn't be with him. This time she spoke without opening her eyes, her words slow and raspy. "Take me to him, Mama, please. Take me to Cody."

CODY WAS COMING around, trying to open his eyes. The room was quiet, but he had the strangest sense he wasn't alone.

He'd been through a surgery, he remembered that much. His lung was gone by now, gone to Ali, where it belonged. But what had happened before the operation? Had he been dreaming or had his father come by with a bandage on his arm, talking about mistakes and seeking forgiveness?

His head was heavy, groggy from the medication, but he opened his eyes and instantly he had the answers. It wasn't a dream. His father was sitting a few feet away, his head in his hands. Next to him was his mother, and standing near the door was—

"Brother!" Carl Joseph lumbered across the room and shook his hand, too excited to contain himself. "Brother, I'm happy to see you!"

"Thanks, buddy." Cody struggled to bring his hand to his face and massage his brow. "I can tell."

Their parents stood and looked at him. His father took a step forward. "Ali's doing great, son. Her father, too. We've all been praying and…the surgery was everything they hoped it would be."

Cody lifted his eyes to his father's. He cared that much? Was he really that different now? In that minute, Ali's request came back to him, the one she'd made on their wedding day. That he might make amends with his parents.

She was right, wasn't she? Life would be better for all of them if forgiveness won out. He'd been given the greatest gift of all—a little more time with Ali Daniels. What right did he have to hold on to anger now, when his whole life was marked by the most amazing sort of love? Life was too short to hate; Ali had taught him that.

"Brother, guess what?" Carl Joseph still had ahold of his hand. He pumped it again. Never mind that Cody had ignored him for the past year, that he'd walked right past him at the last rodeo, the one where Ali had gotten sick. Carl Joseph's love never skipped a beat, never took offense.

"What, buddy?"

Carl Joseph's eyes grew wide. "Dad's here, too. Remember Dad? He's here, brother!"

Their mother took Carl Joseph's hand then and led him back a few steps. Her eyes met Cody's and he saw the fear there, the concern that Cody would break into a fit of rage the way he had before.

Instead, he smiled at her. Then he shifted his gaze and

looked at his father, the two of them unblinking. Whatever his father had done before, the man was sorry. He really was. Cody ached for all the years the two of them had missed, the lonely days when, as a boy, he'd needed his dad. But those days were behind them. Here and now he was overcome with a need to be held by the man again, the way he'd been held by him a lifetime ago.

He held out his arms and said the only word he could manage. "Dad..."

His father came to him, hugging him so tight it hurt the incisions on his chest. But Cody didn't care. A torrent of sorrow released and Cody wept for all they'd lost, all they might never have found if not for Ali.

And in that moment Cody realized that all those years of bull riding, he'd been kidding himself. The battles he'd fought in the arena had done nothing to ease his hatred for his father, the same way the years had done nothing to ease his need for the man.

Only this could empty him of the rage and bitterness and years of unforgiveness, this embrace that tore at the enemy lines and built a bridge that would take them out of yesterday and into tomorrow.

His dad straightened a bit. "I'm sorry about Ali."

"Me, too." He tried to smile, but his chin was quivering too much. "She's a fighter, Dad. I think the doctors are wrong." He sniffed. "I think she'll get ten more years at least."

"At least." His father hesitated. Then he hugged him again, even tighter than before.

That's when Cody realized his father was crying, shaking as the two stayed locked together. Cody's face was wet, and he wasn't sure if it was from his father's tears or his own. Here, in his father's arms, he was a boy facing the biggest battle of all, the battle for Ali's life. If he was to survive it, he needed all the help he could get. When he could talk, Cody mumbled into his father's shoulder, "I'm afraid, Dad. I can't live without her." He grabbed a couple of quick breaths.

His mother and Carl Joseph joined them, adding their arms to the hug. Cody cleared some space and looked at his mother. "I'm sorry, Mom. I was…I treated you awful."

"I always hoped you would find room in your heart for me, Cody."

"Hey!" Carl Joseph jumped a few times. "That's what we always wanted. That Cody's heart would get better, so he could love people. Even you!"

Everyone laughed, but more tears followed. His mother squeezed in and kissed Cody's forehead. "Yes. Even me."

Cody didn't know where the tears were coming from, but they came like a river. He hugged his mom and then his dad again and finally his brother. The whole time, Carl Joseph patted Cody's knee. "It's okay to cry, brother. Big boys can cry."

They were still like that, his entire family basking in the warmth of forgiveness and new love, when Cody heard Ali's mother's voice in the doorway. He eased the others back again and wiped his hands across his cheeks.

"The nurse said it was okay if you had one more visitor." She stepped inside and behind her, led by two attendants, came a gurney through the door into his room. On the gurney was Ali. Her mother shrugged. "She told the doctor she couldn't get better unless she was with you."

He fought back another wave of tears and held out his hand toward her. "How are you?"

"Listen." She inhaled long and slow and grinned at him. "I can breathe."

He wanted to run from the bed and take her in his arms, but instead he reached out his hand a little farther. Chairs were moved and the room quickly rearranged so that her bed could be placed next to his.

When it was, she slowly reached out and took hold of his fingers. "Well, Cody." She sounded tired, but her expression couldn't have been happier. Her eyes traveled around the room at his mother and father and Carl Joseph, and finally back to Cody. "Wanna tell me about my wedding present?"

He bit his lip, stifling a grin. "Yes, I do." He cleared his throat and looked at the others. "Ali, I'd like to introduce you to my family."

Chapter Nineteen

Their time together passed far too quickly.

The doctors' fears—that Ali's body might reject Cody's lung since he wasn't related to her—never materialized. She took to her new lungs as if they'd always been a part of her. Cody wasn't surprised. He was complete only after she came into his life. It was fitting that a piece of him would complete her, also.

He did his best to convince himself that he hadn't lost a step, that he could run his horse three miles and not hurt for oxygen. But the truth was something a little different. Sometimes after ten minutes in the saddle his chest would hurt and he'd have to slow down some to catch his breath.

Ali's father brought it up just once when he caught up with Cody near the barn. Cody had his hands on his knees, catching his breath.

"Gotta pace yourself now, Cody." He grinned. "We both do."

Everything they'd been told about donating a lung was right on. A little more winded once in a while, but otherwise not much to complain about. Cody didn't talk about it or dwell on it or hardly ever even think about it, and Ali's father was the same way.

All that mattered was Ali.

For two years they lived the type of life most people only dream about and never find. Cody stayed away from bulls and rodeos and anything that might take him from her. They moved into her parents' guesthouse, and he continued on with her father, working the cattle and keeping the ranch in good repair.

Dr. Cleary told Ali from the beginning that, like always, horseback riding would shorten her time. Ali talked it over with Cody, and the two agreed she would still ride. She would have to ride. And so—against medical wisdom— Cody and Ali climbed atop Ace once a day and rode the perimeter of the ranch, galloping across the fields toward the foothills, breathing in the smell of sweet summer grass and gardenias, their bodies moving with the horse in a fluid motion that felt as beautiful as it was to watch.

Cody explained it to Ali's parents this way: "The doctors want Ali to spend her days trying not to die." Sincerity rang in his tone. "We believe Ali should spend her days trying to live."

Together they found new and breathtaking ways not only to live, but to love.

Because of her new lungs, Ali was strong enough to hike with Cody on easy trails in the Colorado Rockies. Once in a while they would take a picnic to a remote spot and remember their rodeo days.

Ali would recount specific barrel races, the way she felt tearing around the arena on Ace, how she worked so hard to convince everyone she wasn't sick. And Cody would take a half hour to break down an eight-second bull ride, how the rage drove him and how he willed himself to focus the anger into staying on the bull's back.

But like always with Ali, Cody could talk for only so long before he pulled her into his arms and kissed her, savoring her, loving her the way he'd promised to love her on their wedding day. And sometimes, during those remote mountainside picnics, their bodies would come together and—without climbing another step—they would discover heights they hadn't imagined possible.

One early fall afternoon they rode Ace to the small nearby cemetery where Anna was buried. They climbed off the horse, joined hands, and stood above the marker. *Anna Daniels, 1976 to 1986. Beloved daughter. Sister. Friend.*

Reds and yellows screamed from the surrounding trees, summer's last desperate show of life, but the two of them were silent. What could they say about a ten-year-old girl who'd lost her life? Whose living was over before it really began?

Cody read the inscription again. "I wish I'd known her."

"Yes." Ali bent down and brushed dirt off the corner of the stone. "I wish that, too. You would have liked her."

Ali had talked about Anna before, how she would've laughed when Cody told one of his tired jokes or how she might've been a rodeo queen if she'd had the chance or how she would've enjoyed a certain brilliant sunset. But that day, staring at Anna's tombstone, Ali leaned her back against Cody's chest and brought his arms around her waist.

"Marry again, Cody. Promise me."

Fear grabbed hold of every muscle, and his chest stiffened. "Actually"—he kept his tone casual—"I believe bigamy's still against the law."

"Cody, please." She let her head fall back against his shoulder, her eyes toward the sky. "You know what I mean." Jasmine bushes were scattered throughout the cemetery and the air was sweet with the smell. She tapped the heel of her boot against the toe of his. "After I'm gone I want you to fall in love and get married again." She turned her head and found his eyes. "I want you to have children."

"Don't, Ali." Sorrow and dread and anger took turns punching him in the gut, but anger came out on top. "I want kids with you."

She turned the rest of the way and looped her arms around his neck. "I want kids with you, too. They told us in March, remember? I can't have them—you know that."

"There has to be a way." He hated having no options. "Let's talk to Dr. Cleary again."

"There's no way, Cody. That's why I want you to promise me."

He narrowed his eyes, fighting back angry tears. "Please, Ali…"

"It's all right to talk about it." Her voice was softer than the breeze. "When I go, you'll be too young to live the rest of your life alone."

"No." He pressed his face against hers, and his hands moved up from her waist to her lower back. He couldn't be angry when she was so alive, when his life was so full of her. "You're forgetting something."

"What?" She leaned into him.

"You've got my lung in that body of yours." He touched the back of her neck, making slow circles beneath her hair. "Gunner lungs last longer."

"Is that right?"

"Yes." He kissed her throat and nuzzled his face against hers. "So there."

He thought about what he'd said. It was true; he was strong and in good shape, and so was her father. Maybe the doctors were wrong; maybe with the right lungs, a transplant would give her twenty or thirty years.

Maybe someone would find a cure for cystic fibrosis.

She angled her head, her eyes a mix of patient love and determination. "I still want you to marry again."

He took a step back and put his hands on her shoulders. "You know what I'm going to do?"

"What?" She looked past his jumbled emotions, straight to his soul.

"When we celebrate our fortieth anniversary, I'm going to remind you of this conversation." He raised an eyebrow. "Then you'll feel pretty silly, huh?"

"Yes." Her eyes danced and a smile lit her face. "Pretty silly."

"Okay, then. That's what I think about your request."

She tucked her chin against her chest, her expression as sweet as it was coy. "Can we make a deal?"

He sighed and placed his fingers along her cheekbones. "You're pretty demanding for a woman."

"I know." She grinned. "It's my nature."

"But...since I'm a cowboy and it's a cowboy's nature to be a gentleman, what's the deal?"

"Okay." She bit her lip. "Here it is: If I go before you, you'll get married again and—"

He shook his head. "I told you—"

"Wait..." She held a finger to his lips. "Let me finish. If I go before you, you'll get married again. And if you go first... I'll remarry." She lifted her eyebrows. "How's that?"

His jaw hung open in mock surprise and he mouthed the word, Y*ou?* He took a step back, desperate to keep things light. "You'd remarry?"

She poked her fingers at him and giggled. "Come on, Cody; I'm serious."

The humor left him. He stared at her, not sure what to say. "I can't, Ali."

"You can't?" Disappointment shaded her face. "You can't remarry?"

"No." He didn't blink, couldn't pull himself from her. "I can't believe you'll ever be gone."

THERE WERE OTHER times.

Times when she'd have a checkup with Dr. Cleary and get glowing reports on her lung function tests and bacteria counts, and Cody would believe every lie he'd ever told himself. She wasn't going to die; she was fine, cured, a new person. The disease didn't stand a chance against a competitor like Ali Daniels. The lies helped him sleep at night, but they couldn't stop the passing of days. One after another they came, and each one as it left took with it a small piece of Ali's good health.

The end crept up on them like the last scene in a favorite movie.

Diabetes set in, and Ali's kidney functions fell. Always the fear was a bacterial infection. With cystic fibrosis, some infections could be fought with IV antibiotics. Others would settle in and chip away, taking ground one day at a time until a person's body simply gave up. The pancreas and her digestive system, even her kidneys, could hold their own for years with such an infection. But once a resistant bacteria moved into her new lungs, it would be only a matter of time.

The first pneumonia came just after their third Christmas.

Ali went to bed with a sore throat and an ache in her chest. She woke up coughing as hard as she had before the transplant. Cody thought about running into the main house for a thermometer, but there was no need. She was burning up. He helped her dress, bundled her in blankets, and carried her through a thick layer of snow to her parents' house.

The four of them went together, Ali's father driving, her mother in the passenger seat. Cody sat in the backseat cuddling Ali, stroking her head and telling her to hold on, she'd be well again in no time.

At first it seemed he was right.

Dr. Cleary put Ali on oxygen and gave her high doses of intravenous antibiotics and fluids. Four days later she seemed as healthy as she had before getting sick, with one exception. She was tired.

"We'd expect you to be tired, Ali. But really"—the doctor raised an eyebrow, imploring her—"stay off the horse for a while. A month or two, at least."

Ali looked at Cody, and he saw something in her eyes he'd never seen before. He saw fear. For as long as he'd known her, no matter what illness she faced, even before receiving the new lungs, Ali never looked scared.

But now she was on her last chance.

No lung transplant loomed in the distance for her this time. Rather, if her lungs didn't respond to treatment, if she didn't take it easy and build her strength back, she might never get better.

This time Cody and Ali agreed she should follow the doctor's orders—at least until she recovered and her tests were back to where they'd been. It was winter, so Ali wouldn't miss being on Ace the way she would've any other time of the year. The weeks drifted by; Cody worked less and whenever he wasn't working, he was with her.

They watched old movies—*Casablanca* and *Gone With the Wind* and *An Affair to Remember*—and they spent hours playing backgammon and reading out loud together. Reading was a surprise delight for Ali. All her life she'd stayed away from books, not wanting to waste a single day when she could be outside living.

But books were marvelous now, opening doors to wonder and mystery and magical places Ali had never imagined existed. Her favorites were *The Adventures of Tom Sawyer* and

The Chronicles of Narnia. Ali loved *The Last Battle,* the final book in the Narnia series.

"Listen again, Cody." She would turn to that part of the book, her voice thick with tenderness. "'All their life in this world and all their adventures in Narnia had only been the cover and the title page.'" She would stop, take a breath, and continue. "'Now at last they were beginning Chapter One of the Great Story which no one on earth has read: which goes on forever: in which every chapter is better than the one before.'"

For a moment she would fall silent, staring at the page. Then she would look up, tears in her eyes. "That's how heaven will be, right?"

Cody would draw her near and kiss her cheek, absorbed in her. "Yes." He would search her eyes. "But not for a long time."

She would only smile and take his hand, switching the conversation to Tom Sawyer and the marvels of childhood magic and making memories along the banks of the Mississippi.

Lazy winter days made for early nights, and often Ali was tired. But Cody would argue the fact whenever Ali's parents brought it up.

"I'd like to see more color in her cheeks." Her mother would pull Cody aside every week or so, a frown knit into the lines on her face. "She doesn't look right."

And Cody would find his most confident tone, his most relaxed smile. "It's winter." He'd pat Ali's mother on the shoulder. "Anyone would be pale after a season indoors. Wait till spring; she'll have more energy then."

But by late March, she didn't have more energy; she had a second bout of pneumonia. After another week in the hospital, Dr. Cleary was reluctant to send her home.

"I'd like to keep you here; I think the IV and oxygen tent would help some."

"But not a lot?" Cody was confused. He stood near the head of Ali's bed. He looked at her parents and then at her and finally back to the doctor. "The hospital's always been a good thing for her."

The doctor frowned. It took a moment before he looked up. "In the past we could get her better."

"Meaning?" Ali took hold of Cody's hand, her eyes on Dr. Cleary.

A sad-sounding sigh left the man's lips. "It's not good, Ali; your lung function's way down and"—he breathed in slowly through his nose—"we can't treat the bacteria." He sat on the edge of her bed and took hold of her right foot, his eyes damp. "I'm afraid it's in both lungs."

And like that, the end was introduced.

CODY FELT STRANGE and disconnected.

He wasn't in the room standing next to Ali's hospital bed. He was on a grassy bluff at her parents' ranch, looking into her eyes, knowing she had never looked more beautiful, more whole and well. And he was taking her hand

and placing a ring on her finger and promising to be strong when she could not.

Only how could he be strong now? The doctor was basically telling them she wouldn't get better. Her hand was still in his, and he squeezed it. *Cowboy up, Gunner. Cowboy up.*

He locked his jaw and blinked hard. *Get me through this.*

The room had been silent, the news working its way through the room, through their hearts and minds like a slow, deadly fog.

"So..." Ali's eyes showed no reaction. She coughed twice, rib-jarring coughs, and stared at the doctor. "How long do I have?"

"It depends." He folded his arms tight. "A month, two maybe. Stay indoors, away from your horse, maybe a little longer."

"But if she stays in the hospital, wouldn't that..." Cody couldn't finish, couldn't bring himself to have this discussion. Talking about it would make it true, and it wasn't true; it couldn't be true. Anyone could get pneumonia, right? It didn't mean it was the end.

The doctor was biting his lip. "If it would make a difference, I'd keep her for a month." He gave a defeated shake of his head. "At this point, I think she'd be happier at home."

Ali pulled Cody's hand close and pressed it to her cheek. Her eyes stayed on the doctor. "How will I know? Will there...will there be a sign?"

"It'll get harder to breathe. Harder every day." He angled his head, his expression as honest as it was anguished. "You'll know, Ali."

Three days later, they brought Ali back to the ranch, and the doctor was right. Her breathing grew worse, labored by heavy bouts of coughing that nothing could touch. Not her compression vest or medication or even the prayers Cody and her parents uttered constantly on her behalf.

Cody took to sleeping light, in case she needed him. A glass of water, a cold cloth, or the comfort of his arms around her. One morning, Cody was half asleep when he felt her hand on his shoulder.

"Cody?" She was wheezing, her breathing shallow. "Wake up."

"What?" His eyes were open before she finished his name. He sat up, his heart pounding in his throat.

She met his eyes, the intensity between them so deep, so strong it hurt. "Take me out on Ace." A smile just barely lifted the corners of her mouth. "Please."

Cody hesitated. He wanted to tell her no, she was in no shape to go outdoors, let alone on a horse. But he couldn't. This determination, the will to live no matter the cost, it was part of what he loved about her.

"Okay." He took her hand, helped her to her feet, and found two sweatshirts for her. She was thinner than she'd ever been, and cold most of the time. Some days she wore multiple layers and a jacket. But the air had warmed over the past week, so two should be enough.

Together, without saying anything, they headed for the barn.

Rain would've fit the feelings in Cody's heart, but the morning was clear. Sunshine splashed across the bluest sky of spring and only a few puffy clouds hovered near the distant mountains. Leaves were unfurling from the branches of the oak trees, and clumps of grass grew thick and bright green at the base of the pines on the north side of the house. Everywhere, new life was springing up across the ranch.

Everywhere except in Ali.

Cody kept his arm around her as they walked, protecting her, letting her determine the pace. He was horrified at the changes in her from the day before. She was slower, her steps shaky, a pasty gray had taken over her complexion. And the rattling in her chest didn't go away no matter how often she stopped to cough.

Fear tried to push its way between them, but Cody refused it. If Ali wanted this, he would give it to her. And with everything in him he would pretend things were different, that they were heading out for a ride because the bright spring morning demanded it.

They were almost to the barn doors when Ali turned to him. "Thanks, Cody. This means a lot."

He smiled at her because he couldn't talk.

Once inside, Ace looked up and whinnied, soft and curious. Cody had been taking care of him, riding him when Ali slept in the afternoon. But this was the first time she'd seen him since just after Christmas. When they were a few feet away, Cody let her take the lead.

"Hey, Ace." Ali pushed herself, her pace stronger than before. She opened the gate, and when she was inside she put her arms around his neck.

The horse responded, softer this time. He turned his head, brushing his chin against the side of her face.

She rested her head against his mane. "Ace ...I missed you, boy."

Cody's throat was so thick, he could barely breathe. This was the horse Ali had raised from birth, the one she had broken and trained and taken across the country three times over. Ali had once told him that Ace understood things a horse shouldn't understand. When it was a big rodeo, when a championship or high-stake prize money was up for grabs, Ace would sense her excitement and give her a ride equal to the task. Likewise, he sensed when she was sick and responded with a gentler ride.

Watching now, Cody knew it was true.

There were tears in her eyes when she turned to him. "Ready?"

He gave a short nod and went to work. Once Ace was saddled, Cody climbed on and helped her up in front of him, the way he'd done so many times before. Often when they'd ride around the ranch together, he'd hold the reins by putting his arms around her waist. But this time he handed them to her.

Ali set out at a trot, but as she left the area around the corral, she broke into a run. Not the all-out record-breaking run she and Ace were capable of, but a gentle run that mixed grace and strength and restraint with every stride. He held tight to her, willing her to breathe, to survive this ride without anything worse happening.

It took only a few minutes to realize where she was going. She was taking Ace on the familiar route, the one around the perimeter of the ranch. Cody's heart kept time with the pounding rhythm of the horse's hooves. What if Ali couldn't catch her breath? What if she fainted, too far from the house to get help? Why had he agreed to the ride without telling her parents where they were going?

Halfway around—near the back fence—she brought Ace to a stop and fell back against his chest. "Ali?" He took hold of her shoulders and leaned his face in close. "Are you okay?"

"Yes." Her breathing was hard and fast, but it wasn't raspy like it had been back at the barn. "I feel wonderful."

The tension in his muscles eased some. "Can you breathe? Maybe we should get back just in case you—"

"Cody." She angled herself so she could see him. "I'm fine." She pressed her shoulder into him, and turned Ace so she could see back across the expanse of her parents' ranch. "The day after Anna's funeral, I sat in my bedroom alone. Nothing felt right, so I walked to the window and looked out at all the grassy meadows and bushes, beyond our ranch to the neighbor's farm."

He pictured the scene, studying her so he wouldn't miss a word.

"The neighbor had a palomino horse; every day Anna used to dream of riding him. Only she never got the chance." Ali lifted her eyes to an evergreen a few feet away. "So that day I snuck out of the house and ran through the grass and past the bushes." There was a smile in her voice. "And I knew, I just knew Anna was watching me."

He waited, his fingertips light along her outside arm.

"From the moment I stood next to that horse, I was sure I'd never go back indoors." She smiled up at him. "Except to sleep."

"You're a fighter." He kissed the top of her head.

"I told myself no matter what happened I'd have no regrets." She looked at him again. "But I was wrong."

He shook his head. "No, Ali."

"Yes." Her eyes held his. "My only regret is that maybe…" Her voice cracked. She brought her hand to her throat and hesitated. "Maybe if I'd stayed inside more, I could've had more time with you."

"Ali…"

"I just wanted you to know that." She sat up a little straighter. The familiar wheezing was there, but it was better than it had been in days. She held his eyes with hers. "Every time you ride Ace, every time you look at him, I want you to see me, Cody. I want you to remember how every day with you was a gift. You…" She swallowed, her voice tight. "If you hadn't chased me, I never would've caught you."

"Oh, I see." Cody leaned his chin on top of her head, his tone easy. "You caught *me*, is that it?"

"I was keeping it a secret." She giggled, but the effort led to a short bout of coughing. When she caught her breath she folded her hands around his. "This is my last time out, Cody. The doctor was right."

Cody's heart beat faster. "Ali, please." He shook his head. "Don't say that."

"It is." She drew a long breath, one that made her wince. "The doctor said I'd know, and I do. I knew this morning."

Tears blurred Cody's vision and he blinked hard. Was she right? Was this the last time Ali Daniels would sit on a horse, the blazing Ali Daniels? He remembered her question. "I'll always see you, Ali." He snuggled closer to her. "How could I see Ace and not see you?"

She smiled. "My mama always said we looked alike, me and Ace. I guess it's the blonde hair."

They were quiet for a while. Cody willed his anxious soul to settle down, but it wasn't listening. He couldn't get the thought out of his mind. What if she was right? What if this really was her last ride? The possibility made him crazy with fear.

After a few minutes, Ali took hold of the reins. "Ready?"

"No." He wanted to scream at the heavens, jump off Ace, and run until he couldn't take another step. No. A million times no. He would never be ready to leave their private shared world of horses and open ranchland and April blue sky. He couldn't believe for a minute that this was the last time he and Ali would ride together, the last time he would feel her body against his as they pounded out an ageless rhythm across the fields.

"Cody?" She looked over her shoulder at him. Her breathing was getting worse.

"Okay." He pressed his cheek against hers and closed his eyes.

The whole way back he kept his arms around her waist, his eyes shut, memorizing the feel of her as her back brushed against his chest, the sensation of her silky blonde hair dusting his cheeks.

Just before they turned into the barn, she pulled to a stop. Ace must've sensed she was in trouble, because he lifted his head, offering her his neck to lean against. She smoothed his blonde mane and patted the side of his head. "Attaboy, Ace."

She turned to Cody. "I read something the other day."

He moved his hands up from her waist, running his fingers along her arms again. "Hmmm?"

She looked away and coughed twice. "It was a quote from some guy." A hawk circled overhead and she raised her eyes toward it. "He's dead now."

"Too bad." Cody kept his voice even. He hated talking about death. "What's the quote?"

"Before he died, he told people, 'Soon you will read in the newspaper that I am dead. Don't believe it for a moment. I will be more alive than ever before.'" She looked at him, beyond his confident facade to the terrified places of his soul. "That's what I want you to say about me, okay, Cody? Tell everyone."

"Ali…" He placed his hand on her cheek and cradled her head against his chest. If only she could stay this way, safe in his arms.

"I mean it." She covered his fingers with hers. "It won't be long. Tell them I'm not dead, I'm alive." She hesitated and when she talked again there was a smile in her voice. "Tell them I'm riding with Anna, chasing her across the fields and playing hide-and-seek in the bushes. Okay, Cody?"

"Do you..." He didn't want to say the words. "Do you really think it's soon?"

"Yes." She coughed again, and the struggle was back with every breath. "Will you tell them?"

He turned himself toward her, framed her face with his hands and kissed her, a kiss that willed life into her, one that wanted her to be wrong about the timing. But he wouldn't keep her waiting, not for another moment. He pulled back and searched her eyes. "I'll tell them."

"Thank you, Cody." She pulled the reins to one side and headed into the barn.

He climbed off first and then helped her down. She walked around and stood in front of Ace, the horse she'd ridden and counted on and competed with for a decade. Ace, who for years had been her only friend.

For a long time she stared at her horse. Then she leaned in, looped her arms around his neck and kissed him on the bridge of his nose. "Be good, Ace."

With a single step, she turned to Cody and fell into his arms. Her tears came then, waves of them. Wrapped in his embrace, she shook, ripped apart by a sorrow that knew no limits.

He rubbed her back, and when she had control again, she looked up. "I'm not sad."

A half smile raised his lips. "I can tell."

She made a sound, but it was more cry than laugh. She brought her fingers to her mouth and shook her head. "What I mean is, I didn't sit in a room and watch life through a window." She held on to his shoulders and kissed him. "I didn't win a national championship, but I did everything else I ever dreamed of doing. And now...I'm not afraid." She smiled, her eyes warming him to the core. "I just wish"—her voice caught and she waited a beat—"I just wish I could take you with me."

"Oh, Ali..." He forced himself to find his voice. "Me, too."

Once more she glanced over her shoulder at Ace. Then she turned and held out her hand. "Take me in."

She didn't look back again after that.

Not when they left the barn or when they headed into her parents' house through the back door. From the moment she was inside, her breathing grew worse, more strained with every passing hour. None of the usual methods brought her relief.

Her decline was swift and sure, and she slept through much of it.

By that evening, Cody was convinced. The ride earlier that day, their conversation, all of it had been a miracle, nothing less. Ali might not get better, but they'd been given one single, spectacular morning, a morning that would forever cast light on the broken places of his heart.

Dr. Cleary was contacted, but he gave Ali a choice. She could come to the hospital and have a few more days. Or she could stay home with her family. Ali chose to stay home. The days blurred, Ali fighting her disease the way she'd always fought it, with rolled up sleeves and gloves off.

"I'm trying to hold on, Cody," she told him one night as he lay beside her, studying her. "I'm still trying."

"I know." He ran his fingers through her hair, willing life into her, believing that somehow, someway, they still had a chance. "Don't ever stop; there's still a chance."

Ali smiled. "That's what…I love about you." She swallowed, every word a breathless struggle. "You never stop… believing in me."

"No, baby, never." He leaned in and brought his lips to hers. "You can do anything."

"Hold me."

He worked his hands beneath her shoulder blades and hugged her lightly. Any pressure on her chest would make it harder for her to breathe. "Stay with me, Ali."

"I will." She pressed her face to his. "I'll just…never let go."

She lived two days longer than Dr. Cleary thought possible, clinging to Cody and life, and promising to never stop.

But in the end it wasn't enough.

On a clear late-April day, two weeks after their morning ride, Ali died in his arms.

For a long time—after her parents left the room and after someone had been called to come for her body—Cody held her, clinging to her, breathing in the smell of shampoo still fresh in her hair.

The media learned the story overnight. Hundreds of cowboys and barrel racers and organizers from the Pro Rodeo community attended the funeral. Ali Daniels was no longer a mystery, and they were collectively stunned at the truth, rallying together in their support of Cody and her family.

Cody's parents and Carl Joseph flew in, too, surrounding Cody with a sort of love he had craved all his life.

Carl Joseph came up to him before the service. "Brother." His lower lip quivered. "I'm sorry about Ali."

"Thanks, buddy." Cody crooked his arm around his younger brother and hugged him hard, rocking back and forth.

"She was a good horse rider." Carl Joseph pulled back, his brow furrowed, sincerity and sorrow written in the lines of his face. He raised his hand and pointed to the sky. "Up there, you know what I hope?"

"What?" Cody still had one hand on his brother's shoulder.

"I hope God gives her a horse."

Cody closed his eyes and he could see Ali and Ace, running like the wind together, blazing a trail across the fields behind her house. He opened his eyes. "Me, too, buddy." His throat ached from the sadness. "Me, too."

Ali was everywhere that day.

She was in the eyes of her mother, quiet and stoic, mindless of the tears that streamed down her face. She was in the strength of her father, as he placed a bouquet of daisies on her coffin. And she was with Cody, also. In the way he took the microphone and talked about Ali, her determination and grace.

"Ali wanted me to tell you something." He looked at the crowd of familiar faces. "You think she's dead, but don't believe it." Her voice played in his mind. "She is more alive now than ever before."

She was there when he returned to his seat and took his mother's hand, and again in the long hug he shared with his father.

Cody thought it fitting.

Ali had taught him to love; and now that love would be her legacy.

But she never taught him how to let go.

And when the funeral was over, when his parents and Carl Joseph boarded a plane and headed back home to Atlanta, something happened that Cody didn't expect.

The old anger came back.

Or maybe it wasn't the old anger, but a new, unfamiliar anger, a feeling of rage and helplessness and a strange sort of not knowing. Not knowing what to do or where to go or why he should climb out of bed or how he was ever supposed to feel right again.

Whatever it was, habit suggested he keep it inside.

He stayed the summer at her parents' ranch, most of it on the back of Ace. Out on the ranch, missing her, doubts peppered him like springtime hail. Why wasn't she allowed to live? Heaven would have her for eternity; all he'd wanted was a few decades.

And why hadn't she won the national championship? Strange, but some days that bothered Cody most of all. One barrel? One lousy barrel had made the difference? It wasn't right.

"Cody, we're all missing her," her mother would say every few days. "If you want to talk, I'm here."

Every hour made the strange feelings inside him clearer,

more intense. Finally he figured it out. The pain wasn't anger at all; it was sorrow. A sorrow with fingers that sometimes squeezed his soul, creating an ache that spread from his chest to his shoulders and knees and feet. Other times sorrow was an ocean, deep and wide and vast, and he a lone swimmer, drowning, without any hope of reaching the shore.

Sorrow was a lot like anger.

He could hide it from people, but it was there when he woke up, and when he closed his eyes at night. And nothing, not the act of saddling Ace or tending the cattle or fixing fences or talking to Ali's mother, made it any better. Cody Gunner knew only one way to deal with the pain.

By the sixth month he made up his mind.

He contacted the PRCA and, given the circumstances, permission was granted. Another rider gave him a room at his ranch in California where Cody practiced two months straight. That January in Denver, when the season started, Cody took a seat on his first competitive bull in three seasons. By then he had a reason, an intensity, a battle even greater than the one he'd waged against anger or disease.

This time the dragon that needed slaying was sorrow, a sorrow that would kill him if he didn't fight it. With every amazing bull ride that season, he battled the sadness, the aching way he missed her. And with every ride he could feel her there, beside him. In him. He didn't fly from one rodeo to the next the way he used to. This time he bought a trailer like Ali's, and parked it in familiar places adjacent to the rodeos. Places where he and Ali had first found each other, places where he could sit outside and remember.

The season was a wild and reckless one, taking on bulls with a confidence that defied understanding. People in Pro Rodeo circles wondered if grief had made Cody Gunner crazy, getting on the back of a bull when his body held just one lung. A single jab of a bull's horn and he wouldn't make it out of the arena.

Cody didn't care. The season was something he had to do, had to experience, and in December he stood in the winner's circle, the national champion a third time.

A few days later he flew back to Colorado to get his things and tell Ali's parents good-bye. His family was in Atlanta; he wanted to be there, too. That week, one afternoon he found Ali's mother in the garden and handed her his championship buckle.

"It belongs to you," he told her.

And it did. Because without Ali, without knowing her and loving her and missing her with an intensity stronger than any bucking bull, he would never have competed. He certainly never would've won. So the buckle belonged to her family—it was the one Ali had always wanted.

The season served its purpose.

Along the way Cody learned the truth about sorrow, and that was this: it would never leave. And so he did what Ali would've done. He took a deep breath, held it, and rushed full on toward it. He embraced it and entertained it, and finally he made peace with it.

Epilogue

C ody opened a horse farm on a ranch outside Atlanta, and a year later his parents and Carl Joseph moved onto an adjacent piece of land. Some days, on warm evenings when Ace was in the pasture, Cody would squint from the back porch of his house, and always he would hear her voice.

Every time you ride Ace, every time you look at him, I want you to see me . . .

And he did, but not the way she had looked that last morning, thin and pale, breathing good-byes. Rather, he saw her alive and well and holding her breath, strong in the saddle, flying around a cloverleaf of barrels.

The way he would always see her.

Now that the rodeo world knew Ali's story, Cody had no choice but to leave everything about her competitive years to the ages, a story that would be told again and again as young riders came up through the ranks. But the real story, who Ali was away from rodeo, would always belong to only a handful of people, the way she had belonged to a handful of people.

And most of all, she would belong to him.

His favorite photo of Ali was taken on their wedding day. She was smiling, wearing her long white dress, daisies in her hair, eyes shining, convinced she would beat cystic fibrosis, that the bond between the two of them was stronger than medicine or disease or even time.

Whenever Cody stopped and looked at the picture, he was convinced of the same thing. Though she'd been wrong about beating the disease, she was right about one thing: The bond between them would remain until his dying day.

Flesh had failed Ali Daniels. But love never did; it never would. No matter how far the years took him from Ali's life, her love would live on.

Because it lived on in him.

Author's Note

This story was inspired by the hundred or so people each year who donate a lung to someone they love, someone with cystic fibrosis. All for the chance to buy a little time, maybe a thousand tomorrows, maybe a few more or less.

Ali Daniels' experience with CF was individual to her, the way the disease is to each person who has it. Her situation was not intended to illustrate an average case or average limitations. I tried to keep her situation within the realms of possibility and reality.

Exercise is encouraged for people with cystic fibrosis, but not in a place with allergens and irritants that might harm the lungs. My research showed that it would be highly unusual for a person with CF to run barrels on the Pro Rodeo circuit. But determination and will made Ali Daniels special.

I chose to write about CF because of a little boy named Matt who has the disease. He plays basketball on my husband's fourth-grade team. For Matt, there's no talk about his future in the sport. No worries about potential scholarships down the road. These *are* the good old days for Matt. He plays today because he loves it. He plays like an all-star, with his entire heart. In the same spirit that Ali Daniels rode horses.

In 1970 a child born with CF was expected to live only to age ten. That number has risen to a life expectancy today of thirty-two years. If you're interested in volunteering or helping out the Cystic Fibrosis Foundation, you can contact them at www.CFF.org. Their motto is *"Adding tomorrows every day."*

In addition, though I set this story within the context of a real Professional Rodeo Cowboys Association tour, the characters are completely fictional. Any similarities to real characters or events are entirely coincidental and unintentional. I received a great deal of help from professional cowboys and rodeo organizers in researching this book. Errors in accuracy are mine.

A Thousand Tomorrows is about the sort of love that is patient and kind, a love that always protects, always trusts, always hopes, always perseveres. A love that never fails. Cody and Ali showed us that love is not the way around our problems. It is the way *through* them. Remember, when all things have passed away, these three remain: faith, hope, and love. But the greatest of these is love.

You can find out about my other books or our family's adoption story or my Red Gloves Christmas series by visiting my website, www.KarenKingsbury.com. Sign up for my newsletter, and I'll update you every month or so about new books or speaking events. Drop me a note at my guestbook or by emailing me at rtnbykk@aol.com.

May God bless you and yours...until next time,

Karen Kingsbury

Reading Group Guide

1. Why do you think Cody buries his feelings inside when his father leaves?

2. Carl Joseph looks up to his older brother, Cody. But Cody learns some invaluable lessons from Carl Joseph. What kind of role does Carl Joseph play in Cody's life?

3. At the end of chapter two, we learn that Cody rides bulls because it is the only way he can live with his rage. Why do you think this is?

4. Why does Ali keep her illness a secret? How do you think keeping this secret makes her feel?

5. How did Ali's sister's death shape the person Ali became?

6. How do you feel about the way Ali's mother handled her daughter's choices? How would you have handled a sick child's decision to do something they loved that might shorten their life?

7. At the end of chapter four, Ali gives Cody bull-riding advice. Why does Ali choose that moment to talk to him if they hadn't spoken in the two years they'd been competing side by side?

8. How do you think Cody's and Ali's isolation from their peers draws them together?

9. After his and Ali's lung surgeries, Cody forgives his father and reunites with his family. How does Ali's love influence his decision? On a personal level, have you experienced reconciliation in a key relationship? Explain.

10. In their last month together Ali gives her dearest possession, her horse Ace, to Cody. What does her gift symbolize to both her and Cody?

11. How does Cody show he has strong beliefs? How does Ali?

12. Cody and Ali know their life together is limited, yet they choose to enjoy each day as if there were no tomorrow. How do you think their lives would have changed had Ali lived longer?

13. If you knew someone you loved had only three years to live, would you marry him or her? Why? Why not?

14. What did this story teach you about cystic fibrosis? What personal experience do you have with this disease?

15. Has reading *A Thousand Tomorrows* affected your life in any way? How?

Just Beyond the Clouds

Donald, my prince charming.

We've reached a new year, another season in life, and still I cannot imagine this ride without you. Our kids are flourishing, and so much of that is because of you, because of your commitment to me and to them. You are the spiritual leader, the man of my dreams who makes this whole crazy, wonderful adventure possible. I thank God for you every day. I am amazed at the way you blend love and laughter, tenderness and tough standards to bring out the best in our boys. Thanks for loving me, for being my best friend, and for finding "date moments" amidst even the most maniacal or mundane times. My favorite times are with you by my side. I love you always, forever.

Kelsey, my precious daughter.

You are seventeen, and somehow that sounds more serious than the other ages. As if we jumped four years over the past twelve months. Seventeen brings with it the screeching brakes on a childhood that has gone along full speed until now. Seventeen? Seventeen years since I held you in the nursery, feeling a sort of love I'd never felt before. Seventeen sounds like bunches of lasts all lined up ready to take the stage and college counselors making plans to take my little girl from here and home into a brand-new big world. Seventeen tells me it won't be much longer. Especially as you near the end of your junior year. Sometimes I find myself barely able to exhale. The ride is so fast at this point that I can only try not to blink, so I won't miss a minute of it. I see you growing and unfolding like the most beautiful springtime flower, becoming interested in current events and formulating godly viewpoints that are yours alone. The same is true in dance, where you are simply breathtaking onstage. I believe in you, honey. Keep your eyes on Jesus and the path will be easy to follow. Don't ever stop dancing. I love you.

Tyler, my beautiful song.

Can it be that you are fourteen and helping me bring down the dishes from the top shelf? Just yesterday people would call and confuse you with Kelsey. Now they confuse you with your dad—in more ways than one. You are on the bridge, dear son, making the transition between Neverland and Tomorrowland and becoming a strong, godly young man in the process. Keep giving Jesus your very best, and always remember that you're in a battle. In today's world, Ty, you need His armor every day, every minute. Don't forget… when you're up there onstage, no matter how bright the lights, I'll be watching from the front row, cheering you on. I love you.

Sean, my wonder boy.

Your sweet nature continues to be a bright light in our home. It seems a lifetime ago that we first brought you—our precious son—home from Haiti. It's been my great joy to watch you grow and develop this past year, learning more about reading and writing and, of course, animals. You're a walking encyclopedia of animal facts, and that, too, brings a smile to my face. Recently a cold passed through the family, and you handled it better than any of us. Smiling through your fever, eyes shining even when you felt your worst. Sometimes I try to imagine if everyone everywhere had your outlook—what a sunny place the world would be. Your hugs are something I look forward to, Sean. Keep close to Jesus. I love you.

Josh, my tender tough guy.

You continue to excel at everything you do, but my favorite time is late at night when I poke my head into your room and see that—once again—your nose is buried in your Bible. You really get it, Josh. I loved hearing you talk about baptism the other day, how you feel ready to make that decision, that commitment to Jesus. At almost twelve, I can only say that every choice you make for Christ will take you closer to the plans He has for your life. That by being strong in the Lord, first and foremost, you'll be strong at everything else. Keep winning for Him, dear son. You make me so proud. I love you.

EJ, my chosen one.

You amaze me, Emmanuel Jean! The other day you told me that you pray often, and I asked you what about. "I thank

God a lot," you told me. "I thank Him for my health and my life and my home." Your normally dancing eyes grew serious. "And for letting me be adopted into the right family." I still feel the sting of tears when I imagine you praying that way. I'm glad God let you be adopted into the right family, too. One of my secret pleasures is watching you and Daddy becoming so close. I'll glance over at the family room during a playoff basketball game on TV, and there you'll be, snuggled up close to him, his arm around your shoulders. As long as Daddy's your hero, you have nothing to worry about. You couldn't have a better role model. I know that Jesus is leading the way and that you are excited to learn the plans He has for you. But for you, this year will always stand out as a turning point. Congratulations, honey! I love you.

Austin, my miracle child.

Can my little boy be nine years old? Even when you're twenty-nine you'll be my youngest, my baby. I guess that's how it is with the last child, but there's no denying what my eyes tell me. You're not little anymore. Even so, I love that— once in a while—you wake up and scurry down the hall to our room so you can sleep in the middle. Sound asleep I still see the blond-haired infant who lay in intensive care, barely breathing, awaiting emergency heart surgery. I'm grateful for your health, precious son, grateful God gave you back to us at the end of that long-ago day. Your heart remains the most amazing part of you, not only physically, miraculously, but because you have such kindness and compassion for people. One minute tough boy hunting frogs and snakes out back, pretending you're an Army Ranger, then getting teary-eyed when Horton the Elephant nearly loses his dust speck full of little Who people. Be safe, baby boy. I love you.

And to God Almighty, the Author of life, who has—for now—blessed me with these.

Acknowledgments

This book couldn't have come together without the help of many people. First, a special thanks to my friends at Hachette Book Group, who continue to believe in my books, and my ministry of Life-Changing Fiction™. Thank you!

Also thanks to my amazing agent, Rick Christian, president of Alive Communications. I am more amazed as every day passes at your sincere integrity, your brilliant talent, and your commitment to the Lord and to getting my Life-Changing Fiction out to readers all over the world. You are a strong man of God, Rick. You care for my career as if you were personally responsible for the souls God touches through these books. Thank you for looking out for my personal time—the hours I have with my husband and kids most of all. I couldn't do this without you.

As always, this book wouldn't be possible without the help of my husband and kids, who will eat just about anything when I'm on deadline and who understand and love me anyway. I thank God that I'm still able to spend more time with you than with my pretend people—as Austin calls them. Thanks for understanding the sometimes crazy life I lead and for always being my greatest support.

Thanks to my mother and assistant, Anne Kingsbury, for her great sensitivity and love for my readers. You are a reflection of my own heart, Mom, or maybe I'm a reflection of yours. Either way we are a great team, and I appreciate you more than you know. I'm grateful also for my dad, Ted Kingsbury, who is and always has been my greatest encourager. I remember when I was a little girl, Dad, and you would say, "One day, honey, everyone will read your books and know your work." Thank you for believing in me long before anyone else ever did. Thanks also to my sisters, who help out with my business when the workload is too large to see around. I appreciate you!

Especially thanks to Tricia Kingsbury, my sister who runs a large part of my business life. God brought you to me, Tricia, when things in my office were insanely crazy, and I'll be grateful for always. You are my sister, my friend, and now my assistant. It doesn't get any better than that. Don't ever leave, okay? And to Olga Kalachik, whose hard work helping me prepare for events allows me to operate a significant part of my business from my home. The personal touch you both bring to my ministry is precious to me, priceless to me … Thank you with all my heart.

And thanks to my friends and family, especially my sister Sue, who is a new addition to my staff, and to Shannon Kane and Melissa Kane, my nieces, who helped me with major projects this past year. Thanks to Ann and Sylvia, and to all of you who pray for me and my family. We couldn't do this without you. Thanks to all of you who continue to surround me with love and prayer and support. I could list you by name, but you know who you are. Thank you for believing in me and for seeing who I really am. A true friend stands by through the changing seasons of life and cheers you on not for your successes but for staying true to what matters most. You are the ones who know me that way, and I'm grateful for every one of you.

Of course, the greatest thanks goes to God Almighty, the most wonderful Author of all—the Author of life. The gift is Yours. I pray I might have the incredible opportunity and responsibility to use it for You all the days of my life.

Forever in Fiction™

A special thanks to Al and Sandee Kirkwood, who won the **Forever in Fiction™** auction at the YWCA benefit in Washington State. The Kirkwoods chose to honor their daughter, Kelley Sue Gaylor, by naming her **Forever in Fiction™**.

Kelley Gaylor is thirty-nine, married to Dean, her husband of sixteen years. They have three children: Allie, twelve; Matt, ten; and Joey, five. One of Kelley's many blessings is the fact that both sets of their parents live close by, and that the entire family gets together often.

Kelley enjoys vacationing with her family at Black Butte Ranch in Central Oregon and spending time with the people she loves. She is the oldest of three siblings and spends much of her free time watching her kids play sports, or biking, skiing, and doing weekly Bible studies. She helps out at her children's school and loves her reading time.

In addition, Kelley does charity work for children and

started a group called "For the Children," which provides basic clothing to kids at four schools. Her parents have a thoroughbred racing and breeding business in Washington, and Kelley has had the privilege of attending the Kentucky Derby and the Belmont Stakes. She is a good listener and is liked by everyone who knows her.

You'll notice that Kelley Gaylor's character is a volunteer in *Just Beyond the Clouds*. She works with handicapped people and helps them find their greatest potential. I chose to name this character after Kelley because it was closest to how Kelley is viewed by the people who love her—giving, generous, attentive, and caring.

Al and Sandee Kirkwood, I pray that Kelley is honored by your gift, and by her placement in *Just Beyond the Clouds,* and that you will always see a bit of Kelley when you read her name in the pages of this novel, where she will be **Forever in Fiction™**.

For those of you who are not familiar with **Forever in Fiction™**, it is my way of involving you, the readers, in my stories, while raising money for charities. To date, this item has raised more than one hundred thousand dollars at charity auctions across the country. If you are interested in having a **Forever in Fiction™** package donated to your auction, contact my assistant at Kingsburydesk@aol.com. Please write *Forever in Fiction* in the subject line. Please note that I am able to donate only a limited number of these each year. For that reason I have set a fairly high minimum bid on this package. That way the maximum funds are raised for charities.

Chapter One

The eighteen adult students at the front of the classroom were a happy, ragtag group, mostly short and squatty, with sturdy necks and squinty eyes. All but two wore thick glasses. Their voices mingled in a loud cacophony of raucous laughter, genuine confusion, and boisterous verbal expression.

"Teacher!" The one named Gus took a step forward, lowered his brow, and pointed to the student beside him. "*He* wants the bus to the *Canadian* Rockies." Gus rolled his eyes. He gestured dramatically toward the window. "The buses out *there* go to the *Colorado* Rockies." He tossed both his hands in the air. "Could you tell him, Teacher?"

"Gus is right." Twenty-six-year-old Elle Dalton—teacher, mentor, encourager, friend—looked out the window. "Those are the *Colorado* Rockies. But our trip tomorrow isn't to the mountains." She smiled at the young men. "We're going to the Rocky Mountain Plaza. Rocky Mountain is just the name."

"Right." Daisy stood up and put her hands on her hips. She knew the Mountain Metropolitan Transit system better than anyone at the center. Daisy wagged her thumb at Gus. "I told you that. Shopping tomorrow. Not mountain climbing."

"Yes." Elle stood a few feet back and studied her students. She'd been over this two dozen times today already. But that was typical for a Thursday. "Everyone take out your cheat sheets."

In a slow sort of chain reaction, the students reached into their jeans pockets or in some cases their socks or waistbands for a folded piece of paper. After a minute or so, the entire group had them out and they began reciting the information—all at different times and with different levels of speaking ability.

"Wait"—she held up her hand—"let's listen." Elle knew the routine by heart. She approached the line and waited until she had their attention. "Everyone follow along with me." She walked slowly down the row of students. "Bus Route Number Ten will take us from the center at Cheyenne Boulevard and Nevada Avenue south past Meadows Road, left on Academy Boulevard to the shops."

"Academy Boulevard?" Carl Joseph stepped out of line, his forehead creased with worry. Carl Joseph was new to the center. He'd been coming for three months. His ability to become independent was questionable. "Is that in Colorado Springs or somewhere else?"

"It's here, Carl Joseph." Daisy patted his shoulder. "Right here in the Springs."

"Right." Elle grinned. Daisy could teach the class. "The whole bus trip will take about fifteen minutes."

He nodded, but he didn't look more sure of himself. "Okay. Okay, Teacher. If you say so, okay." He stepped back in line.

And so it went for the next half hour. Elle broke down the directions. The color of the bus—orange—and how much time they'd have to climb aboard and how long it would take to make the drive down to Academy Boulevard, and how many stops would happen between getting on and getting off the bus.

For many of them the lesson was a review. They tackled a different route every week, memorizing it, drawing it out, play-acting it, and finally incorporating it into a field trip on Friday. When they reached the end of the thirty most common bus routes, they'd start again at the beginning. But Elle's students had Down Syndrome, so most of them experienced varying degrees of short-term memory loss. Reviewing the bus routes could never happen often enough.

At the thirty-minute mark attention spans among the group were fading fast. Elle held out her hands. "Break time." She looked out the window again. It was a late April morning, and sunshine streamed in from a bright blue sky. "Fifteen minutes…outdoors today."

"Yippee!" Tammy, a student with long brown braids, jumped and did a half spin. "Outdoor break!"

"Ughh! I hate outdoors!" Sid scowled and punched at the air. At thirty, he was the oldest student at the center. "Hate, hate, hate."

"Don't be a hater." Gus shook a finger at the complaining student. "Ping-Pong is good for outdoors."

"Tag, you're it!" Brian tapped Gus on the shoulder and ran out the door laughing. Brian was a redhead who'd been coming to the center since Elle took over two years before. He was the happiest student by far. As he ran he yelled: "We could play tag and everyone could play tag!"

"Yeah!"

"I hate tag." Sid crossed his arms and stuck out his lower lip. "Hate, hate, hate."

The students headed for the door, all of them talking at once. Straggling behind and lost in their own world were Carl Joseph and Daisy. He was pointing outside. "No rain today, Daisy. Just big bright sunshine. That's thanks to God, right?"

"Right." She looked up at him with adoring eyes. "God gets the thanks."

"I thought so." He laughed from deep in his throat and clapped his hands five quick times. "I thought God gets the thanks."

Elle smiled and went to the back room. She poured herself a cup of dark coffee and returned to her desk. Her job at the center had everything to do with Delores Daisy Dalton. Her favorite student, her little sister. Her project. How different life was for Daisy here in the Springs. Two years ago Daisy had spent all her life with their mother an hour east of Denver in Lindon, Colorado—population 120.

The oldest of the Dalton daughters was only nine when their big strapping father left home one morning for his office job in Denver and never made it back. A patch of black ice on a back country road took his life, and he was dead before the first police officer made it to the scene. There was life insurance money and a settlement against the drunk driver who hit him—enough to allow their mother to stay home, to continue schooling them in their small wood-paneled living room. Enough so that life wouldn't change in any way other than the most obvious and painful.

Because their daddy had loved his girls with everything he had.

Time flew, and one by one the Dalton girls left home and moved to Denver to attend the University of Colorado. Elle was no exception. She pursued a teaching credential and then her master's. But Daisy was the youngest, and when she turned nineteen one thing was certain.

If she stayed in Lindon, Daisy was out of options. And that wouldn't do, because their mother had never dreamed less for Daisy than for the other Dalton girls. Never mind what the doctors and textbooks of that day said about Down Syndrome. From an early age their mom believed Daisy was capable of great things. She believed in mainstreaming and immersion, which meant if the math lesson was about counting money, Daisy learned to count. If it was time to clean the kitchen, Daisy was taught how to run a dishwasher.

When the short bus for handicapped students drove by, it didn't stop at the Dalton house.

"You girls will show Daisy what to do, how to act and think and behave," their mom said. "How else will she learn?"

As it turned out, their mother's thinking was innovative and cutting-edge. When Elle earned her master's degree in special education, mainstreaming was all the rage. People with learning disabilities could do more than anyone ever expected as long as they were surrounded by role models.

When she was offered the director position at the Independent Learning Center—or ILC as everyone called it— Elle formed an idea and presented it to her mother. They could sell the house in Lindon and the three of them could buy a place in the Springs. Elle would run the center, Daisy would be a student, and their mother could find work outside the home.

Sentimental feelings for the old farmhouse made their mom hesitate, but only for a minute. Life was not a house, and family was not limited to a certain place. The move happened quickly, and from her first day at the center Daisy blossomed. Her friendship with Carl Joseph was further proof.

Elle sipped her coffee, stood, and made her way to the window. She sat on the sill and watched her students. A center like this one would've been unheard of fifteen years ago. Back when most of her students were born, their parents had few options. Half the kids were institutionalized, shipped off to a facility with little or no expectation for achievement. The others were sent to special education classes, with none of the stimulation needed for advancement.

Elle took another sip of coffee. The ILC was good not just for her students—most of whom came five days a week, six hours a day. It gave her a purpose, a place where no one asked about the ring she wasn't wearing anymore. She glanced at her watch, stood, and headed for the door. Some days her work at the center not only gave her a reason to move forward, it gave her a reason to live.

She opened the door. "Break's over. In your seats in two minutes."

"Teacher, one point!" Gus waved his Ping-Pong paddle in the air. With his other hand he grabbed the table. "One more point. Please!"

"Okay." Elle stifled a smile. Gus was adorable, the student who could best articulate his feelings. "Finish the game, and get right in."

The transition took five minutes, but after that everyone was seated and facing her. The center took up a large space, with areas designated for various activities. The bus routes were practiced in a carpeted alcove with a large blackboard on one wall and several benches framing the area. Another corner included a kitchen and three kitchen tables with chairs. Social skills, cooking, and appropriate eating behavior were taught there.

The next session was speech and communication. The learning area was again carpeted, and students sat on sofas and padded chairs—simulating a living room setting. The idea was to get the students comfortable in everyday living situations, learning how to read social cues and interact correctly with others.

Elle looked at her students. "Who would like to share first?"

Daisy's hand was up before Elle finished her question. "Me, Teacher!" Daisy got a kick out of calling Elle "Teacher."

Daisy tipped her head back and laughed, then looked at Carl Joseph for approval. "Right? We're ready, right?"

"Uh…" Carl Joseph pushed his glasses up the bridge of his nose. He seemed confused, but his eyes lit up as he connected with Daisy. His words came slow and thick and much too loud. "Right, Daisy. Right you are."

"Shhh." Daisy held her finger to her lips. Her eyebrows rose high on her forehead. "We can hear you, CJ." There was no disapproval in her tone. Just a reminder, the way any two friends might encourage each other.

Carl Joseph hunched his shoulders, his expression guilty. He covered his mouth and giggled. "Okay." He dropped his voice to a dramatic whisper. "I'm quiet now, Daisy."

The others were losing interest. Elle motioned to the spot beside her on the carpet. "Daisy and Carl Joseph, come up and show us."

"Yeah." Sid scowled and punched at the air again. He was the most moody of the students, and today he was in classic form. "All right already. Get it over with."

Undaunted, Daisy stood and took Carl Joseph's hand. His cheeks were red, but when he focused on Daisy, he seemed to find the strength to take the spot beside her at the front area of the class. Daisy left him standing there while she went to the nearby CD player and pushed a few buttons. The space filled with the sounds of Glenn Miller's "In the Mood."

Daisy held out her hand and Carl Joseph took it. After only a slight hesitation, the two launched into a simple swing dance routine. Carl Joseph counted the entire time—not always on beat—and Daisy twirled and moved to the rhythm, her smile filling her face.

Elle's eyes grew damp as she watched them. Neither friendship nor love had ever been this easy for her. But this … this was how love should look, the simple innocence of caring that shone between these two. The way Carl Joseph tenderly held Daisy's hands, and how he led her through the moves, gently guiding her.

Today's date hadn't escaped her. It would've been her fourth wedding anniversary. She rubbed the bare place on her ring finger and bit her lip. How many years would pass before the date lost significance?

Then, midtwirl, Carl Joseph accidentally tripped Daisy. She fell forward, but before she could hit the ground, Carl Joseph caught her in his arms and helped her find her balance again.

"You okay, Daisy? Okay?" He dusted off her shoulder and her hair, and though she had never hit the ground, he brushed off her cheek.

"I'm fine." Daisy had years of dance experience. It was how their mother made sure Daisy got her exercise. No question the slight trip-step hadn't hurt her. But she balanced against Carl Joseph's arm and allowed him to dote on her all the same. After a long moment, she and Carl Joseph began again, laughing with delight as they circled in front of the class.

The music's effect was contagious. Gus stood and waved his hands over his head, swaying his hips from one side to the other. Even Sid pointed at a few of the other students and managed the slightest grin.

When the song ended, Daisy and Carl Joseph were out of breath. They held hands and did a dramatic bow. Four students rushed to their feet, clapping as if they'd just witnessed something on a Broadway stage. Daisy waved her hands at them. "Wait...one more thing!"

Elle stepped back. A situation like this one was good for Daisy. She had spent all her life around able-bodied people, people blessed with social graces. She wasn't skilled at trying to command a group of people with Down Syndrome.

"Hey..." She waved her arms again.

The other students danced merrily about, clapping their hands and laughing. Even Sid was on his feet.

"I said...wait!" Daisy's happy countenance started to change.

But before she could melt down, Carl Joseph stepped up. "Sit down!" his voice boomed across the room.

Instantly the students shut their mouths. Most of them dropped slowly to their seats. Sid and Gus stayed standing, but neither of them said another word.

"Thanks, CJ." Daisy looked at him, her hero. She turned to the others. "We have one more thing."

"Yeah." Carl Joseph chortled loudly and then caught himself and covered his mouth again.

Daisy nodded at him. "I go first, okay?"

"Okay." The loud whisper was back.

"Here it is." Daisy looked at Elle and grinned. Then she held out both hands toward her classmates. "M-I-C..."

Carl Joseph saluted. "See you real soon."

"K-E-Y..."

"Why?" He put his hands on his hips and then pointed at Gus. "'Cause we like you."

Then he linked arms with Daisy and together they finished the chant. "M-O-U-S-E."

Sid tossed his hands in the air. "Yeah, but did you go to Disneyland yet or what?"

"Not yet." Daisy grinned at Carl Joseph. "One day very, very soon."

The two of them sat down as Gus jumped to his feet and scrambled to the front.

"Gus...you want to go next?" Elle moved in closer.

"Yes." He said it more like a question, and instantly he returned to his seat. "Sorry, Teacher." He raised his hand.

"Gus?"

"Can I go now?"

"Yes."

The training continued for the better part of an hour. Each student was progressing toward some form of independent living—either in a group home or in a supervised setting with daily monitoring. Already twelve graduates had moved on to find independence. They attended twice-weekly night sessions so that they could hold jobs during the daytime.

Elle leaned against the wall and watched Gus begin a dramatic story about playing a game of chess with Brian, a redhead who at sixteen was the youngest student. After Gus had received a standing ovation for his story, they heard a poem by Tammy, the girl with long braids—Sonnet Number 43 by Elizabeth Barrett Browning.

When the girl struggled with one line, Carl Joseph stood and went to her side. He pointed at the paper and put his arm around her shoulders. "You can do it," he whispered to her. "Go on."

Daisy raised an eyebrow but she didn't say anything.

Tammy was shaking when she finally found her place and continued. Her next few sentences were painfully slow, but she didn't give up. Carl Joseph wouldn't let her. When the poem was finished, Carl Joseph led her back to her spot on the sofa, then returned to his own.

Finally Sid told them about a movie his dad had taken him to see, something with dark caves and missing animals and a king whose kingdom had turned against him. The plot was too difficult to follow, but somehow Sid managed a question-and-answer time at the end.

They worked on table manners next, and before Elle had time to look at the clock, it was three and parents were arriving to pick up their students.

Elle spotted Daisy and Carl Joseph near the window waiting for his mother. She went to them and patted her sister on the back. "Nice dance today."

"Thanks." Daisy grinned. "Carl Joseph has good news."

"You do?" Elle looked at the young man. There was an ocean of kindness in his eyes. "What's your good news, Carl Joseph?"

"My brother." He flashed a gap-toothed smile. "Brother's coming home tomorrow."

"Oh." Elle put her hand on Carl Joseph's shoulder. He'd talked about his brother before. The guy was older than Carl

Joseph, and he rode bulls. Or maybe he used to ride bulls. Elle wasn't sure. Whatever he did, the way Carl Joseph talked about him he might as well have worn a cape and a big S on his chest. She smiled. "How wonderful."

Carl Joseph nodded. "It is." His voice boomed. He pushed his glasses back into place. "It's so wonderful!"

"CJ...shhh." Daisy patted his hand. "We can hear you."

"Right." He covered his mouth with one hand and held up a single finger with the other. "Sorry."

Elle glanced at the circular drive out front. It was empty. She settled into a chair opposite Daisy and Carl Joseph. "Does your brother still ride bulls?"

"No...not anymore."

"Did he get tired of it?" Elle could imagine a person might grow weary of being thrown from a bull.

"No." Carl Joseph's eyes were suddenly sad. "He got hurt." Daisy nodded. "Bad."

"Oh." Elle felt a slice of concern for Carl Joseph's brother. "Is he okay now?"

Carl Joseph squinted and seemed to mull over his answer. "After he got hurt, he rode bulls for another season. But then he didn't want to." He raised one shoulder and cocked his head. "Brother's still hurt; that's what I think."

"What's his name?" Elle spotted Carl Joseph's mother's car coming up the drive.

"Cody Gunner." Carl Joseph's pride was as transparent as his smile. "World-famous bull rider Cody Gunner. My brother."

Elle smiled. She was always struck by her students'

imagination. Carl Joseph's brother was probably an accountant or a sales rep at some firm in Denver. Maybe he rode a bull once in his life, but that didn't make him a bull rider. But that didn't matter, of course. All that counted was the way Carl Joseph saw him.

"Your mom's here, CJ." Daisy pointed at the car. She stood and took Carl Joseph's hand. "It's your big day. Your brother's coming home tomorrow."

Carl Joseph's cheeks grew red and he giggled at Daisy. "Thank you, Daisy. For telling me that."

They walked off together, and at the door Daisy gave him a hug. They hadn't crossed lines beyond that, and Elle was glad. Their relationship needed to progress slowly. What they shared today was enough for now. As the last few students left, she and Daisy straightened chairs and tables and closed up for the day.

On the way home, Daisy was quieter than usual. Finally she took a big breath. "We should pray for Carl Joseph's brother. For the world-famous bull rider."

Elle was heading down the two-lane highway that led to their new house. "Because he might still be hurt?"

"Yeah, that." She furrowed her brow. "It's hard when you get hurt."

"Yes, it is." Elle looked at her empty hand, the finger where her ring had been four years earlier. "Very hard."

Daisy pointed at her. "You pray, Elle. Okay?"

"Okay." Elle kept her eyes on the road. "Dear God, please be with Carl Joseph's brother."

"Cody Gunner." Daisy opened one eye and shot a look at Elle.

"Right. Cody Gunner."

"World-famous bull rider." Daisy closed her eyes again and patted Elle's hand. "Say it all."

"Cody Gunner, world-famous bull rider." Elle allowed the hint of a smile. "Please help him get well so he isn't hurt anymore."

"In Jesus' name."

"Amen."

For the rest of the ride Elle thought about the anniversary of a moment that never happened, and the picture of Daisy dancing in Carl Joseph's arms. The world would look at her and Daisy and think that Elle was the gifted one, the blessed one. Elle, who had it all together, the beautiful, intelligent daughter for whom life should've come easily and abundantly. Daisy—she was the one to be pitied. Short and stout with a bad heart and weak vision. A castaway in a world of perfectionism, where the prize went to high achievers and people with talent, star athletes and beauty queens. Daisy was doomed from birth to live a life of painful emptiness, mere existence.

Better to be Elle, that's what the world would say.

But the irony was this: Nothing could've been further from the truth.

Chapter Two

Cody Gunner sat next to professional bull riding's best-known cowboy and tried to find the passion for another go-round. They were in Nampa, Idaho, the last day before a six-week break. Cody wasn't signed up for the second half of the season. The way he felt now, he wasn't sure he was coming back.

"Folks, we've got a ton o' fun in this first bull." Sky Miller, four-time national champion, sat on Cody's right. He was the primary announcer for tonight's event. Cody would handle color. "No bull rider's lasted eight on Jack Daniels since February in Jacksonville."

Cody looked to the side, to the place where the barrel racers would've been warming up back in the days when the best bull riders rode the Professional Rodeo Cowboys Association circuit, back when he and Ali had toured together during that handful of amazing seasons.

Good thing he'd switched over to the PBR, the way most

of the bull riders had. Here there were no blonde horseback riders tearing around the barrels, making him think even for a fraction of a moment that somehow—against all odds— she was here, in the same arena with him. The way she had been all those seasons ago.

"What do you say about Joe Glass, Cody? One of the tough guys, right?" The glance from Sky told him he'd missed his cue.

"One of the toughest." Cody grabbed a sheet and scanned it for the bull rider's information. "Joe's won three events this year and stayed on more than half the bulls he's drawn. That's one reason why he's sitting pretty at Number Nine in the overall standings."

Cody stayed focused for the next nine riders. When the network went to a longer break, he stretched. "Sorry 'bout that." He patted Sky on the shoulder. "Something to drink?"

"Coke. Thanks." Sky gave him a wary look. "You some-where else tonight, Gunner?"

"Maybe." Cody took a few steps back.

The legend held his eyes for a beat. He knew better than to ask if the reason had something to do with Ali. It was common knowledge in the rodeo world that Cody hadn't gotten over her. *There goes Cody Gunner,* they'd say. *Poor Cody. Still pining away over that wife of his.* Yeah, he'd heard it all, the whispers and well-intentioned remarks about moving on and letting go. That was okay. Cody climbed down seven stairs to the dirt-covered arena floor. Let them think he was crazy for holding on this long.

They hadn't loved Ali. Otherwise they'd understand.

It was eight years ago that they'd shared their last season on the circuit. Back when her cystic fibrosis had seemed like merely one more mountain they'd need to climb on the road to forever. Not like the eliminator it turned out to be. He steeled himself and stared at the ground as he walked back to the network food tent.

He and Ali had that one last season, and then they married. Cody gave her everything he had to give that year—his heart and soul, a lifetime of love, and one of the lungs from his own chest. "What happened?" people would ask when they heard about the lung. "You gave her a lung and it didn't take?"

Cody would only narrow his eyes and remember Ali, her honesty, the depth in her voice. "It worked." That's all he would say. *It worked.* Because it did. The doctors had told them the transplant would buy them only three years. And in the end that's exactly what it did. Three years. About a thousand tomorrows.

He would've given her his other lung, if he could've.

"Gunner!" The voice was familiar.

Cody looked up and into the eyes of Bo Wade, a cowboy Cody had competed against that last year—after Ali died, when Cody came out of retirement to do it all one more time, to win the championship for her, the one Ali never managed to win. Bo was in the top five back then, but he had hung it up a few years ago. Cody held out his hand and found a smile. "Bo Wade, watcha up to?"

"Workin' for the network." He grinned. "Hoping to be in your spot someday."

"Yeah." Cody grinned. "Same old story."

They talked for a minute or two about the season and the rise of the PBR. "Things are different now."

"No doubt." Cody checked his watch. He had ten minutes to report back. "Some of those bulls are wicked mean."

"And huge. Makes you wonder what they're puttin' in the feed."

Cody was about to wind up the conversation when it happened.

Bo's expression changed. He looked down at his dusty boots and then back up again. "Hey, man. I'm sorry about Ali. I never got to tell you."

Cody's breath caught in his throat, the way it always did at the mention of her. He'd tried a lot of different answers when people brought her into the conversation. He would sometimes shrug and say, "Things happen," or he'd look up at the bluest piece of sky and say, "She's still with us. I can feel her." Once in a while he'd say, "She's never really gone." All those things were true, but for the past year he'd kept his answer simpler.

"Thanks, Bo." Cody squinted. "I miss her like crazy."

"I bet." The corners of Bo's mouth lifted. There was no awkwardness between them. The two had ridden the circuit together for five years. That made them family on a lot of levels. "I remember back before the two of you got together." He shook his head. "Nothing could stop you like seeing Ali Daniels on a horse." He paused. "We had no idea she was sick."

"No one did." The conversation was too painful, the

subject still too raw. Cody clenched his jaw. "Good seeing you." He shook his friend's hand again and nodded toward the arena. "Gotta get back."

"Okay." Bo slapped Cody's shoulder. "Take it easy, man. Maybe see you around the second half of the season. The network just made me permanent tech advisor."

Cody congratulated him, found a Coke and a bottle of water, and headed back to the booth. He kept his eyes straight ahead, but all he could see was Ali, her blonde ponytail flying behind her, racing around the barrels on Ace, her palomino, or standing in the tunnel after a ride, gasping for air while Cody brought her the inhaler. Ali in her compression vest back at the ranch her family owned. Ali beside him on a grassy bluff promising to love him until death had the final word.

He pursed his lips and blew out. He had to hold on to the little details. The smell of her clothes after a ride, the mix of horse and perfume and lavender soap. The feel and exact color of her favorite faded jeans. The sensation of her breath on his face when they kissed.

He had to hold on to his memories, because otherwise they would fade and there would be no getting them back. But he had to live in a world without Ali. That was the balancing act working in rodeo. Here—among the smell of horses and bulls and arena dust—he could think of nothing else.

Cody reached the stairs and stopped. He still had three minutes. He slipped into a shadowy spot beneath the bleachers and leaned against the cool metal bars. He needed out.

Otherwise the memories would drive him crazy. Besides, bull riding had taken enough of his time. A change in careers would be good for him. Maybe something closer to home.

Concern shot a burst of adrenaline through him. His mother's phone call this morning stayed with him, made him glad he was going home tomorrow. There was trouble with Carl Joseph. Big trouble. The kind they'd always feared for Cody's younger brother.

Yes, something closer to home would be better than this, than walking every day through a hallway of memories he couldn't escape. He could go home and be a rancher, raise cattle or competitive bulls. Or maybe find a job in sales, commodities—that sort of thing. He pictured Carl Joseph, the way his brother had clung to him last time he was home. Buddy was never happier than when Cody was home. So maybe he would go back and open a sports camp for kids with disabilities.

He heard the music blaring through the arena. Less than a minute before they went on again. He took the steps two at a time, dropped into the seat beside Sky Miller, and placed the Coke on the table between them. "Sorry, man. Got hung up."

Sky popped the top on the Coke and took a long drink. "Get in the game, okay?"

"I will."

He was sharp in the second set, but his heart wasn't in it. When he helped pack up the booth that night, he had the feeling that this was it, that he wouldn't be back for a long time. Maybe forever. Sky must've known, too.

When it was time to leave, Sky pulled him aside. "You're good, Gunner. You know your stuff."

"Thanks." Cody shifted, anxious to go.

"You could ride this gig for a lotta years." Sky paused. "Thing is, Gunner, you need to figure it out."

Cody didn't want to ask. "What?"

"Ali. Your past." Sky rubbed the back of his neck and exhaled hard. "You take her with you everywhere you go. You'll never be the best until you can walk in here"—he waved at the arena—"and see the stands, hear the bulls knocking around in the chutes, smell the sweat." He hesitated. "And not see her, too."

"That's the problem." Cody put his hand on his friend's shoulder. "I'm not *trying* to see her, man. She's just there, that's all. She's there."

Sky studied him, and for a minute it looked like he might launch into a speech about moving on and putting the past to rest. Instead he grabbed his bag. "Maybe over the break, Gunner. Maybe you can figure it out then."

"Maybe." Cody smiled, but he could feel the tears clouding his eyes. He looked down, and in that one simple movement, he gave it away.

"You're done, aren't you?"

"I'm not sure." Cody backed up, putting distance between them. The dam in his heart was breaking. He didn't want anyone around to see it happen. "Good working with you, Sky. I'll be around."

With that he turned and swung his bag over his shoulder. The hotel was across the street, and he had a flight home in the morning. He was waiting at the light when a carload of girls screeched to a stop.

"Hey, Cody Gunner—wanna ride?" The brunette behind the wheel wore red lipstick and had eyes that looked a little too bright.

"Yeah!" A girl in a cowboy hat and a tight T-shirt leaned in from the passenger seat. "We know every hot spot in Nampa."

The light turned green and the walk sign appeared. Cody tipped his hat at the girls. "Gotta get my sleep tonight, ladies." He started jogging across the crosswalk.

"Come on, Cody," the brunette called after him. He ignored them. Another thirty seconds and he was inside the doors of the hotel and headed for his room. Every stop on the tour, every year he'd been a part of rodeo, he'd had offers from girls like that. Before Ali, he agreed to an offer here and there. But never now. The idea made him sick to his stomach, like throwing dirt in the face of everything Ali stood for.

Inside his room he washed his face, brushed his teeth, and crawled into bed. He pulled the framed photograph of Ali from the hotel nightstand and stared at it. The way her smile reached the depth of her eyes, how even now she seemed to be watching him, looking at him.

"Ali, girl"—he ran his thumb over the smooth glass—"I feel you everywhere tonight." His voice was a raspy whisper. "Like you're right here beside me."

But she wasn't. No matter how long he looked at her picture or thought about her, she was gone. They'd had that last year on the circuit and then three more years, and then she left him. Her body, anyway. Her spirit was still with him—always with him. Whether he was in a rodeo arena or not.

Some nights, like tonight, if he looked at her picture long enough, he could still hear her voice. They were riding double on Ace, taking the path out to the back of her parents' property where the clouds and trees and mountains all came together in a piece of paradise.

Cody ... I want you to love again.

"What?" He had been outraged, of course, horrified at her request. "I'll never love anyone but you, Ali. Never."

But she insisted. *I mean it, Cody. I want you to love again. When I'm gone, you can't waste your life thinking about me.* She leaned up and kissed him—and for the sweetest moment he was there again. *Promise me, Cody. Promise me when I'm gone you'll find love again.*

She pushed him until finally, against everything in him, and only because it was what she wanted to hear, he promised. He blinked and the distant conversation faded. He wiped the tears off the glass frame. "Ali ... I can't." He brought the framed photo to his face and pressed the glass against his cheek. "I can't do it."

Then he set the frame on the edge of the table so that her smile was facing him. He might forget the details but he wouldn't forget this—the sparkle in her eyes or the way she could see right through him when no one else ever could.

When she was alive he would've done anything for her. He forgave his father for her, and he gave up bull riding for her—to protect his lung, that piece of himself that belonged to her. The piece that bought them a few more years together.

But there was one thing he could never, ever do. No matter where the next season in life took him, he couldn't keep that one promise. The promise to love again. Because the idea was crazy. He hadn't known how to love at all before he met Ali. With her, love became real for the first time. She defined it.

He looked at her again. "You understand, Ali. Right?"

Wherever she was, whatever place in heaven shone a little brighter because of her presence, she would have to understand. Because the promise to love again was overshadowed by a bigger promise. The one he'd made to her that day on the bluff overlooking her parents' ranch. The promise to love her forever and always. He touched the frame once more. "Good night, Ali."

Death might've had the last word for Ali, but not for him. So he would love her and he would carry her with him every day, every painful step. Year after year after year.

As long as his remaining lung drew breath.

Chapter Three

Carl Joseph stood at the window next to the front door and waited.

He didn't mind waiting. Brother was coming home, and that was worth waiting for two minutes or two hours. Even two days.

"Cookies are ready!" Mom came to him and smiled. "Want a chocolate chip cookie, Carl Joseph?"

They smelled really good. Chocolaty and warm all through the house. Carl Joseph thought about saying yes. But he couldn't. "First cookies with Brother." He looked out the window. "I wait for Brother."

Mom said okay and went back to the kitchen.

One way to make the time go faster was to count. He counted the squares on the windows at the front of the house. Then he counted the lines on the sidewalk outside— the part he could see. And he counted the tree branches on the big tree out front. He was on the thirty-seventh branch when Dad pulled up.

"He's here!" Carl Joseph shouted loud, but that was okay. Daisy wasn't here to tell him to be quiet. "Brother's home! Brother's here!" He jumped up and punched his fist in the air. "Yea for Brother!"

When he opened the door, he was out of breath. He bent over and blew out, and then he stood up and there he was! Brother! Brother stood up from the car and grinned. The same kind of grin like when he was on TV all those times and he lasted eight seconds on a bull. That grin.

"Buddy!" He had his bag tossed back over his shoulder because he was strong. Brother was very strong. He ran to the porch and dropped his bag. "Give me a hug!"

Carl Joseph wrapped his arms around Brother and lifted him up. Then Brother did the lifting, because Brother was stronger. Brother spun him around in a circle and set him down. "I missed you, Buddy."

"Missed you more!" Carl Joseph stretched up and looped his arm around Brother's neck. "Come on! Mom has chocolate chip cookies. Just like every time you come home!"

They went in and ate cookies and milk and all day, the whole time, Brother stayed with him and talked to him.

It was the best day Carl Joseph could remember for the longest time. And the whole time he kept talking to God about his number-one wish. That one day Brother would stay at home. Because as good as hellos were, as good as it was to share warm chocolate chip cookies with Brother, there could be something better.

To never have to say good-bye.

⌒⌒

BROTHER HAD BEEN home for a full day and life was happy times.

Carl Joseph planted his feet in the play yard and studied the sky. Clouds. All clouds. And clouds were not good for Daisy. They were on a short break, so maybe the rain would stay locked up there until they got back into the classroom.

"Fresh air is good." He linked his arm through Daisy's. "Tetherball?"

Daisy squinted up at the sky. "I guess so."

"Don't be afraid, Daisy. It won't rain today."

She looked at him and nodded. Very slowly. "Okay, CJ. Okay. I'm going to believe that."

They walked across the yard to the tetherball pole. Carl Joseph let go of her arm and walked backward a few feet in front of her. "Knock knock."

The first part of a smile was on her face. "Who's there?"

"Lena." Carl Joseph clapped his hands and laughed. Because if he laughed, maybe Daisy would forget about the clouds and maybe she would laugh, too.

"Lena who?" Daisy smiled bigger.

Carl Joseph stopped walking backward. He took a step toward Daisy. "Lena little closer!" Again he clapped, and he laughed harder than before.

"Lena little closer?" Daisy thought about that for a

minute. Then her hands shot up in the air and her eyes lit up like sparkly diamonds. "Oh ... I get it. Lean a little closer!" She put her hands on Carl Joseph's shoulders. "I like that one the best."

A funny feeling swirled around in Carl Joseph's stomach. His cheeks felt hot, the way they felt when he stood close to Daisy. He took her hand and skipped with her to the tetherball pole.

"I'm going to win today." Daisy hopped around beside him. "I'll beat you, CJ. Watch out!"

Carl Joseph laughed again. Daisy wasn't thinking of the clouds anymore. He could tell. He covered his face. "What do you see, Daisy?" His voice was muffled, but it was loud. When he covered his face he had to talk loud. That way Daisy could hear him.

"I see you're hiding from me!" Daisy took hold of his wrists. "Come on, CJ, take your hands down."

"Surprise!" He dropped his hands and held them out to his sides. "You see me, Daisy? I'm the winner. That's what you see. The winner of all."

Daisy grabbed hold of the tetherball and gave it a hard shove. "Ready, set, go."

"Awww!" Carl Joseph squealed out loud. "I wasn't ready."

"Just kidding." She caught the ball by the rope and waited. "Ready now?"

"Wait." He held up one finger. His breath was fast, too fast. He put his head down and blew out—the way Brother had taught him. After seven breaths he looked up. "Okay ... ready."

She slapped the ball and it came at him fast. Then he hit it so hard it soared up and over Daisy. Carl Joseph leaned his head back and laughed, but when he stopped laughing, the ball was already past him. "Ooops!"

Now it was Daisy's turn to laugh, but she didn't miss the ball. She smacked it loud, and it went round and round and round until it touched the pole.

"Winner!" She danced a pirouette. "Winner, CJ. I'm the winner!"

"Fine." He didn't want to play anyway. He pointed at the bench against the wall. "Let's sit there."

They each took one half of the bench, because it wasn't nice to make a girl feel crowded. When he had his breath back, he smiled at her. "Brother's home."

"I know. You told me." She swung her feet. "Is he better yet?"

"No." Carl Joseph looked at the ground. "He's riding Ace a lot."

"Ace the dog?"

Carl Joseph laughed so hard his glasses fell onto his lap. He helped them back up onto his nose. "That's funny, Daisy. You made a good joke."

She put her fingers over her lips and giggled. "Riding a dog, CJ. That's funny, right? Real funny."

"Yeah." Carl Joseph waited until he stopped laughing. "Ace isn't a dog. He's Ali's horse. When Brother's sad he rides Ace."

"Oh." Daisy patted his hand. "I'm sorry about that."

Just as she said the word "sorry," the first raindrops hit

Carl Joseph's forehead. He opened his eyes wide and looked at Daisy. "Uh-oh."

At first she didn't know what was happening, but then she felt drops on her arm. "Rain! Raaaaain!" She spread her fingers over her face, stood up, and began turning in tight circles. "Rain!"

"It's okay." Carl Joseph looked at the sky. He felt scared and nervous all at once. He reached out and tried to catch her, tried to make her stop turning circles. But by the time she stopped, the rain was falling harder and harder. He pulled off his jacket and held it over her. "Come on, Daisy."

"CJ...I'm scared!"

He kept his jacket over her head and ran next to her toward the building. There was an overhang outside, and they reached the place beneath it at the same time as the other students. Everyone else walked past them into the classroom. A few girls patted Daisy on the back as they passed. "It's all right, Daisy. It's just rain, that's all."

When they were alone, Carl Joseph pulled her into his arms. "It's okay, Daisy. I'm here." He wiped the water off her back and patted her hair. Daisy was scared to death of rain. She had been ever since they met. Teacher said it was a good thing they lived in Colorado where the rain didn't come very often.

But when it did...

Daisy was crying. She put her face against his shoulder, and when she was done crying she looked at him. Fear was still in her eyes. "Water melted the Wicked Witch of the West, CJ. Do you know that?"

"I do." Carl Joseph nodded. "The witch in *The Wizard of Oz*. She died from water."

"Right." Daisy peered out at the stormy sky. "That's why I'm afraid."

He patted her cheek. "But you're not a witch, Daisy. You're not a witch at all."

"I know." She hugged him again. "But it's still water."

Carl Joseph thought about that. "True." The rain stopped then and he led her to the edge of the dry area. "Look out there, Daisy."

"I'm scared." She clung to him, and she wouldn't look up.

"Please, Daisy. Please look." He put his arm around her. "I have a secret for you."

That seemed to make her think. She relaxed her shoulders and sniffed. "What?"

"Good!" Carl Joseph clapped his hands together loud. "I knew I could make you look."

"But why?" Daisy shook her head. She looked ready to run away.

Carl Joseph didn't want her to run. "Look up there." He pointed at the sky.

She looked, but she stayed close to him. She was still afraid. "What?"

"There's sunshine up there, Daisy." He put his hand over his eyes and squinted. "Just beyond the clouds."

For a long moment she thought about that. "Really?"

"Really." He laughed but not because he had told a joke. Because he was happy. "Sunshine just beyond the clouds."

He was about to take her back into the classroom when Teacher came out. "Daisy…I was in the supply room. I didn't know it was raining." The two sisters hugged. "Are you okay?"

"Yes." Daisy looked at him, and her eyes were sparkly diamonds again. The fear was gone from her eyes. "CJ helped me."

"He gave you his coat." Teacher smiled at him. "That's very nice, Carl Joseph."

"No, not that." Daisy moved back beside him. She linked her arm through his the way she sometimes did. "He told me about the sunshine."

Teacher looked unsure about that. "Sunshine?"

"Yes." Daisy led Carl Joseph back to the place where they could see the sky. "Up there. Just beyond the clouds."

Teacher looked up at the sky and little bits of tears came into her eyes. She hugged herself and then she said something quiet mixed in with her breath. "Yeah…I never thought about it that way."

They went back into the classroom, but before they took their spots in the living room area, Carl Joseph watched Teacher. That's when he remembered something. Daisy had prayed for Cody. She had told him a few times already that he should, too. So maybe it was his turn to pray. He could ask God to help Teacher. He found his seat and covered his face.

God…help Teacher, please. Whatever she needs. That's all. Amen.

He opened his eyes and looked at Teacher again. She still

looked sad. And those were for sure tears on her cheeks outside a minute ago. He understood when Daisy cried. She had a reason to be sad, because she was afraid of the rain. But Teacher needed a lot of prayers said for her. Because she was just as sad but there was no reason.

Teacher wasn't afraid of the rain even one tiny bit.

Chapter Four

Cody finally felt as if he could breathe again. His parents owned twenty acres in the foothills near Colorado Springs, and after two days at home Cody wondered why he'd ever left. He had a small house at the far western end of his parents' ranch. He didn't need his own place; not while he was living on the road. The PBR season ran from January to November with only a six-week break.

He could get a house later.

For now, his parents' place was enough. Ace was here, Ali's horse. He could ride and remember and spend time with Carl Joseph. And now he could even think clearly. He showered early that morning and walked over to his parents' house. The bad news about Carl Joseph was worse than Cody expected. He had epilepsy. Several times a week lately he'd fallen into major seizures—the type the doctors called grand mal. The seizures came along with another diagnosis.

Carl Joseph's heart disease was worse. Not just his arteries, but the heart itself.

His prognosis for a long life was dim.

Cody wasn't willing to settle for that, any more than he'd been willing to settle for Ali's diagnosis. There had to be something they could do to help Carl Joseph strengthen his heart.

His buddy must've seen him coming, because he opened the back door and came running out. "Hi, Brother! It's a good morning!" He pointed at the sky. "See that? A bright sunny good morning."

"Yeah, Buddy." Cody smiled. What was it about the kid? Every time Cody was with him he felt happier, like he might just survive after all. "It's a great day."

"You know what?" Carl Joseph put his hands on his knees. His eyes lit up. "I think I wanna be a bull rider like you."

"I know, Buddy." Cody messed up his brother's hair. "You tell me that every time."

"Because I wanna be a world-famous bull rider like you, Brother."

"Bull riders get hurt." He put his arm around Carl Joseph's shoulders and they headed toward the back door.

"Yeah." Carl Joseph's smile faded. "That's true."

Cody pushed the door open and they moved inside to the breakfast table. Their mother was fixing scrambled eggs, cheese, and bell peppers. His favorite. When they were seated, Cody planted his elbows on the table. "You could work at the ranch here, Buddy. That's good work for you."

"No." Carl Joseph shook his head. It took a lot to fluster

him, but this time talk about bull riding seemed to be more than a lighthearted way to carry on a conversation. "No, that's not okay. I wanna be a bull rider." He slammed his fist on the table. "Starting today."

"Whoa..." Cody looked from Carl Joseph to their mother. "What's this all about?"

His mother was stirring the eggs. She looked over her shoulder at Carl Joseph. "You wanna tell your brother what this is all about?"

"Okay." Carl Joseph sat up straighter in his chair. "Daisy likes bull riders. She told me so."

Cody blinked. "Daisy?" He looked at his mother. Inside, the beginnings of something unsettling stirred in his gut. "Who's Daisy?"

"She's my girl." Carl Joseph slapped himself on the chest. "My girl, Brother. She likes bull riders 'cause I told her you were a bull rider and she smiled really, really big. So you teach me, Brother, okay?"

"Tell you what"—he tried not to sound bothered—"let's start with Ace. You can take a ride around the arena with me. How 'bout that?"

"'Cause that's a start, right?"

"Right." Cody stood. He tapped the table between them. "I'll be back, Buddy."

"Okay." Carl Joseph chuckled and clapped hard. Then he looked straight up. "I'm gonna be a bull rider. Thank You, God."

Cody turned his attention to his mother. She was stirring the eggs again, but she had to know he was coming her way.

He reached her elbow and leaned around so she could see his face. "Who's Daisy?"

"He told you." She kept her eyes from his. "Daisy's his friend."

"I've been home for three days." He made an exaggerated move and looked out the window. "I haven't seen any girls hanging around the place. So who's Daisy?"

His mother released a loud sigh. "Look, Cody, don't over-react." She put the spatula down on the counter and faced him. "Your brother's getting older. He has friends now."

Cody's head was spinning. Carl Joseph had friends? "Is this that class thing you were telling me about?"

"Yes." She sighed and met his eyes. "I take him to a center in town. Everyone there has Down Syndrome."

"Including Daisy?" He felt himself relax. The idea of an able-bodied girl falling for Carl Joseph seemed wrong. He couldn't stand the idea that maybe his brother had fallen for a girl who would never have feelings for him. But if she had Down Syndrome like him...

"Yes." His mother picked up the spatula again and started stirring. "Daisy has Down Syndrome. She's twenty-one, four years younger than Carl Joseph." She turned off the stove and wiped her brow with the back of her hand. "They like to swing dance and sing Mickey Mouse songs, and they dream of going to Disneyland one day. Daisy helps Carl Joseph talk quieter, and he helps her not be so afraid of the rain. It's a simple, sweet friendship, Cody." She moved the pan to the island countertop. "It's good for your brother."

"Okay." Cody felt much better. "So he's getting out more,

socializing. This class thing is...I don't know...sort of a play group kind of thing." He looked over his shoulder at his brother, then back again. "Right?"

His mother tilted her head sideways, considering his definition. "Sort of. It's good for him, that's all I know. I've seen differences."

Cody hesitated. "Good. Differences are good."

"If he can keep going." Her expression changed. "With the epilepsy...the doctor isn't sure..."

"We can talk about it later." He reached for a stack of plates in the cupboard just as he heard his dad's voice behind him.

"Carl Joseph, you look good."

"Thanks, Dad. I'm seeing Daisy today."

"Yeah, I just found out about Daisy." Cody set the plates next to the pan of eggs and gave his dad a tentative smile. "I guess I never thought about Carl Joseph having, you know... a girl."

"It isn't like that." His mother pulled a stack of napkins out and set them on the counter. "Come and eat, Carl Joseph."

Come and eat? Cody started to say something, but he stopped himself. The last time he was home, Carl Joseph was served at the table—same as always. He wasn't stable enough to fill his plate and carry it across the room without spilling or dropping it altogether. Cody tapped softly at his mom's arm. "He learned this?"

"Yes." His mom looked proud. "And table manners, too."

"Really?"

His dad joined them in the kitchen. "Really. Carl Joseph

is capable of much more than we ever thought, Cody. It's amazing."

Carl Joseph was still on his way into the kitchen from the dining room, so he hadn't heard any of their conversation. Cody stared at his father and tried to think of a comeback. His comments bugged Cody. Maybe because Cody knew he was never happy about having a son with Down Syndrome. Back when Carl Joseph was two years old, their dad had left home and stayed away for nineteen years because he couldn't bear to be the father of a handicapped child.

So what was this? His dad's attempt at making Carl Joseph more like normal kids? Cody kept his thoughts to himself. He hung back and watched Carl Joseph choose a plate, scoop up a serving of eggs, and take a napkin and fork from the counter. He carried the plate back to the dining room table and sat down without even a little shakiness.

"Okay..." Cody filled his plate and took the place across from his brother. "Buddy, you're doing great."

"Thanks." All his life, Carl Joseph had held his fork like a shovel, and after a few bites when his balance weakened, the food would fall back to the plate and he would shovel it into his mouth with his fingers. Then he would chomp hard, his mouth open, bits falling back to his plate as he chewed. Not today. He was concentrating, no doubt. But he lifted a forkful of eggs into his mouth, chewed with his mouth closed, and swallowed. Then he used the napkin to dab at the corners of his mouth.

"Cody's right." Their dad smiled at Carl Joseph. "You're doing very, very well. We're all proud of you."

"Daisy's proud." Carl Joseph put his fork down and folded his hands in his lap.

Cody watched his brother for a few more minutes. The classes must've been a very good thing for his brother. A few lessons on social graces, a little social interaction...Carl Joseph should've gone to the center years ago.

Carl Joseph focused on his breakfast, and Cody turned his attention to the reason he was home. He set his fork down and looked at his parents. "I need a change."

His mother hesitated midbite. "A change?"

"Yes." He pushed his plate back and rested his forearms on the table. "I'm not under contract for the rest of the season. They want me, but I haven't agreed yet."

His parents waited for him to continue.

"I love bull riding, don't get me wrong." Cody raked his fingers through his dark hair.

"Me, too." Carl Joseph looked up. "Brother's going to teach me to bull ride, right, Brother?"

"One day." Cody smiled at him. He turned back to his dad. "I want to do something different, something that matters. Maybe open a sports center, or raise bulls here at the ranch. So I can be around family more."

"You could do just about anything." His dad sat back in his seat and crossed his arms. "I didn't know you were considering a change."

His mother sat a little straighter. Her eyes were thoughtful. "I've been hoping for this."

Cody took a drink of his orange juice. "That I'd leave the circuit?"

"Yes." She dragged her fork through her eggs. "Because until you do, you'll never get over Ali. You carry her with you every time you hit the road."

For a long moment, Cody held his breath. His mother meant nothing by her comment, he knew that with every heartbeat. But how could he make them understand that he wasn't a victim of Ali's memory? He was the owner of it. He didn't want to move on or let her go. He just needed a place where her image wasn't around every corner.

"Don't be angry, Cody." She reached toward him and put her hand over his. "I loved Ali. We all did."

"But Ali makes you sad, Brother." Carl Joseph waved his fork in Cody's direction. At the same instant, he seemed to notice what he was doing. He brought his fork back down to his plate. "I think Ali makes you sad."

"What your mother's trying to say, son, is…well, it's been four years." His father's voice was tender.

Anger rose inside Cody. He focused on his eggs and ate them more quickly than he planned. When he was finished he stood and took his plate to the kitchen. "I'll be out back."

"Cody…" his mother called after him. "We're only saying that—"

He was out the door before she finished her sentence. He knew what they were saying, and it wasn't their fault. Four years was a long time. But not for him. He stormed out to the barn and a memory flashed bold and brilliant in his mind. The time when Ali had rushed out of her parents' house, the day she found out that he knew the truth about her illness.

She ran to the barn and climbed onto Ace just as he reached her.

"Ali, get down. We need to talk." He stood in front of her, his heart pounding.

"I didn't want you to know. Not yet." She pressed her fingers to her chest. "It was my place to tell you."

No matter what he said, she wouldn't climb down off the horse, so finally he climbed up behind her. With her at the reins, the horse raced across the open field to the trail and on out to the back fence. By then, Ali was so upset she could barely breathe. She fell into an asthma attack. He held her and coaxed her, and by some sort of miracle she found space in her damaged lungs to grab a breath.

Cody held on to the memory as he rounded the corner of the barn and saddled Ace. He brought the horse to a full run and set out on the trail that led to his house on the other side of the property. Atop Ace, he could almost feel Ali in front of him, almost sense her slight back against his chest, her hair in his face.

When his parents' house was out of sight, Cody stopped. His sides heaved and he had to concentrate to catch his breath. It had been that way ever since the transplant operation. He stared at the sky, at the white cumulus clouds dotting the blue. Of course he carried Ali with him every time he hit the road. Was he supposed to leave rodeo because of that?

Cody leaned over Ace and rested his forehead on the horse's mane. No one understood. It wasn't only the rodeo. He carried Ali with him everywhere he went. This break was supposed to give him a chance, an hour or two when he didn't see her face or hear her voice. When the sights and sounds and smells didn't make him think it was eight years ago and she was still by his side.

But now he was home, and things were no different.

She was still there when he fell asleep, there when he woke up. He saw her whenever he saw Ace, and when he looked into the wide open Colorado sky, and when he heard the crunch of dirt beneath his boots on the walk from his house to his parents'. She was everywhere, and until now that had been fine with him.

But his mother was right. Maybe that's why he couldn't shake the anger.

Four years was enough time, enough that it was no longer healthy to see her face and feel her breath against his skin every hour. Every few minutes. And so he was here because he was running from that truth and trying to find a way to embrace it—all at the same time.

"Ali..." He lifted his chin and stared into the blue.

There was no response. Only the whisper of wind in the distant pines.

How was he supposed to move on? The rodeo was over. He could feel it as soon as he stepped onto the plane in Nampa, Idaho. He couldn't take another cowboy coming up and offering condolences, couldn't stand another sad glance from the friends who knew how he was feeling, the way he was stuck back on some long-ago spring day when Ali was still alive, still sharing his bed and his life. When the lung he'd given her was still working.

He was finished with rodeo. He knew that for sure now.

So what was next? He'd read once in a book on grief that the only way to find new life was to get out of bed each morning and put one foot in front of the other. Breathe in, breathe out...and go after the next thing. In time, the pain would dull. One day, morning would come and the memories would no longer be part of every breath. Rather they would have stepped to the side, a favorite friend in a favorite place. Worth visiting every now and then.

Cody drew a long breath and ran his fingers through Ace's blond mane.

The horse whinnied and turned slightly, as if to say, "Well, where is she? Hasn't she been gone long enough?"

"Atta boy, Ace. It's okay."

He touched the horse's sides with his heels and they started moving. One foot in front of the other, huh? If that was true, then he had to find something to do with his time. He'd invested well. His prize earnings, his pay for three years' announcing on the circuit, and a consultation fee for two cowboy movies: All of it added up to a seven-figure bank account and land investments in three states. Money wouldn't be a problem, but what job would allow him to be as passionate as he'd been about the rodeo?

He removed his cowboy hat and ran his fingers through his hair. Only one person besides Ali had ever made him love so much it hurt. His brother, Carl Joseph. He thought about the conversation over breakfast, the idea that Buddy seemed smitten with a girl named Daisy.

Cody worked the muscles in his jaw. Of course the kid

was smitten. He'd never been exposed to any sort of social environment until now. A group of friends was a good thing for Carl Joseph. But how was a daycare ever going to help him find long life and health here at home? His brother was forty or fifty pounds overweight, plagued by the same weak muscle tone that afflicted most people with Down Syndrome. That and the epilepsy and heart disease.

A few years back, Cody had studied the idea of rehabilitation, finding exercises and routines for Carl Joseph that would help him overcome the limitations of Down Syndrome. At the time, he thought Carl Joseph would gain strength if he rode horses. And once in a while he'd helped his brother onto the back of a horse and led him around an arena. But that wouldn't help him find the strength and health he needed to live a long life.

Maybe the answer was a sports complex. He could look around the Springs and buy out a failing gym. Then he could turn it into a place where disabled people could come for physical training. Sort of a rehab program. The exercise would make Carl Joseph stronger, maybe buy him a decade of good health. Cody could run the place and the people who attended could be matched with trainers or placed in special classes. That way people like Carl Joseph could use their energy on something productive, something that would build their self-esteem. It would be a program that would complement the daycare thing Buddy was already involved in.

Cody eased Ace around and galloped the horse back to the barn. As he did, he was struck by a thought—something that proved the accuracy of the information he'd read a long time ago in the grief book. Do the next thing, the book's author had stated. And here—over the last few minutes—he'd done just that. He'd thought about his next move, his next career. His next passion. The book said that by doing such a thing, the memory of a lost loved one would naturally be pushed to the side. That must've been true, because when he was thinking about a center for kids like Carl Joseph a surprising thing had happened. Nothing else had filled his mind.

Not even his precious Ali.

Chapter Five

Elle sat with her mother at the kitchen table and tried to concentrate on their heated game of Scrabble. But Daisy's distractions were relentless. She was dancing in the kitchen, twirling and spinning and singing a song she was making up about field trips and the steps of a bus. It was Thursday, which meant tomorrow was another field trip day. Daisy would be dancing and giggling and celebrating until bedtime.

Field trips had that effect on her.

"Your turn." Her mother stood and headed toward the sink. "Elle, I'd swear your mind is somewhere else tonight. You don't usually let me get this close in Scrabble."

"I'll still beat you." Elle leaned down and scratched Snoopy's ears. The beagle was ten years old now, the hair around his eyes and nose more gray than brown. "I haven't had good letters all game."

"Shoulda swapped 'em!" Daisy twirled past Elle's chair. "I'd swap 'em."

"You're probably right."

Their mother poured three glasses of iced tea. She set one on the counter for Daisy and brought the other two to the table. "You ignored my observation."

"What?" Elle lifted her eyes and feigned innocence. "About beating me at Scrabble?"

She raised one eyebrow. "About your mind being somewhere else."

"Nah. Just thinking about tomorrow's field trip." Elle reached for her tea and took a sip. "Thanks for the drink."

"Tomorrow's field trip!" Daisy jumped in the air, both hands straight out in front of her. She began to hum. "I could've danced all night…I could've danced all night."

Their mother looked doubtful. "Where are you going?" She raised her voice so she could be heard over Daisy's gleeful singing.

"The park and out to lunch. Everyone's bringing money." Elle took four of her letter tiles and built the word "guilty" down along a double-word square. She grinned at her mother. "There. That should put me ahead."

Daisy stopped, out of breath, and dropped to the chair next to Elle. "Do you like bull riders, Elle?"

Elle looked at her sister and blinked. What was the fascination with bull riders lately? Ever since Carl Joseph mentioned his brother and how the guy had ridden bulls, Daisy brought it up nearly every day. "Not particularly."

Their mother leaned on her elbows and looked from Elle to Daisy. "How'd you hear about bull riders?"

"From CJ." Daisy beamed. "His brother's a bull rider."

Elle gave her mother a side glance and the slightest shake of her head. With her eyes she conveyed her doubt. "He's probably an accountant or something. Just moved back to the Springs."

"He's a bull rider." Shock and indignation filled Daisy's face. "I said he's a bull rider and he's a bull rider."

"Okay." Elle patted her sister's hand. "He's a bull rider."

Daisy took a long drink of her iced tea. One ice cube plopped onto the table, and she quickly picked it up and dropped it back into her cup. "You didn't see that, okay, Elle? But he *is* a bull rider." She finished her tea with three big swallows and stood.

When she was out of earshot, Elle whispered toward her mother: "And I'm a ballerina."

Her mother smiled. "It doesn't really matter."

"Except Daisy's all caught up in the idea of bull riders now. Today at class Carl Joseph wore a cowboy hat and announced that he was taking up bull riding and one day he'd be a world champion like his brother." She made an exasperated face. "It's getting a little out of hand."

"I could've danced all night…" Daisy spun around the kitchen counter and into the living room. "I could've danced all night."

Her mother grinned. "Watch this." She used six of her tiles with the word "sugars," placing the *s* at the end of "cage" and racking up points for both words. "That should seal it."

"Okay, okay." Elle added her mother's points to the score sheet. "I have to let you win once in a while. Otherwise you won't play."

"So"—her mother leaned back and ran her fingers along the damp sides of her iced tea glass—"is this bull rider brother guy single?"

"Mother..." Frustration poked pins at Elle's mood. "You promised."

Daisy skipped up to the table. "His wife was a horse rider. That's how he met her."

"Oh." Their mother sounded almost guilty. "So he's a married bull rider."

Elle was surprised, but not because she cared particularly. She hadn't heard about the guy's wife until now. "They're all married." Elle stared at her letters. "And that suits me fine. I'm not looking for a relationship, Mom." She lifted her eyes. "Remember?"

"I know. It's just..." Her mother checked the Scrabble board. "You need more than Thursday night Scrabble with us. You have your whole life ahead of you, Elle. I keep thinking God's going to bring the right man into your life, but weeks turn into months, months turn into years—and still nothing." Discouragement filled her tone. "It isn't right."

"You know what?" Elle met her mother's gaze straight on. "People think my students are handicapped. They look different, so they're disabled." Her voice fell and she looked at the board again. "But all of us are handicapped one way or another." She looked up. "The men I've met don't know how to love. Or they're married and looking for a cheap

affair. That's more disabled than Daisy or Carl Joseph. Don't
you think?"

Her mother sighed. "You're jaded, Elle. You had one bad
experience."

"One?" She looked at her mother, astonished. "I got left
at the altar on my wedding day! That's a little different."

"I'm just saying, you can't condemn all men because of
what happened." Her mom sounded tentative, as if she knew
she was pushing the subject a little too hard. "I'll drop it,
but please, Elle...maybe talk to someone at church. Broken
hearts are meant to be healed."

Elle had a standard answer when people asked her about
love. She steeled herself against the pain and smiled at her
mother. "I've said it before. If I'm supposed to fall in love,
it'll have to find me. Grab me around the neck and sit me
down face-to-face. Because I'm no longer looking."

Daisy pushed a button on the CD player that sat on the
kitchen counter. Waltz music filled the room, and she leaned
her head back, overcome with joy. "I wish CJ was here." She
swept around the table and held out her hand. "Come on,
Elle. Dance with me."

The Dalton girls had always danced. Daisy's love for music
and movement was probably the reason she didn't struggle
with her weight the way so many people with Down Syndrome did. Elle took her sister's hand, stood, and began
waltzing around the table. As they did, Daisy laughed the
open-hearted, no-holds-barred laugh she was known for.

Her happiness was contagious, and Elle began to giggle.
Never mind that her mother wouldn't give up on hoping

she'd find a man. She'd already been down that road. This life—the one she lived at home with Daisy and her mom, the one she lived each day with her students—was fulfilling enough.

Snoopy stood and stretched and fell into line behind them. As they waltzed into the living room, he followed, and that made Daisy laugh harder. "Snoopy is a dancer! He's a dancer, Mom!"

"Yes, he is." Their mother stood and moved in time to the music. When she reached Elle and Daisy, she waltzed close to the beagle. "Snoopy's my partner this time."

Round and round the room they went, and Elle relished the feeling. When the song ended, they were all breathless from dancing and laughing. Daisy plopped down on the sofa and called Snoopy to her side. "Time for movie night."

"You're right." Elle went to the kitchen, found a bag of popcorn, and slipped it into the microwave. "Ten minutes to show time."

The movie that night was *Sweet Home Alabama*, starring Reese Witherspoon. Only a few minutes in, Reese's character daydreamed about a long-lost childhood love, and Elle felt the familiar ache in her chest. She could dismiss her mother's concern and laugh about the idea of needing more than she already had. But deep inside there was no denying the obvious. She had tried love once and failed. Badly.

Even if she were looking, she'd never find the sweet, guileless love that lived every day in the eyes of her students, a love built on honesty and transparency, a love strong enough to tear down the walls around her heart. Only that sort of love was worth letting go of her independence and trusting one more time. And that was the problem. Outside of Daisy's world, that sort of love wasn't just rare.

It was nonexistent.

THE FIELD TRIP to Antlers Park was in full swing, and Elle was proud of the way her students were handling their time in public. The bus ride had gone smoothly, all of the students demonstrating their ability to show their passes and stay seated until the appropriate stop. As always, Daisy led the way, with Carl Joseph right behind her.

Once in a while, Elle would watch the two of them and wonder what the future held. Daisy would be ready for independent living sometime in the next few months. Even now she could be successful, though Elle wanted to be sure Daisy understood her medical needs—monthly checkups because of her weak heart. She also needed a job. Already Elle was helping Daisy put together a resume.

The problem was Carl Joseph. He wouldn't be ready for at least another year. And with his epilepsy, his parents were thinking about pulling him from the program. When she tried to talk to Daisy about the situation, her sister only smiled and said, "I won't move out until CJ can move out."

Elle watched them now, Daisy and Carl Joseph, arms linked. They were at the front of the group, heading down a walkway toward Engine 168, the historic railroad car that had been placed in the park decades ago. It was a point of interest—something Elle wanted her students to understand.

She thought about her sister again. One of these days she'd have to sit down with Carl Joseph's parents and try to convince them. Epilepsy was fairly common for people with Down Syndrome. With the right medication and regular checkups, Carl Joseph could live an independent life even with his condition. Maybe they'd be more open to a group home setting where Carl Joseph and Daisy could live in the same complex. Not as some sort of romantic set-up, but as the best friends they'd come to be. For now, anyway.

They were twenty yards from the railroad car when Gus began to gallop around in circles. "We're going on a train... Hey, everyone, look!" He laughed loud and long and bobbed his head several times. "We're going on a train!"

Sid gave his classmate a disgusted look. He marched to the front of the railroad car and pointed at the ground. "Yeah, but no tracks." He shouted in Elle's direction. "See, Teacher. No tracks."

"No tracks is very dangerous." Carl Joseph stopped and looked around. "What's going to happen if no tracks for the train, Teacher?"

Elle held up her hands. "Everyone come here."

Slowly, with a variety of response times, the group formed a half circle around her. Sid was still mumbling something about the whole day being a disaster because no train could run without tracks. Elle waited until they were mostly quiet. "We are not going on a train today."

Gus pointed at the railroad car. "There it is, Teacher. That's the train."

"That's part of the park." She spoke loud enough for all of

them to hear. Her tone was rich with compassion and confidence. "Today is a park day. The train is part of the park."

She had chosen Antlers Park intentionally, because she knew the sight of a full-size railroad car in the park would be enough to throw most of them. This was why they took field trips, so they could work through everyday obstacles on the quest for living an independent life. She motioned to the group. "Follow me."

When they reached the train, Elle positioned herself near a sign and directed them to come as close as they could. "This is a marker, a sign that explains why a train is here in the middle of the park. Who would like to read it?"

Daisy had her hand up first. About a third of the students could read, but Daisy was easily the most skilled. Their mother had worked hours each week making sure her youngest daughter could read—and she'd done it at a time when conventional wisdom held that a person with Down Syndrome might not be capable of such a feat.

It was one more area where Carl Joseph was far behind Daisy.

Daisy stepped to the front of the group and bent over the sign. Her eyes were worse than they'd been a year ago. She needed to squint in order to make out the words. But one line at a time she read the message on the sign out loud to the class. When she reached the part about the railroad car being a gift to the people of Colorado Springs, something to commemorate the railroad's part in the founding of the city, Gus waved his arms.

"I get it!" He pointed at the train. "It's a tourist trap. My mom told me about tourist traps."

Elle smiled. They finished up with the train and headed for the crosswalk. There, Elle reviewed the traffic signals. Sid lagged behind, and when they crossed, he was last to step into the road. By the time he did, the light had changed and a car honked at him. In times past, Sid would've shaken a fist at the driver or maybe dropped to the ground, weeping, reduced to the abilities of a five-year-old child.

Not this time. With Elle behind him, he stopped, looked at the driver and then waved at the man. Then he turned his attention to the other side of the street and, head high, finished his walk.

Progress! Elle stepped up onto the curb, stopped him, and smiled. "Sid! That was wonderful!"

"He didn't need to honk." Sid looked back at the driver, already speeding down the road.

"No, he didn't."

Elle and Sid joined the others at the Subway on the corner. Restaurants gave the students a chance to face other tasks that might've been daunting without the training they'd received at the ILC. They had to decide what type of bread and meat and fixings they'd have on their sandwich, and whether they wanted a meal package. And each of them needed to count out the right money to pay for the meal.

Twenty minutes later, when they had their sandwiches, the students found seats at five tables all on one side of the restaurant. Another improvement. A year ago, most of them would've wandered aimlessly around the dining area trying to figure out where to sit and who to sit with.

As they began eating, they fell into natural conversations. Another sign of independence. When one of them grew too loud, someone at their table would hold up two fingers— the sign that voices needed to be quieter. Elle sat at Daisy's table with Carl Joseph and Gus. It was one of those moments when she knew with every breath that this was the place God wanted her. Never mind love and relationships, here— with these students, she was making a difference.

They were halfway through their meal when she saw a pickup truck park out front. A rugged dark-haired man in a white T-shirt and jeans climbed out and headed for the front door of the restaurant. Elle was struck by the guy's looks. In her world of working at the center and stopping at the grocery store and heading back home again, there were few guys who looked like this one. But the set of his jaw and his determined pace shouted that he was preoccupied.

She turned her attention back to her sandwich just as Carl Joseph dropped his sandwich and stood up.

"Brother!" He waved at the man. "Over here. Come sit with us!"

The guy's expression eased. Several students let out similar shouts. "Hi, Carl Joseph's brother!" "Come sit here!"

Daisy tugged on Carl Joseph's shirt. "Is that the bull rider?"

He puffed out his chest. "I'm a bull rider, too."

"Okay, everyone." Elle stood and looked at her students. "Let's remember our restaurant manners."

The guy gave a sheepish wave to the others and one at a

time the excited students sat back down. Then he came to Carl Joseph's side and looked straight at him. "You remembered, right, Buddy?" His tone was kind, but his eyes looked troubled. Maybe even angry. "You and I have a date today?"

Carl Joseph did an exaggerated gasp. He covered his mouth and looked from Daisy to Elle and back to his brother. "I forgot, Brother. I'm sorry I forgot."

The guy gave a short laugh. In a way that made it clear he had no choice, he pulled up a chair and sat next to Carl Joseph. "Can you finish up?" A strained smile lifted his lips. "I have something to show you."

"But..." Carl Joseph pointed slowly at Daisy and Elle and Gus and then at the other tables. "These are my friends and...and this is Field Trip Day."

"Yeah." For the first time he looked at Elle. There was suddenly enough ice in his tone to change the temperature of the room. "Mom told me."

Elle held out her hand. "I don't believe we've met. I'm Elle Dalton. Director of the Center for Independent Living."

He took Elle's hand for the slightest moment. Long enough for her to see his wedding ring. "I'm Cody Gunner, Carl Joseph's brother."

"World-famous bull rider." Daisy's entire face lit up. She bounced in her seat. "Right here with us. World-famous bull rider."

Carl Joseph whispered to her, his frustration written into the lines on his forehead. "I'm a bull rider, too, Daisy. Remember?"

"Uh"—Cody gave an uncomfortable laugh—"sorry about this. I need to take my brother. We have plans."

"Okay." Elle looked at Carl Joseph. "The field trip is almost over. It's okay if you go with your brother."

"But Daisy and me wanna dance in the park." Carl Joseph's face fell. He implored his brother. "I didn't get to dance yet."

"Hold on, Buddy." Cody's pleasant facade seemed to be cracking. He dropped his voice to a whisper and turned his attention to Elle. "Can I talk to you? In private?"

Elle felt her defenses rise. She stood and looked at her students. "I need to speak with Mr. Gunner outside. I'll be right back."

She led the way, and once they were out of earshot, he met her eyes. "What is all this?"

"Excuse me?" Elle could feel the anger flash in her eyes.

"This." He gestured toward the students inside. "Putting them on display so everyone can gawk at them." The guy kept his voice controlled, but just barely. "I thought my brother was taking social classes." He laughed, but there was no humor in it. "Now I find out it's some kind of independent living?"

Elle was too surprised to speak.

"Look—" Cody seemed to be trying to find control. "I'm sorry, it's just..." He paced a few steps away from her before whirling around and staring at her. "My brother's sick. He'll never live on his own. Someone should've told you."

Elle was still shocked by the guy's outburst. But now at least she understood it. "His epilepsy, you mean?"

"Epilepsy, heart disease...the fact that he can't read." Cody tossed his hands. "It's wrong to fill his head with ideas of independence." He turned his attention toward the students inside. "How can it be right for any of them?"

"Mr. Gunner." Elle worked to keep her tone even. "I care about each one of those students in that restaurant. I would never bring them into public to be laughed at." She narrowed her eyes. "This is part of their curriculum. If you'd like to know more about what your brother is learning, I'd advise you to make an appointment with me. I'm available every morning an hour before class."

"What's the point? My brother won't ever be well enough to leave home." He shook his head. "Don't you get it?"

"He can be independent even with his limitations." Elle worked to keep her anger in check. What right did Carl Joseph's brother have to disrupt the field trip?

"Never mind." He took a step toward the door and held it open. His voice was still thick with frustration. "Thanks for your time."

Elle thought of a dozen things she could tell this guy, but why bother? Ignorant people like him came along every now and then. She didn't need to validate him by defending her work at the center. He was still holding open the door for her, so she went in.

Cody walked up to Carl Joseph and bagged the uneaten half of his sandwich. "Come on, Buddy. Let's get out of here."

"Wait!" Carl Joseph's voice was much louder than usual. "You didn't meet Daisy."

Cody smiled, but it was laced with impatience. "Fine." He looked at Daisy. His tone was kinder than before. "I'm Cody. You must be Daisy."

"Hi, Cody." Daisy gave him a bashful look. She batted her eyes. "You're cute."

"Hey, what about me?" Carl Joseph turned to Daisy, hurt flooding his eyes.

Daisy took his hand and pressed it to her heart. "You're the cutest of all, CJ." She whispered, "Even cuter than your brother."

At that moment, Cody seemed to notice the way his brother smelled. "Buddy? Are you wearing cologne?"

"Yes." Carl Joseph stood and beamed at Daisy. He pushed his glasses back up the bridge of his nose. "Mom bought me some. I wear it for Daisy."

Daisy leaned close to Elle. "He smells like a bull rider."

"Thank you." Carl Joseph puffed out his chest.

"This is crazy." Cody mumbled the words. He gave a curt nod to Daisy and Elle. "Nice to meet you." As he headed for the door, he stopped and looked back at Elle. "I'll stop in one day this week. Like you suggested."

Elle flashed her most professional smile. "You'll have to make an appointment, Mr. Gunner."

The two left, amidst a chorus of good-byes from the other students. As soon as they were outside, Cody put his arm around Carl Joseph's shoulders. Regardless of his intensity or his intrusion into the field trip, this much was clear: Cody Gunner was crazy about his younger brother. Cody opened the passenger-side door of the truck and gave Carl Joseph more help than he needed getting inside.

As the two drove off, Elle looked around the dining area at her students. Cody's visit had left a dark cloud of uncertainty over the group. But they knew this much: Carl Joseph's brother didn't approve of their field trip.

It was one of the things that made a person with Down Syndrome so special. Part of their makeup included an extraordinary sense of perception. Independent living courses were designed to help people with Down Syndrome recognize their feelings and talk about them.

Elle stood and cleared her throat. There was no time like the present for such a lesson. "Would someone like to tell me how you're feeling right now?"

At first no one responded. Finally Daisy raised her hand. "Daisy?"

"I don't really think CJ's brother is cute." She shook her head. "Not anymore."

Sid tossed his hands in the air. "He didn't like us." He looked around. "Could anyone else see that? Carl Joseph's brother didn't like us."

Tears stung at Elle's eyes. As hard as it was to hear Sid voice his feelings, this, too, was progress. She moved between the tables so she was closer to Sid. "Why did you think that?"

"Because—" Sid pushed his sandwich back. His tone was more hurt than angry. "He didn't look at us."

"And something else." Gus raised his hand.

Elle pointed at him.

"He..." Gus looked at Daisy as if maybe this part might hurt her feelings. "I'm sorry, Daisy. I'm sorry to say something bad about Carl Joseph's brother."

"That's okay, Gus." She touched his shoulder. "You can say what you want."

"Okay..." Gus swallowed. "He said, 'This is crazy.' Maybe that means he thinks...he thinks we're crazy."

Elle's heart hurt. In that moment, if she could've, she would've whisked her students instantly back to the ILC, where they were safe and accepted, where living a life on their own seemed like one more fun activity. This reality was something entirely different. She went to Gus and lowered herself to his level. "Gus, no one thinks you're crazy."

Gus bit his lip and hung his head. "I think...maybe Carl Joseph's brother does."

"No." She stood and met the eyes of the students at every table. "Carl Joseph's brother is an angry person. Carl Joseph said he was hurt, so maybe he's in pain. His back or his knees, maybe." She wished he could see how his appearance had hurt her students. "We can pray for him."

"Yes." Tammy, the girl with the long braids, clapped her hands. "That's a positive idea. Right, Teacher? A positive idea."

"It is." Elle blinked back tears. If Cody Gunner were here she'd grab him by the collar and shake him. Then she'd tell him exactly how his careless words had hurt her students. But she couldn't think about that now. Not with them looking for her to turn things around. "Tammy's right. If we pray for someone who's angry, then that's a very positive idea."

Gus looked around and then dropped from his chair to his knees. He folded his hands together and bowed his head. Elle was about to tell him he could pray from his seat, when around the room the others followed his example. Before Elle could find the words, every one of her students was kneeling in the dining area at Subway, head bowed.

"Dear God," Gus began, "be with Carl Joseph's angry brother. Anger is not a healthy choice. It's not a healthy life skill." He opened his eyes and smiled up at Elle. Then he closed them again. "So please be with Carl Joseph's brother, because maybe bull riders are angry people. Make him happy, Jesus. Amen."

Around the room, more than a dozen amens came from the group. Only then did Elle notice a table of teenage kids at the back of the room. The prayer had caught their attention. But instead of laughing at the handicapped people down on their knees, the teens were doing something entirely different.

They were smiling.

And at the end of the prayer, a few teens even stood and walked over, patting the shoulders of the students. Finally they nodded at Elle, and she mouthed the words, "Thank you," toward them. Then she sat down next to Daisy once more.

Two steps backward, three steps forward. That's the way it was with her students. The world was still getting used to the idea that people with Down Syndrome might be bagging their groceries or sweeping the floor at Wal-Mart. For every ignorant person like Cody Gunner, there was a group of people who understood, kids who had probably attended school with disabled students—because things were different today than they'd been a decade ago.

Elle was too choked up to take another bite of her sandwich. She sipped her water instead and watched as the cloud lifted and her students began interacting again. She could tell them later that it was probably best not to kneel in a public restaurant, that praying could be done in a chair as well as on their knees.

Or maybe not. Maybe if people had the chance to see an entire Subway dining room filled with people on their knees every once in a while, the whole world would be a little better off.

Chapter Six

Cody didn't say a word until they were a mile away from the Subway. He'd been wrong to storm in and demand that Carl Joseph leave right in the middle of his field trip. But why had no one explained the situation to him before? Here he'd thought Carl Joseph was involved in some kind of daycare program, a way to give him social interaction…

But a center for independent living?

Cody's knuckles were white from his grip on the steering wheel. The entire truck reeked of Carl Joseph's cologne, the smell a pungent reminder of everything Cody hadn't understood until today. It had all come together that morning. He'd gotten a late start, and when he walked into his parents' house, he'd found his mother instead of Carl Joseph.

"Where's Buddy?" He grabbed an apple and peered into the living room. "I wanted to take him out today."

His mother was sitting at the dining room table writing a letter. "He had to be at the center early."

"The center?" He took a bite of the apple. "You mean the club, the social place?"

"Yes, Cody." His mother looked up. If he didn't know better, he would've thought she'd been crying. Her eyes looked weary, and there were circles beneath them. "He had a field trip today."

"What?" Fear took a stab at Cody. He walked closer to his mother. "Who's chaperoning?"

"The teacher's in charge. Her name's Elle Dalton. She has eighteen students like Carl Joseph. Friday is Field Trip Day."

"One teacher?" Panic welled up inside him. "You let Carl Joseph go on a field trip with just one able-bodied person? Are you kidding?" He paced to the other end of the dining room and then back again. "Where'd they go?"

"To Antlers Park and to Subway." She set her pen down. "Relax, Cody. Your brother's been going on field trips every Friday for three months." His mother explained that Carl Joseph had been to shopping malls and a skating rink and the zoo. "He'll be fine."

"No, he won't." Cody tried to picture Carl Joseph crossing a city street. "Buddy gets confused. He has epilepsy. You know that. He could wander off and get lost, have a seizure, and then what? He doesn't even know his own phone number."

"He does now."

The conversation had gone in circles, but in the end he made his decision. He and Carl Joseph needed a day to themselves. They'd talked about it when he first got home from the circuit. Cody had even mentioned that Friday might work. And today was Friday—field trip or not.

Cody took a left turn now and eased off the gas. Cody had read something in an issue of *USA Today* at a hotel in Montana earlier that year—how there was a push among educators to help adults with Down Syndrome and other disabilities find functioning independent lives outside their family homes.

Cody had shuddered at the idea. Innocent, tender-hearted Carl Joseph out in the real world, being laughed at and mocked and getting lost in the rat race? He wouldn't survive three days in that environment. And with his epilepsy, the idea was unthinkable. His mother even agreed that they were contemplating pulling him from the program. One of the quotations in the article said it all.

"We must be careful," a person who disagreed with the program was quoted as saying. "Sometimes in our rush to minimize disability, we unwittingly place a handicapped person in danger. The simple truth is that people with mental disabilities are not able to live on their own without great risk."

Cody agreed wholeheartedly. He had asked his mother why Carl Joseph was still taking part in field trips when he could have a seizure at any moment.

"Elle will take care of him," she'd said. "Elle knows what to do."

But now he'd seen Elle. She couldn't stay at Carl Joseph's side, and even if she did she wouldn't be strong enough to catch him if he fell. One seizure and he could crack his head open.

"Brother?" Carl Joseph turned to him.

"What, Buddy?" Cody glanced over.

Carl Joseph, the one who never got mad at anyone, had been quiet since they left the Subway. Now he looked hurt. "You weren't very nice to my friends."

"I'm sorry."

"So then"—he licked his lips—"why, Brother? Why weren't you nice?"

"I was afraid." Cody pulled up at a stoplight and looked at Carl Joseph. "I don't like you out on the streets, Buddy. You could walk into traffic or wander off. You could have one of your spells. Do you understand?"

Carl Joseph looked straight ahead. "Green, Brother. Green means go. Red means stop. White walk sign means walk."

Cody stared at his brother, and only after someone behind them honked did he finally press his foot to the accelerator. "Where did you learn that?"

"From Teacher."

They didn't talk again until they reached the parking lot of the old YMCA. Rumor around town was that the owner wanted to sell it. The city had passed on buying it, so now the place was open to anyone with the money to take it over. Cody parked his truck and turned to Carl Joseph. "Tell me about the center, Buddy."

Carl Joseph took a long breath. He twisted his fingers together, the way he did when he was nervous. "It's for independent living."

"You said that earlier." Cody was careful to make his tone kind. He reached out and took one of his brother's hands. None of this was Carl Joseph's fault. "Don't be nervous. I'm not mad."

"You seemed mad." He licked his lips again. "At Daisy and Gus and Teacher and Sid and Tammy and—"

"I'm not mad, Buddy. Just please ...tell me about the center. Why ...why do you need to go on field trips?"

"Because, see ..." Carl Joseph looked out the window and then back at Cody. "Field trips get us closer to Goal Day."

"Goal Day?" Cody could feel his heart sinking inside him. There would be no goal day for a person as sick as Carl Joseph. "Tell me about it."

"Goal Day is when students move out and live on their own." Perspiration appeared on Carl Joseph's forehead. "All on their own. Independent living."

Cody felt sick to his stomach. So it was exactly what he'd feared. This Elle Dalton was running a program that had somehow taught Carl Joseph to believe something impossible for his future. "Is that what you want?" The blood drained from Cody's face. "To live away from Mom and Dad, out here in the world all by yourself? Even with these spells you've been having?"

"Uh ..." Carl Joseph began to rock. He looked at his feet and then held his hand up and examined it. "Yes. Buddy wants that."

For a moment Cody wasn't sure what to say. He'd already upset his brother. He had to undo this flawed way of thinking, the ridiculous and dangerous notions Carl Joseph had been taught at the center. But he had to do it in a way that didn't hurt his brother. Finally he squeezed Carl Joseph's hand. "Okay, Buddy. I understand." He hesitated. "We can talk about it later."

"Later." Carl Joseph nodded. He still looked uncertain, but he turned his eyes to Cody and smiled. "Goal Day can come later."

"Right." Cody's head was spinning. He wanted to get home as fast as possible and find his parents, confront them about how—since getting his recent diagnosis—they could possibly have allowed Carl Joseph to continue this way of thinking. He released his brother's hand, climbed out of the car, and went to Carl Joseph's side.

But before he got there, his brother climbed out and turned curious eyes in his direction. "Do you have your keys?"

"Yes." He held them up. What was this? Carl Joseph had never even comprehended the idea of keys before. When they went out on the town, Cody would open and close the door for him, helping him to the pavement and back into the car.

"Good." Carl Joseph pushed the lock button on his door and shut it. "You have to check first. Keys get locked in sometimes."

Cody was stunned. How much had his brother learned? Already more than Cody would've thought possible. They started to walk toward the building, and Cody focused on the reason they were here. "I'm thinking about buying this place."

"Really?" Carl Joseph was still trembling, still upset. But

he was clearly trying to move past the earlier incident, same as Cody. "Why, Brother?"

"It's a gym." Cody kept his pace even with Carl Joseph's. "I thought maybe I could turn it into an exercise facility for people like you and...and your friends."

"You think we need exercise?" Carl Joseph stopped. His eyes lit up. "Teacher thinks that, too. She makes us dance and do sit-ups and stretches."

Cody felt his anger rise again. The woman was taking over every area of his brother's life. And what good was coming from her exercise program? Carl Joseph was no more fit than he'd been last time Cody was home. His heart was no stronger. "Well." He kept his voice upbeat. "I think maybe you could use a little more exercise than that. A regular exercise program."

"Okay."

"Yeah, and maybe you'll like this place better than the center." He made a funny face at Carl Joseph. "Might make you big and strong."

"Like a bull rider?"

"Right. Exactly."

"Oh, goodie." They went inside and Cody met the owner at the front desk. "I called about the facility here. I'm interested in purchasing it."

"Yes." The man shook his hand. "Thanks for coming." He hesitated. "But I'm afraid the other owner and I haven't decided whether or not we're going to sell."

Cody was about to ask how much longer before the owners might know more, when he heard someone laughing.

He turned and saw Carl Joseph standing at a butterfly press machine, but instead of using it correctly, he was doing squats over the bench. A couple of scrawny guys in their thirties—long hair and pierced ears—had stopped to watch. One of them was pointing at Carl Joseph. "What's this—comic relief?"

"Yeah, since when do they let retards in?"

By the time Cody reached his side, Carl Joseph had brought his hands up and covered his face. Cody shoved the first guy he reached. "Leave him alone."

The guy had a beard and a mean face. He pushed Cody in return. "What's it to you?"

"That's my brother." Cody grabbed the guy's sweaty T-shirt. This time he pushed him hard enough that the guy fell to the floor.

At that point, the owner stepped up. "I'm going to have to ask you to leave." He took hold of Cody's arm. "The club is for members only."

"Club?" Cody jerked his arm free. "Place is a dive." He snarled at the bearded man, still scrambling up from the floor. "Bunch of lowlifes." He glared at the owner. "No wonder you're going bankrupt."

The two men started to go after Cody, but the owner held them back. Cody led Carl Joseph out the door and back to the car. This time he didn't bother opening his brother's door. As soon as they were inside, Cody let his head fall against the steering wheel. What was happening? Nothing was going the way he planned it.

"Brother?" Carl Joseph touched his arm. "I think I like the center better."

Cody lifted his head. "I'll bet you do." He straightened and turned toward his brother. "I'm sorry about that. Those guys..." He swallowed his anger so Carl Joseph wouldn't think it was directed at him. "Those guys have a problem, Buddy. I'm sorry."

"Maybe they don't have life skills." Carl Joseph reached back and grabbed his seatbelt. He buckled it as if he'd done so a hundred times before. "Life skills help."

"Yes." Cody started the engine. Who would stand up for Buddy the next time some ignorant jerk laughed at him? Who would come along and take his hands down from his face and help him past the situation? He reached over and patted his brother's knee. "Let's get home, okay?"

"Okay."

As they drove, Cody asked more questions about the center. "How does a student get ready for Goal Day? Can you tell me?"

Carl Joseph seemed less upset than before, but he was still nervous. As if he could sense that Cody's questions were being asked not merely out of mild interest but because Cody disapproved. "You have to know the bus routes."

"How to get on a bus, you mean?"

"No." Carl Joseph brought his hands together and began twisting them again. "You have to know that Route Number Eight goes to the Citadel Mall and that Route Ten goes downtown."

Again the shock was so great, Cody could barely concentrate on the road. "You know the bus routes?"

"Not..." Carl Joseph looked up at the ceiling and for a

long moment he moved his fingers against his hand like he was counting. "Not Bus Route Number Twenty-three or Twenty-five. Not Number Thirty-seven. Not Forty-one either."

"But you know the rest?"

"Not like Daisy knows them." He gave a weak smile. "Remember Daisy, Brother? She was at the Subway."

"Yes. She was nice." Cody clenched his fist. He'd been awful earlier. "I should've stayed and talked to her."

"Yes." Carl Joseph stopped twisting his hands. "She had a pretty shirt. You should've said she had a pretty shirt."

"Right." Cody stared at the road ahead. "Was the field trip fun? Before I came?"

"Yes. Gus wanted to ride a train."

"Through the park? I don't think there's a train that goes through Antlers Park."

"There isn't." Carl Joseph laughed. It wasn't as loud and carefree as usual, but at least it was a start, proof that he would recover from the events of the day—events that Cody knew he was completely responsible for.

Cody played along. "Okay, so why did Gus want to ride a train?"

"Because of the landmark at the middle of the park. Old Engine 168."

Carl Joseph was right. There was an old railroad car at the center of the park—something donated to the city ages ago. Cody looked at his brother, disbelieving. In all his life, he'd never had a conversation like this one with Carl Joseph. "Did someone explain that to Gus?"

"Yes." Carl Joseph rocked forward and laughed a little louder than before. "Sid told him, 'Look, no tracks.' And Teacher said, 'Read the sign.'"

This time Cody nearly hit the brakes. "You can read?"

"Not yet." Shame crept into his tone. "I'm learning my ABCs. Daisy's helping me."

"Daisy can read?"

"Daisy's a super-duper reader, Brother. She can read signs and bottles and recipes and *Adventures of Tom Sawyer.*"

The idea was entirely new to Cody. A person with Down Syndrome could learn to read? That wasn't what the teachers had told their mother back when Carl Joseph was in grade school. But since then...Cody wasn't sure. Was he that out of touch?

It all came together. Carl Joseph wasn't involved in the center by his own choosing. Someone had to have found the place and convinced him that independent living was a good idea.

And that person could only have been his father.

The truth brought with it a host of familiar feelings— anger and resentment toward the man. Cody had hated his father most of his life. Ali had brought them together after a lifetime of being apart. Ali, who thought family was too important to hold grudges and harbor hatred. But that didn't mean Cody had forgotten.

Cody was seven and Carl Joseph two when their father climbed into a yellow taxicab and drove off—all because he wasn't willing to raise a son with Down Syndrome. Cody spent the next decade living with the growing understanding that something was different about his little brother. His father had been mean and unfeeling to reject a boy like Carl Joseph. Cody's entire bull-riding career was driven by the rage inside him, a rage that took root that day when his father's cab pulled away. Yes, Ali had brought healing between the two of them. His dad was back, and his parents were happy together. But maybe his father was still embarrassed by Carl Joseph. Why else would Buddy be attending an independent-living center even with a diagnosis of epilepsy?

As Cody parked the car, he spotted his father's sedan. His dad was owner and manager of a restaurant—the same job he'd had since he moved home—and today he was home early. Cody was glad. He could hardly wait to talk to him. There were things he'd never said to the man once he returned, things that had seemed unimportant in light of everything with Ali. Back then Cody's days were too busy loving Ali, finding a way to soak a lifetime out of the three years they had together.

Cody climbed out of the car and waited for Carl Joseph to join him. He could already picture his father, sitting at the kitchen table with his mother, sharing a coffee break. What was he thinking, putting Carl Joseph's life at risk? And what had he been thinking all those years ago, when he climbed into that yellow cab and drove away? Carl Joseph never held any of it against their father. He was happy to see the man when he showed up again. But the things Cody had wanted to tell his father when it came to Carl Joseph stayed with him, stuffed in a corner of his heart.

And that was going to change in a few minutes.

Chapter Seven

Mary Gunner was aware that her world was about to be rocked.

She had called her husband minutes after Cody stormed out of the house. "There's trouble, Mike." She explained that Cody knew about the center, and that he was angry and scared about Carl Joseph being on his own. "Get home early."

Mike tried to downplay the brewing trouble. "Cody will get used to the idea, Mary. He has no say over Carl Joseph's future."

Mary did not like any sort of confrontation where Mike was concerned. They'd had more confrontation in their early years than most married couples had in a lifetime. Mike had played football in the NFL, and when an injury cut his career short, he found his ego best fed in the arms of other women.

When Mary learned the truth, she confronted him, ready

to forgive him if he was sorry, if he promised to change. But Mike wasn't ready to make promises. Instead he told her that he couldn't be a father to Carl Joseph, and with almost no warning or conversation, he took two suitcases and met a cab in front of their house. He left that day with Carl Joseph crying in her arms, and he had never looked back until seven years ago.

By then Mary and Carl Joseph had built a life on their own. They had a comfortable routine, and Mary had only one source of heartache—the way Mike's absence hurt her oldest son. Cody lived most of his years angry, and for that Mary ached day and night.

If it weren't for Ali, healing might never have happened at all. But like an angel sent from heaven, Ali had a way of making people around her see love where before only hatred existed.

Eventually Mike returned home—full of apologies and regret. And every day since then he'd been the model husband, loving her and caring for her, and making up for all the years they'd lost.

In Ali's presence, Cody couldn't stay angry. His painful feelings toward his father faded until finally there wasn't a trace of hatred left. Mike gave blood before Ali's lung transplant, and as Ali grew sicker, Cody and his father grew closer. When she died, Cody wept in his father's arms. The past seemed as distant as if it had happened to someone else.

Until this morning.

So when Mike made light of the situation, when he complained that he was supposed to stay through the dinner shift at the restaurant, she did what she almost never did. She pushed. "Mike, this is serious. More than you know. Please..."

Mike must've heard something in her voice, because he hesitated for only a moment. "Okay." His tone expressed his change of heart. "I'll be there."

And now here they were, waiting, when they heard Cody's car pull into the drive. They were silent, side by side on the living room sofa, as the garage door lifted, and they heard Cody pull the car in.

"I don't want to talk about this in front of Carl Joseph." Mike paced to the window. "He doesn't need to listen. It'll confuse him."

Mary studied her husband, amazed. Sometimes it was hard to believe that this was the same man who had walked out on them. "You're right." She went to meet her sons at the kitchen door leading to the garage.

Cody looked from her to Mike and back again. He opened his mouth to speak, but she held up her hand. "Wait." She turned to Carl Joseph and smiled. "How was your field trip?"

"Good." He gave Cody a nervous look. "Pretty good."

"Carl Joseph, could you do me a favor?"

"Sure." Her younger son stood a little taller. He loved being trusted with assignments from her.

"Okay." This was something new, something that had come as a result of the center. Before, Mary would've assumed Carl Joseph was capable of only the simplest jobs. Not anymore. "Could you go out back and clear the weeds from the flower garden? And then could you spray the fertilizer on the stems? I meant to do that earlier today"—she looked at Cody—"but I didn't get to it."

"Sure." Carl Joseph nodded. He headed toward the back door. On the way, he waved at Mike. "Hi, Dad. How are you?"

"Good, son." Mike was still standing by the window. "Did you see Daisy on your field trip?"

"Yes. We didn't get to dance in the park, though."

"Oh." Mike stuck his hands in his pockets. "I'm sorry about that. Maybe next time."

Cody shifted his position. Mary could feel his anger.

"Next time. Yes, maybe next time." Carl Joseph opened the slider and stepped onto the porch outside. "I'm gonna pull weeds for Mom and fertilize, okay?"

"Okay. Do a good job."

"I will." He smiled, and pride shone in his eyes. "I'll do my very best."

Mary wanted to follow him and pull him into her arms. The turmoil in their home wasn't his fault. And no matter how the doctor's recent diagnosis complicated things, Carl Joseph did want his independence. He'd been proving that ever since he started at the center. Mary returned to her spot beside Mike and braced herself for what was coming.

Cody waited until Carl Joseph was outside. Then he stepped into the living room and waved his hand at the sliding door. "You're trying to get rid of him. Is that it?"

"Lower your voice." Mike's tone was stern.

Mary could feel her husband's body tense up beside her.

As in all those years when Cody was growing up, it would be her role to keep her son's anger at bay. "No one's trying to get rid of Carl Joseph. That's not what this is about."

"Yes, it is!" Cody paced toward the patio slider and back again. "Independent living?" He laughed, but the sound was colored with fury. "That's like packing an eight-year-old's bags and sending him on his way." The muscles in his jaw flexed. "Carl Joseph is as gentle and innocent as a little kid. He has epilepsy. I mean, come on. You can't really think you're going to send him into the world and everything'll be okay."

"The center has a plan for each student, a list of goals that have to be met before the student is introduced to independent living." Mike was calmer now. He moved to the sofa and Mary followed. When they were seated, Mike put his arm over the back of the sofa and leaned into the cushions. "You haven't been around, Cody. You don't know how much this means to him."

"Oh, sure." Cody bent at the waist, his words directed at Mike like bullets. "It's not how much it means to Carl Joseph. It's how much it means to *you*, right, Dad? Big Mike Gunner, former NFL hotshot." He pointed at Mike. "You walked out on him because he wasn't like other kids. Remember?" Tears worked their way into Cody's voice.

"You're right." Mike leaned forward, his elbows on his knees. "I was young and ignorant, and I didn't know how to handle things."

Mary couldn't sit by and let Cody say these things. Not when Mike had so completely changed. "Things are different now. Your father loves Carl Joseph very much." She held her hand out toward Cody. "Can't you see? Both of us only want what's best for your brother. Whatever that is."

Cody let his hands fall to his sides. "I'll tell you what that is." He looked back toward the sliding glass door, out to the place where Carl Joseph was smiling and making his way around the garden, tossing weeds into a bucket. When he spoke again, Cody's words were squeezed through clenched teeth. "What's best is keeping him home where he can be happy and loved, where no one will laugh at him and call him a retard the way they did when we were out today. Where he'll be safe if he has a seizure, and he can get emergency medical help if he needs it." Cody's eyes were wet, and his emotion spilled into every word. "Carl Joseph is the most precious kid I know, but regardless of his age he's just a kid. Keep him home and protect him. Love him the way he deserves to be loved." Cody dragged the back of his hand across his cheek. "That's what's best for him." He hung his head and made both his hands into fists. Then he glared at Mike. "What do you have to say to that?"

Mike waited. He was calmer than Mary had ever seen him. "Are you finished?"

"Yes." Cody spat the word.

"Okay." Mike took a long breath. "First of all, everything we're doing for Carl Joseph these days is because we love him. We love him very much." Mike stood and went to the far window. He sat against the sill and faced Cody. "Have you watched your brother lately?"

Cody's voice rose. He pointed to the place where Carl

Joseph was still working. "I watched him cover his face and start rocking when the guys at the gym called him a retard. So, yes. I guess I've been watching him."

"Getting made fun of is part of life." Mike was unfazed. "I'm talking about his day-to-day activities, the way he lives now. Six months ago, your brother would struggle out of bed, drag himself to breakfast, and barely be able to feed himself when your mother set a plate of eggs in front of him. After breakfast he would curl up on the couch and watch cartoons for a few hours. He'd eat again and maybe walk outside to visit Ace. Then he'd play video games until lunch." Mike grabbed a quick breath. "After lunch he'd fall asleep watching Nickelodeon until I got home at five." Mike paused. "It wasn't much of a life, Cody. You have to admit."

"But he was safe and he was loved." Cody's response was immediate. He took a step closer to his father, his words filled with passion. "The doctor said he won't live very long, anyway. Another ten years, maybe. At least let him live it here, where he's loved. Where he has everything he needs."

Mike didn't blink. "He doesn't want that."

"No, of course not." Cody shook his head. "Not now that you've filled his head with impossible ideas."

"Cody." Mary leaned forward and waited for him to look at her. "What your father's saying is, Carl Joseph's not the same person he was back then."

"He's not." Mike looked out the back glass door and a smile tugged at the corners of his lips. "Even with the dangers of epilepsy, your brother gets up early now. He comes to the kitchen wanting to make his *own* eggs. He eats with table manners and then he helps with dishes. He talks about his friends at the center, the issues they're struggling with, and when he walks around this place he stands three inches taller than before." Mike turned his attention back to Cody. "You know why? Because he's proud of himself. He has a plan and a purpose. He's excited about life." He paused. "And you mean to tell me you'd deny your brother all of that?" He let out a single, frustrated laugh. "You're supposed to love him most of all."

"I do!" Cody shouted the words. Then he gritted his teeth and forced himself to lower his voice. "I love him the most because I love him the way he is. I don't need him to perform some sort of circus act in order to feel good about him."

"That's not fair, Cody." Mary went to him, but he pulled away. "You were with Carl Joseph today. Didn't you see how different he is? How he gets into a car by himself and buckles his own seatbelt? He has more to talk about, and he's excited about reading and getting around by himself. Didn't you see that?"

"And that's worth risking his life?" Cody stared at the ceiling for a moment and then back at her. "Okay, fine. Take him to the center and let him learn how to buckle his seatbelt. But don't fill his head with ideas about independence. Can you imagine it, Mom? Can you picture *Goal Day?*" Cody made the last two words sound ominous. He pointed to the entryway. "Carl Joseph packs his bag and walks out that door and what? He gets an apartment? He'll burn down his place or get hit by a car the first week, Mom! He'll have a seizure and choke on his dinner. It's insane."

"We understand the risks. More now, since our meeting with the doctor." Mike's expression fell. "Independent living might not be possible for Carl Joseph." His eyes lifted to Cody's. "But we have to try. It's what Carl Joseph wants."

Cody's anger eased some. "So maybe I can help him feel more independent. We can run errands together and he can keep taking classes—so long as he doesn't make a plan to move out."

"We've thought about that. We're even thinking about taking him out of the center." The struggle they'd been living through was evident in Mike's voice. "But that's not what Carl Joseph wants."

"Of course he wants the center." Cody's tone softened. "He thinks it'll make you happy. If you asked him to drive the car out onto the interstate, he'd do that, too. Whatever it takes to get your approval. But here's the problem. Carl Joseph doesn't know how dangerous this is. He's trusting you." He looked from Mike to Mary. "And you. And that Elle Dalton teacher of his. He's a kid. He doesn't know the difference. He's believing the adults around him, with no idea what independent living really means."

For the first time, Mike didn't have a response. He hung his head, and when he looked up, his focus returned to Carl Joseph working outside.

Before he could think of something to say, Cody crossed his arms. "I'm sorry for my temper. It's been a long day." He headed for the front door, but then he stopped. "Please... think about the doctor's diagnosis. Don't let Carl Joseph dream about something that can never happen. I love that kid." His voice broke. "I love him too much to see him hurt."

When he was gone, Mike pulled Mary into a hug. "What're we supposed to do?"

She searched his eyes. "Maybe it's time to pull him out."

Mike was quiet for a minute. "Elle's been doing research on people with Down Syndrome and epilepsy living on their own, right?"

"That's what she said."

"So we can't pull him out yet. Not while there's still a chance he could reach his goal."

Mary wasn't sure, but she didn't want to talk about it anymore. She leaned up and kissed his cheek. "Okay, Mike." She eased back. "I'm going for a walk."

He looked over his shoulder. "I'll be outside with Carl Joseph."

Mary nodded, but only because she couldn't speak. If she did, the torrent of tears building inside her would release for sure and she wouldn't have any strength left to make it to the front door.

On the way out, her eyes fell on a picture of Carl Joseph at age twelve, back when she knew without a doubt what was best for her son. His past, his present, and everything about his future. Back when independent living for a child like Carl Joseph would've been absolutely ridiculous.

The way maybe it still was today.

Chapter Eight

When Mary stepped outside, she looked around for Cody, but her oldest son was gone. Probably jogged back to his house on the other side of the property. She sighed and began walking toward the long, winding driveway. When she needed to think, this was where she went. She would set off down the drive and then right and up the hill to the end of the road. The area was wide open with only a few clusters of pine trees and mesquite bushes and enough sky to clear her head.

But today she kept her eyes down, and for the first few minutes she replayed everything Cody had just said. It was easy to mistake Cody for an angry man with no willingness to bend, opinionated, always thinking he was right. But that wasn't the true Cody.

Cody wasn't trying to be right or strong-headed. He loved Carl Joseph. For most of his childhood and adolescence he cared more about his little brother than he did about anyone else. He was Carl Joseph's friend and mentor, and together those two boys had filled her heart with joy.

When Cody first started riding bulls, he'd come home every few weeks and Carl Joseph would be waiting for him at the door, a big, wide grin on his face. He'd fling open his arms and run toward Cody. "Brother! You came back, Brother!"

Mary felt tears in her eyes and sniffed. She could hear him still, the joy in his voice, the anticipation whenever Cody came home. Almost always, Cody would bring video from the rodeo events, and he and Carl Joseph would sit in front of the TV watching Cody's rides over and over and over again. "You're a good bull rider, Brother. Very, very good!"

Even now, Carl Joseph wanted nothing more than to be a bull rider like Cody. Yes, because Daisy was impressed by the idea. But also because it would make him a little bit more like the brother he idolized. Four years ago, when Ali died, Carl Joseph brought Cody more comfort than all the rest of his friends and family combined. Carl Joseph was the one who pulled Cody aside at Ali's funeral and pointed toward heaven. "You know what I think, Brother?" he said as he put his arm around Cody's shoulders. "I think up there in heaven Ali has the fastest, most beautiful horse of all."

Mary had been standing close enough to hear the conversation. "Yeah, Buddy. Maybe you're right." Cody looked up, his eyes filled with pain.

"I am right, Brother. God would definitely give Ali a horse in heaven."

It was the first time that terrible day that Mary saw Cody

smile. Because Carl Joseph had known exactly what Cody needed to hear in the wake of such a devastating loss.

Of course Cody didn't want anything to happen to Carl Joseph—none of them did. But was that reason enough to hold him back, to keep him home in front of a television when there was a chance he could manage his epilepsy and heart disease on his own? Mike was right about the changes in Carl Joseph.

Mary hugged herself and slowed her pace. This was never how she'd pictured things going with Carl Joseph, not since the day she first held him.

Mary reached the end of the driveway and turned right. As she did, as she faced the long hill before her, the years disappeared and she was there again, in the hospital, celebrating one of the happiest days in her life—the birth of her second son.

The day they laid Carl Joseph in her arms, Mary knew something was different about him. His cry was different from Cody's, and his neck looked shorter and thicker. The thought of Down Syndrome crossed her mind—because she remembered once during her pregnancy, when she'd stopped to admire a newborn in the grocery store with her mother. Conversation between Mary and the woman lasted the better part of thirty minutes, and at the end, the woman stroked her baby's forehead. "She has Down Syndrome. The doctors think she'll need to be institutionalized." Tears glistened in the woman's eyes. "But I won't let that happen. Not to my little girl."

The scene had terrified Mary and plagued her for the

next week. But then she let the possibility go. She wouldn't have a child with Down Syndrome. It wasn't something that ran in her family, and besides, she was taking great care of herself. Her child would be even healthier and stronger than Cody, because she knew more about being a mother the second time around.

But that day in her hospital bed, looking down at Carl Joseph, the fears returned. What if there was something wrong with him, something that would affect him all his life? She shuddered at the thought. Her baby was perfect. Beautiful and whole and healthy, no matter what doubts plagued her.

Not until the end of his first week did doctors do a blood test to confirm her fears. Carl Joseph had Down Syndrome; there was no doubt. One in a thousand babies were born with the chromosomal defect, and in this case, he was that one. He had an extra chromosome 21.

The doctor went on to say that had Mary submitted to an amniocentesis, they might've found out about the birth defect sooner. "Then"—the doctor pursed his lips—"you might've had options."

"Options?" Anger flooded Mary's veins. "You mean abortion? I could've aborted my baby if I'd known—is that what you're saying?"

"Just a minute." The doctor held up his hand. "I'm only saying I advise all my patients to have an amnio. You declined." He looked at Carl Joseph. "Now your options are far more limited."

"Look"—Mary pointed to the door—"you can leave

now. I never...never would've aborted Carl Joseph just because he isn't like other children. And I never want to see you in this room again."

The doctor left, and Mary sat in her bed trembling. The baby in her arms looked up at her, all innocence and tenderness and love, and Mary realized something. This child needed her more than Cody ever had. "You're a miracle, little Carl Joseph. A miracle from God. Everything's going to be okay."

She cooed and kissed Carl Joseph's cheeks until an hour later when a new doctor entered the room, a man with kind eyes and a gentle manner.

"I'm Dr. West," he told her. "I understand you've heard the news about your little boy."

"Yes." She didn't realize it until that moment, but she had tears on her cheeks.

"Your son will always be different, but that doesn't mean he won't bring a great deal of love into your life."

"Are you...are you recommending an institution?" The thought horrified her. She couldn't imagine taking her baby home, feeding him and holding him and rocking him, all so when he was three or four years old she could drive him to some brick building and say good-bye.

She didn't wait for Dr. West's response. "I can't put him in an institution, Doctor. I can't do it."

Dr. West put his hand on her shoulder. "I wasn't going to recommend that. That's an old way of thinking, the idea of institutionalizing children with Down Syndrome. Now most doctors will tell you to take your baby home and love him. You feed him and read to him and cuddle him."

"Until…" She wasn't sure she understood.

"Indefinitely." Dr. West smiled. "Having a child with Down Syndrome is like having a child that will never grow up. Your baby, Mrs. Gunner, will level off in cognitive thinking and social interaction at about the age of a second grader. He won't learn to read or write or live on his own. But these days, we're finding that children with Down Syndrome who are allowed to live at home live longer than those who are placed in institutions." He opened the folder in his hands and studied the information inside. "Carl Joseph has a healthy heart for now. He could live into his forties, if things go well for him."

The doctor talked to her for a few more minutes. Then he smiled and patted Carl Joseph's head. "You and your baby need some time alone."

"Yes." She held Carl Joseph closer. "Thank you."

After Dr. West left, Mary wept over her tiny baby. He would never talk clearly or walk normally, and he wouldn't look like other children. He wouldn't have a first day of kindergarten, and he'd never play high school football. He wouldn't graduate and he wouldn't have a career goal. He'd never fall in love.

But he would be hers forever.

And as her tears fell that day, she felt herself bonding to Carl Joseph as she'd never connected to anyone or anything in her life. Mike spent much of his time away from home, and Cody was independent from the moment he could walk. But Carl Joseph…Carl Joseph might have Down Syndrome, but he would be hers and always hers. Forever and ever.

Now as she walked away from the house, images from that day filled Mary's heart and overflowed into her soul. She kicked at a few loose pebbles as she made her way up the hill. After Mike left all those years ago, her feelings for Carl Joseph only grew stronger. She protected him from strange glances and mean comments, and she made sure he never wanted for anything. If he needed his shoes tied, she tied them. If he wanted breakfast, she made it. She waited on him and looked after him and treasured the times when they cuddled together in front of the television. When he left for his special school on the short bus, she thought about him constantly until he returned home safely.

School taught Carl Joseph very little, as it turned out. He learned to color and stack blocks and how to share a puzzle during carpet time. But after a few years it became clear to Mary that special education—at least at their small-town school—was little more than glorified babysitting. She pulled Carl Joseph out after fifth grade.

When Mike's child support wasn't enough to pay the bills, Mary took a night job. And throughout those years she comforted herself with the truth that was a balm to her hurting heart: Carl Joseph would always be hers. That was the balm. Never once during Carl Joseph's childhood or teenage years had she ever considered that he might want to move out on his own one day.

She slowed her pace. Independent living was Mike's idea, of course. Cody was right about that part. But not for the reasons Cody guessed. Mike was not embarrassed by Carl Joseph, nor did he want their youngest son to achieve great things to make the two of them feel better about having a handicapped son.

After Mike returned to their lives, it took only a few weeks before he came to her on the front porch one day. His eyes were red, his cheeks tearstained. "Mary, I'm sorry."

She looked long and deep into his eyes. "About what?"

"About all I've missed." He coughed, struggling with his words. "I'm so sorry. I never...never should've left."

"Aw, baby." She put her arms around his waist. "You've already told me that a dozen times. It's okay. We're together now; everything's different."

"But..." He fought back another bit of sorrow. "I haven't told you how sorry I am about Carl Joseph. I ran from him, the affairs, the other women. I was always running away from Carl Joseph. When...when I should've run *to* him. I should've embraced him." He pressed his fist to his chest. "That kid has worked his way in here so fast it makes my head spin. He's wonderful, Mary. I love everything about him."

Mary blinked and remembered how it felt to hear those words, how it made her want to shout to the heavens that finally Mike understood how wonderful it was to have Carl Joseph as a son. Mike had missed so much, all the years when Carl Joseph's wonderment at the world around him was enough to make Mary see all of life through new eyes.

She reached the top of the hill and looked out over the fields. Ever since that day, Mike had grown more and more attached to Carl Joseph. But Mike was also busy, making a name for himself in the restaurant business. When Cody was home, Carl Joseph never left his side. And Mike was usually at the restaurant. It would've been easy for Cody to miss how close Carl Joseph and Mike had become.

But that didn't change the facts.

The idea of independent living came up quite innocently. One day after work, Mike went to the doctor for a checkup. When he came home that evening, his eyes were shining. He handed her a brochure. "Read this." His voice held a sense of awe. "I had no idea."

Mary looked at the flyer. Written across the top it said, *Independent Living Center—give your disabled child every chance for a bright future.*

She drew a deep breath and closed her eyes. Never in a million years would she forget how she felt in that moment. Her heart skipped a beat, and she almost handed the pamphlet back to Mike, almost told him to rip it in half and never mention the words "independent living" again.

She'd heard of such a thing more than once in the years leading up to that moment. She'd heard about it, and every time she'd felt sick to her stomach. Carl Joseph, independent? The boy would be lost in the world without her, without the safety and security of the home she'd made for him.

But with Mike standing there, she had no choice. She read about the full-time program offered at the center, and the testimonials from family members of people with Down Syndrome. How they were grateful to the center for giving their son or daughter a chance at the sort of life everyone deserved.

Mary wanted to scream at those parents. At first, she'd felt the same way Cody felt, that a child with Down Syndrome couldn't possibly understand what he did or didn't deserve. The entire idea felt like something created by able-bodied people and from the viewpoint of able-bodied people. A program that tried to force people with Down Syndrome into a mold that seemed normal and acceptable to people without disabilities.

But it was the photo on the inside page that caught her attention. There, smiling bigger than life, was a young man with Down Syndrome. Beneath his picture it said, "I'm a man now, not a little kid. This is my life. All my dreams are coming true—Gus, Age 22."

Mary stared at that photograph, and everything she'd believed about her life with Carl Joseph began to crumble before her eyes. Was this the life Carl Joseph deserved, the one she'd unwittingly denied him?

Mary stared at the brochure for a long time. Then she handed it back to Mike and in a voice pinched with emotion, she said, "Let's talk to Carl Joseph."

Mike had done the talking when they brought the topic up to Carl Joseph later that night. Mike explained that maybe it was time for Carl Joseph to attend adult school, time to learn how to handle money and take the bus places. Maybe even time to get a job.

Carl Joseph took a minute or so to absorb what was being said. But as it all started to click, he sat up and looked from Mike to Mary. "You mean…I get to be a man like Daddy?"

What was left of Mary's doubts fell away in that instant. She crossed the room and knelt in front of Carl Joseph. Then she put her arms around him and hugged him. Independent living was the most terrifying thing she could imagine. But if it made Carl Joseph feel like a man, how could she possibly deny him the chance?

They enrolled him at the center the next morning.

Mary smiled at the memory. Gus was one of Carl Joseph's friends now, someone who was also working very hard toward his Goal Day.

She reached the bottom of the hill and turned left into their driveway. There, standing on the front porch, was Carl Joseph, his hand shading his eyes. "Mom?" he shouted.

She was too far away to yell back, but she waved at him, big so he could see. With that he hopped down from the porch and ran to her. Mary stopped and admired him. He did not run with the grace of an able-bodied person, but he ran with gusto and determination, huffing and puffing as he came. When he reached her, he stopped and fell into place beside her. "Hi, Mom." He gave her a big, open-mouthed smile.

"Hi, Carl Joseph." Mary swallowed her sadness. Never mind Cody's anger. What they were doing was right—as long as they could feel safe about Carl Joseph's epilepsy treatment. The classes were helping Carl Joseph feel good about himself and good about life. "Did you finish weeding?"

"Yes." He spread his arms out wide. "I did the whole thing. All of it."

"Good." She nodded. "You're a hard worker, Carl Joseph."

"I am." He stuck out his chest. "Teacher says I can have a real job by Christmastime."

"Really?" A chill ran down her arms. "By Christmastime?"

"Yes." He held up one hand and made an exaggerated show of counting, his brow knit in concentration. "Seven months, Mom. It'll happen in seven months." He laughed out loud, the excited laugh of a child. "Then I'll be almost ready for Goal Day."

She hid her fears. "That'll be exciting."

He moved closer and took hold of her hand. "It's okay if I hold your hand still, right, Mom? Even if I'm a man?"

"Yes." She felt her heart melt. "Of course. It'll always be okay."

"Good." They walked for a few seconds in silence. Then Carl Joseph turned to her. "I'm not sure about Cody."

Mary smiled. "Me, either."

"'Cause you wanna know why?" Carl Joseph's smile faded. Concern filled the lines in his forehead.

"Why?"

"'Cause he was mad at Teacher today." He shifted his jaw to one side and looked away. "He was mad at my friends, too."

"Mad at them?" As difficult as the idea of Carl Joseph's independent living was for Cody, Mary couldn't picture him being rude to his brother's friends.

"He came into Subway and said I had to go. He said it was crazy."

"What was crazy?"

"Something Daisy said." Carl Joseph wrinkled his brow a little more. "He said it was crazy."

"Oh." Mary wasn't sure she understood, but that wasn't

the point. Carl Joseph had always been perceptive about people's feelings, and this was no different. If Cody was upset, Carl Joseph was bound to pick up on it and feel confused. "Well, honey, I don't think he thought you or Daisy were crazy."

"Maybe the field trip."

"Maybe."

"'Cause know what I think?" They were almost to the house. Carl Joseph peered at the porch as if he was looking for Cody.

"What?"

"I think Cody's heart needs fixing again." Carl Joseph stopped and turned to her. His eyes were very serious. "The way it did before he met Ali, the horse rider."

"Yes, maybe that's it." Mary felt a familiar sadness. Ali had been so good for Cody. She had taught him to love when it didn't seem—outside his feelings for his brother—that he'd ever learn. And now, the best thing for him would be to meet another girl, to find those feelings once more. But it would be easier for Carl Joseph to earn his independence than for Cody to fall in love again. She took Carl Joseph's other hand. "How can we help fix Cody's heart?"

"We can pray." Carl Joseph gave a series of small nods. "We can close our eyes and pray to Jesus."

Though once in a while Mary would pray in the quiet of her heart, prayer wasn't mentioned around the Gunner household with any consistency. She smiled at her youngest son. "Okay, honey. You go ahead and pray."

"Close your eyes." Carl Joseph waited until she'd closed

them. "Okay. Dear God, here I am. Carl Joseph Gunner. This time I have a prayer for Brother. His name is Cody. Please help him…" He hesitated, as if he were trying to remember what help Cody needed. When he spoke again, his words were rushed and so thick it was hard to understand him. "Oh, yes! Please help him have a fixed heart. So he isn't mad at me and my friends, and so he doesn't say it's crazy. Amen."

He squeezed Mary's hands and she opened her eyes. "That was wonderful, Carl Joseph." Mary pulled him close and hugged him. "How did you learn to pray like that?"

They began walking toward the house again. Carl Joseph shrugged. "It's a life skill. Teacher says we can't be independent if we don't know how to talk to God."

"Of course." Mary could barely draw a breath. Carl Joseph went into the house, but she stayed outside on the porch. Prayer, a life skill? She sat on the glider a few feet from the door and stared at the distant mountains. Her fears about Carl Joseph's independent living had always seemed to be about him. She was afraid he wouldn't survive without her. But maybe she wasn't really worried about how Carl Joseph would do without her.

She was worried about how she would do without Carl Joseph.

Which was exactly how Cody was feeling. Now it would be up to her oldest son to see that, too. Because not until Cody understood his own fears would he stop fighting the idea of Carl Joseph's independence and do the one thing Carl Joseph wanted his brother to do.

Let him go.

Chapter Nine

All weekend, Cody ran from his anger. He didn't want to talk to his parents, didn't want to go online and look at studies about independent living or hear testimonials from other people with Down Syndrome. He wanted his brother to stay the way he used to be. Safe and loved and accounted for, without any threat of a life that could bring him harm.

So he spent the weekend with Carl Joseph.

Saturday morning he helped his brother onto Ace and led him around the arena.

"This is a start, right, Brother? Every bull rider starts on a horse, right?"

"Right." He patted Carl Joseph's leg as they walked. "Not everyone who gets on a horse can get on a bull, though. You know that, right?"

Carl Joseph didn't hesitate. "But I will." He grinned. "Daisy likes bull riders."

Cody tried another approach. "But you need a bull first."

That stopped Carl Joseph cold. He frowned, and as he did, he pulled back on the reins. Ace stopped sharply, irritated.

"Buddy, let up. You shouldn't pull back so hard."

"Right." Carl Joseph relaxed his hold. "Sorry." He gave Cody a concerned look. "Where are we gonna get a bull?"

"We might not get one." Cody had to be honest. "But that's okay. Know why?"

"Why?" Disappointment rang in Carl Joseph's voice. "Daisy likes bull riders."

"Yeah, but Daisy likes cowboys, too, right? Wasn't that what you told me?"

"Yes."

"Okay, so see!" He took a step to the side and waved his hand at the picture Carl Joseph made atop the horse. "You're already a cowboy. So she'll already like you."

"Oh." Carl Joseph pondered that for a moment. "I never thought about how she already likes me."

"Yeah, Buddy."

"But, Brother"—he knit his brow together, his lips slightly open—"are you still mad at me?" He had asked the question ten times on Saturday alone.

Cody sighed and gripped Carl Joseph's knee. "No, Buddy. I'm not mad, remember? I was never mad."

"But you said it was crazy."

"I was wrong. I'm sorry." He tightened his hold on the lead rope and tried to think of another way to make his brother understand. "I was having a bad day. That's all."

"Oh." Carl Joseph sounded relieved. He faced straight ahead. "Bad days happen."

"Yes, Buddy. Bad days happen."

"Like when Ali died. Ali the horse rider."

"Yes." Cody swallowed back the pain. He patted Ace. "Yes, Buddy—like that."

After riding horses that day, they watched old footage of Cody's bull-riding days, and then they settled in for back-to-back movies, one of their favorite ways of spending a day together. By Sunday afternoon, Carl Joseph was no longer asking whether Cody was mad or not. It was a victory, and Cody promised himself he would never again act in such a way as to make Carl Joseph doubt him.

But that didn't mean he was going to sit by and let his brother be pulled along toward some sort of crazy idea of living on his own. He would keep warning his parents of the dangers, begging them to remove Carl Joseph from the center. And he would make the appointment with the teacher— so he could explain his fears in person. When Monday came, he showered and dressed and appeared at the breakfast table, relaxed and smiling.

He hadn't said more than a few words to his parents all weekend, so his mother gave him a wary glance. "You look nice."

"Thanks." He dished himself a bowl of oatmeal and took the seat next to Carl Joseph. The smell of his brother's cologne was so strong he could taste it, but he didn't say anything. Instead he smiled. "Buddy and I are going to school together today."

Carl Joseph looked at Cody for a long moment and then dropped his eyes to his oatmeal. "Right," he muttered. "Me and Brother are going to school together."

"Really?" Their mother gave Cody a disapproving look. But when Carl Joseph turned his attention to her, she smiled. "I...I didn't know that."

"Well, we are." Cody kept his tone upbeat. "He's going to show me what they do at the center."

"That's not crazy." Carl Joseph cast an innocent look at their mother. "Right, Mom?"

"Right. Not at all."

She waited until they were finished eating. Then she stood and turned to Cody. "I'd like to talk to you for a minute, please."

"I have to brush my teeth." Carl Joseph cleared his bowl, rinsed it in the sink, and loaded it into the dishwasher. He didn't clank his dish or drop anything or let the water run too long. He waved at them and headed down the hall. "Teeth need brushing."

When he was gone, Cody turned to his mother. "I know what you're going to say. But it's my right to go. His teacher asked me to come in before class and talk with her. I want to hear her thoughts on epilepsy." He walked a few steps toward the dining room, and then back again. "I want her to know that we're all worried."

She looked distraught. "Maybe she'll tell you her plan. She has a way she thinks it could work. Carl Joseph living in a group home, taking medicine for his seizures."

"No." Cody said the word a little too loud. He had to keep a grip on his temper. "You can't let that happen." He went to her and gently took her hand. "You and Dad need to get him out of that center. It's only going to hurt him when he can't reach Goal Day. And clearly he can't." He paused, quieter than before. "That's what the doctor said, right?"

His mother had never come right out and said so. But now she looked down and after a few seconds she nodded. "Yes. The doctor doesn't think it's possible."

Cody felt the weight of Carl Joseph's disappointment. He gestured down the hall where Carl Joseph had gone. "Think how hard it's going to be for him, Mom. When he finds out he can't live on his own."

Cody took a breath. "Even if Carl Joseph could manage his epilepsy on his own, he couldn't live by himself. He couldn't live in a group home without people helping him every hour of the day." He looked down the hallway toward Carl Joseph's room again. "I want to see what this Elle Dalton is teaching them. Let me see a person with Down Syndrome who can manage all those things, and maybe I'll feel differently."

His mother held his gaze for a long time. "Okay. Go, then. But your brother's already nervous. He knows you're not going just because you're interested." She let loose a sad sigh. "He senses everything you feel, Cody. Don't forget that."

"I won't." Cody allowed his tone to soften. "I don't want to fight. It's Dad who wants Carl Joseph out of the house, not you."

"No." She shook her head. "You're wrong." Her voice rang with sincerity. "I see what the center has done for Carl Joseph, how it's made him happier." She paused. "I want it, too, Cody. Don't make this a battle with your father. We're both in this."

Cody could hear Carl Joseph coming. He didn't want anything to trouble his brother that morning. "Okay." He leaned in and kissed her cheek. "I'll try to remember that."

"Good."

They spent the next half hour getting ready. Carl Joseph needed to bring a bag of flour and a bottle of vanilla to class, because Monday was Cooking Day. "We're making shortcake, Brother," he said as he rummaged through the kitchen. "Everyone loves shortcake. People at Disneyland love shortcake."

"Disneyland?" Cody stood back and let his brother do the work. If he wanted to be independent, he needed to be able to locate ingredients in the kitchen.

"Yes." Carl Joseph heaved a bag of flour onto the counter. He looked intently at the label. "F-l-o-u-r. Flour." He turned to Cody. "Teacher said she had strawberry shortcake at Disneyland once."

Carl Joseph set the ingredients in a paper bag, grabbed his backpack, and grinned at Cody. "Time for school."

The drive to the center took fifteen minutes. The whole time Cody wrestled with his purpose for going. He didn't care if Carl Joseph knew how to make shortcake. How would that keep him from getting lost or running out of food? How would it help him know how to handle a seizure by himself? What was Elle Dalton teaching her students that would keep them from getting run down by a car on their way out the door of a grocery store?

As they walked up to the center, Carl Joseph twisted his hands together. He stopped just as he reached the door. "Brother, you're not mad?"

"No, Buddy." Cody hugged his brother's shoulders. "I'm not."

Carl Joseph didn't look sure. But he nodded anyway. "Good."

"Let's go in, okay?" Cody was suddenly anxious to let the teacher know he was there.

"Okay, right. Let's go in." Carl Joseph opened the door and led the way.

Inside the room was full-blown chaos. Loud music filled the place, and even louder voices and laughter. There were more than a dozen young adults with Down Syndrome— the same students who had been on the Subway field trip. A few were sitting on an old sofa, talking animatedly to each other, and three others were huddled over a stuffed turtle, laughing their heads off.

In another corner of the room were Daisy and three students, all of them swaying and twirling and clapping to various rhythms in the loud music. An able-bodied older woman was talking with two students at the far end of the room, but no one seemed to be in charge.

Carl Joseph gave him a nervous look. "Free time comes first."

Cody could barely hear him. "I see that." He was about to find a seat where he wouldn't be noticed, when Daisy spotted him.

Her eyes grew wide and her mouth came all the way open. "Carl Joseph brought his brother to class!" She skipped toward Cody, took his hand, and began pumping it. "I'm Daisy. Remember me?"

"Yes." Cody was very comfortable around Carl Joseph. When he looked at his brother, he never saw a handicapped person, but only the kid who adored him. But he didn't know Daisy. He tried to hide his discomfort. "I remember you, Daisy."

She came closer and made a dramatic show of smelling him. Then she nodded her head at Carl Joseph. "You're right, CJ. He smells like a bull rider, same as you."

The other students gradually stopped whatever they'd been doing and gathered around Cody and Carl Joseph. One stepped up, his expression blank. "I'm Gus."

"Hi, Gus." Cody shook his hand.

"So you like us now? But not the other day?" Gus looked at the other students around him. "Carl Joseph's brother doesn't like us, that's what we said at Subway."

"I liked you then, too." He laughed, but it sounded weak. "I was in a hurry the other day. I'm sorry about that."

"We prayed for you." A girl with long brown braids waved her hand. "You might not have life skills so we prayed."

Cody felt his cheeks grow hot. The entire class had prayed for him because he didn't have the life skills to be cordial? That had to be Elle Dalton's doing. He was about to ask where she was, when he spotted her near a doorway at the back of the room. Her eyes met his, but she directed her words to the students. "Okay, everyone. Let's give our visitor some space." She turned off the music and moved to a section of the room with two rows of chairs and an oversized blackboard. "We're getting a new bus route today. Everyone find your seats."

She held Cody's eyes a little longer and then turned to her students, making small talk with them. As Cody watched her, something inside him stirred. She was the enemy, no doubt. She was willing to risk Carl Joseph's life to see her idea of independence played out. But there was no denying that she cared for her students. She took time with each of them, speaking to them at an adult level instead of talking down to them the way people did who weren't used to being around someone with Down Syndrome. And from his place by the door, Cody couldn't help but notice something else.

Elle Dalton was beautiful. Breathtaking, even.

Not in the way some girls were, with flashy clothes and makeup and jewelry. She had a quiet beauty about her, and something that could only have come from inside. Cody clenched his teeth and turned away. None of that mattered. He wasn't here to admire her.

Cody turned his attention to his brother. Carl Joseph was sitting next to Daisy, talking with his hands. His cheeks were red and his smile took up his entire face. Cody realized what was happening. Carl Joseph didn't come to the center to learn about independence. He came because of Daisy. This was his first crush, and that was innocent enough. He watched his brother for another minute, watched him play with Daisy's hair and her hands. It might be innocent, but where could it possibly lead?

He shifted, and without meaning to, his eyes returned to Elle, to the graceful way she moved in and out of the rows of students, speaking to each of them. Finally she took her spot at the front of the area. "Everyone turn to a partner and go over the details of Bus Route Eleven, the one we used last week on our field trip."

"Subway eat fresh!" The girl in braids stood up and grinned with the proclamation. She clapped her hands the way Carl Joseph sometimes did. Fast and loud, with her hands raised up close to her face. "Subway field trip. Eat fresh."

"Thank you, Tammy." Elle wasn't flustered by the student's outburst. "Please sit back down and turn to your partner."

Cody watched Carl Joseph turn to Daisy and take her hands. In that moment Cody saw something in his brother's eyes he'd never seen before. The sort of adoration and puppy love that indicated he was right about Carl Joseph. His brother was completely taken by the girl.

Great, he thought. Carl Joseph would never give up the idea of living on his own if it meant letting go of Daisy.

As soon as the students were busy, Elle said something to the older woman—who was obviously an aide or an assistant. Then Elle walked over to him. The kindness he'd seen in her eyes a few minutes ago was gone. She never broke eye contact as she approached, and when she reached him, she nodded to the door. "I'd like to speak with *you* outside, Mr. Gunner."

He followed her. What was this about? She had no reason to be angry with him. Not yet, anyway.

When the door shut behind them, Elle put her hands on her hips. "I didn't appreciate the way you disrupted our field trip last week."

"Yeah, well." He forced himself to stay focused. He wasn't angry, but his frustration was rising. "If all it takes is an unexpected visit from me to disrupt things, maybe you shouldn't be taking field trips."

Elle searched his eyes. "What exactly is your problem? The entire class felt bad after you left."

Cody fought his emotions. Guilt and shame and anger and confusion. He looked down and rubbed the back of his neck. He clenched his jaw. "I heard. I'm sorry." Cody met her eyes, and he felt his breath catch in his throat. Even angry, her hazel eyes were gorgeous. He had to work to remember his point. A grin tugged at his lips. He didn't want to fight with Elle Dalton. He only wanted Buddy home where he belonged. "You asked the whole class to pray for me, right? You told them I didn't have the right sort of life skills."

Elle's anger dimmed, but only a little. "Based on my limited experience, you don't."

Cody wasn't sure what to say. And his attraction to Buddy's teacher was irritating. He pursed his lips and inhaled sharply through his nose. He pointed at the classroom. "What you're teaching those young people isn't right for all of them."

"I disagree." Her eyes flashed, indignant.

"Okay." He held up his hands and took a step back. "I'd like permission to watch class today, but I have to be honest. My goal is to have Carl Joseph removed from your program as soon as possible."

The anger in Elle's face became sadness. "You're serious?"

"Yes. This morning Carl Joseph said something about making shortcake."

"Monday's Cooking Day." Elle held her ground. Her gaze didn't waver.

"And how, Ms. Dalton"—he leaned against the stucco wall and slipped his hands into his jeans pockets—"will making shortcake help Carl Joseph when he's lost on a bus route somewhere? When he's bagging groceries at the market and someone calls him a name or pushes him or confuses him? Is he supposed to whip up a batch of shortcake then? Or maybe drop down on his knees and start praying? Is that your answer?"

Elle looked at him for a long time. The emotions in her eyes changed from outrage to hurt, and finally to quiet resignation. "I can see I have a lot of work ahead."

"No work, Ms. Dalton. I'll sit in the back and keep to myself. Don't change your routine for me."

"I won't work to impress you." She lifted her chin, pride smoothing out the concern in her face. "I'll work to convince you. Because you're wrong. And before you and I are through, you'll see that for yourself. I promise."

"Is that right?" Cody wanted to laugh at her spunk. If things had been different, if life had been different, he might've been drawn to Elle Dalton. But even if he had room in his heart to love another woman, it wouldn't be the arrogant young teacher standing before him.

She took a step toward the door. "I know what you're thinking, Mr. Gunner."

"You don't know the first thing about me." He gave her a lazy grin. Why did he have to find her so attractive? She was the single reason their home was in turmoil. He reminded himself to focus on that, and not the way her hazel eyes caught the morning sunlight.

She lingered at the door for a moment. "I'm not the only one intent on proving something here, right?"

"Exactly." His tone grew more serious. "Independence is more than being able to eat at a Subway, Ms. Dalton."

She gave him a final look and then returned to her students. His heart was pounding as he followed her into the room and took a seat near the door. The longer he watched Elle, her gentle way and patient voice, the more he felt convinced that he'd pegged her wrong. She wasn't the enemy. She was a confused do-gooder. Someone whose intentions were right, but whose ideas were way off.

So maybe he wouldn't ask his parents to pull Carl Joseph from the class after watching for just a day. Maybe he'd come every day this week and prove to Elle Dalton that he wasn't an irrational, irate, overly protective older brother. He would earn her trust, and then they could sit down and talk about the reality of what she was trying to pull off. Especially with a sick student like Carl Joseph. She was an idealistic teacher. She hadn't spent her life with a Down Syndrome sibling. Cody settled back in his chair and tried not to notice the way Elle walked or the way her face lit up when one of her students made her laugh. Yes, he would come every day that week. He would come for the simple reason that he needed to invest time at the center in order to gain Elle Dalton's trust. Not for any other reason.

Even if at times that morning it took all his strength to focus on anyone or anything in the classroom but her.

Chapter Ten

Elle could barely concentrate on the coursework that day. Having Cody Gunner watching her from his seat near the door was a distraction that rivaled any she'd ever had. Not because of his dark good looks. He was married, after all. No, he was a distraction because of the threat he represented. If Cody convinced his family to pull Carl Joseph from the center, Daisy would be devastated. So would every one of her students.

Carl Joseph's departure would raise countless questions, fears, and anxieties for them. No doubt they would figure out the reason he left. The truth that his family no longer supported his plans to be independent would be glaringly obvious. And that could quite possibly start a chain reaction of events that would undermine everything the center stood for. Everything she was passionate about.

Elle maintained her composure until break time. It was nice outside again, not a cloud in the sky. She dismissed them to the outdoors, and then, without a glance at Cody Gunner, she retreated to the break room.

And there she fell back on the one life skill she couldn't live without. She poured herself a cup of coffee, held the warm mug close against her chest, and closed her eyes. *God... what's happening? Who is this Cody Gunner and why did he have to come home in the first place?* She kept her eyes closed and thought about that. The timing was all wrong. If Cody had come home six months from now, he could've seen for himself how independent Carl Joseph had become. They would have a plan to manage his heart disease and his epilepsy.

Instead Cody could see only the early stages of progress.

Lord, I'm up against a wall here. Help me show Carl Joseph's brother that it's possible, that even sick people with Down Syndrome can lead independent lives. Please, Father.

She opened her eyes and her breath caught in her throat. "Mr. Gunner!"

"Sorry." He was leaning in the doorway, watching her. "I was a little harsh earlier. You have a way with your students." He studied her. "I'm impressed, Elle Dalton."

She flashed proud eyes at him. "Is that why you're standing there? To tell me that?"

Regret colored his expression. "I don't want to be enemies."

She waited, suspicious. "You're opposed to what I'm doing here, Mr. Gunner. That much is obvious."

"I am. For my brother." He straightened. "But I'm willing to hear you out, willing to see what the program's all about." He sighed, and the conflict in his heart was obvious. "I love my brother, that's all. I want what's best for him. What's safest."

"I understand." Her tone softened. Still, she wasn't sure where he was headed with this. "What are you saying, exactly? That you'll stay around the rest of the day without making a judgment?"

"I'll stay all week." He took a step back. "If that's okay. But at the end of the week, let's talk about whether this"—he looked back at the class space—"all of this is really good for Carl Joseph."

She narrowed her eyes. What had Carl Joseph said? That his brother was hurt, that he'd been injured in bull riding, right? Whether the bull riding was true or not, maybe the guy had been injured somehow. Maybe that's why Cody didn't want to see anything happen to Carl Joseph. Because he understood that one injury could change everything. "You've spent all your life protecting your brother, haven't you?"

"Yes." He held her gaze for a long moment.

Elle took a sip of her coffee, but she never took her eyes off him. Behind his brash approach and bitter words, Cody Gunner cared. "There were times"—he caught her eye again—"when Carl Joseph was the only person who kept me going, when everyone else felt like a stranger." A steely look came over him, and his eyes penetrated to her soul. Not with anger, the way they had before class started, but with a passion that caught her off guard. Each word was measured, full of intensity. "I can't let anything happen to him. Do you understand that, Ms. Dalton?"

"Yes." She considered him. "I hope at the end of the week you'll see that I feel the same way. I would never put your brother in danger. Not for anything."

"Okay." Cody gave her a polite nod. "I'll be in the classroom, then." He hesitated. "No hard feelings about my attitude earlier?"

"None." She didn't smile, but she did feel more relaxed. The rest of the day went smoothly. Cody stayed glued to the action as she went over the bus route again, and then directed the students to move into the kitchen.

"We're making shortcake today." She found an apron in a drawer and tied it around her waist. "Who remembers why we make shortcake?"

Daisy shot her hand in the air. She grinned at Carl Joseph and then at Elle. "Because people at Disneyland like shortcake."

"Disneyland is good for shortcake." Carl Joseph held his hands toward the other students, looking for their approval.

A chorus of nods and affirmations came from the crowd.

Elle smiled. "Okay, yes. There's a little restaurant in Disneyland that makes the best strawberry shortcake." She thought she caught Cody grinning at the back of the room. "But that's not *why* we make shortcake. Anyone remember why?"

Sid made an exaggerated sigh. "I know." He raised his hand. "Pick me, Teacher."

"Sid, why do we make shortcake?"

"So we can entertain."

"Right. Very good." Elle held up a laminated oversized

card with a photo of shortcake. "Shortcake is a dessert, and it can be used in many ways when you entertain."

This time she saw Cody shift his position. She could read his mind, even midstream in front of her class. What was the point of teaching people with Down Syndrome how to entertain? That's what he was thinking. She tried not to let the negativity she felt from him ruin her mood. She'd been looking forward to this cooking assignment since last week when they'd learned how to prepare broccoli.

"Shortcake is very attractive." Tammy swung her braids and smiled. "Very attractive."

"I think I could entertain twelve people if I had short-cake." Gus looked around at the others.

Carl Joseph reached back and patted Gus on the knee. "I would come to your party if you had shortcake, Gus."

"Okay, then." Elle regained control. She moved to the long countertop area that separated her from the students. "First let's take a look at our ingredients."

"I brought flour and vanilla, Teacher." Carl Joseph stood up. He slid his glasses back up his nose and then grinned at Daisy. "Flour and vanilla."

Before a landslide of comments followed, Elle motioned to Carl Joseph. "Could you get nine mixing bowls from the supply cupboard? Then place them in a row along this counter, okay?"

Carl Joseph looked as if he'd won the lottery. He jumped up and hurried to an oversized cupboard. He was the newest of her students, and even he knew where everything was kept. Elle continued explaining the ingredients, but she kept watch on Carl Joseph. Clearly his brother would be scrutinizing this assignment, seeing whether Carl Joseph could follow multiple orders without needing help.

Sure enough, he took the mixing bowls out one at a time and set them in two stacks. Then he counted them again, just to be sure, and distributed them along the counter. The counter area had been built so that a team of two people could stand facing each other and work on a recipe together. Elle had nine copies of the shortcake recipe. "Okay, find a partner and station yourselves near one of the mixing bowls."

Daisy danced her way over to Carl Joseph. She stood opposite him and laughed a few times. "Is this spot taken?"

"No, madam." He hunched over, giving her his shyest giggle. "Not unless Mickey Mouse shows up."

Daisy laughed at that as if it were the wittiest thing she'd ever heard. "Mickey Mouse! CJ, you're funny."

Over the next hour, with Elle and her aide overseeing the project, each team of two students followed the shortcake recipe and created a bowl full of batter. At one point, Cody stood and circled the work area from a distance.

As he walked near Carl Joseph and Daisy, Elle expected her sister to get excited again and say something about Cody smelling like a bull rider. But this time the laughter that had marked their work time faded as Cody came closer. Carl Joseph gave Daisy a secretive look, and she nodded in a way that wasn't quite subtle.

"Good job, Buddy." Cody peered over his brother's shoulder at the bowl. "I bet your shortcake is best of all."

"Yeah...thanks." Carl Joseph didn't look up. He kept his eyes moving between the batter and Daisy. Then he looked at Cody. "I don't need help, Brother. Thanks, but I don't need help."

"Okay." Cody angled his head and glanced across the room at Elle. "I'll try to stay out of the way."

"Yeah, 'cause then it'll be a surprise." Carl Joseph waved at his brother. "Go back to the chair and thanks anyway."

Cody raised his brow and chuckled, clearly not sure how to take the gentle rebuffing from Carl Joseph. One at a time, Elle directed the teams of students to spoon their batter into greased pans and place their shortcake in one of the center's two ovens. The hardest task, the one that would matter most when they were living on their own, was to work against their short-term memory problems and remember the shortcake after it was in the oven.

Elle and the aide oversaw the project, but neither of them would rescue the students. Sure enough, the first two teams forgot about their shortcake. Elle waited until the cake was burned but not on fire before reminding the teams. "Gus's team and Tammy's team, do you smell something burning?"

All four students lurched into panic mode. They ran into each other, and then across the room into the kitchen, all of them talking at once. Elle stood with her arms crossed. "You'll need potholders."

"Potholders." Gus raced to the right drawer and found one for each of them.

"What next?" Elle could feel Cody watching, disapproving. If she hadn't reminded them about the shortcakes, they eventually would've caught fire. But this was part of learning. If Cody didn't understand that, then maybe by the end of the week he would. "What next, people?"

"Turn off the ovens." Tammy had an oven mitt on her hand. She stared at the oven and did a nervous little dance in place. "We should turn off the ovens."

"Yes, do that." Elle kept any frustration from her voice.

Gus and Tammy each reached for the controls on their separate ovens and turned them off. Elle felt a ripple of satisfaction. At least here, even in a time of panic, they remembered how to turn off the ovens. She moved in closer. "What next?"

"Take out the shortcake!" Gus looked at his baking partner and swallowed hard. "I'll do it, okay?"

The other young man nodded. "I'll get the hot pad."

Gus pulled a blackened shortcake from the oven, while a few feet away Tammy did the same thing with hers. They set the burned desserts on the hotpads, stepped back, and stared at them dismally. Gus looked at Elle. "No entertaining tonight."

"No." Elle smiled. "But we learned something."

All four students stared at her, mouths open, as if they weren't sure what they'd learned by burning their shortcake. Then Gus gasped and his hand shot straight in the air. "We learned not to forget." He pointed back at the oven. "We could use a timer."

Elle felt her heart soar. "Exactly." She hadn't mentioned that to any of them, because the timer was something all of them should've known by now. The other students gathered around to gawk at the blackened shortcake.

"Gus, you can have some of mine," Daisy said.

"Yeah, mine, too." Carl Joseph tapped his fingers on the counter near the burned dessert. "'Cause yeah, a timer would be better." He turned to Daisy. "They use timers at Disneyland."

It was a victory. Without her prompting, Gus had remembered that a timer would've saved the shortcake from burning. Carl Joseph and Daisy were one of the teams to use the ovens next, and Carl Joseph raised his hand. "We'd like a timer, Teacher. If that's okay."

She laughed. "Yes. Go right ahead."

With textbook precision, Carl Joseph and Daisy worked to get their dessert into the oven. Carl Joseph checked the oven while Daisy set the timer. Then, using a potholder, Carl Joseph placed their pan of shortcake batter onto the hot rack and Daisy shut the oven door.

Elle wanted to hug them both, but she couldn't overreact. This was the sort of thing that would have to come easily for them before they could celebrate Goal Day. Thirty minutes later, when the timer went off, all four students promptly and calmly found their oven mitts and potholders, turned off their ovens, and removed their shortcakes. Both were a light golden color on top, cooked perfectly.

"Carl Joseph." Elle walked up and whispered to him. "I think maybe when it cools, your brother would like a piece."

"Yeah." Carl Joseph's eyes sparkled. "Brother should get a piece."

An hour later, when Carl Joseph brought a piece of

shortcake to his brother, Cody thanked him and complimented him. And as he took his first bite, he raised his fork in Elle's direction. She gave him a sly smile and then turned back to her students. Maybe they would find common ground yet.

The day wore on, and by the time her students left, Elle was exhausted. It was twice as hard, teaching and trying to make things work well for Cody Gunner all at the same time.

"You look tired, Teacher." Daisy came up, her backpack slung onto her shoulder. She twisted her head upside down and stared at Elle. Then she straightened and laughed at her own silliness. "Are you tired?"

"School's over, Daisy." She gave her a knowing look. "You call me Elle now, remember?"

"I know." She laughed again. "Elle...Elle...Elle." She set her backpack on the floor, unzipped it, and peered inside. "The shortcake's in there."

"Yes." All the students took home a large piece of shortcake. "We can entertain tonight. You and Mom and me." She jumped into the air and came down in a perfect ballet first position. "And we can dance for fun."

"First we need to go to the market." Elle had none of her usual energy. It had been draining being watched by Cody all day. He was giving her a week to prove that the students were learning skills that would one day make them capable of living on their own. One week. She sighed and grabbed her bag. "You ready to go to the store?"

"Yes." She stuck out her tongue and curled it up over her

lip, something she did when she was concentrating intently. She looked through her backpack, rummaging around and finally pulling out a calculator. She grinned and held the calculator straight up over her head. "I'll keep the budget."

Daisy had been at the center longer than most of the students. That she was thinking about staying on a budget at the mere mention of grocery shopping was further proof that she was almost ready. Depending on how the next few months went, she could have her Goal Day before the holidays.

A sense of bittersweet joy came over Elle. Letting go of a sibling with Down Syndrome would never be easy. There would always be risks, but then life for able-bodied people held risks, too. She was proof.

"Okay, Daisy." They linked arms and headed out toward the parking lot. Elle turned off the lights and locked up on the way. "You keep the budget. Let's make sure we don't spend more than a hundred dollars today, all right?"

Daisy did a few short laughs. "Wow, Elle. A whole hundred dollars."

For the rest of the ride to the market and even after they parked and were heading inside, Daisy kept a running dialogue about what they might be able to buy with a hundred dollars. When she'd hit just about every combination of groceries, Elle thought of a way to change the subject. "Daisy."

"And peanut butter and mayonnaise and string cheese and—"

"Daisy." Elle's frustration rose a notch.

Her sister fell silent. She pulled out a cart and opened her eyes wide at Elle. "I was making a budget."

"I know, but I have a question."

Daisy pushed the cart into the store and they walked toward the produce section. She looked a little put out, but she turned her attention to Elle anyway. "What question?"

Elle wanted to know more about whatever exchange had happened between her sister and Carl Joseph while they were making the shortcake batter. It was the first time Daisy hadn't acted thrilled about Cody Gunner. "About Carl Joseph's brother."

As soon as Elle said the words, Daisy's expression closed. She lifted her chin, pride having its way with her. "I don't like CJ's brother. Not anymore."

"I thought he smelled good and he was a world-famous bull rider."

Daisy allowed the hint of a smile. "He does smell good." Her smile fell off. "But I don't like him anymore."

"Why?"

"CJ's brother doesn't want him at the center." She looked straight ahead and stopped at a display of bananas. "He doesn't want him there because he doesn't like us."

Elle took a bunch of bananas and weighed them. "Three pounds, Daisy. Let's start with that."

Daisy took her calculator from her pocket and squinted at the sign above the bananas. "Forty cents a pound." Her mouth hung open while she punched in the numbers, but after a short time, she laughed aloud. "One twenty. One dollar and twenty cents. That's how much so far."

"Excellent." Elle gave her sister a look that expressed how proud she was. "You're doing so well, Daisy."

A shadow fell over her expression. "But Cody Gunner doesn't like us."

"He will." Elle allowed Daisy to take the lead as they moved to a display of apples. "One day he will."

And as they finished shopping, as she allowed her sister time to gain the experience of finding eggs and peanut butter and mayonnaise and string cheese along with a cart full of other items all for under a hundred dollars, she could only pray quietly that what she'd told Daisy was right.

That someday—by some sort of miracle—Cody Gunner would like not just the students at the ILC. But he would also like her work well enough to believe in Carl Joseph's place there.

Chapter Eleven

Carl Joseph was at his parents' computer trying to write a letter. But he was having trouble. Something maybe was wrong with Brother. He had heard the yelling and shouting that day when he was pulling weeds. And now it was Wednesday and Brother was still coming every day to the center.

Daisy said he was coming because he didn't like them. "Your brother doesn't want you at the center," she had told him earlier that day.

And maybe Daisy was right. But maybe not. Because Brother had a smile and a happy voice when he was at the center. He sat in his chair and he watched and he thought a lot. And sometimes Brother would get up and find him next to Daisy and see what they were doing. Three times he said, "Good job, Buddy."

Also he thought Teacher was pretty. Carl Joseph knew because Brother's eyes were the same at Elle as they were at

Ali the first time. When Brother and Ali were at the rodeo together. Because Carl Joseph would come with his mother and sometimes with his dad, and he could see Brother's eyes then. His eyes for Ali. And that was the same as his eyes for Teacher.

But even all that didn't mean he was happy.

Carl Joseph looked out the window and bit his lip. Plus the letter was hard 'cause he was a little scared 'cause of the bus routes. And that kept filling his head. He knew Number Eight and Number Three. But Number Eleven was scary because there were two changes. And two changes had to happen. Otherwise no Goal Day. Yes, bus routes were scary.

He turned his eyes to the computer screen. There was nothing on it so far. He adjusted his glasses and looked at the keyboard. He could at least type her name. He found the *D* and tapped it. Then he tapped out the rest of her name. A-*I-S-Y*.

He lifted his eyes and made a happy laugh. Daisy. That's what it spelled: Daisy. He wanted to write Daisy a letter because of Disneyland. Teacher said that when you entertain you have to invite someone. And he wanted to entertain Daisy at Disneyland. So maybe he had to write her a letter and invite her first.

He heard a noise and he saw Brother's truck pull into the driveway. That made him feel nervous, because he wasn't sure about Brother anymore. He didn't want to make him mad. 'Cause maybe Brother was mad that he and Daisy were friends and maybe he wanted Carl Joseph to leave the center.

He watched Brother park his truck and head up the walk. "Uh-oh." He grabbed the mouse. But not Mickey Mouse, 'cause that was different. Then he moved the arrow fast, faster. Fast as he could until he found the X marks the spot. Then he clicked and the letter was gone. 'Cause he could write a letter to Daisy later.

But he didn't want Brother to be mad. Not ever.

Because Daisy was his number two best friend, but Brother...Brother was his best friend of all. So he could hide letters to Daisy. Because he didn't want Brother to see what he was doing and be mad. He stood and slammed the chair back against the desk. His heart pounded like a drum. He moved quickly away from the computer and over to the door. That way Brother wouldn't see what he was doing. Then he ran and held open his arms. "Brother!"

"Hey, Buddy." He came up and they hugged. "Whatcha been doing?"

"Nothing." Carl Joseph answered fast. "Not writing a letter to Daisy. Not me."

Brother stopped and crossed his arms. He looked around at the computer and then back again. "Are you lying to me, Buddy?"

"Yes." Again his answer was fast. Because Mom said you don't love someone you lie to. And you don't lie to someone you love. He nodded, very serious. "Yes, Brother. I'm lying."

"How come?" Brother put his arm on his shoulder and looked at him. Straight at him.

Carl Joseph felt his heart slow down a little. Brother still loved him. 'Cause he put his hand on Carl Joseph's shoulder and that meant, "I love you, Buddy." Carl Joseph put his hands on his knees and breathed out like when he raced Gus at break time. When he looked up he licked his lips first. "You don't like Daisy."

"What?" Brother looked hurt. So maybe he did like Daisy. "Buddy, that's not true. I like her a lot. She has cute blonde hair."

"'Cause she has cute blonde hair and she likes Minnie Mouse." Carl Joseph looked down at the floor. His heart was pounding again. "And Brother likes Minnie Mouse."

"That's right." He sounded tired. He led Carl Joseph back into the office and pulled out the computer chair. "Sit here."

Carl Joseph did as he was told. He sat down and looked at the blank screen.

"You were writing a letter to Daisy, right?"

"Yes." He didn't look around. He didn't want to see if Brother was mad or not. "A letter to Daisy."

"Okay, Buddy. Then go ahead." He reached down and hugged Carl Joseph from the back. "Go ahead and write to Daisy. I like when you write letters."

"'Cause"—Carl Joseph turned around and looked at Brother's eyes—"I was inviting her to Disneyland with me." He looked at the screen again. "Teacher says when you entertain, you need to invite someone."

Brother sounded a little more tired. "Fine. Go on and write your invitation. I'm not mad at you, Buddy." He came around and sat on the edge of the desk. Then he looked straight at Carl Joseph. "I love you, Buddy. Okay? Remember that?"

Carl Joseph thought for a moment. "Yes, I remember."

"Good. I'm not mad and I like your friends."

"'Cause after Daisy I can write a letter to you." He smiled at Brother. "And maybe you think Teacher is pretty."

Brother opened his mouth but no words came out. Carl Joseph closed his eyes because this might be where Brother got mad. But instead, laughter came from him. Lots of laughter. Carl Joseph opened his eyes. "Brother?"

"How do you know I think your teacher's pretty?" He leaned in and messed Carl Joseph's hair.

"'Cause your eyes looked at her like..." Carl Joseph stopped. Every time he talked about Ali the horse rider, Brother got sad. Brother was laughing now, so he didn't want to make him sad. He pushed his glasses back up his nose. "'Cause your eyes said she was pretty."

"Well." Brother stood and took a step away. "You're right about your teacher. She is pretty. But that doesn't mean we agree about everything. Okay?"

"Okay, Brother. Except Disneyland. We can agree about Disneyland."

Brother was still smiling, and his face said he thought Carl Joseph was silly. "We can definitely agree about that."

"You and me and Daisy."

"Yes, Buddy." Brother waved at him. "You and me and Daisy."

When Brother left, Carl Joseph remembered everything he wanted to say to Daisy. Because he wasn't afraid anymore about Brother. Brother liked Daisy and that meant no more heart like a drum. But before he started back on the letter, he closed his eyes and folded his hands and talked to God out loud.

"One day, God, please let Brother and me and Daisy and Teacher go to Disneyland together. 'Cause the Magic Kingdom has shortcake and Mickey Mouse and Minnie. And thanks that Brother isn't mad. So maybe we can all go there. Amen."

When he opened his eyes, he felt ready for the letter. 'Cause Teacher said it felt good to use life skills. And praying to God was one of the best life skills of all. You could say what you want to God anytime, anywhere. Teacher said that. And talking to God meant God was with you. And sometimes being a grownup was scary. Except with God it was never scary at all.

Even when you had to know all the bus routes in the whole wide world.

Chapter Twelve

Elle couldn't wait to get Snoopy out on a leash. All afternoon she'd been looking forward to taking her dog to the park up the street. It wasn't a big park like Antlers. Just a patch of grass in the middle of twenty rows of modest homes. A place where mothers could take their preschoolers and find a swing set and a slide and a set of monkey bars. The park was one of Elle's favorite places after a long day.

The sunshine from earlier had disappeared behind a layer of clouds, and she was about to find something warmer to wear when her mother approached her.

"You look tired."

Elle chided herself for not hiding her feelings better. "I'm fine. Just a long day."

"That's nearly a whole week of long days." She frowned. "What's happening at the center?" Her mother touched her arm, her eyes curious. "You've been more tired, quieter."

Daisy overheard the question. She stepped up and clucked

her tongue to the roof of her mouth. "CJ's brother. He happened this week."

Their mother wrinkled her nose. "The world-famous bull rider?"

Elle rolled her eyes. "Please, Mother. Don't feed the fantasy." She headed for the coat closet and found an old sweater. "I'm taking Snoopy for a walk."

Her mother stayed on her heels. "So he's not a bull rider?"

"I don't know what he is." Elle looked past her mom. Daisy hadn't followed them. "The guy shows up Monday morning unannounced, and now he's a regular fixture at the center."

"Oh." Her mom stepped out of her way as she slipped on the sweater and moved back toward the kitchen. "Is he curious?"

"No." She stopped and looked at her mom. After being calm and gentle with her students all day, she didn't have the patience for this. Even so, her mother didn't know what was happening with Cody Gunner, and Elle couldn't blame her for being curious. She exhaled and tried to explain the situation better. "He wants Carl Joseph removed from the center. That's his bottom line." She leaned against the nearest wall. Everything about Carl Joseph's brother made her feel worn-out.

"Why on earth?" Her mother's expression told the story. She couldn't fathom someone opposed to independence for people with Down Syndrome. "Are you sure?"

"Yes. He thinks that Carl Joseph is safer and happier at

home, that because of his epilepsy and heart disease, we're filling his head with impossible ideas. That sort of thing."

"Oh." She wrinkled her brow. "Of course it's up to Carl Joseph's parents."

"Since his diagnosis, they're unsure, too. Cody's opinion could be enough to sway them."

"I see." Her mother looked into the next room, where Daisy was sitting in a weathered old recliner. She was reading *Heidi* for the third time. "Regardless of his health, I can't imagine standing in the way of someone with Down Syndrome. Not when there are so many options for them now."

"I know. Me, either." Elle leaned in and kissed her mother's cheek. "Let's talk about it later. I need to get out."

"Okay." Her mom patted her arm. "I'm sorry, Elle. You don't deserve that."

"I just wish he didn't make me doubt myself." She gave her mother a tired smile. "It feels like I'm spending my time defending myself, instead of getting my students closer to their goal."

"It'll pass."

"I know." She pulled Snoopy's leash from a drawer in the kitchen and headed for the door. Their small house was one of hundreds in this part of Colorado Springs. It was the best they could do with the money from the sale of the old house, and it was cozy. More than they needed. She smiled at her mother. "I'll be back in an hour."

The moment she stepped outside, she felt her mind begin to clear. She walked more slowly than usual and studied the new leaves on the branches of the trees that lined the street.

Colorado Springs didn't have many deciduous trees, but this neighborhood's developers had seen to it that there were at least a few mixed in between the common evergreens.

She took in a long breath and walked a little taller. Cody Gunner had been driving her crazy this past week, between his wary glances and his subtle smiles. He wasn't critical or mean, exactly. But his scrutiny exhausted her. Once in a while, for a brief moment at a time over the past several days, she would catch herself watching him, admiring his strong jaw and intense eyes, or the way his broad back tapered down to his waist.

Each time she would turn away, angry with herself. He was married. That she would find him attractive was appalling.

No, she definitely couldn't be attracted to Carl Joseph's brother. But now that she was outside, now that the cool evening breeze played against her face and the smell of jasmine filled her senses, she had to be honest. Her attraction to him was part of the problem.

Not only did she want him to finish the week convinced that her work at the ILC was necessary and important, and that it was the right place for Carl Joseph, but she wanted him to go back to whatever he used to do with his days. Go back home to his wife and leave the educating to her. She spotted another dog owner across the street. They nodded to each other and Snoopy looked up and whined.

"I know…you want to play." She stopped and patted the old beagle's head. "Too bad, Snoopy. We have ground to cover."

At the end of the street, Elle turned right. The park was

just three blocks up on the left. It was impossible to think about Cody Gunner and not let her mind wander back to where the damage had been done. If things hadn't fallen apart, she would be into her fourth year of marriage, maybe talking about having children or buying a first home.

She narrowed her eyes and tried to fight the memories. But then, in a rush, they came at her with a gale force and she could do nothing to hold them off. It wasn't as if she thought about the past every day. For the most part she could live without thinking about it. But once in a while it helped to go back. The memories reminded her of why she was the way she was, why she had no intention of trusting love again unless God Himself brought the right person into her life.

Anyway, Elle wasn't waiting around. It was better to keep existing, keep following her passion for helping her students, keep playing Scrabble with her mother. That way no one could ever hurt her the way she'd been hurt that terrible spring.

She looked ahead as she walked, but she no longer saw the cars passing by or the budding trees or even the park. She was seeing all the way back to the beginning.

His name was Trace Canton, and he was the principal at Pinewood Elementary where Elle received her first teaching job. She was just out of college at Colorado University and she'd taken an apartment not far from campus. She applied to four schools—all in separate districts—and Pinewood was the first to offer her a job.

The ironic thing was she didn't meet Trace until after she was hired. He was on vacation during the hiring process, so the assistant principal and the district superintendent had made the decision without him.

That fall she was hanging posters in her classroom when she felt someone watching her. She turned and jumped. "Oh, sorry." There was a man standing in the doorway, and not just any man. He wore designer slacks and a button-down silk shirt. He wasn't built like the guys she'd dated in college. He had the slender frame of a model—like someone who had stepped out of the pages of *GQ* magazine. Elle set the poster down on the desk and cleared her throat. "I didn't know you were there."

"Don't mind me." Trace smiled at her, and that simple smile cut straight to her heart. "I wanted to get a look at your classroom, that's all."

Elle figured the guy was the father of one of her students. "Did someone in the office tell you about Back-to-School Night this Friday?" She glanced at his hand, his ring finger. It was bare.

He chuckled and took a few steps into her classroom. "I'll be there."

She was flustered by his confidence. He acted as if he owned the place, and suddenly she wondered. Should she be nervous? Was he some psycho who had stumbled into her classroom off the street? She took a step back. "Excuse me, I didn't get your name."

"Trace." He stopped a few feet from her and grinned. "Most everyone around here knows me as Mr. Canton."

Elle was mortified. She could've slithered under the carpet and wormed her way to the parking lot. How could she have missed that this was the principal? She felt her cheeks grow hot. "I didn't ... I had no idea that ... I guess I haven't ..." She sat on the edge of her desk and made an exasperated sound. "I'm sorry." She shrugged and gave him a crooked grin. "I didn't know you were back."

"Don't worry about it." He pressed his shoulder into the wall and studied her. "Everyone in the office tells me you're beyond dedicated." He surveyed the room. "I wanted to see for myself."

It took that long for Elle to catch her breath. "Well"— she waved her hand at the walls, at the work she'd already done—"what do you think?"

"I think the staff is right." He cocked his head and held her eyes. "Welcome to Pinewood, Ms. Dalton. I'm sure you'll fit in very nicely." He nodded at her and turned to leave. He stopped at the door and looked at her again. "Oh, and I'll make a point of stopping in on Back-to-School Night." He grinned, and then he was gone.

That visit was the first of many.

It was an unspoken rule that there would be no fraternizing between staff members. Two of the teachers were married to each other, but that was the exception, not the rule. Still, Elle felt a connection between herself and the principal every time they were together. A month into the school year, she found the courage to mention him to one of the old-timers, a teacher who had been there since before Trace Canton arrived at Pinewood.

"What's his story? He doesn't have a wedding ring." They were in the teachers' lounge, so Elle kept her voice low.

"No one knows." The older woman gave Elle a curious look. "He's a looker; everyone can see that. But in the five years he's been here, no one has learned a thing about his private life."

"Strange." She kept her comments casual. She didn't want to appear too interested.

"Want the rumor?" The teacher looked around. When she was sure there was no one else around she lowered her voice. "People say he's gay. That would explain a lot."

"Gay?" Elle felt her stomach drop. That wasn't possible, was it? Not based on the way he looked at her. Even so, it gave her a reason to keep her distance. If he wasn't interested in her, then she wouldn't make a fool of herself by talking to him more than was absolutely necessary.

Over the next few months, Elle stayed away from Trace Canton. Better to learn more about him from afar than to put herself at risk for humiliation.

Just before Christmas break, Trace found her alone in her classroom. "Is it true you're reading the Nativity to your children?"

Elle taught a second-grade class. She was working at her desk but she set her pen down to give him her full attention. "Yes, sir."

"Please"—he smiled at her—"don't call me sir. It makes me feel old."

"Okay." She swallowed and glanced at her desk, at a stack of papers her students were to color the next day. Each one had a picture of Mary and Joseph and the manger, with an enormous star overhead. She looked back at Trace. "Yes, I'm reading them the Nativity story. I researched it with the district. We're allowed to talk about religious holidays, right?"

"Definitely." He walked up to the desk and sat on the edge of one of the student tables. "I'm not upset, Ms. Dalton. I admire your determination." He crossed his arms. Whatever cologne he was wearing, it made her knees feel weak. "I'm a Christian. The day we lose the meaning of Christmas in our public schools will be a sad one, indeed."

She could barely find the wherewithal to speak. "Yes. Indeed."

Before he left her classroom that day, he took his time examining her wall of papers and posters. She returned to her work, preparing the blackboard for the next day's lessons. When she turned around, she caught him looking at her, his eyes glancing at the length of her. In the same heartbeat, he refocused and held her gaze a little longer than necessary. "You impress me, Ms. Dalton." He headed for the door, but stopped and spoke the next words straight to her soul. "More than you know."

When he left that afternoon, she was convinced of two things. First, there was something special developing between her and the principal—however complicated that might be. And second, the man was not gay. He was a Christian, after all.

The rest of the school year was made up of a series of casual meetings and conversations between them, none of which Elle sought. Once he came close to asking her out for coffee, but he stopped himself. At the end of the school year he called her into his office.

"Ms. Dalton, there are some things you need to know." He was sitting at his desk, and he looked broken. The confidence he carried as he strolled the halls of Pinewood was completely missing.

Her heart skipped a beat, and then slid into a strange rhythm. Was this where he would bare his deepest secrets? Was the old teacher in the lunchroom that day right about him, despite everything she'd come to believe? She sat forward and folded her hands. "Okay."

"First—"he adjusted his tie and glanced at the door. He looked so nervous she felt sorry for him. "First, my role as principal of this school is one I take very seriously. My plan has always been to work here for ten years and then move into the district office. It's my dream, and I wouldn't harm that dream for anything in the world. Education has been my life since I entered college. It's left me no time to pursue anything personal."

Elle had no idea where he was headed with this. "I see," she said, simply because it seemed right for her to answer somehow.

He rested his forearms on his desk and slumped his shoulders forward. His eyes met hers and he looked tormented. "Second, I've developed feelings for you, Ms. Dalton. Feelings that go"—he looked down for a moment and then back at her—"far beyond my admiration for you as a teacher."

Relief spilled into her veins, and her heart found its normal beat again. Trace Canton was not gay. She didn't break eye contact with him. "Really?"

"Yes." He laughed, and it relieved much of the tension between them. "Whew." He shook his head. "That's one of the hardest things I've ever said."

"I…" She felt shy now that his intentions were clear. "I sort of wondered. I mean, I guess I hoped you might feel something for me."

His eyes danced as he realized what she was saying. But just as quickly, he grew serious again. "The trouble is, it would be completely inappropriate for me to ask you out, for us to see each other given our current working relationship."

"I agree." The palms of her hands were damp. "It's one thing for teachers to date. But you're my boss."

"Exactly." He slid a document across his desk. "Look at this. It's a request to have you transferred to Barrett Elementary three miles west of here. It's the same district, but it would allow us…" He paused, and she could hear a tremble in his voice. "It would allow me to do what I've wanted to do since the day I met you."

Elle could hardly believe her good fortune.

All along, she'd been telling her mother about Trace, how he was a cheerful man, great with the kids, but how his private life was a mystery. Now, though, the mystery was solved. Trace had been so caught up in education and working his way into the role of principal that he hadn't had time to date. No wonder he was single.

Elle accepted the transfer the next day, and when school let out for summer, she and Trace went to dinner. That night, for the first time, he called her by her given name as he opened the car door for her. "You look beautiful, Elle."

Before she climbed in, their eyes held. "I've wanted to call you that since September."

The connection between them happened quickly and with an intensity that left her dizzy. Of course, they'd already spent nine months pretending they didn't have feelings for each other. Now that they were able to express themselves, the romance between them took on a life of its own.

All summer and into the next school year, they were inseparable. They hiked Pikes Peak and three other trails into the mountains surrounding the Springs. They went snow skiing in Vail over a four-day weekend, and golfing at the Broadmoor.

The subject of purity was one they both agreed on. God wouldn't bless their relationship unless they put off temptation. On the trip to Vail, they stayed in separate rooms and never considered breaching the boundaries.

"He's a perfect gentleman," Elle told her mother that Christmas. "I never dreamed I'd meet a man like him."

Her mother listened, but it took a moment before she said anything. "He sounds a little too good to be true."

"Not really." Elle didn't want anyone saying anything to mar the way she was feeling. "He's a man of God, Mother. What more could I ask for?"

One afternoon, her mother explained her concern. "How old is he?"

"Thirty-one." Elle grinned. "Eight years older than me, but that doesn't bother us. He says I'm more mature than him most of the time."

Her mother nodded, thoughtful. "Thirty-one and never been in love. Sort of unusual, don't you think?"

"No." Elle bristled. "He's been getting his education and training. That's not unusual, Mother. It's dedication."

Her mother dropped the subject and pulled Elle into a tender hug. "I'm glad you're happy, honey. You deserve this."

Elle's happiness grew tenfold that New Year's Eve when Trace took her to dinner at the Broadmoor, and after dinner—out on a patio overlooking the beautifully lit golf course, he lowered himself to one knee and pulled a velvet box from his pants pocket. His eyes were damp as he searched hers. "Marry me, Elle."

"Trace…yes." She brought her fingers to her lips and then took the box. Inside was a diamond solitaire surrounded by a ring of smaller diamonds. She gasped, and before she could take a breath they were in each other's arms, hugging and kissing and laughing.

Their engagement was more of the same, one amazing day after another. The plans came together quickly, and the wedding was set for May. Elle and her mother went to Denver and found a stunning dress, tight along the bodice with a spray of glittery white that made up the skirt and train.

Three hundred people were invited—the staffs at both elementary schools and family on both sides. Together they picked out the DJ and the ballroom—at the Broadmoor, of course. They laughed as they strolled through Nordstrom, registering for new dishes and crystal and fine china.

Elle didn't notice anything amiss until a month before the wedding. They had plans for dinner and a walk, time to talk about the wedding plans and go over the details of the reception. But Trace called half an hour before he was supposed to pick her up. "Um, Elle…I can't make it tonight. Something's come up."

She was puzzled by his behavior, but she figured it had something to do with the wedding. Maybe he was meeting with someone about the honeymoon. Or maybe he was cooking up some other surprise. She let the incident pass without commenting. But when it happened again later that week, she felt the first tremblings of fear.

"Trace…is everything okay? With us, I mean."

"Of course." His answer came fast, his tone a little too forced. "Don't worry, Elle. This is about me."

She tried not to think too long about his answer, but his strange behavior continued into the next week and the week after that. Finally, one day after school she showed up at Pinewood and strode into the reception area. She nodded at the woman still seated at the front desk. Then she walked past and into Trace's office.

"Hey." He was on the phone, but at the sight of her he slammed the receiver down and stood. "You can't walk in here unannounced."

"I just did." She couldn't make out the emotions in his eyes, but they were nothing she'd ever seen before. "We need to talk, Trace." She shut the door behind her. "I'm sorry I didn't call first. But I couldn't wait. What's happening with you?"

He lowered himself to his desk and shielded his eyes with his fingers. He exhaled, almost as if he was still recovering from the sight of her. When he lowered his hands, his expression had changed to one she was more familiar with. "Honey, I told you. This isn't about you."

"Okay, so what's it about?" Panic coursed through her. She wanted to scream at him. "We're getting married in ten days, Trace. And you can't keep a dinner date. Doesn't that strike you as strange?"

"I know." He uttered a weak laugh. "I can imagine how it looks." He reached across the desk.

For a moment she didn't respond. She was too angry. "I can't live this way. With you keeping things from me. Secrets." She looked around the room as if the answer might be tangible. "Whatever it is, I can't take it."

"I'm sorry." He stretched his hand out a little farther. His expression was still pinched, his voice nervous. "Elle, come on, honey. I love you. I told you this isn't about you."

She didn't want to, but she took his hand anyway. Whatever damage had been done, feeling his fingers against hers was necessary if they were going to find their way back to where they'd been before. She blinked back tears. "I'm about to commit my entire life to you, Trace. Whatever you've been dealing with, you need to talk to me about it."

"No, Elle." Something cold flashed in his eyes, and just as quickly it was gone. "No, Elle. It was my problem, and I took care of it. Just some leftover business from my old life." He smiled at her, the smile that had won her heart. "The lonely life I lived before I met you."

She wasn't satisfied with his answer, but she didn't know what to do to change his mind.

Finally, he stood and came around to her side of the desk. "I'm sorry for reacting when you walked in." He eased her to her feet and drew her into his arms. "I've been dealing with a lot, Elle. One of the new teachers isn't adjusting very well, and I've been needed more because of that." He touched his lips to hers. "Nothing's changed. Trust me."

Despite Trace's reassurance, Elle's suspicions remained, but there was nothing that justified her breaking things off. She loved Trace, and if he was feeling stressed about the pending wedding, that only made him human, right? Over the next week, he slipped back into his usual self, making time for her and spending evenings at her apartment going over the details of the wedding.

The Saturday of the ceremony dawned with thick clouds. Looking back, Elle should've seen it as an omen. Especially since the forecast had called for nothing but sunshine. Her mother and Daisy were in town, staying at her apartment, and her other two sisters were at a nearby hotel. The five of them gathered early that morning and fussed over each other's hair and makeup. Finally, at ten-thirty, they were ready to go. The wedding was slated for eleven, and the drive to the church took just ten minutes.

A friend at school knew someone who owned a limo service, and arrangements had been made to have one free of charge for Elle and Trace's big day. The limo whisked them off to the church and they arrived fifteen minutes early. Lots of guests were already there, but the pastor found them in the bridal room. "Have you heard from the groom?"

Fear colored black streaks across Elle's perfect morning. "He's coming by himself. The groomsmen are meeting him here."

"Very well." The pastor looked at his watch. "Is he usually punctual?"

Elle caught her mother's nervous glance. She cleared her throat and adjusted her veil. What could she say? Trace was one of the most punctual people she knew. She smiled at the man. "Usually. But if we have to wait for him, we'll wait."

"Absolutely." He smiled. "See you in a few minutes."

Elle's insides tied in knots. She couldn't look at her mother, couldn't imagine the unfathomable thoughts whispering in her mind. Instead she turned to Daisy. "Are you excited about today?"

"I love to dance." Daisy smiled. She came to Elle and looked her dress up and down. "You look like an angel, Elle. A pretty angel."

"Thanks, Daisy. That's sweet." She kissed her sister's cheek. "You look like an angel, too."

The bridesmaids' dresses were red. Daisy looked down at herself and adjusted her skirt. Then she cast a questioning look at Elle. "Maybe I look like Minnie Mouse."

Elle laughed, and for a moment she didn't feel suffocated with doubts. "Yes, Daisy. You look like Minnie."

The minutes slipped away slowly, painfully. When the time reached five till eleven, Elle stationed herself near the window. Her sisters had gone out into the foyer to mingle with the guests. Only her mother remained in the room with her. "Go, Mom. Please? Find out if he's here."

Her mother didn't say anything. Her pale face said it all. At eleven o'clock sharp, she returned and shook her head. "Does he have a cell phone?"

"Yes." She was shaking by then, shivering from head to toe. She could hear her veil crinkling from the way her shoulders shook. She dug through her purse and only then realized that she'd had her phone set to the vibrate mode. When she opened it, she saw that she had four missed calls.

Frantically she scrolled through them. Each one was from Trace. Her head was spinning and she could barely concentrate. She sat on the edge of a desk chair and put her head down. Anything to get the blood to flow to her brain so she wouldn't pass out.

"Elle…what is it?" Her mother knelt by her side, her hand on her shoulder. "Talk to me, sweetheart."

"It's Trace." She lifted her head. "He's called four times."

"Okay, then." Her mother nodded to the phone. "Call him back. He's probably just running late."

Elle couldn't stop the spinning in her head. Running late? She clung to the idea. Yes, that had to be it. He had gotten stuck in traffic or his car had broken down, or a pipe had burst beneath his sink. Or maybe he'd stopped to help someone in trouble. There had to be a reason.

She tried to swallow but her throat was too dry. She lifted the cell phone, but she was shaking too badly to dial his number. "Here." She handed it to her mother. "Call him for me. Please."

Her mother looked as frightened as she was. She took the phone and scrolled through the missed calls. Then she hit the send button. After a few seconds she handed it back. "It's ringing."

On the third ring, Trace answered. From the beginning she could tell he was crying. Weeping, even. "Elle…I'm sorry, honey. I'm so sorry." Every word was another sob.

Her heart pounded so hard she was certain it would burst through her chest or stop altogether. She gripped the phone and paced to the window. "Talk to me, Trace. What happened? Were you in an accident?"

"No." He had never sounded so distraught. "I can't do it, Elle. I can't marry you." He moaned. "God, why do I feel this way? Why is this happening?"

She was seeing black spots now. Was he praying? And why now, why his doubts at the very hour they were supposed to be saying their vows? "Trace..." She steadied herself against the window sill and closed her eyes. "I...I don't understand."

"I've fought it all my life, Elle." He stopped crying long enough to explain himself. Even so, his words were punctuated with quiet sobs. "I'm in love with someone else. Another teacher. I tried...I tried to let him go, but I couldn't."

Elle's breathing grew shallow and she gasped for air, grabbed at any way to understand what he'd just said. "*Him? You're...*you're in love with a man?"

Across the room, her mother dropped to another chair. "Dear God, no...no."

Trace was going on, saying something about it being wrong. "All my life I've had to choose. God and His goodness, or the desires of my flesh." He let out a cry that cut through her. "I can't promise you forever when...when I'll be looking for every chance to be with him. Oh, Elle...I'm so sorry."

It wasn't happening. The only way Elle was able to fill her lungs, to keep from passing out or having a heart attack, was by convincing herself that what she was hearing was all a lie. It was impossible. Trace Canton, her one true love, wasn't leaving her stranded at the altar for a man. No way.

She let the shock work its way through her body, through her heart and soul. He was still going on about getting counseling and knowing it was wrong and wanting God's will, when she interrupted him. "I have to go, Trace." Her voice was cold, unfeeling. "Good-bye."

Her phone felt like a burning piece of coal. She closed it and dropped it at the same time. Then she turned to her mother, but the words wouldn't come. Not that she needed words. Everything that could've been spoken had already been said. Her mother, too, looked ready to pass out. Always in their growing-up years, Elle had been the strong daughter, the one who rubbed her mother's back when the task of raising four daughters without the help of a husband seemed daunting to her.

Elle was the daughter who took responsibility for Daisy, helping her with kitchen tasks and reading to her when their mother was busy with the other girls, and she was the one who, of course, had gone into teaching—just one more way she could help people. But here, with three hundred wedding guests sitting in the sanctuary down the hall, Elle couldn't take another step.

Her mother must've known. Because she stood and drew a long breath. "I'll talk to them. I'll say there's been a change of plans."

The shock was still exploding through her, but Elle had never loved her mother more than in that single moment. An hour later, when the wedding guests were long gone and she and her mother and sisters had wept together until they had no more tears to cry, they went back to Elle's apartment.

She stayed the summer with her mother and Daisy, unwilling to talk about Trace or the disastrous wedding day. In July, she received a letter from him. He had quit his job as principal of Pinewood and had relocated to Los Angeles. He was still seeking God's will, still aware that acting on his passions was sinful. He asked her to pray for him.

A year later, on what would've been their first anniversary, she pulled the letter out and realized that God had been healing her heart even when getting up every day had been a struggle. Because on that day, with tears streaming down her face, she did the thing she couldn't do until that moment.

She prayed for Trace Canton.

And then she folded up the letter and tucked it into a box with the invitations and napkins, and the guestbook that had never been used.

People who knew her well said things intended to make her feel better. "Better to find out now, Elle. Better than living your life with him and having him leave you three years from now." Or, "You're not the first one to be left at the altar. It's not a reflection on you, Elle. It was his problem, and it's his loss."

The truth about why he left never came fully to the surface, although the whispering in the lunchroom at Barrett Elementary must've been only a fraction of what it was at Pinewood. People talked, and she assumed they knew. But no one ever said a word to her.

No one but her mother and her sisters. "It's a lie," her mother told her one evening, a week after the broken wedding. "Trace is believing a lie. The truth is we all struggle with sin and we all have a choice whether to live life for God or against Him." She ran her fingers over Elle's hair. "Don't let this change how you feel about yourself or about love, Elle. Please, sweetheart."

But there was nothing her mother could say or do to undo the damage. If the devil was lying to Trace, he was doing the same thing to her. Because from the moment Trace explained himself on the phone that day, from the moment she stepped out of her wedding gown, sobbing so hard she could barely breathe, she became convinced of one thing.

Love was a lie.

And she could live the rest of her life without having anything to do with it.

That was her determination. Yes, she could love her mother and her sisters. And over the next two years she threw herself into getting a master's degree in special education so she could help Daisy find a better life.

But she would never open her heart to a man again.

꒰ꔫ꒱

SHE AND SNOOPY finished two full laps around the park, and Snoopy started whining again. He didn't like to walk more than two laps, not this close to suppertime. She stopped at a bench and he took the spot on the ground next to her, his warm body pressed against her ankles.

Once in a while, when she felt particularly close to God,

she would allow herself to imagine that if love burst through the doors of her heart some far-off day, she wouldn't stop it. She wouldn't pursue it, but she wouldn't resist it, either. Not if God had a plan for her to find love again. Even that was a stretch. She thought about the past few days, and the visitor who had plagued her classroom and her thoughts. Yes, God might bring love into her life again. But not in the form of a married man. The one thing she could never, ever do was allow herself to have feelings for Cody Gunner. Because the first time her heart was broken, she was lucky to escape with her life. Elle had no doubt that the next time wouldn't merely set her back a few years.

It would kill her.

Chapter Thirteen

Cody had planned to make his mind up about his brother's involvement at the ILC before the Friday field trip. But the closer it got to Friday, the more he knew he wanted to attend the trip with Elle and her class. He loved her compassion, loved the way she worked with her students.

Or maybe he just loved watching her.

Whatever it was, he didn't want to stop spending time with her. The days with Carl Joseph at the center had given him the distraction he'd been looking for. Even if he hadn't been looking for a girl with hazel eyes.

After watching her work with the young adults at the center every day that week, he couldn't deny the obvious. She was helping them. Even if a person with Down Syndrome lived at home in a safe, loving environment all his life, it wouldn't hurt for him to know how to cook or eat correctly, how to shop on a budget or take the bus.

Elle Dalton was dedicated to her students in a way that surprised him. He had studied her all week, trying to see past her beauty. Whatever drove her, it wasn't a temporary incentive. She was committed to changing the lives of handicapped people, and she went about it as if that alone were the purpose of her life.

At the end of class Thursday he found her in the break room again. Most of the students were gone, but Daisy and Carl Joseph and Gus were outside taking turns at the tetherball pole. "Mr. Gunner"—she was making copies of something, probably the bus route—"thanks for not scaring me this time."

"You're welcome." He smiled, but he was careful to keep the moment professional. "Look, Ms. Dalton—about your field trip tomorrow. I was wondering if I could join you. If it wouldn't be too much trouble."

Elle stopped and put her hands on her hips. She studied him for a moment before she answered. "You've already made up your mind about me"—she waved to the room beyond—"about the work I'm doing here at the center." She wasn't angry, merely pointing out what she clearly thought was a fact. "Why come with us?"

"Because—" He wanted to look away, but he couldn't. She had that effect on him. "The truth is, I'm impressed by your work here. You're giving your students skills they wouldn't have otherwise."

She raised an eyebrow. "Really? I changed your mind that easily?" There was teasing in her tone.

He smiled. "You haven't changed my mind about putting

people like Carl Joseph out in the world to fend for themselves. But"—his voice grew more serious—"your work,
your passion for these people, is a great thing. A very great
thing."

"Thank you." She glanced down at her feet. Her cheeks
grew red and she turned back to the copy machine and
pressed a few buttons. When she spoke, it was hard to hear
her. "You can come with us, Mr. Gunner." She faced him
once more. This time her expression was no-nonsense. "But I
take these field trips very seriously, and so do the students."

"I know that." He hated how she thought of him, critical
and ogre-like. Maybe that's why he needed to spend more
time with her. Not so she could change his mind about the
purpose of the center, but so he could change *her* mind about
him. "The Subway thing…it won't happen again."

She narrowed her eyes. "Do you know where we're going
tomorrow?"

"To a dance class downtown?"

"A dance class and then to an old church. One of the oldest in Colorado Springs. It has a midday Friday service."

Cody clenched the muscles in his jaw. He and God had
been on a roller-coaster since Ali died. She had faith enough
to move mountains, but it hadn't helped her in the end. After
her death, there were times when he wanted nothing to do
with Ali's faith, and other times when it made perfect sense,
when he was thankful beyond words to Ali's God for giving
them as much time as they had.

Even so, over the last few years he'd fallen away from even
thinking about faith. It hadn't been a part of his life before

Ali, and truthfully it hadn't helped much to believe there was a higher power, a Great Being who watched over the moves of His people and helped when He was called upon. Cody crossed his arms. "Carl Joseph has never been to church. Our family, we've never been churchgoers."

"I know that." She no longer seemed flustered. "I talked to each of the students. Every one of them wants to go."

"Because prayer is a life skill." It wasn't a question. He had seen Elle remind them about prayer time and again during the week.

Elle drew a long breath. "Yes, Mr. Gunner. Because prayer is a life skill." She studied him. "Are you opposed to God in some way? Do you want to keep Carl Joseph from attending the church service?"

"No." He shrugged. "I guess I haven't seen a lot of proof of God, that's all. If you want to take your students to church, I won't stand in the way."

"And you won't mumble under your breath or give angry looks to the pastor, rolling your eyes, that sort of thing?" The hint of teasing was back in her voice.

He was beginning to understand Elle Dalton, at least the public Elle. She hid behind a layer of professionalism and mild sarcasm. He understood that. But the time he spent with her left him no closer to knowing the real her. Not in the least. He considered her question. "I'll sit in the back. You'll never know I'm there." He angled his head. "I might even learn something."

"All right then." She went to a filing drawer and pulled out a single sheet of paper. "We're meeting here an hour earlier than usual." She handed him the paper. "Here are the details."

He thanked her and was headed toward the door when he stopped and faced her again. "What's your interest, Ms. Dalton? That's the part I can't figure out."

"My interest?"

"Yes." He wasn't being combative, not this time. He was simply curious. Maybe if he understood her motives, he could consider the reasons for putting someone like Carl Joseph out into the world by himself. He searched her eyes. "Why isn't it enough for people with Down Syndrome to live at home with their parents, safe and loved and cared for?"

"Because"—passion filled her tone—"people with Down Syndrome have dreams and hopes, Mr. Gunner. Did you know that? They look at magazines and television, and they picture themselves dressed in a suit, headed off to work. They see married couples, holding hands and kissing, and they dream of knowing love like that."

Cody could feel himself frown, despite his determination to stay neutral. "They want to be married?"

"Yes." She leaned against the counter. "Before I took this job, I interviewed a married couple with Down Syndrome. They had assistance from a twice-weekly caregiver, but they managed just fine on their own. Even with a variety of health issues." She stared at him, her voice intense. "Do you know how long those two people waited for permission to marry?" She didn't wait for him to answer. "Twenty years, Mr. Gunner. Because people like you and me kept denying them the right to be together."

"It's like letting grade-school kids get married."

"No, it isn't." She crossed her arms. "Down Syndrome makes a person less capable cognitively. But not emotionally. They still mature at an age-appropriate rate."

"You mean, Carl Joseph has the feelings and desires of any other twenty-five-year-old guy?" Cody let loose a single laugh, and it expressed how ludicrous he thought the idea. He had never considered such a thing. Carl Joseph was a child; he would always be a child.

"That's exactly right." In that instant, Cody could think of only one person. His precious Ali. Wasn't that her philosophy? People had to choose life every day if they were going to really live. He blinked back her image and took another step toward the door. "We'll be here in the morning, Ms. Dalton. Thank you."

He left the break room and headed across the center's main area. He stepped outside and saw that Gus was gone. Only Carl Joseph and Daisy remained in the yard, and neither of them heard him walk out. He stood near the door and studied them.

They were singing as loud as they could, though it took a minute for Cody to understand them. When he did, he was struck by the simplicity of the moment. Daisy was dancing in a sort of box step, and Carl Joseph was trying to follow her lead. Together they were singing, "M-I-C...K-E-Y... M-O-U-S-E!"

Something stirred in Cody's heart. Even now Carl Joseph was in danger. He could have a seizure at any time, though Carl Joseph hadn't had one since Cody had been home. He was on a new medication, but the risk remained. That's what the doctor had told his parents yesterday at Carl Joseph's appointment. The doctor was adamant.

Carl Joseph's condition was unstable. Independent living couldn't even be considered unless his health improved.

Cody felt a rush of sadness as he watched his brother. Carl Joseph put his hands around Daisy's waist and the two of them waltzed to something Daisy was humming. Whatever the future held, he hoped Carl Joseph could keep his friendship with Daisy.

For both their sakes.

⌒

"I LOVE DANCING with you, Daisy. 'Cause you're the best dancer in Disneyland!" Carl Joseph smiled so big it became a laugh.

Rain was in the forecast, and Carl Joseph kept looking up, checking the clouds. Cody felt a surge of protectiveness for his younger brother. Lately Carl Joseph had been almost obsessed with clouds, peering at them and staring at them, frowning at them, as if a tornado were in the forecast when all that floated overhead was a layer of cumulus clouds.

It was this exact sort of thing that would make him a danger to himself if he were on his own in the world. He could be walking across a street and get distracted by the sky. That quickly he could step off a curb into the path of a bus.

Carl Joseph and Daisy had moved on to some other playacting. They were doing some other kind of dance step—and but for Carl Joseph's awkward clumsiness, it almost seemed they were following a regular pattern.

That had to be Daisy's doing. Clearly she was as taken with Carl Joseph as he was with her. No doubt she encouraged his new interest in faith, since she'd been attending the center longer than he had.

A gust of wind blew across the courtyard, and the first raindrops began to fall. In the distance, a low rumble of thunder echoed across the valley. Suddenly Daisy began to cry, loudly and in short bursts. She covered her face and turned in a tight circle, frantic. At the same time, Carl Joseph sprang into action. He pulled off his jacket, put it around her shoulders, and whispered something into her ear. Then he led her with fast, jerky steps to a covering of trees and a small cement bench.

Cody watched, mesmerized. As they reached the dry area, Daisy began brushing the raindrops off her arms and legs and face, her movements quick and compulsive. If Cody didn't know better, he'd think the raindrops were burning her skin. He moved closer, but before he could make his presence known, he saw Carl Joseph put his arm around her shoulders and gently, tenderly, rock her.

Cody was close enough now to hear what they were saying, though they were too distracted to notice him. Carl Joseph was still rocking her. "It's okay, Daisy. The rain won't hurt you. Not the rain."

She looked up, her expression paralyzed with fear. "I could melt."

"No, Daisy. That was the Wicked Witch of the West. You're not a witch and...and you're not a wicked witch. You're Minnie Mouse."

A slight smile appeared in her eyes. "And you're Mickey."

"Right." He laughed hard, the laugh that would tell anyone within listening range that he was not like other people. The laugh that made Cody love him more than anything in life. "Right, Daisy, I'm Mickey. Mickey Mouse." He pointed at her, his eyes big. "And I'm writing you a letter. So I can entertain you at Disneyland."

For a moment Daisy's eyes lit up, too. But the rain was falling harder and she looked out at it. As she did, terror filled her face. "But the rain..." She began to cry. She pressed her forehead into Carl Joseph's shoulder. "Keep me dry, CJ. Okay? Keep me dry."

Cody was stunned by the scene. His throat felt thick as he watched it play out. This was why Carl Joseph had become obsessed with clouds. Because he was driven to protect Daisy from her obvious fear of the rain. His heart swelled inside him. The friendship between the two of them was painfully genuine.

He gave a little cough so he wouldn't startle them. "Buddy...it's time to go home."

Carl Joseph gave him a frustrated look, the sort of look he had never given Cody in all his life. "Not yet." He tightened his hold on Daisy's shoulders. "Not with rain." He pointed at the wet pavement. "Not now."

"Okay." Cody wasn't sure what to do next. Behind him he heard a sound and he turned. Elle was locking up, and as she came out she realized what was happening. "Carl Joseph, are you helping Daisy again?" She smiled at the two and headed toward them. Along the way she glanced at Cody, and her eyes told him how Carl Joseph's display of friendship touched her as well.

When she reached Daisy, she touched the young woman's shoulder. "Are you okay?"

"CJ keeps me dry." She looked up but made no effort to move.

"Carl Joseph has to go home with his brother." Elle tilted her head. "I'll make sure you don't get wet, okay?"

Carl Joseph lifted his eyes to Elle and then turned to Cody again. He stood, his hand still on Daisy's back. For a moment he looked unable to express himself. That happened often with Carl Joseph, and when it did he sometimes hid his face and resorted to a slight rocking motion.

Not now.

With his options limited, Carl Joseph looked around and spotted the covered area near the center door. He pulled his jacket up around Daisy's shoulders again and over her head. "Come on, Daisy. Run with me."

Her blank expression made it clear she didn't know where Carl Joseph was taking her or why they were supposed to run. But she trusted him. Because she ducked her head and with quick steps, the two of them ran across the rainy yard to the covered area.

There Carl Joseph eased his jacket down around Daisy's shoulders. Cody could barely make out what he was saying.

"Brother wants to go."

Daisy smiled at Carl Joseph, but then glared at Cody. "I want you to stay."

"Me, too." He stood squarely in front of her and patted her shoulders. "You stay dry with Teacher."

"Okay." Daisy ran her tongue over her lower lip. "Come tomorrow, CJ."

"I will." He pulled her into a hug then, and for a moment the two held on as if they might never let go.

Cody watched, awed. He barely noticed Elle coming up beside him. "See?" Her tone was gentle. "Carl Joseph doesn't want you making his decisions. Can't you feel it?"

"Yes." Cody kept his eyes on his brother. "I feel it." But in that moment, he felt Elle's nearness more. The softness in her voice and the subtle smell of her shampoo. He tried to focus. "Does Daisy have a ride?"

"I'll take her."

"Oh." He had sensed that Elle was fonder of Daisy than some of the other students. That was fine; maybe Daisy had no other way to the center. He tipped an invisible hat. "See you tomorrow."

In the car on the way home, Cody looked at his brother. "Daisy's afraid of the rain?"

"Yes." Carl Joseph was grumpy. His short answer was loaded with attitude.

"Why's she afraid?" Cody turned his attention back to the road. He tried to keep his tone upbeat, casual.

Carl Joseph uttered a loud breath and turned impatient eyes toward Cody. "She isn't the Wicked Witch of the West.

She's Minnie Mouse. And Minnie Mouse doesn't melt in the rain."

"Oh." Cody blinked. He made one more try. "So she's afraid she'll melt, Buddy? Is that it?"

"Yes." Carl Joseph lifted his hands and let them drop in his lap. "I keep her dry, okay?"

"Okay." They rode the rest of the way in silence.

Not until they pulled into the driveway did Cody sense that Carl Joseph had cooled down some. "Are you okay now, Buddy?"

"Yes, I'm okay." He reached out and patted Cody's knee. "Sorry, Brother. Sorry for being mad. We still wanted to dance, okay?"

"You and Daisy?"

"Yes." He smiled, even though the look of it was still a little subdued. "Me and Minnie Mouse."

That night Carl Joseph couldn't stop talking about the field trip. They were going to get a dance lesson from a real dance instructor. "So maybe I can learn the Lindy Hop," he told their parents after dinner. He hopped around the table, laughing as he went. "Hop...hop...hop!"

Neither of his parents had spoken to Cody about the center since he started attending with Carl Joseph earlier that week. Now, though, his mother caught his eyes, and the concern in her face told Cody she'd been worrying about the situation since their last conversation. "You're going on the field trip?"

"Brother wants to dance!" Carl Joseph's mood was

considerably better than it had been in the car on the way home. He grinned as he danced past Cody. "Right, Brother?"

"Dancing and church." He raised a forkful of mashed potatoes in a mock sort of cheer. "Should be interesting."

Carl Joseph stopped in his tracks. His smile faded. "But you're happy to go, right, Brother? Not mad like the Subway field trip?"

Elle's request ran through his mind. Remorse hit him like a truck, and he immediately changed his tone. "Yes, Buddy. I'm very happy." He held his hand out, the sarcasm from earlier gone. Carl Joseph took hold of his fingers. "The field trip will be lots of fun."

Doubt lingered, but only for a moment. Then Carl Joseph smiled again, the big open-mouthed smile he was known for. He pushed his glasses back up his nose. "Goodie! Field Trip Day is fun!"

The rest of that night and the next morning as they pulled up in front of the center, fear shot darts at Cody. What if Carl Joseph had a seizure today? He could fall and get hurt and... the worst scenarios played out in his imagination in as much time as it took him to draw a single breath. He couldn't lose Carl Joseph, his buddy. His friend. Not after losing Ali. He wouldn't survive it.

He could only hope that of all days, Carl Joseph's medication wouldn't give out today.

Chapter Fourteen

Cody kept his thoughts to himself as the group waited inside the center. Once they were all together, Elle took her place at the front. "Everyone remembers the bus route?"

Several voices began talking at once. Elle held up her hand. Her patience seemed to know no limits. "One at a time."

Daisy raised her hand. "Me, Teacher."

"Let's ask someone else. We all know that Daisy knows the bus routes." She gave Daisy a quick smile. "Gus, why don't you tell us the bus route today."

"Uh..." Gus pulled a piece of crumpled paper from his pocket and opened it. He turned it one way and then another and for a few seconds he did nothing but stammer.

Cody raised his brow, waiting.

Finally Gus looked at Elle. "Walk to Adler Street. Take the west bus past four stops to Cheyenne Street. Get off."

He looked up at the ceiling and tapped one finger on his temple. He checked his paper again and suddenly his eyes got big. "I know. Take the orange bus south to Pine Street. Get off and take the south bus to Main Street." His mouth hung open, eyes unblinking. "Right, Teacher?"

"Yes." Elle beamed. "Exactly right."

With that, the group gathered their things and left the center, walking toward Adler. Cody lagged behind, watching. Every now and then a car would slow down as it passed. Cody wanted to shout at the driver to keep moving and not to stare. It was hard enough for this group to get anywhere without people gawking at them.

Like every other day, Carl Joseph walked next to Daisy. They were the same height, but Carl Joseph stood taller in her presence. When he seemed to think no one was looking, Carl Joseph linked his baby finger through hers. It was something Cody tried not to notice. Because Carl Joseph loved this life, these friends. So what would happen when his parents did what they needed to do? When they broke the news to him that independent living wasn't possible for him?

As they reached the first bus, Carl Joseph walked more slowly. This time Daisy put her arm around him. "It's okay, CJ. This bus is right."

Carl Joseph stopped at the bottom of the steps. He pulled the directions sheet from his pocket, looked at it, and scratched his head. Then he pulled his bus pass from the other pocket and looked at it. "This bus is for Cheyenne Street?"

"Yes, CJ." Daisy tugged gently at his arm. "This bus."

Cody shuddered to think how Carl Joseph would handle this moment without the support of Daisy and Elle and his classmates. His brother tucked the papers back in his pocket and looked up at the bus. He was stiff with worry, and he began wringing his hands. "This bus?"

"Come on, CJ." Daisy released his arm and moved onto the first step. There were still four other students waiting to board.

One of them peered around the others. "Move it, people. Teacher wants to move it."

Elle was hanging back, watching the drama unfold. She kept from saying anything, and after a minute, his legs trembling, Carl Joseph followed Daisy onto the bus.

Cody came up behind Elle. She smelled wonderful, and for a crazy minute he wished it was just the two of them on the trip. "Is he always like this?"

"Yes." Elle didn't look troubled. "Most of the students are nervous about the bus until they get used to it. That's the purpose of the field trips."

Cody swallowed. His heart was beating faster than usual. "How can you know they won't act this way when they're by themselves for the first time?"

Elle reached the top step. She looked back at Cody. "We don't just drop them off at an apartment and wish them luck, Mr. Gunner. Every stage is carefully monitored."

"Oh." He held her gaze a beat longer than necessary. Then he swallowed. "I didn't know."

They reached the dance studio on Main Street and filed into the lobby. The instructor was an older woman, and she and Elle seemed to know each other. The students moved into the dance room, and for the next two hours they learned a variety of swing dance moves, including the Lindy Hop. Cody couldn't help but smile as he watched the smiles on the faces around him. Clearly they loved to dance.

As they left, Cody caught up to Elle and walked beside her. "You taught them about dance, right?"

"Yes." Her eyes sparkled. Then her gaze dropped to his left hand and her guard seemed to go up again. "People with Down Syndrome need more exercise than other people. Dance is an exercise they enjoy, so it's something they'll do without being told."

"They could benefit from something tougher—weight training or cycling." He put his hands in his pockets, his pace easy and in line with hers. She had a dizzying effect on him, something he couldn't shake. "I was thinking of starting something before I came home."

"Really?" Her enthusiasm took him by surprise. "The owner of the center wants to expand. He wants a fitness center, an addition to the existing building." She looked at him, her eyes thoughtful. "He won a grant from the state, so the money's already in place." She angled her head. "I'm supposed to find someone who could run it, develop a fitness program for the students. That way we could open it up to other disabled people, as well. People who don't have the opportunity to learn independence." She gave him a curious look. "Are you returning to work, wherever you were before you came home?"

"No." He waited for the usual comments about rodeo and

how difficult life must be on the road. But they didn't come. He smiled to himself. She was maybe one of the first women he'd ever known who wasn't part of the rodeo world. He looked straight ahead. "I'm sort of at a crossroads. Looking for the next thing."

"Oh." Her look became the more familiar subtly sarcastic one. "That's why we were blessed to have your scrutiny this past week. Because you have nothing better to do."

"Look, Elle..." He wanted to keep the air between them light. Her nearness was intoxicating, but his feelings went beyond that. He liked her, liked the way she didn't back down from him and the way she cared for her students. He liked her passion most of all. But still he had to make himself clear. "I'm here for one reason." He nodded at Carl Joseph walking next to Daisy a few people ahead of them. "I love that kid."

She hesitated and then moved over some, creating more space between them. "I understand that, Mr. Gunner." She gathered the students in a circle there on the sidewalk. "Who besides Daisy can tell me the next bus route?"

The students pulled out their direction sheets. One of the students gave the right answer and they were off again, this time toward the church service. As they climbed off the bus across from the old downtown church, Elle threw what must've been a curve at them. "Who would like to eat lunch?"

Several hands shot up.

"I'm very hungry, Teacher." Gus looked at the others. "We're starving."

"Yes." Tammy twirled one of her braids. "I could eat a cow."

"Cow isn't always good for you." Sid pointed at her. "Cow should be cooked."

Elle stifled a smile. "Very well." She took in the faces around her. "How many of you brought money?"

All week, Elle had talked to them about field trips, and how if they were going out on the town they should be prepared. Preparation was a life skill, she told them. They should have their directions, and a cell phone, and ten dollars in case they needed to eat while they were out.

Now all but two students raised their hands. Some of them actually raised their money.

Elle told them to put their money back in their pockets. "Tommy's Burgers is one block south." Elle pointed in the right direction. "We have an hour before the church service. Let's go eat."

"See," Tammy announced loudly. "We are having cow." She stuck her tongue out at Sid as she walked past. "Cooked cow, Sid. Burgers are cooked cow."

The first trouble of the day came at the restaurant.

One minute everything seemed to be going smoothly, and the next Tammy was standing and screaming, pointing at Gus. "Help him! Someone help him!"

Gus's face was deep red, and he was grabbing at his throat. Drool hung at the corners of his mouth and he was stomping his feet in panic.

"Help him!" Tammy's scream incited the rest of the group, and in an instant, all the students were on their feet shouting the same thing. "Help him! Someone help him!"

Cody was sitting by himself. As soon as he realized what was happening, he cut his way through the crowd, reached Gus, and positioned himself behind the young man. "Stand up straight, Gus."

The guy did as he was asked. By now Elle was at their side. "Dear God." She covered her mouth, her voice filled with fear. "Help us, Lord."

Cody stayed behind him and slid his arms beneath Gus's. He made a fist with one hand and cupped it with the other, then he pressed the fist against Gus's stomach, in the hollow where his ribs met just below his chest. He pressed hard, jerking his hand in an upward motion. Then he did it again.

Some of the girls were screaming now, moving in tight circles. On the third thrust, a large piece of barely chewed hamburger flew from Gus's mouth out onto the floor. He gasped for air. His eyes wide, he dropped to his knees and grabbed his throat with both hands.

Cody put his hand on the young man's shoulder. "Gus, you're okay. Breathe out."

But panic still had the best of him. He shook his head, fast and frenzied.

"Gus." Cody used a stronger tone this time. "Breathe out. You're okay, now just breathe out."

Elle worked her way through the students, telling them that Gus was fine and asking them to sit back down. Two of the girls were still crying.

"Breathe out, Gus." Cody leaned in closer. "You're okay."

Finally Gus did as he was told. He pursed his lips and blew out. He still had his hands around his throat, his eyes still bugged out of his face. But after a minute he struggled to his feet. He stared at Cody and then at Elle and back again. "I laughed."

Tammy was shaking, but she approached Cody and explained what had happened. "Gus was telling a funny story." She looked at the other two students who had been sitting at her table. "And he was eating and telling a funny story."

"And"—one of the others grabbed his throat and stuck his tongue out—"no more words."

Cody didn't realize until then that he was shaking. Gus had waited longer than necessary to stand up, probably because choking was an unfamiliar concept to him. Carl Joseph had choked once when he was around ten or eleven. Cody still remembered their mother giving him the Heimlich maneuver and saving his life.

Gus finally relaxed the hold he had on his throat. He lowered his hands and, moving like a ninety-year-old man, he returned to his table. When he reached his chair, he turned and pointed at Cody. "He likes us now."

"Yes, he likes us." Tammy bent over in dramatic fashion, catching her own breath. When she straightened, she lifted both her hands toward the ceiling. "Thank You, God. Carl Joseph's brother likes us."

Cody felt the sting of tears in his eyes. It had taken this, but at least now the students trusted him.

Elle made her way to his side and touched his elbow. "Mr. Gunner..."

"Call me Cody." He braced himself against the nearest chair and tried to catch his breath.

"Cody...thank you." Her eyes still held fear, but it was mixed with an undeniable admiration. Maybe even an attraction. Her tone was drenched in relief. "Nothing like that...That's never happened before."

Cody looked at Carl Joseph. His brother had his hands over his face, and he was rocking. Daisy was talking to him through the spaces between his fingers. Cody sighed and turned to Elle again. "People with Down Syndrome sometimes have trouble swallowing."

"I know. It's one of the reasons we make sure the students are paired up when they move out on their own."

Cody looked deep into her eyes. "Even then..." He wasn't being defiant, just honest. "This sort of thing could always happen." He walked over and crouched next to Carl Joseph. "Buddy, it's okay. Gus is fine."

Carl Joseph opened his fingers wider and peered at him. "Gus?"

"Yes, he's okay." Cody wasn't sure if his brother was reacting this way because he remembered what had happened when he was younger. Either way, the event had traumatized him.

It took a half hour before the group relaxed enough to set out for the church. They walked together, and again Cody hung back. Ali had always wanted him to go to church with her, but they'd never gone. Their time was too short, and being around other people always represented a possibility of infection for her.

The day was overcast again, but Cody looked up and saw a slice of blue. *Ali, you'd be proud of me. I'm going to church.* A sad smile lifted his lips. It was happening. Her memory no longer consumed him. Thoughts of her were never far away, but they weren't a part of every breath anymore. That would explain the feeling in his heart, the emptiness. He looked up ahead at Elle. She walked between Gus and Tammy, the three of them laughing.

And maybe it explained why he couldn't stop thinking about a certain young teacher.

When they reached the church, Elle brought her finger to her lips and shushed the students. Cody was last in line, and she repeated the motion for his benefit. Then she added, "I mean it."

Cody saluted her and filed in. A change had happened today, maybe because of the incident with Gus. There was a bond between him and Elle now, something he couldn't quite define. He took a pew just behind the students, and watched how they filed in and found their seats. Two of the guys wore baseball caps. As they reached their seats, they removed their caps and placed them on the floor. Awe and wonder filled their faces. Gus dropped to his knees and bowed his head immediately, and several of the others did the same. A few merely looked around, spellbound by the old church.

An organist played two hymns, and then the pastor got things started. He welcomed Elle's students and explained that God has a plan for every one of His children. Cody swallowed back a rush of emotion. *Down Syndrome, God?* Is that the plan You have for Carl Joseph and his friends?

There was no answer, nothing audible. But he remembered something his mother had said over the years when she spent time with Carl Joseph.

"Here on earth, we think Carl Joseph is handicapped. Won't it be funny if we get to heaven one day and find out it was the other way around."

Cody watched Carl Joseph, his head bowed in prayer. Their mother had a point.

He crossed his arms and lost focus on what was being said up front. Instead he thought about Ali, how she had believed so firmly that she would go to heaven, that she would meet up with the sister she lost as a child, and the two of them would ride horses forever across endless fields of green.

Cody wasn't so sure.

He caught very little of the rest of the sermon, but when it was over, collection baskets were passed. Cody sat a little straighter and felt his blood begin to heat. Certainly the church wouldn't be so bold as to take money from handicapped people. He slid into a pew adjacent to the group so he could see better.

Sure enough, the basket made its way back to Elle's students, and one at a time they pulled out wads of one-dollar bills and coins and tossed them in. When the basket reached Carl Joseph, Cody watched him take out a stack of money, count five twenty-dollar bills, and place them in the basket.

Cody was on his feet before the basket could make it to the next person. A hundred dollars? Where would his brother have gotten that sort of money, and how could he throw it into a collection basket? He quietly approached the pew where his brother was sitting next to Daisy. When the basket reached the end of the row, Cody dug in and discreetly took out the five twenties. Then he whispered toward his brother. "Buddy, we need to go."

"What?" Carl Joseph pushed his glasses up. He looked stunned by Cody's request. He glanced at the students around him. Several of them noticed Cody and were clearly waiting to see what Carl Joseph would do. He looked back at Cody, and his face reddened. He leaned over Daisy's legs and whispered loud, "Not now! This is church."

"Come on." Cody couldn't wait another minute. They needed to catch a cab back to the center and get home. He gave his brother a stern look. "Now."

Carl Joseph respected him too much to argue. Despite his angry expression, he stood and moved past Daisy out into the aisle.

It was at that moment that Elle noticed what was happening. She excused herself and came to them, her eyes full of alarm. She, too, kept to a low whisper. "What's going on?"

"We're leaving." Cody could feel the apology in his eyes. "My brother just dropped a hundred dollars in the plate." A sad, whispered laugh escaped. "This isn't for us. I'm sorry."

He led the way and despite the horrified looks from the other students, Carl Joseph followed. When they were outside on the front steps of the church, Cody turned to Carl Joseph. He held up the five twenties. "What's this, Buddy?"

Carl Joseph's anger became sorrow. His shoulders fell a little. "My gift, Brother. My gift for Jesus."

"Jesus doesn't need a hundred dollars, Buddy." Cody

waved the bills at his brother. "You don't know the first thing about money."

"I know the first thing." Carl Joseph held up his hand and stared at his fingers. He was so nervous, his entire arm shook. He appeared to be counting and after several seconds he held up his pointer finger. "I know one thing. Gifts are for Jesus."

Cody's heart broke for his brother. He found a kinder tone. "Where'd you get this money, Buddy?"

His brother made a series of exasperated sounds and turned in small half circles. Then he stopped and pointed at Cody. "I worked, Brother. I worked for that money."

"Doing what?" Cody hated his tone, hated that this would be yet another time when he and Carl Joseph would struggle to find the friendship that had always come so easily for them. But he had to make a point. He had never heard about his brother holding a job. He softened his tone again. "Are you lying, Buddy?"

"No!" Carl Joseph shouted the word.

Cody hesitated. "Let's get a cab." They crossed the street at the light, and Cody scanned the traffic in either direction. As he did, a soft rain began to fall.

"Buddy…" Cody couldn't believe it. Less than a hundred days of rain a year, and today had to be one of them.

"Rain!" Carl Joseph gasped and looked up at the sky. "Daisy! Daisy might get wet!" He reached his hand out toward the church across the street. "Daisy, don't get wet!" Then, before Cody could stop him, he lurched off the curb and straight into oncoming traffic.

In a blur of motion, a van swerved to miss Carl Joseph, but its rearview mirror caught him by the arm and knocked him to the ground. Traffic screeched to a halt, and several drivers laid on their horns.

"Buddy!" Cody ran into the road. Carl Joseph lay on his stomach, sprawled out and unmoving. His arm was bleeding where the vehicle had hit it. "Buddy!" Cody dropped to his knees next to his brother. "Talk to me, Buddy."

The driver of the van, a young guy, was walking toward them, his face pale. "I'm sorry....He jumped right in front of me."

Cody screamed at the guy. "Call 911! Now!"

He lowered his face close to Carl Joseph's. "Buddy, I need you to talk to me."

The rain was falling harder, and after a few terrifying seconds Carl Joseph lifted his head and looked at the church. His cheek was scraped, but otherwise he looked okay. This time he held out his good arm, the one that wasn't bleeding. "Daisy hates the rain."

Cody's eyes filled with tears. "Where are you hurt, Buddy? Tell me."

"In my heart." Carl Joseph heaved himself into a sitting position, oblivious to the traffic stopped all around him. He put his hand over his chest and gave Cody a condemning look. "I hurt in my heart."

Cody carefully helped his brother to the curb. By the time the ambulance arrived, Cody was pretty sure his brother was going to be okay. Physically, anyway. He was given permission to accompany him to the hospital, and the last thing he saw as they closed the door was Elle Dalton and several students on the front steps of the church.

His eyes met hers, and there was no need for explanation. Carl Joseph had been hit by a car, the very thing Cody had feared. But it hadn't happened because of anything Elle Dalton had taught or failed to teach. It was his fault, entirely. Why had he overreacted? So, his brother gave a hundred dollars....They could've talked about it later, at home. Carl Joseph had been having the time of his life—sitting next to Daisy, surrounded by his friends, praying to a God he believed in. What was Cody thinking pulling him from the service like that?

The ambulance took a sharp turn. Cody was thankful that they kept the sirens off. He put his hand on his brother's foot. "You okay, Buddy?"

"Daisy..." He covered his face and shook his head. "Daisy needs my coat."

Cody silently cursed himself. "I'm sorry, Buddy."

He lowered his hands and slowly lifted his head enough so that their eyes met. Hurt and betrayal filled Carl Joseph's expression. "I didn't lie, Brother." He rested his head back on the stretcher and began whispering, "Sorry, Daisy....Sorry about the rain."

Cody hated this, hated what he'd just done. Since he'd been home he'd only worked to make Carl Joseph unhappy and uncomfortable. Maybe he belonged back on the circuit, after all. He closed his eyes. If he hadn't pulled his brother from the service, Carl Joseph would be fine. Instead, the accident would likely sway his parents that the doctor was right. Carl Joseph was not suited to a life of independence. And in the big scheme of things, the doctor was probably right. Carl Joseph was safer at home.

After today, the answer would be obvious to everyone in his family. Carl Joseph's days at the Independent Living Center were over.

Chapter Fifteen

Carl Joseph was lying in a big white hospital bed. He stared out the window at the rain. It kept falling and falling but he couldn't help Daisy. He couldn't give her his coat. He didn't even know where she was.

Brother was sitting next to him, but he didn't want to talk to Brother, except sometimes. He looked at him now. "I didn't lie."

"I know." Brother put his hand on the bed. "I'm sorry, Buddy. I know you didn't lie."

"I didn't." He looked out the window at the rain again. "Mom gave me jobs, and I worked for Mom. 'Cause all winter I brought in firewood. Every time she asked. And I stacked firewood."

"Mom and Dad will be here any minute, Buddy. Everyone's glad you're okay."

Carl Joseph turned to Brother again. "'Cause my heart is not okay. Daisy might get wet."

"I know what you're thinking." Brother stood up and walked to the door. Then he came back again. His eyes looked red. "You think this is all my fault, Buddy, and you're right. It is my fault. I didn't understand about the gift for Jesus." He breathed hard. "I'm sorry. I should've let you stay."

"Yes." Carl Joseph nodded. His cheek hurt and it hurt to turn his neck. "The field trip was not done."

"I know." Brother sat back down in the chair near the bed. "You didn't want to leave yet."

Carl Joseph touched the owie on his face. He looked back at the rainy sky. "Daisy might get wet. 'Cause I tried to get her, but the traffic ..."

"Daisy is fine. I talked to your teacher. She wanted you to know that Daisy is not wet, okay?" Brother sounded sad. "Remember?"

"Yeah, 'cause Daisy might want my jacket." Carl Joseph saw his parents in the doorway.

His mother took a deep breath and ran to him. "Carl Joseph!" She leaned over and hugged him. "I was so worried!"

"Be careful. He has a bruised sternum, Mom." Brother crossed his arms. He stepped back so Dad could get in close. "No internal injuries, though. Just a few bruises."

Carl Joseph looked at his mother. He felt glad to see her. "'Cause my heart hurts."

"He's talking about Daisy." Brother leaned in and looked at her. His voice had a lot of sorry in it. "The doctor said he's going to be fine."

"'Cause Daisy might get wet." He pointed at Brother. "He took my gift for Jesus."

Brother didn't say anything. He just hung his head down low.

"Carl Joseph"—Mom hugged him again—"I was so worried about you."

"Me, too." Dad touched his face. The good side. "Thank God you're okay."

"Yeah, 'cause Brother took my gift for Jesus."

"Okay, well, we'll talk to Cody about that." His mom kissed his head. She gave Brother a look, and Dad did, too. Then Mom pointed to the hall and Brother nodded. She turned back to him. "We need to talk to Cody. We'll be right out in the hall, and then we'll come back, okay?"

Carl Joseph didn't want to say it was okay. He didn't want Mom and Dad to talk to Brother in the hall 'cause that's where they might think of bad news. Very bad. He felt tears, and he blinked four times fast. Then he looked from his mom to his dad. "Hurry."

They said they would, and they followed Brother out into the hall. Carl Joseph tried to stop the tears, 'cause sometimes kids at school said, "Baby, baby," if he had tears. He looked at the rain and the tears came harder. 'Cause Daisy might get wet and she might need his jacket.

And 'cause Mom and Dad and Brother had bad news in the hall.

Very bad.

HIS PARENTS WAITED until they were far enough away from Carl Joseph's room that he couldn't hear them. Then Cody's father stared at him. "Tell us what happened."

"Was it a seizure?" His mom's face was pale. She gripped his father's arm, and there was a cry in her voice. "The doctor warned us about this."

And like that, Cody had his chance. His parents were afraid, the way he knew they'd be. A week ago, he would've been grateful that finally they had their proof. Evidence that Carl Joseph couldn't make it on his own.

But that wasn't the truth, not now, anyway.

"It wasn't a seizure." Cody folded his arms and looked at the floor. "It was my fault." He lifted his eyes, but instead of finding his voice, he was seized by sorrow. Because of his careless actions, Carl Joseph had nearly been killed.

His father took hold of his shoulder. "Son, it's okay."

"No, it's not." He gritted his teeth. "I've been wrong." He searched his parents' eyes and the entire story tumbled out, every honest detail.

He explained about the incident in the church, how Carl Joseph had placed a hundred dollars in the collection basket. "Which is crazy." He held up his hands. "A hundred dollars?"

Something came over his mother's expression. "Oh, no..." She covered her mouth with one hand and shook her head. "I knew about that." Her face was ashen. "I forgot to tell you."

His father looked confused. "I didn't hear about this."

Mary sighed and absently massaged her neck. "Carl Joseph worked for me all winter, bringing in firewood, stacking it, making sure we always had enough to keep the house warm. He made four hundred dollars."

Cody felt his heart sink another notch. "Still…he doesn't understand the value, Mom."

"He does." She smiled, but another layer of tears filled her eyes. "He said his gift was half an iPod, fifty bottles of milk, or about four bags of groceries. He told me it was four pairs of jeans or ten T-shirts. He knew how much money it was."

Cody moaned. He let his head fall back against the wall and stared at the ceiling. Why did everything have to be so confusing? No matter how kind Carl Joseph's intentions, a person with so little income-earning potential should never throw a hundred dollars in an offering plate. But did that mean he couldn't live on his own? If living on his own was what he wanted?

"I think…" He drew a slow breath and tried to put his thoughts in order. He'd been thinking about this moment since they arrived at the hospital, since he'd known Carl Joseph was okay, and he'd had time to analyze the situation. He looked from his father to his mom. "I see what you mean about the center. I think it might be good for Carl Joseph."

For half a minute his parents only stared at him, mouths slightly open. Then his mother exchanged a worried frown with his dad. "Cody"—she turned her attention back to him—"we've made a decision. Carl Joseph's health is too unsteady."

"We're pulling him from the center."

Cody could hardly believe it. The tables had turned, but after Carl Joseph's accident and the doctor's advice earlier that week, there wasn't much to say. "I don't know about independent living"—he shifted his weight—"but that center's good for Carl Joseph." Angry tears clouded his vision. "He loves it there."

"We've made up our minds." His father's voice was calm, but certain. "Your mother and I have talked about having you work with Carl Joseph."

"You were looking for a way to be more involved, remember?" His mother touched his elbow. "That's what you said when you came home."

Cody didn't respond. Anything he might say would make him sound delusional. After all, he had wanted safety for Carl Joseph whatever the cost.

They went on about how Cody could teach his brother ranch work, how to help with Ace and how to keep the fence around the property in working order. How to clear land and trim hedges—that sort of thing.

"Eventually he could take over for one of our ranch hands." His father sounded as if he'd been thinking about this for a while. "Carl Joseph could make a living right at home."

"Yes." His mother's tone was hopeful. "I found a program at the park for people with Down Syndrome. Something social, without the goal of independence. Something to help replace the center."

Nothing would replace the center. Cody understood that now. The idea sounded safe. Constructive. But would it give Carl Joseph a reason to look forward to Fridays? Cody's heart ached. He pictured Carl Joseph, the way he'd looked earlier today, basking in the light of his special friend. He peered back toward the hospital room and then at his parents. "What about Daisy?"

"She can visit." His mother's answer was quick. "Her parents can bring her over any time."

"He has friends at the center." Cody's argument was only half-hearted.

"He'll make new friends." His father sighed. "We have no choice, Cody."

Defeat settled in around Cody's soul. He could hardly argue. After the accident, Carl Joseph might need a month before he was stable enough to leave the house. Based on the doctor's advice and today's accident they had little choice, really.

Cody felt his determination build. If this was a season in Carl Joseph's life when Cody could help him get stronger or teach him how to be a ranch hand, so be it. He'd take him to the new classes and help him get stronger. He'd do it to the best of his ability. He owed Carl Joseph that much. Especially after today. His parents' plan might work, even if it wasn't what his buddy wanted.

Now it was only a matter of breaking the news to Carl Joseph.

Chapter Sixteen

Mary Gunner hovered over a stack of dishes in the kitchen sink and watched Cody pound out of the barn on Ace. His frustration was at an all-time high. Mary watched him go, and she felt her anxiety grow. So far the new plan wasn't coming together the way any of them had hoped. She sighed and adjusted the drain plug so it was tight against the base of the sink. Then she squirted dish soap in and around the plates and cups and turned on the hot water.

The old farmhouse didn't have a dishwasher, but Mary had never minded. She enjoyed washing dishes. It gave her time to look out the window at the distant fields and foothills. Here, with her hands in warm, soapy water and her eyes on the endless ranchland, she always believed that somehow everything would work out.

But today she had her doubts.

Carl Joseph had stayed in the hospital overnight while they watched his heart. It had slipped into a weak rhythm after the accident, and his doctor wanted to be sure he was completely back to normal before he came home. By the time they released him, all his tests were fine, and Carl Joseph was ready to go home, ready to get back to his life.

His new life.

That afternoon, she and Mike and Cody sat down to explain the situation to Carl Joseph.

Mike had started the conversation. "We're proud of you, son. You know that." He leaned over his knees and rested on his forearms. He never broke eye contact with Carl Joseph.

"'Cause I'm growing up and Teacher is teaching me." Carl Joseph looked nervous. He shifted his attention from Mike to her, and finally to Cody. "I was on a field trip."

Mary could see the accusation in Carl Joseph's eyes. He might not have confronted Cody, but he was angry. He hadn't acted the same around his older brother since the accident. Cody stared at the old wooden table. Mike cleared his throat. "We have some new ideas for you, son. All of us think they could be a very good change for you."

"Change?" Carl Joseph pushed his glasses up his nose and knit his brows together. "At the center?"

Mary couldn't bear to drag the inevitable out any longer. "Carl Joseph, you're not going back to the center. Not for now, anyway."

"What?" His mouth hung open, and he took a few seconds to stare at each of the faces around him. A loud exasperated sound came from him. He stood and walked a few steps, then he came back and sat down. All the while the shock never left his face. "I like the center."

"But it might not be safe." Mary reached out and held Carl Joseph's hand. "You were nearly killed on Friday."

Carl Joseph stared at Cody for a long time. Then he turned back to his mom and said, "'Cause Daisy might get wet."

"I know." Mary felt her throat get thick. If only there was a way to make Carl Joseph understand.

Mike took over then. "We thought maybe Cody could work with you, teach you how to be a cowboy here on the ranch. That would be a great life skill."

"Brother..." Carl Joseph turned a blank look at Cody. "Brother is not Teacher."

"But I can teach you a lot about working a ranch, Buddy." Cody's voice was tender. "Give it a try, okay? I have some good ideas."

Carl Joseph seemed to sense defeat. He nodded and his shoulders slumped forward. Then, without saying another word, he stood and headed slowly down the hall toward his room.

Mary had replayed the scene a hundred times since then.

Since that day, Carl Joseph had spent a few hours each afternoon learning ranch skills, but his heart wasn't in it. That much was clear to everyone. Mary blew at a wisp of hair. So what was the answer?

She heard the pounding of hooves across the grass out back. Cody came into view, he and Ace flying across the ranch toward the old farmhouse. As they drew closer to the barn, they slowed and came to a stop. Cody was breathing hard, Mary could see that much through the kitchen window. He leaned close to the horse's mane, the way he often did.

All last week, he'd been a different person. Happier, more engaged in conversation. But now...now he was the same sad Cody he'd been for the past four years. She studied him, the way he held himself, the way grief still tugged at his shoulders and his jaw line. Poor Cody. He missed Ali so much. The day she died, she took with her so much more than his lung. His excitement and love and laughter. She took those, too. He was lost without her. He wore his sorrow like a thick cloak—especially when he was on Ace.

Mary watched Cody and Ace head back out toward the far fence again. Cody was struggling with more than missing Ali. No matter how he tried, he couldn't find the familiar friendship with Carl Joseph. They hadn't visited the park program yet, but Cody had his doubts. They all did.

She drew a breath and returned to the dishes. Something would have to give soon, because neither of her sons was happy. Carl Joseph mostly kept to his room. Once in a while Mary would catch him at the computer trying to compose a letter to Daisy. But his frustration generally won out before he finished.

He was missing her badly, and though Cody had called Elle Dalton to inform her of the family's decision to remove Carl Joseph, so far Daisy hadn't been able to come for a visit.

Too soon, Elle told Cody. Daisy needed more time to get used to the idea that Carl Joseph wasn't coming back. A visit now would confuse her.

And so these days Mary Gunner didn't stand at the kitchen sink looking out the window admiring the view. She spent her time doing something she'd learned from Carl Joseph.

She prayed.

For healing and hope and love. And most of all she prayed that God would allow the sunshine to break through the clouds that had gathered around their home. Before the sad changes in her sons became little more than a way of life.

As MUCH AS Elle wanted to believe Cody and his parents would change their minds, by Monday there was no denying the obvious. Carl Joseph wasn't coming back to the center.

Elle had asked for a week to convince Cody Gunner, but she'd failed. She could see that when her eyes met Cody's as he sat in the back of the ambulance moments before it pulled away with Carl Joseph inside. Cody had probably convinced his parents before sundown that Carl Joseph couldn't return to the center.

Carl Joseph's accident had been deeply traumatic for Elle's students. She was still trying to reassure them that Carl Joseph was okay, that the accident hadn't done serious damage. The questions about his condition came every hour at first, but by Friday—a week since they'd seen Carl Joseph—the questions had stopped. Even so, nothing was the way it had been. The students entered the classroom more slowly, and the first thing they did was look around and take stock. When they saw that once again Carl Joseph wasn't there, they frowned, wrinkling their brows and muttering his name under their breath.

Of course the one most affected was Daisy.

It was Monday morning and Elle was in the break room, waiting for the students to arrive. Her sister was sitting at the art table, coloring a picture. For a week she'd done almost no talking. She didn't volunteer information when Elle asked a question, and she wasn't enthused about their latest field trip to the bowling alley.

The coffeemaker needed cleaning, so Elle took it to the sink and began rinsing it out. She could remember every detail of her conversation with Cody Gunner, the one that had taken place the day Carl Joseph got out of the hospital.

"We've made a family decision," he told her.

At first she'd been distracted, trying to hide the effect his voice had on her. But then she realized what he was saying. His tone didn't sound harsh or judgmental, the way he'd come across at times before. If she hadn't known better, she'd have thought she heard regret. "Carl Joseph won't be coming back to the center."

And that was that. It served her right, because there was no denying the feelings she'd developed for Cody Gunner. What sort of woman was she? Looking forward to the company of a guy whose wife was sitting at home waiting for him? Elle was disgusted with herself because after a week with Cody, she was doing it again, letting herself fall for the wrong man. Now he would no longer be a temptation. He wasn't coming back, and neither was Carl Joseph.

But where did that leave Daisy?

Her sister still looked at the door every fifteen minutes, longing for Carl Joseph. When the music played, Daisy sat in her seat staring at her hands or looking at a blank part of the wall. All the while Elle allowed her sister to believe that maybe her friend would return.

But it was time to tell her the truth. No matter how much she hoped the Gunners would change their minds, they clearly weren't budging. Carl Joseph wasn't coming back.

Elle studied her sister. She would tell her today, after class.

The students were arriving, and Elle went to meet them. But as the day progressed, an undeniable cloud of sadness hung in the air. Even bad-tempered Sid was concerned about Carl Joseph. Sid raised his hand in the middle of an explanation on the new bus route. He didn't wait to be called on. "Has anyone seen Carl Joseph?"

Elle didn't give the others a chance to answer. "He's getting better, remember? He had an accident."

"So..." Sid held up his hands. He squinted, the confusion written across his face. "Is he still on the orange bus?"

"No, Sid. He's home getting better."

"He could get better here." Gus looked around for approval. Several of the students nodded and started a chorus of voices agreeing that yes, certainly he could get better just as easily at the center as he could at home.

The rest of the day Elle had trouble keeping them focused. Finally when the last student was gone, she looked around and found Daisy back at the art table. *God...how am I going to say this?* Sadness filled her heart and stung at the corners of her eyes. Dear sweet Daisy. She would be devastated by the news.

Her sister didn't seem to notice her approaching, and Elle had a moment to stand behind Daisy before beginning the conversation. Her sister was drawing a picture of Mickey Mouse, each line meticulous, the colors exactly the ones used in the real Mickey.

"Nice, Daisy." She took the seat beside her sister. "I like it."

"Thank you." Daisy didn't look up. She switched the black crayon for a red one and kept coloring. "It's for CJ."

"Oh." The pain in Elle's heart doubled. "I'm sure he'll like it."

"When he comes back." She paused and looked straight at Elle. "For when he comes back."

"Yes." Elle turned her chair so she was facing her sister. "Daisy, I have to tell you something. It's not something I want to say."

Daisy didn't answer, but her head began to bob ever so slightly. When Daisy was frightened, this was always the first sign, long before she was able to articulate what she was feeling. Elle put her hand over Daisy's. "Stop for a minute, okay? I need you to look at me."

Daisy put down her crayon. She turned to Elle, but she didn't lift her eyes. She was still rocking, and now a soft humming came from her throat. Everything about her mannerisms told Elle that she wanted to shut out whatever was about to be said.

Elle wanted to tell her to look up, but instead she took her sister's hands and held them softly. "Carl Joseph is going to stay at home for a while." She had decided this was the best way of putting it, better than to say that her friend was gone for good. She leaned down so she could see her sister's face better. "His brother told me we can visit him."

"CJ wanted to entertain me." Finally she lifted her head. Tears left a shiny layer over her eyes. "He wanted to entertain me at Disneyland. With shortcake." She sniffed. "And dancing at Disneyland."

"I'm sorry, Daisy. Maybe you can still go to Disneyland one day." Elle wanted to hold her close, but she needed to be clear at the same time. "Do you understand? About Carl Joseph?"

Daisy looked around and nervously twirled a piece of her blonde hair. "CJ isn't here. He's at home."

"Yes. Right." Elle felt her own tears gathering. "He needs this time."

Daisy cast her eyes back at the picture she was coloring. As she did, a single tear landed with a splash on Mickey's nose. Daisy tried to rub it, but it only smeared the black, leaving a smudge at the center of her artwork. Daisy put her hands to her face and pushed her chair back.

"Honey." Elle put her hands on her sister's shoulders. "It's okay. Everything's going to be fine. Your Goal Day is coming, and then you can go visit Carl Joseph any time you want."

Daisy shook her head. Anger was clearly throwing itself into her hodgepodge of emotions. She stood and went to the window, wobbling more than usual as she walked. When she reached the sill, she braced herself and stared out at the overcast sky. "Why, God?" she whispered in a voice that was loud and slurred. "Why?"

The moment was too heartbreaking. Elle made her way next to her sister and slipped her arm around her shoulders. "What, Daisy? Talk to me."

She was crying harder now. She pointed at the sky. "Sunshine...just beyond the clouds." Her eyes found Elle's. "That's what CJ says."

"He's right." Elle put her fingers to her throat. The lump there made it almost impossible to talk. "In a rainstorm and in life."

Daisy hung her head then and cried like a little child. The sort of gut-wrenching tears that only time could comfort. After five long minutes, Daisy wiped her eyes and pulled away from Elle. She went to the desk, took a tissue, and blew her nose.

Then she moved across the room to the CD player and pushed a few buttons. Glenn Miller's "In the Mood" broke the silence, its rhythmic horns and strings filling the room. Daisy held out her hand the way she'd done when she danced with Carl Joseph on a number of occasions.

This time, though, she kept her eyes on a vacant spot just in front of her. She smiled and took a step forward. Her feet began to move in time to the music, and with both hands up around her pretend partner, she danced across the floor.

They needed to get home, and Elle couldn't take much

more. The day was sad enough without watching Daisy dance by herself. She went to her sister and touched her elbow. "Daisy...it's time to go."

"But"—she was out of breath—"I'm finding something."

"What, honey?" Elle was about to turn the music off. "What are you finding?"

Daisy stopped, her chest heaving. "Sunshine." She pointed toward the window. "I'm finding sunshine."

Chapter Seventeen

Nothing about his parents' plan was working, but after only two weeks, Cody wasn't ready to give up. Carl Joseph was sulking, missing his friends at the ILC. That was to be expected. Cody missed the routine, too. But maybe if he realized the joy of working outdoors, helping with Ace and checking the fence around their ranch, the pain of missing the center would ease a little.

Working so hard with Carl Joseph had brought about only one benefit so far.

Cody was thinking of Ali less.

Not that she wasn't still there in his heart. She was. But now when he found himself missing someone, more often it was Elle. Her sweet and subtle sarcasm, the way she held her own with him. And her eyes—the way he could get lost in them without meaning to.

It was Monday, start of the third week. Cody walked from

his house to his parents', and as he reached the back door he dug down deep for another dose of patience.

Inside, Carl Joseph was sitting at the dining room table. His face almost touched his plate of scrambled eggs.

"Hi, Buddy."

Carl Joseph mumbled something, but he didn't look up.

Maybe it was Cody's imagination, but it seemed that Carl Joseph was regressing on purpose. As if he were smart enough to know that if he acted disengaged, maybe someone would decide to take him back to the center where he'd been doing so well.

Cody sucked at the inside of his cheek and studied his brother. "I'm going to teach you how to stack hay today, Buddy."

"It might rain." Carl Joseph poked at his eggs. "It might."

"That's okay. Guys who work on ranches have raincoats." Cody had wished more than once that the weather would go ahead and clear up. It was one of the rainiest late springs the area had ever experienced. And every drop reminded Carl Joseph of Daisy and his friends back at the center.

They headed out to the barn, where a neighbor had dropped off twenty bundles of hay. All of it lay in a heap near the entrance to the arena. "Okay, first I'll teach you how to pick up a bale of hay."

Cody positioned himself in front of one of the bales. "Always bend like this, Buddy. You don't want to hurt your back."

"Gus hurt his back one time in cooking class." Carl Joseph

turned toward the door, his back to the hay. "One time he did that."

"I'm over here." Cody held his breath. He didn't want his frustration to show in his voice.

Slowly Carl Joseph turned toward him and moved behind a bale of hay. "'Cause not to hurt my back." He pushed his glasses back into place, spread his legs wide, and bent at the knees. But as he did, he rose up on his toes and lost his balance. He toppled forward and didn't get his hands out in front of himself in time. He hit the hay face-first and fell to the ground. He had hay sticking in his hair and small cuts across his cheeks—including along the newly healed section where he'd gotten hurt in the car accident.

Cody hurried to his side and helped him brush the hay off his shirt and out of his hair. "Not that wide, okay? You can't spread your legs that wide." He helped his brother to his feet. But by then, Carl Joseph was shaking from the fall.

"Fine, let's try something else."

CARL JOSEPH DIDN'T want to learn about the ranch. But he didn't want to say that to Brother or Brother might get mad at him. Also, this was his home, and Brother said boys should help out at home. He would get paid if he could learn all the jobs.

But he didn't want to.

Brother said it could be a break from the prickly hay, but Carl Joseph didn't clap or smile or laugh. 'Cause what about Daisy? What about Gus and Tammy and Sid? What about Teacher and the bus routes and the field trips?

Brother said they were going to fix a fence. So Carl Joseph walked with Brother out across the dirt where Ace liked to run, to a fence at the far back. Brother pointed to a broken part. "See that, Buddy?"

"Yes." He squinted through his glasses. They still had hay on them. He took them off and rubbed them with his shirt. Then he put them back on. There. "I see that now."

"First thing we have to do is cut a piece of wire." Brother had a roll of something and he knelt on the ground and took cutters from his pocket.

Carl Joseph didn't care about the wire. He sat down on the ground while Brother worked, and he dragged his finger through the soft sandy dirt. Where was Daisy right now? He looked at the sky. It was darker than before. He studied the dirt again. He could write in the dirt. He'd done it before.

"Then you take the wire," Brother was saying, "and you wrap it several times around the post and..."

The dirt felt good on his fingers. Better than the hay. Carl Joseph drew lines one way, and then another. Then he erased the lines with his whole hand. Then he had an idea. He began drawing letters in the sand. All the letters he knew how to spell.

"Buddy?" His brother was standing beside him. He sounded upset. "What are you doing? You're supposed to be watching me fix the fence. So you can learn how to do it."

Carl Joseph leaned back so Brother could see better. "I'm writing my favorite letters."

"You are?" Brother moved around so he could see the letters better. "What's it say?"

Carl Joseph felt sadness deep inside. "D-A-I-S-Y....It spells D-A-I-S-Y."

Brother tossed his cutters onto the ground and he dropped onto his behind. "I know you want to be back at the center, Buddy. I want that, too." He took off his hat and wiped his forehead. "But the doctor says no, and Mom and Dad say no. You need to understand."

"D-A-I-S-Y."

His brother was going to say something, 'cause his eyes looked tired. But then the rain started hard and fast. Carl Joseph gasped and looked at the letters in the sand. He covered them with his body so they wouldn't get wet. So they wouldn't melt.

But then he felt sadder than ever before. 'Cause the rain fell on everything and Daisy might melt. She might get wet and melt. Even if she wasn't the Wicked Witch of the West. Water fell onto his cheeks, but it wasn't from the rain.

"Your teacher will take care of Daisy. She won't get wet."

"'Cause I'm not there." He covered the whole word "Daisy" with his body. "She might get wet."

"Buddy, what can I do?" His brother breathed out hard. He slid closer on the wet ground. "How can we get you excited about working at home?"

Carl Joseph wasn't sure what Brother meant. He thought and thought, and then he knew what to say. He kept his body over her name, but he looked at Brother's eyes. "Remember Ali, the horse rider?"

Brother pulled up one knee and laid his forehead on it for a minute. "Yes." He lifted his head. "I remember her."

"You miss her, Brother. You said so."

"I do." His brother's voice was quiet. "I miss her a lot."

"That's how I miss D-A-I-S-Y."

Brother looked at him for a long time. Then he said, "I'm sorry, Buddy."

And that's when the rain stopped, and Carl Joseph had an idea. He could pray. So he prayed the rest of the day that maybe sometime soon Brother would take him back to see Teacher and the students and Daisy. Because praying was a life skill.

The most important of all.

ALL ALONG—FROM the start of his parents' plan—Cody figured the club meeting at the park would be a highlight for Carl Joseph. The day dawned warm and sunny, but no amount of small talk about the weather on the ride to the park lifted Carl Joseph's dark mood.

"Are you excited, Buddy?" Cody tried again as they reached the front door of the park building.

"I don't know." Carl Joseph kept his gaze straight ahead.

The two of them walked inside and saw an older man at the front desk. He was busy writing something, but when he noticed them he smiled and stuck his pencil behind his ear. "Can I help you?"

"Yes." Cody wasn't sure where to begin. He decided to keep the explanation simple. "My brother's name is Carl

Joseph Gunner. He'd like to take part in the club meeting today."

Next to him, Carl Joseph folded his arms in front of his chest and scowled.

Cody managed a weak smile. "Are we on time?"

"Yes. The others are all here, but they always come a little early." The man was kind; his expression and voice were warm and welcoming. He took a piece of paper from a stack on his desk and handed it to Cody. "Fill this out for him"— he pointed beyond his desk around a corner—"then take him in with the other adults."

Cody took the piece of paper and a pen from the counter. The questionnaire was simple and straightforward. Name of club member, condition of club member, any health or allergy problems, any behavioral problems, any triggers. Cody answered as quickly as he could.

"Teacher says I should write the words," Carl Joseph mumbled under his breath. The man at the counter took a phone call and didn't notice.

Cody stopped writing and looked at his brother. "The man asked me to fill it out, Buddy." Cody returned to the paper.

At the bottom of the sheet was a contact list, where Cody provided their home number, his cell phone number, and his parents' cell phone numbers. The man was off the phone by then, and he smiled as he took the paper from Cody. He studied it and nodded. "Looks good." He reached out his hand to Carl Joseph. "Welcome to Club!"

Cody held his breath and willed his brother to respond

the way he should. Carl Joseph was the kindest person Cody knew. He wasn't used to this new depressed, sulking Carl Joseph. Cody did a nervous laugh to ease the tension of the moment.

The internal struggle Carl Joseph was going through played out on his face. With his arms still folded tightly in front of him, his scowl became a mild frown, and then more of a fearful look. Finally he relaxed his shoulders and his arms released to his sides. He found a tentative smile for the old man. Then he took the man's hand and shook it.

"Good." Relief filled Cody's voice. He gave the man a grateful look. "Thank you." He put his hand on Carl Joseph's back and guided him around the corner. "Come on, Buddy. It's this way."

In the next room, art supplies were set up at a number of tables. Molding clay took up one, paints and paper another, and yarn and felt another. Moving around the room and between the tables were maybe fifteen Down Syndrome people, all ages and sizes.

Sitting at a desk near the back of the room was a woman who looked familiar. Cody led Carl Joseph to her desk, and as he came closer she looked up. In a rush he remembered where he'd seen her before. She was his mother's friend, a woman who used to work at the bank near his parents' house. Her name was Kelley Gaylor, and she and Cody's mom had done volunteer work together over the past few years.

"Mrs. Gaylor..." Cody reached out and shook her hand. "My brother's joining the club for today."

"Cody! My goodness. Your mother said you were taking

a break from the rodeo circuit. I keep wishing we could hire you to help run our family's thoroughbred farm." She stood and a smile brightened her eyes. She looked at Carl Joseph and came around her desk to greet him. "Carl Joseph, I'm glad you're here."

Cody tried to remember what his mother had said about her friend. She was much younger than his mom, maybe in her late thirties, and very pretty. She was married with three kids, and very involved in charities for children.

And now she was here helping with handicapped adults.

"Did you leave the bank?"

"Yes." She leaned on the edge of her desk. Her blue eyes were filled with a warmth that put Cody at ease. "I'm doing some accounting work for my parents, and spending more time with my kids, and volunteering. Actually this is only my second day working with the club. I was going to tell your mother about it, but..." She hesitated. Clearly she didn't want to talk about Carl Joseph with him standing there. She motioned to him. "Why don't you follow me, Carl Joseph? Let's start you off at the painting table."

Cody looked at her desk. There were framed photos of her and her husband, and another of a daughter and two young boys. On the other side of the desk were two framed pictures of beautiful horses. He had finally found the perfect place, led by someone he knew and was comfortable with. What could be better?

He turned his attention to Kelley and Carl Joseph, making their way to the paint table. Things had been rocky until now, but this place, this club, was exactly what Carl Joseph needed. Maybe his parents were right. Tuesdays here would give him a safe way to be creative and social.

Carl Joseph didn't resist. Maybe because of the woman's gentle approach or because of her compassionate voice. He followed her to the table where the paints were, and she introduced him to another young man who was deciding on a color. Carl Joseph's expression was blank, but he took a piece of paper and a small jar of red paint. Then he sat at a nearby table and began to work. For a long moment, Kelley stayed with him, helping him and making him feel comfortable.

Kelley waited until Carl Joseph was working on his own, then she came back to Cody. She kept her voice low. "Your mother told me Carl Joseph was working with the ILC, heading toward his Goal Day." She looked concerned. "Did something happen?"

Events from the past few months flashed in Cody's mind. Cody explained about the accident and the doctor's suggestion—that Carl Joseph be kept at home where he would be safer in light of his epilepsy.

Kelley was quiet for a moment, but her eyes never left his. "What about Carl Joseph? Does he like being home?"

"He misses the center." Cody's answer was thoughtful. "He's always been the happiest kid. But now he knows about life away from home." He narrowed his eyes and looked at his brother. "The risks are just too great."

Kelley smiled. "All of life is a risk, Cody. Bull riding and loving a sick barrel racer. Giving up one of your lungs." She paused. "You, of all people, should know that."

Her words cut him deep. It took a few seconds for him to catch his breath, and when he did, he no longer wanted to talk. He had figured Kelley would be on his parents' side, but instead she sounded just like Elle Dalton. The way maybe he should've sounded if he'd tried harder to convince his parents that Carl Joseph still needed the center. Cody exhaled. He felt as if he'd aged a decade in the past week. "The club meeting is three hours?"

"It is." She touched his arm. "You can come back then. Don't be upset by what I said. Whatever you and your family decide for Carl Joseph, I'm sure you'll all be fine." She angled her head and looked at the club members. "This sort of outing is the answer for many of them. But for some"—she met Cody's eyes again—"independent living is a very real possibility."

He hesitated. "Thanks."

Cody wasn't sure how he made it out to the parking lot and climbed into his truck. He didn't remember any of it. All he could think about was what Kelley Gaylor had said. Cody, of all people, should know that life took risk. So why wasn't he trying harder to be his buddy's advocate? The way Elle Dalton would be if she had a voice in the matter. He started his engine and headed to the mall. He needed a pair of jeans, and he wanted to pick up a few CDs for Carl Joseph. Even when all he wanted to do was get his brother back in the truck and head to the center. Because Buddy was going crazy missing the people there.

And just maybe Cody was, too.

Chapter Eighteen

Cody was pulling into a parking spot at the Citadel Mall when his cell phone rang. He checked the Caller ID. *Park and Rec Dept*, it read. His heart skipped a beat. Carl Joseph was fine when he left, but maybe he was having a meltdown, weeping for his friends at the center. He flipped open his phone. "Hello?"

"Cody, it's Kelley." She sounded frantic, breathless. "Carl Joseph's disappeared."

"What?" Cody shouted the word. He felt the blood leave his face. "How could that happen? Have you searched the building?"

"Everywhere. I've called the police. They're on the way." She let out a single sob. "Cody, I'm so sorry. He painted a picture of Minnie Mouse, and he wrote the name Daisy at the top." Her words were choppy, mixed with panic. "Then he asked if he could go outside and look at the park. We have a special yard for our disabled club members. Normally the gate's locked, but today...today the maintenance man left it open."

"So he's gone? No one saw what direction he went?" Cody's heart tripped into a crazy fast rhythm. He started his truck and backed out of the parking space. In a frenzy he headed back the way he'd come. "Where have you looked?"

"Around the perimeter of the park." She moaned. "I can't believe this. When he didn't come back after a few minutes, I followed him. The gate was open. How far could he have gotten?"

Suddenly Cody felt an awful possibility explode in his mind. "Is there a bus stop near the park?"

"Yes, of course. Right out—" She gasped. "You don't think..."

"Just a minute." Cody jerked the truck into the nearest gas station parking lot and did a U-turn. There was only one person who would know the bus routes Carl Joseph might take. He tried to concentrate. "Carl Joseph had his wallet with him. I'm sure he had his bus pass and probably ten dollars."

"What should I tell the police?" Kelley's words came fast, filled with fear.

"Tell them Carl Joseph probably took the bus. I'm heading toward the ILC. Carl Joseph was probably trying to get back to the center."

"How would he know which bus to take?"

Cody forced his head to stop spinning long enough so he could think straight. "His former teacher would know."

"Anything else? I want to get this to the police right away."

"Yes." Cody felt the first tears. His brother was lost some-where on a city bus. What if he got off and ran into traffic again? Or had a seizure? He pinched the bridge of his nose. "Please, Kelley. Pray for Carl Joseph."

When the call ended, Cody reached the center in record time. They never should've pulled Buddy from his friends. Never. Whatever the consequences of this ordeal, they'd have to sort through them later. In the meantime, Cody was grateful for one very good thing.

There wasn't a cloud in the sky.

He hurried inside, but before he reached the door, he stopped himself. He couldn't disrupt Elle's class. Not after all the damage he'd already caused them. Despite his rac-ing heart, he forced himself to exhale. He opened the door slowly, and immediately his eyes found Elle's. Almost on cue, the students turned their attention to him. Shock filled their faces. Two of them cheered out loud and clapped.

Gus pointed at him. "Carl Joseph's brother!" He grinned big and looked at the others. "Hey, everyone—Carl Joseph's brother! That means Carl Joseph is coming in next!"

"No." Cody kept his tone as gentle as he could. Panic was making it hard to draw a breath. Carl Joseph was missing; he couldn't think of anything else. "Sorry, guys. Carl Joseph isn't here." He shot a desperate look at Elle. "Please…can I talk with you outside?"

Elle didn't look pleased, but she must've sensed the urgency in Cody. She motioned to her aide, and the older woman came to the front of the room. The students were talking all at once, guessing where Carl Joseph might be hiding and whether he was still hurt and why Cody would come without his brother.

"Listen." Elle held up her hand. "I need your attention up here. I'll speak to Mr. Gunner and I'll be right back."

She followed Cody outside the classroom. When the door was shut she turned to him, her expression a mix of confusion and concern. "My students have only today stopped asking every ten minutes about your brother. I've asked if you would call before—"

"Elle, I need your help!" Cody's mouth was dry. His mind was racing, picturing his brother catching a bus to Denver or getting mugged. "Carl Joseph's missing. I took him to the park, to a club meeting, and he left." He paused, horrified. "I think he took the bus."

Her eyes grew wide. "Dear God, no…" She took a step back. "Wait here."

Cody stayed outside, but he watched through the window. Elle pulled her aide aside and whispered something.

The moment she was outside, Cody caught her hand and ran with her back to his truck. He tried not to think about how her hand felt in his. All that mattered was his buddy. "You know the bus routes, the ones Carl Joseph knows."

"Yes." She waited until he opened the passenger door. "Get in and drive to Adler Street."

Cody raced around the front of the truck, and as he jumped into the driver's seat he felt a sense of relief. Elle would help him. They'd find Carl Joseph. They had to find him.

Before the unthinkable happened.

CARL JOSEPH FELT bad about what he'd done.

The nice lady, Kelley, was his mom's friend. Carl Joseph remembered her coming to the house. But no one said he had to stay. Cody would come back in three hours. Kelley told him that. Three hours was enough time for a field trip. Teacher said so.

When Carl Joseph went into the yard and out the gate, the bus was just coming. He remembered his wallet. "Every time you go out, Carl Joseph, make sure you have two things with you," Teacher had said. "Your bus pass and ten dollars." So that morning he remembered.

He walked over, and when the bus stopped, he climbed on. All by himself. And the driver was friendly. He asked where Carl Joseph wanted to go. There was no line of people, and no one was pushing him to move along, move along. He licked his lips and pulled his wallet from his jeans pocket. He showed his pass, and then something else. He showed the card from Elle Dalton. The one from the center.

"Here." He pointed at the card. "I want to go to the center."

The man was still friendly. He said to take the bus four stops and then he would say what to do next. Carl Joseph sat down near a window. 'Cause window seats showed the whole world outside. That's what Gus said every time they had a field trip.

But when Carl Joseph sat down, he felt scared and sad. 'Cause maybe he should ask the driver to call his mom or call Brother. The bus was a big place without any other students. And no Teacher, too. And no Daisy, who knew the bus routes better than all the students put together.

He pushed himself close to the window and tapped his feet. Maybe he would call his mom when he got to the center. She could tell the nice Kelley that Carl Joseph was sorry for leaving. Sorry for not saying good-bye. He pressed his forehead against the glass. It felt hot, so he pulled back.

Then he remembered about the life skill. He closed his eyes. "Dear God, I don't like this." He whispered the prayer. But maybe it was loud because the driver looked back at him.

"You okay, pal?"

"Yes, pal." Carl Joseph sat up straighter. "I'm okay." His heart was pounding hard. "D-A-I-S-Y ...D-A-I-S-Y." He spelled her name a few times. Very quietly. Then he talked to God once more. "Help me, God. Help me now."

They reached four stops, because the driver stopped the bus. Then he stood up and came back. Carl Joseph was the only person on the bus. "This is your stop."

Carl Joseph stood, but his legs felt shaky. Like after he rode Ace. He swallowed and pushed his glasses up the bridge of his nose. "What now?"

"Follow me." The driver led him slowly down the middle aisle and slowly onto the steps. On the sidewalk, the driver pointed across the street. "Cross at the light and walk one block. There's a blue bench. Take that bus five stops and you'll be right at the center."

Carl Joseph smiled. See? He could do this. He could take

a bus and go see Daisy. He should've done it sooner. Then Brother wouldn't have to work with him so much. It was better when he and Brother were friends. Now Brother was trying to change him. 'Cause he wanted to change him.

Carl Joseph shook the bus driver's hand. "Thank you, pal."

"You're welcome." He hesitated. "You sure you're okay?"

"A-okay." He felt less wobbly. A-okay was what Tammy said. It sounded professional. "Yes, very a-okay."

The bus driver climbed back up the steps of the big bus. Then he closed the door and drove away. Carl Joseph walked six steps, 'cause he counted them. 'Cause counting was a life skill, too. Then he stopped and looked around. Was he supposed to cross straight ahead? Or straight across? He took two steps straight ahead. His heart started to beat faster again.

Then he turned and took three steps toward the other light. He blinked four times. Which way was it? He covered his face with his hands and turned around and around. First one direction, then the other. The bus driver called him Pal. Then what? Which way was he supposed to go?

"Life skills, Carl Joseph," he told himself. "Think of life skills." He parted his fingers and peered out. Two people passing by looked at him. They had scared faces. "Life skills," he told them. "Time for life skills."

The people kept walking. Carl Joseph couldn't hear. His heart was beating too hard, 'cause he didn't like this. He was alone and he was about to cry. But the first life skill was praying, 'cause praying made you remember that...that you were never alone! Carl Joseph dropped his hands to his sides and looked up at the sky. Straight up. It was bright blue, no rain at all. "God, I want to go to the center. I forget which way."

He was about to look at the lights again, walk up to each crossing line and decide what to do, when he felt a hand on his shoulder. Maybe it was Brother or his mom. He turned around and right away he covered his face again.

'Cause policemen only came when there was trouble. Big, big trouble.

And right there his eyes started shaking back and forth. Back and forth and back and forth. And his mouth came open and he couldn't say anything. 'Cause his legs and arms were shaking and then he was falling.

And everything, everywhere turned the blackest of black.

Chapter Nineteen

Nearly an hour had passed since Carl Joseph's disap-pearance, and Elle was out of options. Beside her, Cody was desperate, his eyes wide, terror written into the worried lines on his forehead.

Elle pointed to the stoplight just ahead. "Turn right, there's another bus stop just down the street." Her heart pounded, and she felt sick to her stomach. No matter how hard she prayed, Carl Joseph wasn't turning up. They'd driven three times by every bus stop familiar to Carl Joseph, but there was no sign of him.

"He could be almost to Denver by now." Cody made the turn, and the muscles in his right forearm flexed from the death grip he had on the steering wheel. A raspy sigh slid through his teeth. "It's my fault. I should've stayed with him. Of course he'd try to find a way back to the—"

The ring of Cody's cell phone stopped him cold. He took

the wheel with his left hand, grabbed the phone, and flipped it open. "Hello?"

Elle couldn't hear the caller's response, but all at once the tension seemed to leave Cody's body. "Thank You, God…" He paused. "We're close. Maybe five minutes."

"He's at the center?" Elle leaned closer, her voice a whisper.

Cody nodded. "Okay…yes, we're on our way." He snapped the phone shut and set it on the seat. Then, as if it were the most natural thing in the world, he took hold of her hand as he sucked in a long breath. "He's safe."

Elle couldn't respond. The feel of Cody's hand in hers burned all the way up her arm, screaming at her to let go. Never mind the high stakes, or how differently things might've turned out. Regardless of the emotion of the past hour, Cody was married. Holding his hand made her the worst of women.

But in that moment she couldn't let go of his hand if her life depended on it. Elle worked to find her voice. "How… how did they find him?"

Cody didn't seem to notice her struggle. He focused on the road ahead, and when it was safe he flipped a U-turn. "I guess he boarded a bus and showed the driver your card. Told the guy he wanted to go to the center." Cody glanced at her. Relief shone in his eyes. "He must've gotten confused between buses." He ran his thumb along the side of her hand. The worry was back in his voice. "He had a seizure just as a police officer found him."

Let go of his hand, Elle told herself. But his touch was intoxicating. "He had a seizure?"

"The officer helped him through it. He's with my mom in the parking lot of the center."

Elle tried to picture Carl Joseph on a bus by himself, trying to make a connection without any of the tools or help he was used to. And if he had a seizure, how come the officer hadn't taken him to the hospital? She still had questions, but they would be answered in a minute or so when they reached the center. All of them but one.

Why was she still holding the hand of a married man?

CODY WAS INTENTLY aware of Elle's presence beside him, the faint smell of her perfume, and the way her hand felt in his. In the past hour the underlying connection he'd been feeling toward her, the attraction, had all but consumed him. Even so, while he was still frantic to find Carl Joseph, he didn't dare act on it, didn't consider taking her hand.

Now, though, in his relief, he had the overwhelming desire to pull over and take Elle in his arms, hold her, and thank her for caring about Carl Joseph the way she did. But the idea was only a crazy passing thought. Elle seemed uncomfortable, and little wonder. With Carl Joseph's accident, he had never had a chance to tell her how she'd succeeded. How much he believed in her work now that he'd seen it for himself.

In some ways, she must've still seen him as the enemy.

He released her hand as they pulled into the parking lot. His mother was parked in the front row, and Cody took the spot beside her. He turned off the engine and let his head fall back against his seat. "I didn't think it would matter."

"What?" She took hold of the door handle.

He turned so he could see her. "Praying." Awe filled his heart, his soul. "I prayed from the moment I heard he was missing, and it worked."

She smiled, but it didn't quite reach her eyes. "Praying always works." Her tone was sad, resigned. "Even if sometimes we don't like the answer." She opened the door. "I have to get back inside." She glanced past him to Carl Joseph. "Bring him inside before you go?"

Cody searched her eyes. He didn't want to upset things any more than he already had. "You sure?"

"Yes." She stepped out, but her eyes held his. "Daisy misses him." She hesitated. "A lot. She's become a different person without Carl Joseph."

"All right." He opened his door. "Give us a few minutes."

Elle nodded and then she hurried back inside the center. Cody watched her go, and he realized he'd been holding his breath. She had that effect on him—and there was no denying it. But even with his lack of experience he could easily read her.

She wasn't interested.

He climbed out and knocked on Carl Joseph's car door.

His brother jerked around and his eyes grew wide. He flung his door open, hurried out. Then, all at once, shame and sorrow seemed to hit him. "I'm sorry, Brother. 'Cause I didn't ask first." Carl Joseph shook his head, his mouth hanging open as if he couldn't find the right words. He pushed his glasses back into place. "I'm so, so sorry."

Cody couldn't take another moment. He pulled his

brother into his arms and held him tight. "Buddy…I'm so glad you're okay." The hug lasted a long time, and when Cody released him, he put his hands on Carl Joseph's shoulders and stared straight into his eyes. "This wasn't your fault, Buddy. I never should've left you."

"No." Carl Joseph shook his head, a little at first and then more strongly. "No, 'cause the driver said, 'You okay, pal?' and I told him yes and then I wasn't sure to cross that way." He pointed straight ahead. Then he pointed out to the side, "Or that way. And so no, Brother, it isn't your fault."

Their mom was out of the car now. She came up and put her arms around both of them. "Did Elle say we could stop in?"

"Yes." Cody wasn't sure what was going to happen next for Carl Joseph. He wanted to hear more about his seizure, and another doctor's visit was already set up for tomorrow morning. His mom had told him that much when she called. But for now, they needed to get inside because that's what his buddy wanted.

Badly enough that he'd risked his life to get here.

The three of them walked toward the center door. Through the window they could hear the sounds of swing music and happy laughter. Clearly the students had been spared news of the ordeal.

"I'll get it." Carl Joseph seemed slower than usual, but he stepped in front of Cody and their mother and held open the door.

A swing dance session was in full progress inside. All except for Daisy. Carl Joseph's friend was sitting at an art table in the far corner of the room, alone. Cody's heart sank. Daisy was the most sociable student in the class. Her solitary behavior could be caused by only one thing.

Elle looked over, and immediately her face lit up. "Carl Joseph!" She smiled and hurried toward him. All signs of the regret and sorrow she'd shown earlier were gone. She took Carl Joseph into her arms and hugged him. "Are you okay?"

"I am now." He grinned at Elle and then at the students, who were one at a time stopping and turning toward him. "I wanted to come here really bad. 'Cause here's where I get my goal one day. Where I grow up like a man." He moved closer to Elle and lowered his voice to what he must've thought was a whisper. "I can't grow up around Brother."

Elle shot a sympathetic look at Cody.

Cody wanted to shout at both of them that he was on their side. But it wasn't the time. Besides, he was still stinging from Carl Joseph's words, playing them again in his mind. *I can't grow up around Brother.* No wonder Carl Joseph had been difficult the last few weeks.

Carl Joseph was going on about how happy he was to be back. "I missed this place bad, Teacher!" Carl Joseph nodded fast. "Really bad."

"That's for sure." Their mother looked exhausted, but she was smiling. She leveled her eyes at Elle. "Thank you...for everything."

Elle's smile softened. She patted Carl Joseph's shoulder just as someone turned off the music. A chorus of voices began talking all at once, the students calling Carl Joseph's name and clapping their hands. Elle raised her voice so she could be heard over the noise. "Your classmates have missed you. Especially one of them."

Carl Joseph laughed, the loud lovable open-mouthed laugh Cody hadn't heard around the house since the accident. "D-A-I-S-Y!"

"Yes, that's the one." Elle led the way to the back of the classroom.

Cody was drained from the scare. He hung back with his mother while Elle linked arms with Carl Joseph and walked him to the students. It took a few seconds, but a chain reaction started.

Gus covered his mouth with both hands and then slid them along the side of his face to the top of his head. He danced in a circle and raised both arms high. "Carl Joseph is back!" He looked at the others and motioned for them to follow. "Carl Joseph is back, everybody!" He ran toward Carl Joseph so fast he tripped. Three other students helped him up, and just like that, Cody watched his brother become surrounded by the support of his friends.

Sid frowned at Carl Joseph. "You should never go that long without coming to class." But after a few seconds, he smiled, too. "Never again, Carl Joseph."

Some of the students were jumping in place, clapping and laughing and talking all at the same time.

"We have a new bus route! You have to know the new bus route."

"Look at my haircut, Carl Joseph. Hair-cutting is a life skill!"

"We cooked asparagus, so now you can cook asparagus if you want asparagus."

Those who weren't shouting came up and patted Carl Joseph's back. A few of them thanked him. "Finally our class is together again." Tammy swung her long braids one way and then the other. "Thank you for coming back, Carl Joseph!"

Only then did Cody see Daisy. She had left the art table, and now she was walking up to the group. Her mouth hung open, and tears streamed down her face. At the same time, Carl Joseph seemed to take inventory of the faces around him, and he must've realized who was missing. In a sudden frantic burst of motion he made one half turn and then another, until finally he saw her coming closer. He smiled bigger than Cody had seen since he'd been home.

"Daisy..." He parted the circle of friends and ran to her, arms outstretched, big oaflike steps, all the way across the room.

But Daisy didn't run to meet him. She hung her head and kept crying, stifling quiet sobs as Carl Joseph made his way to her. Cody and his mother drew nearer so they could hear.

"Daisy, what's wrong?" Carl Joseph put his hand on her shoulder. "I'm here now."

"You...left me." Her words were hard to understand through her deep emotion. She looked up and her nose was red, her cheeks wet. "I didn't know where you were. Even when it rained."

Carl Joseph's eyes grew wide and his lips parted. Cody understood the shock and regret in his expression. He had let his friend down and he felt terrible, wracked with guilt.

He released a quiet gasp. "I'm sorry, Daisy. I wanted to be here. I did."

She seemed to grow calmer in light of his explanation, but still there was something in her expression. Hurt and betrayal. And it was then that Cody felt the pain of Carl Joseph's last several weeks worst of all. What had they done, keeping him away from the center? Away from Daisy and Elle and Gus and everyone here?

Elle caught his eye. Then, dabbing at her own cheeks, she approached him and his mother. "I know you don't agree, but"—she looked at Carl Joseph and Daisy—"he belongs here." She hesitated, clearly struggling with her emotion. "He needs this."

Their mother looked at Carl Joseph, at the way he had both his hands on Daisy's shoulders now, how he was looking straight into her eyes, trying to convince her that he hadn't meant to be gone, that he had missed her as much as she missed him. The wounded look in Daisy's eyes was fading. She gave Carl Joseph the slightest smile. Mary touched her fingers to her throat and turned her attention back to Elle. "You're right." Her voice cracked. "But his health...I don't know how we can do it."

The other students made their way over to Daisy and Carl Joseph. By then Daisy was smiling, and Carl Joseph was doing a silly dance trying to make her laugh.

"Please, Mrs. Gunner. I know of other doctors you can talk to." She swallowed, as if she didn't want to overstep her bounds. "Please consider it."

His mom seemed overwhelmed by the idea. But she nod-ded. "We will."

Cody could've kissed Elle Dalton right there. That was the answer! Another doctor, one who was more open to advancements for sick people with Down Syndrome. He didn't say anything, because he couldn't. He was too mes-merized by the young teacher standing there, talking to his mother.

Before they left, Cody pulled Elle aside. "Thank you." He studied her. Something in her eyes closed off whenever they were close like this. He swallowed a ripple of frustration. "For helping me look, but also for caring."

"Of course." She took a step back and motioned to her students. "I need to go. Maybe…maybe we'll see Carl Joseph sometime soon."

"Maybe." He wanted to ask her what was wrong, but he resisted. "My parents…They have a meeting with his doctor tomorrow."

"Well, then…I guess, have them call me." She gave him a professional smile. Then she returned to her students.

On the way home that afternoon, while Carl Joseph rattled on about Daisy and Gus and Sid and Teacher, Cody couldn't stop thinking about Elle. His feelings weren't caused only by her eyes or the way he felt when he was near her. More than that, it was her love for her students. Her dedica-tion and concern for Carl Joseph. In the hour they'd spent together looking for his brother, she'd taken hold of Cody's heart with an intensity he'd known just one other time in his life. He didn't have to wonder about his feelings for Elle Dalton, not anymore. Today they were as clear as the sky over Colorado Springs. There was only one problem, and it consumed him the rest of the day and into the evening. He'd left a first impression bigger than Pikes Peak.

And now—no matter what he tried—he wasn't sure there was any way around it.

Chapter Twenty

The appointment with the specialist brought more bad news.

When the three of them got home from Denver that evening, Cody's father found him out back in the barn and told him the details. An MRI proved that a degeneration was happening in Carl Joseph's brain. He would be prone to more and stronger seizures, and worse, he was at high risk for a stroke.

"Between that and his heart disease, he might not have long. A few years. Five, maybe." His father's eyes were red and swollen. "So we've made our decision. Carl Joseph has to stay here, where we can care for him." His dad took a quick breath and looked up, fighting a wave of emotion. When he had more control, he searched Cody's eyes. "We want to talk to Elle about having him visit the center. Maybe once a week."

Cody reached out and steadied himself against the nearest

wall. This couldn't be happening, not to Carl Joseph. Losing Ali was enough loss for a lifetime. They couldn't give up, couldn't simply accept the diagnosis when maybe there was something they could do. He swallowed his disbelief and let his hands fall to his sides. "Elle says she knows another doctor..."

"The tests don't lie, Cody." His father gave a sad shake of his head and then moved toward the barn door. "I'm going back inside. Your mother's having a hard time."

When he was gone, Cody tried to draw a full breath, but he couldn't. His one lung fought against the news, against the shock ripping through him. So that was it? Carl Joseph was doomed? There had to be another answer, a way for his buddy to accomplish the goal that mattered so much to him.

The one Carl Joseph didn't think he could reach working alongside Cody.

There was only one place Cody could take all the feelings crowding his heart. Out to the fields with Ace. He hadn't been on the horse in three days, too caught up with Carl Joseph to find even an hour to ride. Now he straightened and adjusted his baseball cap, saddled the horse, and climbed on.

"Let's go, Ace." He blinked back tears. "I need you to run today."

A warm wind blew over his parents' ranch, and it carried with it memories of everything that was gone from his life. Everything that would never be again. His days of bull riding, and his time on the rodeo circuit, and Ali. He breathed deep and peered at the still blue sky. He stopped and let his sadness come to the surface.

He walked Ace out to the trailhead. June evenings in Colorado Springs were always beautiful and this one was no exception. It was eight o'clock and he still had half an hour before sunset. The old horse was still as strong and proud and faithful as he'd been when Ali rode him at one barrel-racing event after another, week after week, season after season. The vision of Ali tearing around the barrels on Ace stayed with him still. The way it would forever.

Cody patted the horse's neck. "Atta boy, Ace." He leaned forward and in a sudden rush he shouted, "Giddyup!"

A strong whinnying came from the horse and Ace set off at a trot that quickly became a full run. The pace fit his mood, made him feel that somehow they could outrun the bad news about Carl Joseph, outrun the ways things had gotten worse for his brother in the weeks since he'd been home.

Usually, riding like this made him think only of Ali, but not so today. With the wind in his face and Ace pounding out a timeless rhythm beneath him, Cody could only think of his brother and the teacher who had given his buddy a chance to truly live.

Elle Dalton.

The sun was making its way toward the mountains, casting that surreal final splash of light against the cactus and shrubs that dotted the back acreage of the property. Cody leaned back and let the rays hit his face, as if the warmth might find its way to the cold dark places of his heart. Gradually, Ace slowed to a walk.

"So, Ace..." He rubbed the horse's mane. "Carl Joseph, too."

The horse took a few steps, then stopped and ate from a patch of grass.

Carl Joseph was dying. Not today, but soon. Cody stared as far as he could toward the horizon. Carl Joseph, his buddy. The kid who had adored him since he was old enough to crawl. The one who wanted to be a bull rider so he could be a little more like Cody. Dying from something Cody couldn't understand, let alone help.

If he was at risk for a stroke, then every day would represent danger to Carl Joseph. Cody settled back in the saddle and drew a full breath. What had Kelley Gaylor said yesterday morning? Cody of all people should know about taking risks.

At least a hundred times since the nightmare of losing Carl Joseph, Cody had played one particular moment over in his mind. Yesterday as he walked into the recreation center, he had been struck by something that hadn't dawned on him until after Carl Joseph disappeared. The young adults at the club meeting were entirely different from the students at Elle Dalton's Independent Living Center.

At the club meeting, people with Down Syndrome were given crafts and simple books and time to visit. But they wore blank expressions on their faces and seemed almost despondent. No challenge was presented, no learning. Just a way to pass the time together. Something to set apart Tuesday from

Wednesday. It wasn't Kelley Gaylor's fault. The club wasn't designed to teach independence or give its members a goal.

Cody stroked Ace's neck again, and the horse lifted his head. There weren't many horses like Ace. He could sense a person's feelings, a person's mood. Now, for instance, when Cody wanted to wrestle with his feelings, Ace was content to graze and take only a few small steps in either direction. And when Ali was sick, when Ace could tell her breathing wasn't right, he would lift his head high, giving her something to rest against until she caught her breath.

Cody looked at his wedding ring, the simple white gold band he still wore. If Ali were alive today, if she were here with him, well enough to ride across the back field with him, he knew without a doubt what she would say about Carl Joseph's situation.

Ali and her sister were both born with cystic fibrosis, and for the first decade of their lives they stayed indoors. Their parents bought special air filters and did everything possible to keep allergens and dust from entering. Ali and her sister would sit by their bedroom window and dream of running across the grassy hills and over to the neighbor's barn and the horses he kept there.

Ali rode horses even after her doctor told her it would take years off her life to do so. She rode because she wanted to live her life, not sit it out. Ali was a dreamer and a doer, and if she had known Carl Joseph longer, she would've been supportive of the ILC from the beginning, and she would've cheered its purpose.

Even when she knew her death was coming, she lived

every day, every final moment to the fullest. He pictured Elle Dalton and her tireless work with Carl Joseph and the other students. Elle wasn't so different from Ali, really. They both understood that risk was a necessary part of living.

Cody gave a light nudge with the reins, and Ace started walking back to the barn. One autumn, a year before she died, Ali was walking beside Cody in the mountains when she stopped and stared at a tree whose leaves were brilliant red with just a hint of gold.

"Funny, isn't it?" She picked up a red one from the ground. "A leaf's most beautiful days are at the very end, just before it dies."

He had listened, watching her, memorizing her.

"Sort of like me." She met his eyes, leaned up, and kissed him. "These are the most beautiful days of all, Cody. The ones I want you to remember."

The sun was behind the hills now. Streaky pinks and pale blues filled the sky. He'd had enough loss to last him a lifetime, without having something happen to his younger brother. But it would be worse to watch him waste away at home, having never done even the simplest things he dreamed of doing.

Maybe he could move out with Carl Joseph, and the two of them could live together. That might make things a little safer for Carl Joseph. But as soon as the thought crossed his mind, his doubts overshadowed it. He and Carl Joseph were better off with the friendship they used to share. His buddy didn't want him acting as the teacher. He wanted to do things on his own. Cody would only hold him back.

Cody sucked in another breath of sweet early night air. Then there was the phone call he'd gotten earlier today. A vice president from the network had phoned. Apparently, Cody's agent had given a verbal commitment that Cody would return to the circuit.

"We could use you, Gunner," the man told him. "The fans love you. I need an answer by the end of the week."

An ache filtered through his chest. In the end, it probably made the most sense to go back. Bull riding was what he knew, what he was good at. And it would take him away from Elle Dalton—a woman who clearly wasn't interested. Either way, his decision about the circuit didn't matter nearly as much as the one his parents needed to make, the one about Carl Joseph's future.

Cody pressed his heels lightly to Ace's sides, and the horse began to gallop. He released the tension on the reins, and Ace moved into a full run. The details weren't clear, but somehow he had to change his parents' minds. Cody leaned down close to Ace's neck and squinted against the wind. Carl Joseph would tell him to pray about it. And prayer had certainly helped yesterday. He was getting closer to the barn, and in the fading sunlight he could see someone standing near the back of the house. As he came nearer, he saw it wasn't one person, but three. Carl Joseph and...He strained forward, trying to make them out, until finally, he knew. His heart skipped a beat and he sat up straight in the saddle.

It was Elle Dalton and her student, Daisy.

Chapter Twenty-one

Elle couldn't take her eyes off Cody. The way he looked in the fading sunlight, flying across the field on the beautiful palomino. Together they made a picture of strength and grace and beauty. She wasn't here to see Cody, but it was impossible not to look.

She turned away and watched her sister and Carl Joseph, slow dancing on the fresh-cut grass. Carl Joseph's mother had called with the news, and Daisy had heard her half of the conversation.

"CJ is sick?" Daisy had tugged on her arm. "Is he sick, Elle? Tell me if he's sick."

Elle held her finger to her lips and gave her sister a sharp look. But Daisy wouldn't be ignored. Finally, Elle had to ask Carl Joseph's mother to hold on while she explained to her sister that CJ was okay. A discussion of epilepsy could come later.

"Take me to him, Elle...I have a Minnie picture for him. Please!" Daisy tugged on her again. "Please, Elle!"

Finally, Elle relented. "Would you mind if Daisy and I came by after dinner?"

Carl Joseph's mother sounded tired, but she said she was grateful for the offer. "We could all use a reason to smile."

Elle had another reason for coming to the Gunner house tonight. She wanted to meet Cody's wife. She scanned the area adjacent to the driveway. Was his wife here? According to Carl Joseph, Cody was home for six weeks. So where was his wife? Did she stay back in whatever city Cody had come from?

The pieces of his story didn't add up.

She heard Cody's horse getting closer, so she shifted back toward the pasture and watched Cody ride into the barn. The news about Carl Joseph must've been devastating for him. If he was hurting, she had to be especially careful. His behavior yesterday when he held her hand, and the way she enjoyed it, still burned in her conscience. She wouldn't cross that line again today.

A few feet away, Carl Joseph was explaining the situation to Daisy. "Brother has to put Ace in there 'cause it's bedtime." He was talking loudly, probably trying to impress Daisy with his horse knowledge.

"But horses don't lay down to sleep, right?" Daisy was standing next to Carl Joseph, leaning against his arm.

"'Cause they don't have beds." He laughed hard, and she did, too. "Isn't that funny, Daisy? 'Cause horses don't have beds."

Cody came out of the barn toward them. The closer he came, the more Elle was sure she could see something different in his eyes, something that hadn't been there before. A compassion and empathy that seemed directed straight at her. She felt her guard go up. *He's married, Elle...Don't be crazy. God, help me keep my head.*

"Hi." He folded his arms and looked at Daisy. "I see your teacher took the long way home."

Daisy laughed. "I'm not allowed to call her Teacher after class."

Suddenly Elle realized how little Cody knew about her. She moved closer to Daisy and took her hand. "Daisy's my sister." She looked at Cody. "You didn't know that?"

Cody's expression went blank, and then filled with wonder. "You're her...she's your..."

Cody was clearly shocked by the news, but more than that, he seemed touched by it. Elle allowed a nervous laugh. How had she missed telling him this detail before? They would've found common ground on the issue of independent living so much sooner.

He was still looking at her, searching her eyes, when Carl Joseph walked up to him and tugged on his denim shirtsleeve. "Brother, look at this." He held out a painted picture. "She drew me Minnie Mouse." The painting was meticulously done, and at the top, Daisy had written, *Daisy wants CJ to come back.*

A smile lifted the corners of Cody's lips. "It's beautiful." He winked at Daisy. "Nice work."

"Thanks." She was beaming. Whatever ill feelings she had

had toward Cody Gunner, they were gone now. Daisy pulled a picture from behind her back. "And look what CJ gave me. Mickey for D-A-I-S-Y. And that's the very best gift of all."

Again Cody appreciated the artwork, and the painstaking way that Carl Joseph had spelled out Daisy's name across the top. Her name was still one of the few words he could consistently spell correctly.

Carl Joseph said something quiet to Daisy, and the two of them laughed again. Elle took the moment to approach Cody. *Keep it professional,* she told herself. She crossed her arms. "Can we talk?"

"Sure." He walked a few yards away from their noisy siblings, and she followed. "My mom told you, huh?"

"Yes. His diagnosis isn't good." Elle kept her distance.

Cody put one foot up on the split-rail fence. It wasn't dark, but shadows were falling across the yard. Cody stared into the distance, heartbreak glistening in his eyes. "Just when he was starting to really live."

The back door of the house opened, and Mrs. Gunner stuck her head out. "I sliced up some apples," she called. "Carl Joseph, maybe you can bring your friend in for a snack."

Carl Joseph cupped his hands around his mouth. "Apples all alone or with peanut butter?"

"Peanut butter." There was a laugh in Mrs. Gunner's voice.

"Goodie!" Carl Joseph clapped loudly and took Daisy's hand. "Come on, Daisy…'cause my mom makes the best apples and peanut butter in the whole Rocky Mountains."

Elle watched them skip toward the back door and

disappear into the house. She moved a step farther away from
Cody. Though the night was warm, a shiver passed over her
arms. The song of faraway crickets mixed with the breeze
and heightened her awareness of Cody a few feet away. She
tried to concentrate. "The other doctor…he has methods
for helping patients remember to take their medicine. Ways
an epileptic patient can be certain not to forget."

Cody studied her, and for a while he said nothing. Then
he leaned back again on his elbows. "You're uncomfortable
around me."

It wasn't a question, so at first Elle wasn't sure how to
respond. But anger mixed with her curiosity and she put her
hands on her hips. "Which might be a good thing, don't you
think?"

Cody wiped his brow with the back of his hand, but his
eyes stayed locked on hers. "Because you still think I'm your
enemy?"

"No." A sound came from her that was part laugh, part
frustration. "Because of your wife."

Disbelief flashed in Cody's eyes, and then faded. He
opened his mouth to say something, but then he must've
changed his mind because he pushed away from the fence
and took three steps toward the barn. He stopped and slowly
faced her again. "You're serious?"

Elle prided herself on being in control of a situation. But
she had clearly lost all sense of it here. What was he imply-
ing? That he wasn't the least bit interested, or that it was
okay for the two of them to have feelings for each other
despite the fact that he was married?

She exhaled in a huff and moved a few feet closer. "Of course I'm serious. I never hear about her, Cody." She looked back at the house and tossed her hands. "So where is she? What's her name?"

This time an undeniable sorrow colored his expression. "Her name's Ali." He stuck his hands in his jeans pockets and his voice fell a notch. "She died four years ago."

Elle felt her heart sink to her knees. "What?" Her voice was a whisper, the news hitting her in waves. All these weeks? The whole time she'd been assuming he was married, when..."Cody..." She covered her face, mortified and humiliated and broken because of the loss the man across from her had faced. She let her hands fall slowly to her sides. "I'm so sorry."

Absently, he rubbed the ring on his left hand. "Maybe you and I need to take a ride."

Elle wasn't sure where to or how long they'd be gone. But she wanted to go wherever Cody Gunner might take her, and she wanted to know his story, wanted to understand every detail.

Because maybe then she would understand the man behind it.

⌒

CODY WASN'T SURE whether to laugh or cry.

It was his wedding ring, obviously. That and maybe something Carl Joseph had said. But either way now he finally understood the way she'd felt around him. She thought he was a married man. Of course she hadn't acted interested.

Not that it mattered much now, because he was going back to the circuit. His life would be on the road, and hers would be here with her students.

But he still wanted the next hour or so to clear the air.

He led her to his pickup and opened the passenger door. When he was behind the wheel, he started the engine and drove through a gate on his parents' property. "There's a road along the side of our ranch….It leads to a bluff." He drove slowly along the dirt road. "From there you can see a million stars."

The ride took only a few minutes, and then Cody parked and grabbed a flashlight from his glove box. As he did, his hand brushed against her knee. He tried not to notice, but it was impossible. They climbed out and he took her hand, using the flashlight to navigate the path the last fifteen feet to an outcropping of rocks at the top of a small hill.

He waited until she was seated before releasing her hand and turning off the flashlight. For a few seconds he said nothing, just let the warm breeze wash over him, clearing the air between them. He leaned back on his hands and looked up. A carpet of stars covered the sky. "See…the first time I found this place at night—about a year ago—I thought it must be a little bit what heaven's like." His voice was quiet, gentle.

"It's beautiful." Her teeth chattered and she rubbed her arms.

"Cold?" He started to get up. "I have a sweatshirt in the back."

"No…" She touched his arm. "I'm fine…just…just

shocked." She pulled her knees up to her chest. "About your wife."

"You saw my ring?"

"That. And Carl Joseph told me you were married." Her sad smile was just barely visible in the light of the stars. "He said your wife was a horse rider. Of course he said you were a bull rider."

"Ali was a barrel racer." His voice grew softer. "One of the best ever."

Elle shifted so she was facing him. "Really? Professional rodeo?"

"Yes." He tried not to picture her, the way she had looked tearing around the barrels. "Buddy was right about me, too."

"You're a bull rider?" Elle sounded embarrassed, frazzled. "Wow...what else have I missed?"

"I rode bulls full-time for a while. Gave it up a year after Ali died." He smiled. "Carl Joseph will always see me as a bull rider, but these days I work the shows. Keeps me involved."

"So...you met her through the rodeo."

"I did. I was the first person outside her family who knew she was sick." The sound of an owl drifted on the breeze from a few hills over. Cody felt Elle shiver again, and this time he didn't wait for her to refuse. He popped up, turned on the flashlight, and took long strides back to the truck. He grabbed the sweatshirt, jogged back up the hill, and handed it to her. "Wear this."

She slipped it on, and in the process she moved closer to him. "She was sick? That's how she died?"

"She had cystic fibrosis." He hadn't told Ali's story for a long time. Doing so now made his time with her seem far removed. Almost as if it had happened to someone else.

"CF." Elle sighed, and for a few seconds she was quiet. "I did a paper on it in college." She faced him again. "You knew, then, when you married her…"

"Yes." He wasn't sure he wanted to tell her the rest of the story, but he'd come this far. He drew a steady breath. "I gave her one of my lungs."

"Cody…" A quiet groan came from her. "You gave her a lung, and it didn't work?"

"It worked." He had no regrets; he never would. "The doctors told us the transplant would buy her three years, and it did." He paused. "About a thousand tomorrows."

Elle's eyes glistened. "The way you love your brother…" She sniffed, sadness spilling into her voice. "I understand better now."

"I can't imagine losing him." Cody turned his gaze up toward the stars. "But I can't imagine him spending his last years at home watching Nickelodeon, either." He reached for her hand. "He has to get back to the center, Elle. Help me find a way."

"I will." She didn't sound convinced. "I guess I had that wrong, too."

"You thought it was me—that I was standing in Buddy's way?"

"Yes. I mean"—she seemed flustered again—"I knew it was your parents' choice, but I figured after the accident you talked them into pulling him out."

"No." He nudged her shoulder, playing with her. "You asked me for a week, and you did it."

"Really?" Their arms were touching again.

"Yeah." The feeling was back, the intoxicating sense of her nearness. "You proved that my brother needs to be there. Whether he's sick or not."

"Think your parents will let him go?"

"I'm not sure." Cody remembered his father's tone from earlier. "They're worried. I even thought maybe I should stay and live with him."

"Hey"—she angled her head—"that's a great idea."

"Except Carl Joseph's never been more frustrated with me than in the last few weeks." Cody gave a single laugh. "He basically told me I wasn't you."

"Oh." Her tone was lighter than before. "I think there's a compliment in there somewhere."

"There is." He tried to look deep into her eyes, but the darkness wouldn't allow it. "You're amazing with your students, Elle. It makes sense now that I know about Daisy."

"Mmm. There's a special sensitivity that comes with having a sibling with Down Syndrome."

"Definitely."

A quiet fell between them again, and Cody broke it first. "I'll be going back on the road again in a week or so. That way Carl Joseph won't feel like I'm watching over him."

"Oh." Her disappointment was subtle, but clear. "I'm not sure about that. I mean…I think he needs you more than you know."

"He needs you and your center." Cody smiled. "I know

that much." It was getting later, and Daisy and Carl Joseph would be wondering where they went. He stood and took her hand, helping her to her feet. "Thanks for talking."

She faced him, her hand still in his. "I'm sorry about Ali."

Cody gave a slow nod. He shifted his lower jaw and looked away for a moment. "We all are."

"It's why...you're so protective of Carl Joseph."

"It is." His eyes found hers again. "I guess we both understand each other a little better now."

"I guess we do."

⁂

CODY HELD HER hand all the way to the truck before letting go. Elle was quiet, leaving some space, some time. They rode back to the house, and when they went inside Daisy and Carl Joseph were dancing, humming something that didn't sound like any swing music Elle had ever heard. She smiled. "I like seeing them together."

Cody didn't say anything, but his eyes shone a little brighter as he watched their siblings. "He missed her."

"Same at our house." She drew a deep breath. She could hardly believe the turn of events tonight, or the roller-coaster of emotions she felt. The man she could feel herself falling for wasn't married, but single. Only now he was determined to stay on the road working for the rodeo? She couldn't imagine telling him good-bye in a week.

The idea hit her on the way back to the house. Actually, it was Daisy's idea, something she'd mentioned earlier today after school: "CJ wants to entertain me at Disneyland. But here's what I think." Her voice was determined, as if she'd given a lot of thought to whatever was coming next. "I think a hike first. First a hike, Elle. Wouldn't that be nice?"

Elle stayed by Cody's side, watching her sister. *Come on, Elle....You can do this.* "So, I have this favor to ask you."

He angled his head, and she saw a teasing in his smile. "Elle Dalton...asking a favor of me?" He took off his baseball cap and tucked it beneath his arm.

His reaction set her at ease. "Yes. Actually, I have this sister who's practically desperate to go hiking with her friend CJ." She raised her eyebrows. "And my guess is they'll both need a little help for a trip like that."

He laughed. "So maybe the four of us might be better?"

"Exactly."

"Well, I'll tell you what." Cody's smile was easygoing and tinged with just a hint of sadness. "If the doctor says my brother's up for a hike—even from the parking lot to the first trail sign—we'll do it this Sunday afternoon." He gave her a light nudge again. "How's that sound?"

"Like I'm going to have one very happy sister on my hands."

He led the way over to Carl Joseph and Daisy. For a few minutes more, the four of them talked and laughed about horses' having beds and whether—if they did—they would have to take off their shoes. Finally, Elle put her arm around her sister's shoulders. "We'd better get going. It's late."

Long after they left that night, Elle replayed her time at the Gunner house. She saw Cody riding in on the palomino, the look in his eyes when he saw her, and the way he treated her with a new level of camaraderie once he understood that Daisy was her sister.

She had felt more emotion sitting on the bluff next to Cody than she'd felt in years. She couldn't get over his story, the way he'd sacrificed out of love for Ali, and all he'd given up, all he'd lost along the way.

As she pulled into the driveway, she was practically desperate to keep her strange new feelings from her mother. Daisy was perceptive, but she didn't recognize more than the fact that her big sister was happy. Her mother would be harder to fool.

She couldn't talk about Cody with her mother, not when she could barely identify the way she was feeling. Was she falling for him? And what was the point if he was leaving? She didn't want to have feelings for a man she could see only a few times a year. But maybe—if God allowed it—Cody might stay. She could ask God every night for the next week to keep him here, to convince him that he should run the fitness center when it opened adjacent to the center.

But what then? Could her heart even remember how to take this walk? If so, she wasn't sure she'd be brave enough to follow.

All she knew was that the stars shone a little brighter tonight and the place on her arm where he had touched her felt a little warmer. Her heart felt lighter, and she could practically hear the hope in her own voice. All because she'd spent a few minutes talking with a man who was more than she had ever imagined him to be.

A rugged, brokenhearted bull rider named Cody Gunner.

Chapter Twenty-two

The doctor didn't endorse a hike in the foothills for Carl Joseph, but he didn't forbid it either. Early Sunday morning, Cody found Carl Joseph in his room before breakfast and poked his head inside. "Hey, Buddy. What're you doing?"

Carl Joseph lifted his eyes and his face lit up. "Writing my hundred words! 'Cause today is hike day so no time later. 'Cause of the hike." He laughed a few times, his excitement spilling into his voice.

The smell of cologne saturated the room. "You smell pretty good for a hike, Buddy."

A shy sort of laugh came from his brother, and he shrugged his shoulders. "'Cause D-A-I-S-Y." He wore khaki pants and a polo shirt—not exactly hiking attire. But he had on sturdy shoes. "I dressed up for Daisy 'cause that's called entertaining." He sat back down at his desk and pointed at the piece of paper there. "Look at this, Brother."

Across the top it read, "One Hundred Most Common Words." Painstakingly, his brother had printed two of the words five times each. Remorse rained on Cody's heart as he came up behind his brother and looked over his shoulder. His parents were debating whether to see the doctor Elle had told them about. In the meantime, Carl Joseph had made a decision. He would keep up on his work at home until the doctor said he could go back. In his buddy's mind, it wasn't a matter of *if* he returned, it was a matter of *when*.

"Watch this, Brother!" Carl Joseph covered his eyes with his hands. "No peeking."

Cody came around to the side so he could see better.

"*At*. A-T. *At*." He took his hands from his eyes and stared at the word. Then he clapped and bounced a little in his chair. "*At*, Brother. I can spell the word 'at.'"

Cody put his hand on Carl Joseph's shoulder and gave it a gentle squeeze. "Good work, Buddy. I'm proud of you."

With those words, Carl Joseph made a slow turn in his chair. He pushed his glasses up a little higher on his nose and stared at Cody. Then, like a gradual drip from a faucet, tears filled Carl Joseph's eyes. "Really, Brother? You're proud of me? Even if I'm not learning new things right now?"

Cody felt his heart breaking all over again. "C'mere, Buddy. I'm so proud of you." He held out his arms and Carl Joseph stood. Slowly, he came to Cody, and the two of them hugged the way they hadn't done since Cody's first day home. "Hey, I have an idea." Cody took a step back and smiled. "Let's go to breakfast before the hike."

Joy flashed in Carl Joseph's eyes, but then just as quickly

his smile faded. He looked at a calendar on his wall where each day of the week was represented in a different color. Carl Joseph had crossed off every day of the month that had gone by. He moved his finger along the small boxes until he reached the first one not crossed off. Today's date.

"Uh-oh." He straightened and turned back to Cody. "Blue means Sunday. Sunday means church."

Once more Cody felt seized with guilt. He had discouraged his brother from giving money to the church, and Carl Joseph hadn't mentioned attending a service since. But here was further proof that Carl Joseph still knew what Sundays were about. What they were supposed to be about. "Yes, Buddy, today's Sunday. But we can still have breakfast out. Restaurants are open on Sunday."

Carl Joseph's expression fell flat for a moment, and he looked at the dresser next to his bed. He reached down and opened the top drawer, then he lifted an envelope from inside. Across the front in their mother's handwriting it read *Carl Joseph's gift for Jesus.* He studied it, then set it back down and shut the drawer again. "Not church today?"

"No, Buddy. Just breakfast. Is that okay?"

He bit his lip, as if the question was perplexing. Then he nodded, and a hesitant smile lifted his lips. "Okay. On Sunday me and Brother have breakfast."

"At Denny's."

"'Cause Denny's has pancakes!" Carl Joseph hurried toward the door. "I need a shower, Brother. I'll be right back."

In a rush, Cody felt his defenses fade away. Who was he

to tell Carl Joseph how he could spend his money? Carl Joseph lived at home, and if he wanted to give a fourth of his earnings to the church, that was his prerogative. He opened the drawer and took out the envelope with his brother's gift.

Cody thought about his years on the rodeo tour, and the lengths people would go for money. Athletes who would shoot themselves with cortisone or painkillers because they wanted to make a thousand dollars. People did crazy things for money.

Guilt ate at him as he ran his thumb over the envelope. He stared out the window and felt the weight of his earlier decision. How come it had taken this long for him to see the gift as what it was? A gift. A decision. One that Carl Joseph had the right to make.

"Okay, God," Cody whispered. He wasn't good at praying, and nothing about it came naturally. He squinted against the sunlight. "Am I supposed to encourage Carl Joseph to put a hundred dollars in the church plate?"

Cody looked around his brother's room, and his eyes settled on a poster near the bed. The words read, "But seek first His kingdom and His righteousness and all these things will be given to you." Beneath the words was a boy with Down Syndrome sitting at a bus stop.

Chills ran down Cody's arms. The message was unmistakable. Seek God first, and everything else would fall into place. He thought of his lung—the gift he'd given his precious Ali. Lots of people would've thought him crazy to let doctors cut into his chest and take out one of his lungs, all so that a dying girl could have a few more years.

Tears stung his eyes again. It hadn't mattered what anyone else said. His gift to Ali made perfect sense to him. But what if he'd had Down Syndrome? What if he'd wanted to give Ali the gift, and someone had stood in the way and forbidden him from giving it? A piece of him would have died right alongside her, no question. The look in Carl Joseph's eyes a few minutes ago came back to him again.

Was that how his brother felt? His hands tied, unable to do something that was so strongly in his heart?

Cody took a long breath and gathered his determination. He would get dressed—khaki pants and a polo shirt, so his buddy wouldn't feel out of place. He'd take his brother out to breakfast and on the hike they'd planned for today. But first, before they stopped at Denny's for pancakes, he would do what he should've done a long time ago.

He would take Carl Joseph to church.

THEY WERE HALFWAY to Denny's when Cody made a turn onto the main highway. His heart felt lighter, happier than it had felt in weeks. In years, even. He drove through the suburbs and toward the downtown area. The closer they got, the more he couldn't stop himself from smiling. Carl Joseph didn't notice anything out of the ordinary until Cody pulled up in front of the downtown church, the one where the field trip had taken place.

Then he stared at the building and his mouth dropped. He looked at Cody and swallowed. "That's not Denny's."

"No, Buddy." He pulled Carl Joseph's envelope from

beneath the seat and handed it to him. "I thought maybe we should go to church first. That way you can give Jesus your gift."

Carl Joseph gasped. He had always been emotional, easily moved to tears, though in the last few months he seemed to have outgrown dramatic shows of his feelings. But here, now, Carl Joseph stared at the envelope and his eyes filled with tears. Once more he gave Cody a curious look. "You mean, it's okay, Brother? My gift is okay?"

"Yes." Cody struggled with the lump in his throat. "It's a beautiful gift." He looked at his watch. "But we'd better get inside. Service is about to start."

The message that day was as if God Himself had spoken it straight to Cody's heart. It was about trust and worry, and how it was fruitless to be anxious about tomorrow. No one could tell the future, the pastor said. "We can only trust God and follow His lead throughout this journey called life. Then when the end comes, we will have nothing left to do but celebrate."

The idea filled Cody's entire being. Trust God every day, so that in the end—whenever that was—there would be a celebration, not a wake. Joyful memories, not painful regrets.

And wasn't that Ali's message from the beginning? People died tragic deaths all the time. The point wasn't how a person died. It was how a person lived.

Cody watched Carl Joseph, the way he knelt and stared earnestly, reverently at the cross up front. Cody struggled with relationships and love, with knowing what his next season in life should be about, and with where God fit in his life.

All the areas where Carl Joseph didn't struggle at all.

When the offering plate came around, his brother took the folded envelope from his pocket, kissed it, and placed it tenderly on top. Then he looked at Cody and grinned. And from somewhere up in heaven, Cody could almost feel God grinning, too.

THEY EACH ORDERED a Grand Slam breakfast, and Cody realized he hadn't enjoyed his brother this much since he'd come home from the rodeo circuit. They talked about bus routes and field trips and Daisy. A lot about Daisy. When the meal was over, though he debated it, Carl Joseph decided against the strawberry milkshake. "Ice cream isn't a healthy choice." He shook his head. "Not very healthy."

"No." Cody stifled a smile. "Water's probably better."

"Probably."

The waitress brought the check and set it at the edge of the table. She was older, their mother's age maybe. Already Carl Joseph had explained that Cody was his brother and that they were just returning from church.

"The pastor said to trust God," he told her when she came to clear their plates. "Do you trust God, waitress?"

Cody was about to interrupt, apologize for his brother's behavior, and let the waitress off the hook. People didn't come out and ask questions like that, not of strangers, anyway. But before he could say anything, the waitress patted Carl Joseph's hand.

"I do." She gave Cody a knowing smile, as if to say they made a nice picture—two brothers sharing a meal this way. She turned back to Carl Joseph. "I trust Him every day."

"Good." Carl Joseph stopped short of clapping, but he was clearly overjoyed that the waitress understood this truth about God.

Again Cody was taken aback. He folded his hands on the table and gave a slight shake of his head. The more he thought he knew about life, the more Carl Joseph redefined it. What was wrong with talking about God, anyway? Carl Joseph's question had given the waitress a reason to smile even in the middle of a Sunday late breakfast rush.

After she left, Carl Joseph took the check and studied it. Cody watched him and wondered again about Elle Dalton's offer. Could he take the next season of his life and devote it to working with adults like his brother? Today, the way Carl Joseph was relaxed around him, made him think it was possible.

He took a twenty from his wallet and set it on the table. Carl Joseph was still studying the check. "Brother?" Carl Joseph had the check in one hand, and the money in the other. "You need more."

"What?" Cody took the check and looked at the total. Fourteen dollars, eleven cents. "But I put a..."

Carl Joseph held up the bill. "This is a ten, Brother. You need a twenty for the food we ate. 'Cause Grand Slams aren't cheap." He laughed at himself. "That's why they're Grand Slams."

Cody was stunned. "How did you know that?"

"I learned it." He grinned and laughed at the same time. "Teacher taught me."

Elle again. The girl with the beautiful eyes and sensitive heart. The one he couldn't wait to spend an afternoon with. "I like your teacher, Buddy."

A quiet laugh came from him. "I know you do."

"What?" A smile pulled at Cody's lips. "How do you know?"

"Because"—he laughed again—"I just know. 'Cause standing close and smiling at her. A lot of smiling."

"Okay." Cody was laughing now, too. He dropped his voice to a whisper. "But it'll be our secret."

"Good." He clapped quietly. "I like secrets."

Long after breakfast and into the rest of the day, Cody felt a peace that hadn't been there since he returned home nearly two months ago. He and his buddy were friends again, that was much of it. But also, the pastor was right. Life really was a matter of trusting God every day so that when it was all over, there wouldn't be sadness over a mountain of regrets.

There would be a celebration.

The sort of celebration that was about to take place on a simple hike with friends.

Chapter Twenty-three

Cody and Carl Joseph would be there in an hour. Elle couldn't find her hairbrush, so she went down the hall to Daisy's room. Her mother and sister were in Daisy's bathroom, working together to put curlers in her fine blonde hair.

Elle stood in the doorway and raised an eyebrow. "Did I get the memo wrong? I thought we were going on a hike."

Daisy peered over her shoulder. "It's a date."

"Oh, it is?" Elle loved this about her sister, her feisty independence, knowing her own mind before anyone could speak for her.

Their mother sent a helpless look back at Elle. "Daisy told me it was a date. She wanted her hair curled."

"It's a date for you, too, Elle." Daisy grinned in the mirror. "You and Cody."

Heat filled Elle's cheeks. "It's not a date for us, sweetie. We're only going along for fun."

Daisy stared at her for a few seconds. "It's a date."

Her mother gave her another look, and there was no denying the twinkle in her eyes. "I don't know, Elle. Maybe you'd better curl your hair."

"Thanks, Mom." She gave an exasperated breath. "You're a big help." But even as she said the words, her heart reacted to the possibility. She forced herself to stay matter-of-fact. Daisy was wrong. This wasn't a date for her and Cody Gunner. They'd discussed nothing of the sort.

Still, if Daisy could curl her hair, Elle could at least wear a nicer pair of shorts. She ran back to her room and changed both her shorts and her shirt. Was it a date? Was that how Cody saw the afternoon hike? She doubted it. He'd made himself clear when they talked about his Ali. Cody never expected to love like that again. Never wanted to. And Elle was the same way. At least that's what she'd always told herself. Now, though, she had to wonder if her heart had a different agenda altogether.

When she was happy with her look, she left the room to rejoin her mother and sister. As she left, the faintest hint of perfume lingered behind her.

THEY WERE AT a stoplight, and Carl Joseph stuck his head out the window and peered at himself in the side mirror.

"Brother...can you help me?"

Cody stifled a smile. He'd never seen his brother so concerned with his looks. "What's up?"

Carl Joseph looked in the mirror again. "I look wrong." He turned an empty expression to his brother. "How come?"

The light turned green, and Cody shrugged. "I think you look perfect."

"Good." Carl Joseph hiked up his pant leg. "I wore my best socks 'cause Daisy is my best friend. Best and best, Brother."

"See?" Cody patted his shoulder. "You're just perfect."

"Yeah, 'cause I tell the best jokes. That's what Daisy says. Also I might ask her to Disneyland. 'Cause I might entertain her at Disneyland."

"Let's do the hike first."

"One thing." Carl Joseph held up one finger. "Can we pray? 'Cause this is a big day, Brother, and we have a lot of driving and we have Daisy and Elle and we don't want to get lost. 'Cause also prayin'—"

"Is a life skill." Cody smiled at him. "I was just going to say the same thing." He kept his eyes on the road and one hand on Carl Joseph's shoulder, and he prayed a prayer about protection and direction and open hearts and trusting.

And then, silently, he asked for one more thing.

That God might calm his nerves sometime before they reached the Dalton house.

⌒

ELLE HADN'T BEEN this nervous as far back as she could remember. She paced to the front window, peered down the street looking for his truck, and then paced back into the kitchen. "No sign of him."

"He's not supposed to be here for five more minutes." Her mother was making a cup of tea. "Right?"

"Cody's always early." She smoothed her jean shorts.

"Elle Dalton." Her mother's voice was low. "You're falling for him."

Daisy was at the sink filling a water bottle, and she didn't seem able to hear their conversation.

Elle stared at her mother. "What in the world gives you that impression?"

"The way you're acting, all flustered. I haven't seen this from you since..." She stopped herself. "I haven't seen it in a long time."

"That's because Teacher likes Cody." Daisy turned around and twisted the lid onto her water bottle. "Right, Teacher?"

"Daisy..." There was a warning in Elle's voice. She raised her brow and looked straight at her sister. "You can only call me that in the classroom."

"Okay." Daisy danced around in a circle, twirling and doing a slightly awkward pirouette. "Elle likes Cody." She shrugged and gave their mother a silly look. "Cody likes Elle, too."

Elle could feel the entire day unraveling into a disaster. "You're wrong, Daisy. And please don't say anything about that today, okay?"

Daisy held her finger to her lips. "Shhh. Not a word." She grinned and then danced her way into the front room. "I'm waiting for CJ outside."

"Great." Elle fell into the nearest chair and stared at her mother. "Did you have to ask in front of her? She'll talk about it for sure."

"No she won't." Her mother pulled the tea bag from her

steaming cup and tossed it into the trash. She gave Elle a pointed look. "Daisy's the one who told me. A week ago, Elle. All that time and she hasn't said a word to you or Cody."

"Really?" Elle felt herself relax.

"Yes."

Elle thought about her sister. Of course Daisy would've seen this a week ago. Hadn't they all learned ages ago not to underestimate Daisy's perception, her understanding of social settings?

There was a sound at the door, and Elle jumped up. She grabbed her backpack and kissed her mother on the cheek. For the briefest instant she hesitated, her eyes locked on her mother's. "What if you're right?" she whispered. Her heart beat in double time. "What if you're both right?"

Her mother smiled and took her hand. "Then you pray for wisdom and proceed with caution." She squeezed Elle's hand and then released it. "And you thank God for breathing new life into that very special heart of yours. Even if it all amounts to nothing."

ELLE WAS WILLING to sit in the backseat with her sister, but Daisy made a fairly dramatic show of pointing to the passenger seat, the one next to Cody. By the time Elle slid in next to him, Cody was hiding a sympathy laugh.

"Don't worry about it." He looked in his rearview mirror at Daisy and Carl Joseph. "They're just excited."

"It'll be fun trying to keep them focused enough to stay on the trail." Elle sat back in her seat. The inside of his truck reeked of cologne, and she sniffed a few times.

"It's my brother." Cody aimed his thumb toward the backseat. "You know…two capfuls of cologne."

"Ooops." Elle winced and allowed a quiet laugh. "We haven't talked about that in our social graces class."

Cody blinked, as if his eyes were burning from the smell. "When you do, Carl Joseph can be the poster boy."

They both laughed, and Cody turned up the radio. It was a country song by Lonestar, and Elle found the lyrics fitting. Something about how the Lord gave people mountains so they could learn how to climb. If that were true, she and Cody should be experts by now.

She looked at Cody, but only for a moment. She was keenly aware of every move he made. The muscles in his shoulders as he turned the wheel, and the details of his handsome profile. She'd Googled him last night and found that Cody Gunner was definitely a legend in bull-riding circles. One Web site said, "To this day, no one has ridden a bull the way Cody Gunner rode. He is bigger than life in and out of the arena, and it'll be a long time before someone else takes his place."

Indeed. That's what she was sensing from him today. The larger-than-life part. Being in his presence here made it hard for her to breathe. And yet for all his professional reputation, the world didn't see what she'd seen. What he'd let her see on a starry night sitting on a bluff at the far end of his parents' ranch.

They reached the parking lot, and when they climbed out

Elle was suddenly aware of Cody's height. This was the first time she'd been around him in anything but high-heeled shoes.

"Ready?" He gave her a quick grin and then patted his brother's back.

"Ready, over and out!" Carl Joseph saluted.

Daisy laughed and did a salute of her own. "CJ, you're so funny!"

Elle mouthed the words, "Oh, brother," for Cody's benefit. Then they set out for the trailhead.

For the first part of the hike, Cody took the lead and Elle brought up the rear. She wanted to make sure there were no problems with Daisy and Carl Joseph keeping to the trail or falling behind. After an hour they found a clearing and took a break. Carl Joseph and Daisy walked over to a patch of clover.

"Over here, CJ. I have a new move for you."

"Dancing in the clover!" Carl Joseph clapped and bounced a few times. "'Cause I like dancing in the clover."

"Yeah, but this is a dance move from class, CJ. So come here."

Carl Joseph went to her, and Daisy started the impromptu lesson.

"They love to dance." Cody bit into an apple and handed a second one to Elle.

She took it and thanked him. "Yes. Sometimes I wish when we do the addition to the facility, we could add a dance room, too. That way they could see themselves in the mirror." She angled her head and looked at their siblings.

"That could help a lot with body control, just knowing how they look."

Cody sat on a chair-sized boulder. He was quiet for a minute, staring at Carl Joseph and Daisy. Finally he drew a long breath. "They look pretty happy."

"They do." She was standing a few feet from him. "Thanks, by the way."

"For what?" He took another bite of his apple.

"Bringing Carl Joseph today. I'm sure the doctor wasn't crazy about the idea."

"No." A sad smile lifted Cody's lips. "But he told us we couldn't protect Carl Joseph from everything." He turned to her. "My parents are thinking about talking to the other doctor, the one you recommended."

Elle felt a surge of hope. "That's what we're praying for."

"Good." He patted the spot next to him. "Sit down. We won't have another rest until we reach the top." He grinned. "The planner of this hike's a real taskmaster."

She laughed and sat next to him. As she did, her arm brushed against his, and the sensation made her dizzy. She gave him a teasing look. "We can go slower if you can't handle it."

"No, no." He held up his half-eaten apple. "My one lung's better than two of yours. Don't worry about me."

"Ugh." She dropped her head in her hands. How come she hadn't thought of that? Here she was pushing Carl Joseph and Daisy up the hill, encouraging them to keep the pace, and she hadn't once thought about Cody's limitations. She peered at him through her fingers. "I completely forgot. I'm sorry."

"Nah." He dropped the pretense and patted her knee.

"I'm fine, really. Just teasing. I went a whole season of bull riding with one lung. I can certainly hike up a mountain."

"I guess." She still felt bad, but before she could say anything more about it, Daisy and Carl Joseph began waving at them.

"So"—Cody searched her eyes—"I told you my story. What about you? Never married?" His expression changed. "Sorry. You don't have to answer that."

"No, it's fine." She leaned back on her hands. She watched her sister and Carl Joseph, still working on the dance step. She took a long breath. "I never dated much through school. My only real love was the principal of the first school I taught at. His name was Trace."

She hadn't told the story often, and it didn't come easily now. She stayed with the main details, how after a year of friendship with Trace, she took a transfer to another school so they could date. Cody listened closely, though her story sounded like any other until she got to the part about the wedding.

"The rumor was that Trace was gay." She squinted against the glaring pain of her past. "I guess I didn't want to believe it. And after we started dating, I had no reason."

Concern colored Cody's expression. "He backed out of the wedding?"

"On our wedding day." She smiled, but she knew it didn't hide the hurt. "We had three hundred guests waiting for the music to start when I got his call."

"Elle..." Cody looked sick to his stomach. He shifted, studying her. "That's awful."

"I should've seen it coming." Elle lifted her chin and stared at a slice of blue through a patch of evergreens.

For a while Cody said nothing. Her story had that sort of effect on people. When he did speak, his tone was softer than before. "So you put everything you have into your work."

"Yes."

"Wow..." He anchored his elbows on his knees and stared at the ground. "I'll bet you haven't told that to many people."

"No. Our friends and relatives think he had a nervous breakdown, a serious case of cold feet."

"Whatever happened to him?"

"Last I heard he'd walked away from the gay lifestyle. He was getting counseling at a Christian center in San Francisco."

Cody straightened, the concern still in his eyes. "How'd you get through it?"

"God alone." She smiled at him, but her heart hurt. The way it always would when she talked about Trace. "I've got a good life. Rewarding. Fulfilling. It's enough."

"Hey..." Carl Joseph waved at them. "Come on, Brother. We have to teach you the dance!"

Elle let the sad feelings pass. She smiled at their siblings. "They're quite a pair."

"They are." Cody chuckled. "Looks like it's lesson time."

"Come on!" Carl Joseph tipped his head back and laughed with the abandon of a child. He twirled Daisy, and she ducked to get under his arm. In the process, she tripped and almost fell, but Carl Joseph caught her.

Elle smiled. People with Down Syndrome were limited

in so many areas. But in so many of the ways that mattered, they weren't limited at all.

"I'm the teacher this time." Daisy ran up and took Elle's hand. When Elle was on her feet, Daisy motioned for Cody. "Come on." She pointed to the patch of clover. "We all have to dance because that's a good dance floor."

Cody followed along, but he shot Elle a wary look. "I can't dance."

"Yes, Brother, 'cause I'll teach you." Carl Joseph met them halfway and helped lead Cody to the middle of the patch.

"Start like this." Daisy put one hand in Carl Joseph's hand, and the other on his shoulder. "Go on." She nodded to Elle. "Like me and CJ."

Elle turned to Cody and made a face. The moment was more humorous than awkward, but even so she didn't want Cody to feel forced into anything he wasn't comfortable with. "I don't think we have a choice."

"No." He straightened, feigning a proper look, and he held out one hand. He placed the other on her shoulder. His voice was too low for their siblings to hear. "I warned you. I have two left feet."

"Okay, here's the beat." Daisy was still in Carl Joseph's arms. She used her hand to set the rhythm. "Five, six, seven, eight." Moving slowly and deliberately, they took a step together and then a step apart. Daisy pointed at their feet. She jumped in place a few times. "Do that!"

Cody imitated the steps.

"Do it better!" She laughed at the two of them.

"We're trying." Elle giggled. "Give us a break."

One step after another Elle and Cody played along, following Daisy's instruction. Partway through the number, Carl Joseph began to hum, and Cody dipped his head near Elle's. "I love that kid."

"I know." She spoke low near his face. "Me, too. He's been so good for Daisy."

The humor of the moment faded, and Elle could think only of how good she felt. Her hand was warm in Cody's, and they were close enough that once in a while she could feel his breath on her face. When she wasn't focused on the dance steps, she felt dizzy from the nearness of him. New feelings, brand-new emotions were taking root in her heart and soul, and she could do nothing to stop them.

"How're we doing, Buddy?" Cody looked over his shoulder at Carl Joseph. "Doing okay?"

Carl Joseph stopped and watched them for a few beats. He gave a firm nod and pushed his glasses back up his nose. "'Cause this is your first time."

"Very good for the first time." Daisy smiled. "Keep making music, CJ."

The dance continued, and Elle couldn't help but savor the feel of it. After Trace, she hadn't imagined herself ever feeling this way again. But here she was on a mountainside overlooking Colorado Springs, dancing on a patch of clover in Cody Gunner's arms, and suddenly nothing felt impossible.

"All right now, spin!" Daisy did a spin beneath Carl Joseph's arms again, only this time she added a second spin. The move didn't look smooth, but they managed it without tripping or falling.

Cody wore a look of concentration as he tried to copy his brother's move, but in the process his feet got in the way and Elle tripped over them. She let out a cry and fell forward into his arms. He caught her around her waist, and for a moment it seemed they'd both fall to the ground. But he steadied himself and they burst out laughing.

"Brother." Carl Joseph stopped and stared at them. He gave Cody a mildly disgusted look. "That is not how you do it."

"Really?" Cody leaned his head against hers. He was laughing so hard he still seemed unsteady, and she was doing the same. He had one hand on the small of her back, the other up between her shoulders.

As they caught their breath, their eyes met, and Cody seemed to realize the way he was holding her. The laughter faded, and something different filled his eyes. A mix of desire and unbridled fear. She felt the change, too. What were they doing, standing here this way, their faces inches from each other? At the same time, she felt something brush against her middle finger. She didn't have to look to know what it was.

Cody's wedding ring.

He must've realized what she was feeling, because he took a step back and moved his hands to her shoulders. The laughter returned to his eyes, and the intimacy of the moment passed. Clearly, he wasn't going to talk about the ring or why—after four years—he was still wearing it.

And Elle wouldn't either. She fixed her hair and nodded at Cody's feet. "You did warn me."

"I did." He dropped his hands to his sides. He was back to the confident, easygoing Cody, the one he'd just recently allowed her to know. But at least he wasn't shutting her off, frightened by their moment of intimacy.

And that's what it had been, no question. Even if it lasted only a couple of heartbeats, Elle had seen in his eyes, his expression, that he wondered about her as much as she wondered about him. The knowing was enough to take her breath.

"You need work," Daisy pointed out. She looped her arm through Carl Joseph's. "Maybe later."

They all agreed that later would be better for the dance lessons.

"I'm thirsty." Carl Joseph pulled his water bottle from his backpack. "See, Teacher. I know this life skill. Drink your water!"

"CJ knows." Daisy patted him on the back.

Elle took a drink, and so did the others. As she did, she watched Daisy and Carl Joseph, the way Daisy had such pride for every milestone Carl Joseph reached, and how he protected her at every turn. They were so comfortable around each other. Elle couldn't help but feel a little jealous. Which of them were really handicapped if relationships came this easily for Daisy and Carl Joseph?

After they'd packed the water bottles in their backpacks, they started up the trail again. But there was a difference. This time Cody let Carl Joseph and Daisy take the lead, and he fell in beside Elle. The trail was narrow in places, and at times their shoulders touched.

Elle wasn't as perceptive as Daisy, but she could sense a slight hesitation from Cody. He wasn't angry or even distant. But though they didn't talk about it, she was pretty sure he was caught off guard by the feelings that had surfaced during the dancing incident. Just as she was.

As they walked, they talked about other hikes Elle had taken with Daisy, and how Cody wanted Carl Joseph to spend more time getting exercise. When they reached the top of the trail, they had talked about everything from Daisy's childhood to Disneyland. Everything except the most obvious thing.

Whatever was happening between them.

The rest of the hike there were no other close calls between them, nothing but two new friends sharing an afternoon. But when Cody dropped Elle and Daisy off at their house, the four of them climbed out of his truck. Carl Joseph walked Daisy to the door and the two hugged. Elle could hear Daisy telling him about the coming week at the center and Carl Joseph trying to guess where the next field trip would take place.

Elle and Cody stayed near the truck. "Thanks." She looked up at him. "That was fun."

"It was." He looked down at his feet and tried a few in-place steps. "I could still use a little help in the dancing department."

"You'll get it next time." Elle's cheeks felt sunburned from the day on the mountain. A gentle wind blew by them, and Elle wondered what he was really thinking, and whether there would even be a next time.

They were facing each other, and then, as if he were wondering the same thing, Cody took her hands in his. And in as much time as it took her to inhale, the moment became deeper, more intimate, exactly what it had been up on the patch of clover. He searched her eyes. "Elle...I don't know."

Her heart skidded into a strange rhythm. "You don't know what?"

The muscles in his jaw flexed and he looked up for a long time, up at the place where big, puffy white clouds punctuated the clear blue sky. He exhaled, and it made him sound beyond weary. Then he faced her again. "I don't know how..." He looked at Carl Joseph and Daisy. They were dancing again, this time on the front porch. "I don't know how to feel or..." He pointed at his brother. "Or how to be like that again."

She willed her heart to slow down, pressed herself to find the right words. "Maybe you don't have to." A sad smile lifted the corners of her mouth. "It was just one dance, Cody."

He rubbed his thumbs along the tops of her hands. "No, it wasn't." He looked past her defenses. "You felt it, too." His lips parted. He looked nervous and determined all at the same time. His voice dropped a notch. "You feel it now."

A part of her wanted to run into the house and never look back. Wasn't this how things had started with Trace? It would be better by far to keep things casual, to laugh and joke about dancing and Disneyland so that they never had to talk about anything more. She gripped his hands a little tighter. She steadied herself and met his eyes again. "My mother once told me that God doesn't give us something new unless our hands are empty." She shrugged one shoulder and looked at his left hand, at the ring there. "You know?"

Cody looked at her for a long time. "I have a lot to think about." He pulled her into a hug, the sort of hug he would give his sister if he had one. "You, too."

"Yes." She took a step back. Her cheeks were hotter now, and with the sun hidden behind the clouds she was certain the heat wasn't only her sunburn. There was something she wanted to say, something she wanted him to know before he left. "Thank you, Cody."

He must've understood that she meant more than the hike, because he waited, studying her eyes. His smile touched her heart to the core. "For what…other than stepping on your feet?"

"For trusting me enough to tell me that." Never mind that it was a summer afternoon. With Cody a few feet away from her, Elle felt a chill run down her arms. "Let me know about the doctor and Carl Joseph."

"I will." He took a step back and waved. "See ya."

After the guys left, Elle put her arm around Daisy's shoulders and the two headed inside. "That was a fun day."

"Know something?" Daisy grinned and made a few silent chuckles, as if she had the biggest secret in the world on the tip of her tongue. "I love that CJ."

Elle hugged her sister. "I'm glad, sweetie. I think he loves you, too."

Daisy nodded, confident of the fact. "Hey, Mom! What's for dinner?"

How easily Daisy handled love. The feelings were there, and that was that. Nothing to hide or act strange about, no need for caution or pretense. Love simply was. Period. Daisy headed back to her bedroom and their mother appeared from the kitchen.

"Help me chop carrots?"

"Sure." Elle knew what was coming. She and her mother had always talked about everything. Spending a day with Cody Gunner would be no different. Especially since Elle had already told her mom about Cody's past, the heartbreaking loss of his wife, and his decision to give her one of his lungs to buy three more years with her.

"People don't usually love like that twice in a lifetime," was all her mother told her. Since then they hadn't talked about Cody, not even when Elle's mom learned that the four of them were taking a hike today.

Now they took up their places at separate cutting boards, a pot of water between them. For a minute, they sliced in silence. Then her mother stopped long enough to look at her. "I saw you outside with Carl Joseph's brother. You looked...very happy."

Elle set down her knife and covered her mother's hand with her own. "We're just friends."

"But what about you?" Her words were gentle. "How do you feel?"

Elle hesitated, and in that single hesitation she knew she was in trouble. She could feel the way her fingers nestled into Cody's hand, feel the way she'd felt safe and protected on the path beside him, and how when she was in his arms she never wanted the moment to end.

"Elle?"

"I'm not sure." She picked up her knife and another carrot and looked back at the cutting board. She grabbed a fast breath and found a smile. "Anyway, you should hear about the hike. Carl Joseph and Daisy were hysterical, dancing on a patch of clover halfway up the trail…"

She launched into a lengthy description of the day that told her mother in no uncertain terms that the conversation about Cody, about the heart of Cody, was over. The fact was, she couldn't tell her mother how she was feeling about Carl Joseph's brother until she found some time alone, time to talk to God. Because before she could talk to someone else about her feelings for Cody Gunner, there was something she had to do.

She had to figure them out for herself.

Chapter Twenty-four

After Cody took Carl Joseph home, after he evaded a handful of questions from his mother, he looked at his watch. Four o'clock. Four more hours of daylight. Enough time to visit the one place he wanted to be.

The one place he had to be.

By the time he returned to his truck and set out along the dirt road toward the back of the ranch, his head was swimming with a thousand different thoughts. Images of the hike and his time with Elle filled his heart and mind and soul. His feelings for her were rising to the surface before he was ready for them. What had happened today? And how was he supposed to make sense of it when he never planned on loving anyone other than Ali?

He focused on the road ahead.

He parked where he had the other night with Elle. For a few minutes he leaned against his truck and stared at the evergreens and craggy outcroppings of rock that circled the place. Then he walked up the hill and sat on the bluff. He could see miles of undeveloped foothills from here, and the serenity of the place allowed him to think. Cody had a number of spots on the ranch where he and Ali had gone to talk about her impending death.

But this wasn't one of them.

He felt the tears come, felt them overflow from his heart into his eyes. Was he moving on? Doing the one thing Ali had asked of him before she died? He closed his eyes because the shock and sorrow were the same every time he thought about her. It seemed like just ten minutes ago that she was lying beside him, still fighting the disease, still breathing the same air as him. So how could she really be dead?

"Ali..." He sat up straighter and pressed his fists to his eyes. *Dear God...will it ever get easier?*

The prayer came unexpectedly, and Cody blinked his eyes open. He looked beyond the foothills, up to the distant horizon. *Please, God...can You hear me?*

At that same moment, a warmth came over him, settling his soul and calming his emotions. A knowing filled his heart, one that gave him the strength to consider the thoughts that had been stirring inside him all day. He looked at his wedding ring, and he was overwhelmed with a certainty, one that had never hit him when he'd come here before.

Ali was gone, but more than that, she had moved on. She was in heaven taking on the tasks and joys that God had for her on the other side. And what she'd left behind was a lesson he hadn't wanted to act on until now. Ali believed in life, in living every minute as if it were her last.

So how was it he'd lived his last four years as if his life were over, too? He'd resisted friendships and conversations, and he'd built up a determination never to love again. When that wasn't what Ali stood for at all. She would've been angry with him for what he'd become—a closed-off man, at first afraid even to let Carl Joseph have the wings to fly. He blinked away another layer of tears. Ali wouldn't recognize him.

Elle's words from earlier came back. What was it her mother had told her? That God couldn't give a person something new unless his hands were empty. He looked at his left hand again, at the wedding ring he still wore. Elle had noticed it, no doubt. He had felt the moment when her body stiffened, when she looked away because of it.

Cody twisted it, and for a moment he was back again, standing on a bluff in her parents' backyard, beneath the big open Colorado sky, pledging forever to Ali Daniels. He could see her eyes, feel her hands in his. But then, like the changing direction of a gust of wind, the image disappeared.

Wearing the ring didn't make her any less gone. It served only as a reminder that his life had ended right along with hers. And that—Cody was sure of it—would've made Ali furious. Ali, who had made him promise to love again, and who had grown frustrated when he dismissed the idea.

"You need to live, Cody." She rarely raised her voice, but the last time they talked about his future, she grew angry with him. "I won't stand for you to lose your passion, your ability to love, just because I'm not here anymore."

Ali hadn't just hoped for him to find a new life after her

death; she'd demanded it. But for four years, one season after another, he'd ignored her wishes. Not because he didn't care what she thought, but because he could barely get out of bed each morning. Her loss made it hard for him to breathe, let alone consider love. He shifted his gaze to the distant hills.

Until now.

He gritted his teeth. He had tried to keep Elle Dalton out of his heart, tried from the moment he saw her. So what if she was beautiful? He could walk away from beauty. But today, on a hike that was supposed to be nothing more than an outing with their siblings, he had learned something about himself.

He couldn't walk away from Elle Dalton's heart.

Elle was passionate about love and life and people with Down Syndrome. Deep inside her wounded heart was a love for Daisy that rivaled his love for Carl Joseph, and in that, Elle was a kindred spirit.

Part of his attraction to Ali, even though he didn't like to think this way, had been her illness, and the fact that he might protect her, shelter her. She needed him, and that drove their love to a level that Cody hadn't known existed.

Elle wasn't sick with a deadly disease, but the damage to her heart was enough to cripple her for a lifetime. Working with people like her sister was enough for Elle. She was willing to put her own feelings on ice while she served others. Better that than to experience the pain and rejection that could come with falling in love.

And that made Cody want to shelter Elle, the same way once a lifetime ago he'd wanted to shelter Ali. He spotted a pair of deer in the distance. They stopped and looked his direction, and then ran off into the hills. Cody leaned back on the rock and thought about the hike.

When he stepped on Elle's feet, when she stumbled into his arms, he had the sudden urge to love away all the betrayal and rejection inside her, to protect her and care for her and teach her that love didn't have to hurt so bad. The strength of his feelings took his breath. Feelings he hadn't acknowledged until that instant.

He breathed in, and as always he felt his body stop short of a full breath, the way it had done since the transplant operation. The tangible reminder of Ali that he would always carry with him.

He looked at his wedding ring one more time. Then he stood and stared into the distance. "I know what I have to do, Ali. And I know somewhere in heaven you understand because…you made me promise."

His eyes were dry now, his thoughts more about Elle and the future than anything from the past. A sense of peace warmed him, the way it had earlier when he prayed. He hesitated a moment longer. He slid his hands into his pockets, took one last look at the sky, and then made his way back to his truck. On the way home, his jumbled thoughts all seemed to right themselves. And suddenly he knew exactly what he was supposed to do next.

When he walked in the door, his family was sitting at the dinner table, just about to eat. The smell of lasagna was thick in the air, and as Cody came closer, Carl Joseph's face burst into a grin. "Brother! You came back in time!"

Cody laughed. He loved the way Carl Joseph made dinnertime feel like a vacation to the Bahamas. "Yes, Buddy. I made it back."

He raised his fork in the air. "Brother's here for Mom's lasagna."

The celebration hung in the air for several minutes after Cody sat down. Only then did he notice the way his parents were looking at each other, as if they had something they could hardly wait to say.

Finally his dad set down his fork. "We talked to the doctor, the one Elle suggested."

"He called us here. On a Sunday." His mom's eyes grew damp, but the joy there was undeniable. "He told us about a new medication."

Cody was dizzy with anticipation. He looked from his mother to his father. "And?"

"I can't keep it, Mom!" Carl Joseph pushed back from the table and jumped up. He danced in a few circles and pumped his fists. "No more secrets! I can't wait!"

A tear spilled onto his mother's cheek, and she made a sound that was more laugh than cry. "Carl Joseph is going back to the center on Monday."

Cody felt his breath catch in his throat. He stood and studied his parents. "You're serious?"

"I can keep working for Goal Day, Brother!" Carl Joseph raised both fists in the air. "'Cause better medicine now."

His mother folded her hands, and Cody noticed that her fingers were trembling. As Carl Joseph danced into the kitchen, she lowered her voice. "He had another seizure this morning." She swallowed, fighting her tears. "It was bad, Cody."

A sobering shadow fell over the moment. "When...when can he try the new medicine?"

"Monday afternoon." She found a shaky smile. "We're meeting with the new doctor then."

"We still aren't sure we're doing the safest thing." His dad crossed his arms. His chin quivered and he coughed, finding his own control. "But it's the right thing. We know that."

"The doctor was very encouraging."

Cody thought about Ali again. She would rather have raced horses for one year than spend ten years in the safety of a sterile room. It would be the same way for Carl Joseph. Suddenly the decisions that lay ahead for Cody were clearer than water.

Carl Joseph returned to the table out of breath. "My turn to pray!" His voice was louder than usual, and he caught himself. He covered his mouth and raised his eyebrows. "Sorry," he whispered. "'Cause it's my turn to pray."

"Go ahead, son." His father smiled at him.

Carl Joseph reached for his mother's hand and everyone closed their eyes. "Dear God, hi. Carl Joseph here." He stifled a quiet laugh. "Everything's perfect now, God. So thanks for the lasagna, and thanks for Mom and Dad and Brother and Teacher." He giggled again. "And Daisy. And medicine." He clapped his hands. "Now we can dig in!"

Cody opened his eyes, amazed. Hours ago Carl Joseph had been in the throes of a terrible seizure. But as far as he could tell, life was perfect. It was one more way Carl Joseph's faith stood as an example to the rest of them.

They let Carl Joseph talk for a while. He told them that he and Daisy had decided the next hike would be at Disneyland. "'Cause we have to get there first and we don't know the bus route."

"You'd probably have to fly." Their dad was finishing his dinner. He had an easy way with Carl Joseph, something Cody hadn't noticed in his hurry to blame his dad when he first returned from the rodeo circuit.

"Yeah." Carl Joseph looked out the window. He'd never been on an airplane, and his anxiety over the possibility was written in the lines on his forehead. "'Cause we could fly."

After a few minutes of talk about Disneyland, Carl Joseph stood and took his empty plate and cup to the kitchen. "I'll wash." He gave their mother a big smile and tapped their father's shoulder. "That would be good life skills."

Dad stood and joined Carl Joseph in the kitchen. "Let's do it together."

"Goodie." He clapped, sheer joy filling his tone.

Cody stood and joined his father and brother in the kitchen. Carl Joseph was relating a comical version of the hike, and how Cody and Elle had danced together.

"Brother is not a good dancer." Carl Joseph made a dramatic shake of his head, so dramatic that his glasses nearly fell to the floor. He caught them and set them back in place. Then he patted Cody's shoulder and gave him a rough embrace. "But he's a very, very good brother."

They played Uno that night, and Cody stayed up later than usual before returning across the ranch to his own house. He'd been anticipating this moment all day, and now—in a

way he was helpless to stop—it was here. He stepped inside
his front entrance, closed the door, and locked it.

What he had to do now, he would do alone—the same
way he had handled the trip to the bluff earlier. He walked
through his living room and stopped at the fireplace mantel.
Perched on top of the polished piece of oak was his framed
wedding picture. Ali and him, when the future still seemed
possible. When a cure for cystic fibrosis was all that stood
between that fleeting moment and forever.

He ran his thumb over the glass, over their faces, smiling
and hopeful. "It's time, Ali." He smiled, even though somewhere inside him he could feel his heart breaking. He looked
at her face, her eyes. "I know you'd tell me the same thing."

Then, feeling a hundred years old, he moved into his
bedroom and opened the top drawer of his dresser. A small
wicker basket sat near the back, a catch-all for things that
didn't quite have a place. His old pocketknife from middle
school and a pair of earplugs he wore when he ran the trac-
tor out on the ranch. And next to that, on top of a mound
of old quarters and nickels and dimes, were the two velvet
boxes.

He took the pale pink one first. The hinges made a soft
creaking sound as he opened it. The ring inside was still
beautiful, mostly because seeing it reminded him of how it
looked on Ali's finger. He took the ring from the box and
brought the cool white gold close to his face.

Once in a while, holding her wedding ring this way made
him feel as if he were holding her hand again. Her fingers

tucked in his. But tonight it was only a cold, empty reminder of all that wasn't. All that would never be.

Cody placed the ring gently back in the velvet box and closed the lid. Ali was not in the grave, and she was not in the small velvet box. She lived in his heart, in a back room where she had recently moved, one that would always belong to her. He lifted the other box, the dark one, and set it on the dresser top.

He'd never come even this close before, so every move was slow, painful. He opened the lid and then looked at his left hand. Ali had placed the ring there seven years ago, and it had stayed there every day since. But here, on a day when he had prayed for answers, he felt beyond certain that this was the next step, the move he absolutely had to make.

The wedding ring fit just as it had the day they were married. So it took only a few seconds to gently twist it up over his knuckle. The ache in his heart spread to his chest and up into his throat. Then, with a sharp breath, he did what he never thought he'd do.

He took off his ring and tenderly set it back in the box. For a few seconds he stared at it. The things he felt about the ring would always stay in his soul. But what it meant to the world was no longer true. He wasn't married, and after four years it was time to acknowledge that fact.

Even if doing so practically dropped him to his knees.

Cody closed the box and set it tenderly next to Ali's. Then he closed the drawer and moved to an old recliner he kept in his bedroom near the window. He sank into it and peered into the dark of the night. God was leading him; Cody could feel His guidance in every step. In the process he had let go of Ali, just enough to take one step forward. And now he was ready to face whatever came next. Because—whether he returned to the road or not—he had the one thing Elle had talked about, the thing he felt God urging him to have.

Empty hands.

Chapter Twenty-five

Elle was about to start class that Monday when the door opened and Cody and Carl Joseph stepped inside. A smile lit up Cody's face, and Elle knew the answer before a single word was spoken.

"Carl Joseph would like to come back to class," Cody said. He and his brother moved closer to Elle and the students.

Gus stood straight up. "You're back? You're really back?"

"I knew it." Sid high-fived the guy next to him. "I told you he'd be back!"

Daisy was on her feet. She tiptoed over to Carl Joseph and flung her arms around his neck. "You're home, CJ! Welcome home!"

Elle was grateful for her students and their loud celebration. Because she couldn't have talked if she wanted to. She stood and went to Cody. "Your parents talked to the new doctor?"

"Yes. I'll tell you about it later." He smiled, and for a long beat he held her eyes. "Whatever time Carl Joseph has, he wants to live it." He turned toward his brother. "He can do that here."

Elle asked Cody to stay, but he shook his head. "I have things to do." He smiled, but there was something deeper in his expression, feelings he was maybe working through.

"Have you decided? About returning to the rodeo?"

"Not yet." He briefly touched her hand. "Let me know if he has any trouble." Cody told his brother good-bye, and he left.

Every day that week was the same, only a few words from Cody when he dropped off Carl Joseph or when he picked him up. Something was happening inside him, and Elle could do nothing but pray for him.

Once in a while he would look at her across the room or share a few words with her, and when he did there was a depth that was constant. A depth full of conflict and vulnerability, one that she didn't dare ask him about—not in what could only be a few minutes' conversation before class.

By Friday morning, Elle wasn't sure what to make of the change, but it scared her. Because she didn't know any way to undo feelings that had already taken root. Especially when she looked forward to seeing him every morning during drop-off time. She thought about asking Carl Joseph, but somehow the idea didn't sit well. If God wanted her to know what was different with Cody Gunner, the information would come to her some other way.

And it did.

It came Friday morning just before their field trip to a

supermarket two miles away. Carl Joseph and Daisy were sitting together, waiting for the rest of the class to arrive. They were talking about shortcake and Disneyland and which pair of socks were their favorite if they got to hike the theme park.

Elle tuned out on their conversation for a few minutes. She was sorting through information packets for the students when she heard her sister's tone change.

"Why would he go on the road?" Daisy pulled her knees up and sat cross-legged, facing her friend.

"He wants to think." Carl Joseph tried to pull his legs up, but they were too short and stout to maneuver and he quickly gave up. He blinked as if he were trying to remember what he'd been saying. "'Cause...Brother wants to think about things."

Daisy looked around the room, clearly confused. "He could think here, CJ." She pointed to the seat next to her on the classroom sofa. "Right here on this spot."

"He could think on top of Ace, the horse."

"Or on his bed." She put her pointer fingers together and made a careful heart in the air between them. "My bed has big hearts."

"My bed has Mickey Mouse." Carl Joseph put his fist in the air in a show of victory. "Mickey Mouse is the best bed."

Elle needed to be alone. She stepped into the break room, braced herself against the counter. Cody was leaving? After all the emotions she'd ridden because of him, he was taking off? *God, is that how this is going to end? You bring him into my life for what, so I can tell him good-bye before anything comes of all this and—*

Her self-pity fell off abruptly. What was she thinking? How shallow to consider that the only reason Cody Gunner had shown up at all was for her. The reason God had brought Cody into her life probably had nothing to do with her. She pictured Carl Joseph, giddy about today's field trip, already back in sync with his classmates and making progress toward independence. Carl Joseph was reason enough, even if she never saw Cody again.

A sense of futility came over her, and she was tempted to let the subject go, walk out of the break room and conduct the field trip and believe that one day in the not-too-distant future she'd forget about Cody. But her eyes fell on a sign posted near the coffeemaker.

Don't forget to pray! It's the most important life skill of all!

A lump formed in her throat, and she swallowed back her tears. *Forgive me, Lord. Even if Cody leaves, we can stay friends. But please...if it's Your will, convince Cody to stay. Convince him to work here at the center so we can share our love for people with Down Syndrome and maybe someday...something more. And if not, Lord...help me let him go.*

She collected herself and returned to the classroom. Most of the students were there, talking about how they would spend their imaginary hundred dollars. She had arranged with the manager of the store that each student could have a cart and choose food within a budget, and then—so they would better understand the sections of a grocery store—they would return the food to the shelves.

And as they set out for the first bus stop half an hour later, she refused to think about Cody and whether he would stay or head back out on the road. God had all the details figured out. If he left, even in her sadness she would know that was God's will.

Even if she would remember for a lifetime how it felt to dance with him on a patch of clover halfway up a mountain trail on a sunny afternoon in June.

CODY KEPT HIS distance on purpose. He didn't want his feelings for Elle influencing his decision to stay or go. Because if he stayed, he wanted to go to her not only with empty hands, but with a full heart. Full of hope and promise and excitement for tomorrow and every day after it.

So that week he kept his distance from Elle and his parents, and in some ways even Carl Joseph. In the process, he took his brother's advice and prayed. He talked to God every chance he had. Should he go and spend a year sorting through his options, his feelings? Or should he stay, roll up his sleeves, and work alongside a girl who filled his senses? Was he ready for that, or would he be better off by himself? Him and God.

The way he'd never really been even after Ali died.

Until now, now that he'd let her go.

Day after day he prayed, stopping in each morning to take Carl Joseph to the center, and forcing himself to stay only a few minutes, so he wouldn't change his mind and stay all day. He was that drawn to Elle. In some ways, he expected the answer to come easily. Should he stay or go? Simple question, simple answer. But God didn't shout at him or whisper in his heart or make the answer clear in any way.

The answer came on Friday, after Carl Joseph's field trip.

Cody had ridden Ace that day, and he was in the barn brushing the horse down, patting his neck. He heard Carl Joseph tromping out to meet him long before his brother appeared at the door.

"Brother!" It was midafternoon, and the sun splashed rays on either side of Carl Joseph. "Supermarkets are fun!"

Cody set down the brush, dusted off his hands, and crossed the hay-covered floor to the door. He wiped his brow and smiled at his brother. "I hadn't noticed."

"What?" Carl Joseph didn't pick up on sarcasm. It was one more innocent way about him.

"Yes, Buddy." Cody patted his shoulder. "Supermarkets are a lot of fun."

"Yeah, and I picked out a melon and"—he held up two fingers—"a two-gallon milk and butter unsalted and wheat bread." He clapped his hands and laughed the way he did when he was practically overcome with joy.

"That's great, Buddy. I'm proud of you." He meant it. Every field trip, every class session was another victory for Carl Joseph, another step closer to Goal Day.

Carl Joseph bounced a little, nodding and explaining in detail about the trip. But after a minute of talking, he stopped and his smile dropped off. He pushed his glasses up onto his nose and squinted at Cody. "Why, Brother?"

"Why what?"

"You didn't go. I like you to go, Brother. But maybe you don't like supermarkets?"

Cody stared at his brother, past the extra chromosome to the tender-hearted boy inside. A boy who had looked up to him and longed for his attention since he was old enough to talk. And there, in the guileless question from his only brother, Cody had the answer he was looking for.

Just as strongly as if God had walked into the barn and hand-delivered it.

CODY AND CARL Joseph walked into the center ten minutes late, but Elle was nowhere to be seen. Cody's heart pounded, but he expected that. He'd taken his answer back to God and prayed about it over the weekend. Time and again the feeling in his heart was the same.

Now it was time to act on it.

Carl Joseph didn't know what Cody was about to do or how today was different from any other day. He bounded into the classroom, stopped, and was about to give Cody a good-bye hug when Cody stopped him. "I'm staying, Buddy."

His brother's eyebrows lifted high up into his forehead. "You're staying?" He made a few disbelieving guffaws. "Really, Brother?"

"Really." Cody patted his brother's shoulder. "I'll sit here by the door. You go with your friends."

Carl Joseph ran to the group, waving his hands. He was just announcing, "Brother's staying! Brother's staying!" when

Elle walked back in from the break room. She must've felt Cody watching her because she turned to him and their eyes met and held. They held while Daisy jumped to her feet and as she danced around Carl Joseph, celebrating the fact that his brother was staying.

Elle put her things down on her desk, turned, and slowly came to him. Her expression told him that she was confused, that she didn't understand whether he was staying for the day, visiting with Carl Joseph's class.

Or staying in Colorado Springs.

When she reached him, a hundred questions shone in her eyes. But she asked just one. "You're staying?"

He hated the way she looked nervous. Elle Dalton, whose heart had been through enough. He stood and glanced at the class. The aide was working with several students. He searched her eyes again. "Can you step outside for a minute?" His pounding heart grew louder, so loud he could barely concentrate. He steadied himself. *Breathe, Gunner. Take a breath.* He could do this. God had made it clear.

Elle announced to the class that it was time for group discussion. She gave a knowing look to her aide and then smiled at her students. "Find your seats, please. I'll be right back."

She followed Cody outside, and a warm wind met them on the patio. He leaned against the cool brick wall and waited until she was a few feet in front of him. "I have a question."

"Okay." She ran her tongue along her lower lip. She looked nervous, no idea what was coming.

He smiled, and never broke eye contact. "Is that position still open? Running the fitness program here at the center?"

Surprise worked its way across her face, but it took only a few heartbeats before her eyes lit up. "Are you serious?"

Cody felt the anxiety leaving him. "On one condition." In this moment there was Elle, and only Elle.

A happy cry came from her. "What?"

"I want a dance studio."

Her reaction wasn't slow or measured or cautious. She threw her arms around his neck and hugged him, the sort of victory hug the moment demanded. But it demanded more than that.

He eased back just enough so he could see her, and slowly she took her arms from him. They stood there, inches from each other, and the mood between them changed with a sudden intensity. He crooked his finger and brushed it against her cheek. "I was right before." He reminded himself to breathe again. "I feel it, too. I felt it then on the mountain." He moved closer, searching her eyes. "And I feel it now."

"Cody..." Fear shadowed her eyes, and she looked away. "I don't know."

"I won't hurt you, Elle." He took her hands in his. "I wouldn't be here if I hadn't thought this through."

When he rehearsed this moment in his mind, he hadn't been sure where exactly it would take place or how it would wind up. But he knew one thing. He wouldn't let her go until she was clear about his feelings. Only now, with her class waiting for her and doubt trying to distract her, he could think of just one way to convince her.

Gently, with a tenderness that he had learned a long time ago, he released her hands and worked his fingers along the sides of her face and into her soft brown hair. Then in a moment he was sure they would both remember forever, he leaned down and kissed her. It was not the kiss of passion and desire, even if those feelings were hidden inside him. Rather it was the kiss of everything new and tender and innocent. A tentative kiss that lasted only a few seconds.

When he straightened, he never took his eyes from hers. "Well." He hugged her again and whispered into her hair. "Do I get the job?"

She didn't answer him, and at first he wondered if she'd changed her mind. Not about him, but about the fitness program. But then he felt the trembling in her shoulders. She wasn't hesitant.

She was crying.

And for the first time in far too long, Cody savored the sound. Because this time Elle's tears did not come from a place of utter despair and heartbreak.

They came from pure, boundless joy.

ELLE SNIFFED AND wiped her tears. "Yes." She pressed her cheek against Cody's chest. "You can have the job."

He stroked her hair, and after a little while they moved apart and he took her hands again. "Good thing, because I don't exactly have a Plan B." He smiled. "Not anymore."

She was about to ask him what happened, how come he'd stayed away all week only to come here now with his mind made up. But with his fingers around hers, she suddenly noticed something.

He wasn't wearing his wedding ring.

"Cody—" she ran her thumb over the smooth indentation, the place where the ring had been just a week earlier. She looked at his finger and then back at him. "Why?"

"I wanted empty hands." Sadness touched his eyes, but only in a distant sort of way.

She could imagine how hard it must've been to make this move, to set aside his wedding ring. As much as she felt giddy and alive, as much as her head was spinning trying to believe what was happening, she couldn't have him doing this unless he was certain. She framed his face with her hands and looked deep into his eyes, all the way to his heart. "Are you sure?"

"Yes." His answer left no doubt, and his eyes told her he wanted to kiss her again. But he resisted; they both did. This wasn't the time or place, and there would be no rushing whatever lay ahead. There were plenty of reasons to take things slowly.

He grinned, and his eyes danced. "So I was thinking that tonight, well, Carl Joseph and Daisy haven't seen each other outside of class for a long time."

"A week." She felt like shouting out loud. She felt that good.

"Right, a whole week." He gave a shake of his head as if to say a week was far too long. "So what about tonight the four of us go out for pizza?"

Elle tilted her head. She could feel the stars in her eyes. "That'd be amazing."

She soothed her fingertips over the empty place where his wedding ring had been. "What made you do it, Cody?"

"I took your advice." The laughter in his voice eased off a little, but the sorrow was gone.

"What advice was that?"

"I used a life skill." He was serious, even though the air between them was light.

"Oh, really?" Already she could see where this was going, how it would play out in the weeks and months ahead. God in all His glory was giving her a new beginning, the one her mother and sisters and even she had prayed for. The future suddenly had all the streaky pinks and blues of a brilliant sunrise and Elle could've shouted her thanks to heaven because she could hardly wait.

She wanted to know what he meant, and she caught his eyes once more as they headed back toward the classroom. She worked to focus, but her head was still spinning. "Which life skill?"

"Prayer." He smiled, and it gave her a window to his soul. "The one that matters most."

Chapter Twenty-six

Mary Gunner stood at the door of her house and waved good-bye. Cody and Carl Joseph were setting off to help move Daisy into her new apartment, the one she was sharing with Tammy, another student at the ILC.

Daisy had reached Goal Day the week before, and Mary and Mike had celebrated with Daisy and Elle's mother, and all the students and their families. She had a job now, taking tickets at a movie theater one mile down from her apartment.

"Just two bus stops," Daisy liked to say.

The moment was bittersweet for Mary. Spurred on by Daisy's efforts toward independence, Carl Joseph was making record progress toward his own Goal Day. His new medicine was working, but he still had terrible seizures every week or so. Mary sucked in a breath and held it. In four days Carl Joseph had a job interview at the western feed store—cleaning floors and stocking shelves. Elle had explained that she was fairly certain Carl Joseph would get the job. The manager understood about his potential for seizures. They didn't worry him.

Mary watched Cody pull out of the driveway and turn left toward the city. The two brothers were closer than ever. Mary smiled and felt all traces of sadness leave her. Yes, Carl Joseph would be leaving home soon. Cody and Elle had found a group home in the same complex where Daisy and Tammy lived. And that was the right thing for her son. She had believed it when they enrolled him at the center, and she believed it now. Even if once in a while her heart wavered.

Long after Cody's truck was no longer in sight, Mary stood there, pondering all that had happened. Elle had said they might be moving Carl Joseph into the group home in six to nine months. Already he had a roommate lined up—Gus. That way they could share the same independent-living coordinator, a social worker who would come once a week to make sure they were following their routines, remembering their medications.

She smiled. For all the amazing growth and change in Carl Joseph, the greatest change was in her older son.

Cody was in love. Deeply and completely, in a way Mary had thought would never happen again for him. Cody and Elle were inseparable, and already she'd heard mention of a wedding sometime in the near future. In a little more than a month, over Presidents' Day weekend, the two of them were traveling with Daisy and Carl Joseph on a special trip. Something that had Carl Joseph literally counting down the days.

Mary leaned her head on the doorframe. Once, a lifetime ago, before she and Mike married, her mother told her something that stayed with her. She said, "A mother knows she's done a great job when she has an empty nest and a full heart."

She pictured Cody and Elle, lost in their own world, helping Daisy move into her apartment while Carl Joseph chattered on about his Goal Day. There were times in the last decade when she wondered if she was an absolute failure as a mother. Back when Cody wouldn't speak to her and anger was his only language, or when she realized that by not expecting more of Carl Joseph, she had nearly doomed him to a life of watching television from his spot on the living room sofa.

But here, with her empty nest right around the corner, and her heart so full it could burst, Mary could only hope that maybe her mother was right.

That maybe between her and God, she'd done something right, after all.

⁓

THE BIG DAY dawned beneath thick, dark clouds.

By the time they reached the airport, a steady rain was falling, and in the backseat Daisy had her head on Carl Joseph's shoulder. "I hate the rain."

"Don't hate, Daisy." Carl Joseph was talking a little more quietly lately. "'Cause it's not nice to hate."

"Okay, I get scared in the rain." She rarely argued with Carl Joseph, rarely tried to be right the way she did with just about everyone else. Cody had noticed, and the fact made him smile.

As much as Cody and Elle were falling faster and deeper every day, Carl Joseph and Daisy were, too. Yes, their friendship was more complicated, but it wasn't impossible.

And Cody had decided if his brother wanted to get married someday, if he was well enough to handle the process, Cody would do whatever it took to help him. That way, the lessons Ali had taught him would live on in Carl Joseph.

Cody reached over and took hold of Elle's hand. "What time's the flight?"

"We have ninety minutes." Her face lit up the morning, in spite of the rain. "I can't wait."

"You?" He chuckled and kept his voice low. "This morning Carl Joseph showed up at the breakfast table wrapped in his Mickey Mouse bedspread. He wanted to wear it today, so everyone would know where he was going."

Elle smiled. "Daisy packed six colored pictures for Minnie. Three for each day we're there. So"—she raised an eyebrow—"I think we're about equal."

Cody kept his eyes on the road. The trip to Disneyland was Elle's idea, but he had been in favor of it from the beginning. They had purposely waited until just a week ago to tell Carl Joseph and Daisy. Otherwise the distraction could've messed up her Goal Day, leaving her too preoccupied to prove she was ready to live in an apartment.

He found a parking spot. "All I know is I wouldn't miss this for the world."

"I know." Elle smiled and it found its way to his soul. "My mom told me to fill a two-gig memory chip with their reactions, everything from start to finish."

"Well"—he looked back at his brother, still comforting Daisy—"let's get going. Disneyland's waiting!"

Once they were at the airport gate, they found a quiet corner where they could wait. The moment they were settled, Carl Joseph gasped and then caught himself. He uttered a softer breath this time and pointed at the ceiling. "Swing music!" He took hold of Cody's hand. "Come on, Brother. We can dance."

"Oh, no." Cody shook his head. He could feel Elle laughing at him from her seat beside him. "Not this time, okay?"

"Yeah, I'll need my feet for Disneyland." She whispered near the side of his face.

"Thanks." He squeezed her hand. "I told you, we have to take lessons. Real lessons."

A few feet away, Carl Joseph was undaunted. He took Daisy's hand instead.

She stood and did a graceful bow. Then they began dancing to the elevator music at Denver International, and with the bustle of activity along the concourse and near the gate attendant, only a few people noticed. But those who did walked away with a smile.

Elle had been teaching Daisy fear-management techniques and ways she could pray when the rain made her feel too afraid to move. Here, then, was progress. It was raining outside, but Daisy had found the courage to dance with Carl Joseph instead of cowering in his arms. Whatever Elle was doing, it was working.

"Did you work out the rooms?" Elle slid her fingers between his.

The closeness of her still took his breath. He loved everything about her, loved her in a way he never could have if not for Ali. He kissed her forehead. "You and Daisy across the hall from me and Carl Joseph."

"Perfect." She was about to settle into the chair when the gate attendant instructed their group to board.

Cody motioned to Carl Joseph and Daisy to get in line, and suddenly—as if she had just noticed the rain again—Daisy clung to Carl Joseph and started to whimper.

Immediately, Carl Joseph put his arm around her and patted her hair. "It's okay, Daisy. 'Cause you won't melt."

It was the same reassurance he always gave her, and it seemed to work. They inched their way past the gate and through the Jetway and onto the plane. It was the first time either Carl Joseph or Daisy had flown, so Cody and Elle had booked the seats with their siblings in the aisle seats. At least until they felt comfortable in the air. Then they could switch so Carl Joseph and Daisy could have window seats.

But as they walked toward the back of the plane and found their aisle, Daisy wouldn't let go of Carl Joseph's arm. Rather than make a scene, Cody sat by Elle so Daisy could sit by Carl Joseph.

"It's okay, Daisy. It's okay." His buddy patted Daisy's arm. "The rain won't melt you."

Carl Joseph comforted her throughout the safety announcements and as the plane lifted off. But then something almost magical happened. As the plane soared into the sky, it burst through the layer of clouds and into a brilliant blue sky.

Daisy sat up straight and looked out the window. "CJ, look!"

Cody leaned forward so he could hear them. Elle did the same.

Carl Joseph clapped his hands, not loudly and obnoxiously, the way he used to, but muffled and with a sense of wonder. He nodded fast and hard. "See, Daisy? I told you so. Sunshine…just beyond the clouds."

Her fear left instantly and she stared at the sky, clearly stunned by this new revelation. Carl Joseph did the same, as if he could hardly believe that all this time the words he had used to comfort Daisy had been right on.

Elle looked past him to their siblings. "Down Syndrome is nothing more than a layer of clouds, really. Clouds that cover up a very bright sunshine."

Cody leaned in and kissed her, the way he'd been longing to do since she climbed into his pickup that morning. Briefly, tenderly, and with all the feeling he held in his heart for her. They were still hiding their kisses from Carl Joseph and Daisy. No need to confuse them, or make them think they, too, should be kissing. Not yet, anyway.

"Good night." Elle closed her eyes. "See you in LA."

Cody settled in against the headrest.

He wasn't sure about the timing, but he wanted to spend the rest of his life with Elle Dalton. He was already looking at rings. He stared out the window at the vast and endless blue. He'd never thought about it that way, but Elle was right. Whether in a rainstorm or living with Down Syndrome, or trying to survive a loss so great it might've killed them, the sunshine had always been there. It always would be.

Just beyond the clouds.

Dear Friends,

Thanks for journeying with me through the pages of *Just Beyond the Clouds*. For a while now, I've wanted to go back to Cody Gunner, to find him in that place where I left him a few years ago—a place of heartache over losing Ali, his wife. But those of you who read *A Thousand Tomorrows* know that Cody wasn't only heartbroken over losing Ali. He was also changed forever by knowing her. For that reason, I was convinced the story wasn't finished.

After all, Ali made Cody promise one thing—that he would find love again.

And so this—like *A Thousand Tomorrows*—is a love story that made me smile as I wrote it. Like so many of my books, it played in my head and heart like a movie, and I had the simple and profound pleasure of capturing the story on the pages of this book for you.

I enjoyed very much writing more about Carl Joseph, Cody's brother. And I enjoyed delving into the world of Down Syndrome, where scientists are still learning so much about what is possible for these special people, and about how very high the bar should be raised for them.

One of the themes that runs through the book on a few different levels is the one represented in the title: *Just Beyond the Clouds*. Life has a way of sending in the clouds—not the clowns. That unexpected diagnosis, the pile of bills that won't go away, the empty mailbox, strained relationships...But the truth is always what Carl

Joseph tried to tell Daisy: There is sunshine just beyond the clouds.

Scripture tells us that God has good plans for us, and so He does. But sometimes it's a matter of holding on to that truth when the clouds come, when the sky is so dark that it's hard to believe there could really be sunshine on the other side. But there is, especially for those who believe.

Carl Joseph's faith is a simple one, and maybe one we can all learn a lot from. He doesn't process things the way most adults do. Rather, he thinks simply, like a child. He loves God, and so he gives God his best in every area. Sort of the way our kids do. If you've found hope in Jesus Christ for the first time while reading this book, then please know that I am praying for you. Your next step is to find a Bible-believing church in your area and get connected. Go to a Sunday service, take in a Bible class, attend a small group. And if reading Scripture is new to you and you can't afford a Bible, write to me with the words *New Life* in the subject line. I'll make sure my office sends you a Bible so you can get started on that new life in Christ.

I pray that this finds you well and walking in His truth and light. And most of all, I pray that you will join me in looking for the miracles around us and in celebrating life! Remember, sometimes His greatest messages come to us while we wait for the clouds to clear.

If you haven't been to my Web site for a while, stop by! My ongoing journal will give you a window into my personal and writing life, and you can connect with other readers in the Reader Room. Also, you can check out my latest contests and post a photo of someone you know who is serving our country. People all over the world are praying for the soldiers pictured on my Web site.

Also, pass this book on to someone who hasn't read it yet, and you can enter the Shared a Book contest. Just send an e-mail to Kingsburydesk@aol.com, and type "Shared a Book" in the subject line. In the e-mail, give me the first name of the person you shared with and why you shared it with them. At the end of every March, I will pick a winner. That person and a friend will win a trip to the Northwest to spend a day with me and my family. I hope to see you there!

By the way, I still love hearing from you! Your prayers and letters remain a very great encouragement to me as I write stories that God might use to change your life and mine.

Until next time . . . keep looking for the sunshine!

In His light,

Karen Kingsbury
www.KarenKingsbury.com

Reading Group Guide

1. Where is Cody Gunner emotionally at the start of this book? What clues lead you to that conclusion?

2. Where is Elle Dalton emotionally at the start of this book? What clues lead you to that conclusion?

3. What does Carl Joseph understand about independent living? How does he feel about reaching Goal Day?

4. Do you know anyone with Down Syndrome? What is your experience with that person, and have you ever been surprised at how much that person is capable of?

5. What do you think about independent living for people with Down Syndrome? Explain your answer.

6. How does Cody feel about Carl Joseph? What causes their relationship to be strained over the course of the story?

7. What are Cody's feelings about independent living at the beginning of the story? Why do you think he feels that way?

8. Describe how Cody's feelings change as the story develops. What causes his change of attitude about independent living for people with Down Syndrome?

9. Do Carl Joseph's feelings for Cody change during the story? Explain Carl Joseph's relationship with his brother and how it affects him.

10. How is Daisy's level of independence different from Carl Joseph's? Discuss their strengths and weaknesses.

11. Discuss Elle's former heartbreak. Has anyone you know had a similar experience? How did this heartache leave Elle feeling about herself?

12. Cody and Elle shared a few misunderstandings over the course of the story. Explore a few of those and how they could have been avoided.

13. Have you or someone you know ever experienced a troubled relationship because of a misunderstanding? Explain.

14. Carl Joseph's situation was complicated by his health issues. When have you seen health issues complicate a goal for you or someone you know? Talk about it.

15. Describe Mary Gunner's feelings about Carl Joseph. How difficult was it for her to accept the idea of independent living despite Carl Joseph's health issues?

16. How does Mary Gunner handle her fears regarding her son? How do you handle fears regarding your children or the lives of people you love?

17. Throughout the story, Elle talks about having an open hand in regard to relationships. What does this mean to you, and how can you apply it in your life?

18. In what ways is Elle a perfect match for Cody? Talk about how important it is to have like interests and passions when making a decision to start a relationship.

19. Fear posed a serious threat many times in this story. Explore those incidents. How should we respond to difficult situations?

20. Describe a time when fear threatened to prevent you or someone you know from making an important decision. How did you or that person work through the fear, and what were the end results?

Other Life-Changing Fiction™
by Karen Kingsbury

9/11 SERIES
One Tuesday Morning
Beyond Tuesday Morning
Every Now and Then

LOST LOVE SERIES
Even Now
Ever After

ABOVE THE LINE SERIES
Above the Line: Take One
Above the Line: Take Two
Above the Line: Take Three
Above the Line: Take Four

STAND-ALONE TITLES
Shades of Blue
Oceans Apart
Between Sundays
This Side of Heaven
When Joy Came to Stay
On Every Side
Divine
Like Dandelion Dust
Where Yesterday Lives

REDEMPTION SERIES
Redemption
Remember
Return
Rejoice
Reunion

FIRSTBORN SERIES
Fame
Forgiven
Found
Family
Forever

SUNRISE SERIES
Sunrise
Summer
Someday
Sunset

RED GLOVE SERIES
Gideon's Gift
Maggie's Miracle
Sarah's Song
Hannah's Hope

FOREVER FAITHFUL SERIES
Waiting for Morning
Moment of Weakness
Halfway to Forever

WOMEN OF FAITH FICTION SERIES
A Time to Dance
A Time to Embrace

CODY GUNNER SERIES
A Thousand Tomorrows
Just Beyond the Clouds
This Side of Heaven

CHILDREN'S TITLES
Let Me Hold You Longer
Let's Go on a Mommy Date
We Believe in Christmas
Let's Go Have a Daddy Day

MIRACLE COLLECTIONS
A Treasury of Christmas Miracles
A Treasury of Miracles for Women
A Treasury of Miracles for Teens
A Treasury of Miracles for Friends
A Treasury of Adoption Miracles

GIFT BOOKS
Stay Close Little Girl
Be Safe Little Boy
Forever Young: Ten Gifts of Faith for the Graduate